THERE, CROW'S FEET STRETCHED THEMSELVES,
SUPINE FORMS TUCKED INTO THE FACE OF EPOCH ITSELF.

THE EPOCH TRILOGY

AWAKENING (2013)
REDEMPTION
THE FINAL REFORMATION

EPOCH

AWAKENING

THE FIRST CHAPTER IN AN EPIC SAGA
OF POLITICAL UPHEAVAL, PERSONAL
GROWTH AND DISCOVERY, AND THE
BURGEONING SPIRIT THAT WILL MARK
THE NEW AGE OF THIS WORLD

JEFFREY PANZER

HARP
UNSTRUNG

Jeffrey Panzer © 2013 Harp Unstrung

First Edition

978-0615924625   061592462X

FACEBOOK.COM/EPOCHTRILOGY

EPOCHTRILOGY.COM

Special thanks to Jessica, Judith, Maurice, and Cass.
I wouldn't have gotten here without your support and help.
The Boys – I am eternally grateful.
Yvette, who puts up with my shit through thick and thin.
My parents, without whom nothing would be possible.

AWAKENING

FOR IRIE ANNEMARIE

TABLE OF CONTENTS

PROLOGUE
IN DARKNESS

They bring him to question in the morning.

Outside can be heard the conversations of various men, ill-defined, words heard through wall, shadow and finite void. These do not interest Peter; he has heard them before, fought the foggy ether of his mind to make them out, to bring sense to this place in which he finds himself.

Words are spoken, questions asked. He has no reply.

In truth he cannot respond nor articulate even a sputter, tongue cast in iron, heavy and too slow to move. His eyes wearily trace the confines of the chamber, empty now except for himself and the questioner.

Let them do their worst.

Turns back to the bench, patient and somber, meets the steel gaze there found. The figure before him speaks, words meaningless, all lies.

This is taking a long time. These clothes do not befit me.

Finally a respite: They have come to take him back to his cell. Trudging through the long corridors he nearly feels alone, solitude yet denied by the shadowy presence to his rear.

Will they again ask me tomorrow? The next day?

He knows the answer. He has been in this routine for a long time: days, years, weeks for all he can recall.

Arriving at his windowless demesne he casts himself onto the hard stone, a willful Titan apart even from sea and eagle. This place has no such acute realities, merely the dreary waiting and questions, always questions.

Lying down he prepares to drift into sleep, without even room to stretch out, not even alone but kept company always by others, countless others.

In the dark one tends to speak to oneselves.

What would you be?

Afraid to reveal too much yet unable to hide anything at all, he inches down the thin line toward his only salvation.

Blessed sleep.

Slow now, slowing down, he turns on his side, toward the oblivion of his lonely soul.

Daniel jerked upright, "I do not know him!"

His scream filled the small space of the room, spilled there from, out into the hallway, beyond, yet no one was there to hear.

CHAPTER 1
OUT ON THE STREETS

A GRIM OUTLOOK AT BEST

She sat quietly, watching him with seemingly calm yet surely measured patience.

That's how they always watch me.

Bide your time, bitch. At the least you'll get your money's worth out of me.

Daniel leveled a slate-blue gaze upon her, their eyes meeting for a moment before she quickly looked down at her pad, scribbled something.

I wonder what she's writing. Something useful?

He laughed, silently, grim vocalizations in the awkward confines of his mind.

Maybe she's doodling.

Their time, marked by the steady, inexorable tick of the clock on the wall behind him, inched passed, slowly, painful.

"Is there anything else you'd like to share with me?" she asked mildly, pursing her lips and bringing her pen to her lap.

Fucking likely. I'd like to share a big dick with you, but you probably don't want that.

"No," he shrugged. "I dunno..."

Perhaps he should tell her what a waste this was, of her time not his, or how little he could afford her hourly fee, that is if he actually planned to pay the bill that would no doubt find its way within the week to the P.O. box he infrequently checked yet nonetheless maintained, but instead he merely shrugged and continued to watch her.

Her well hidden discomfort, visible at the margins of her movements, the tilt of her breath, was tangibly humorous to him, amusing in its effect on her... not so much her discomfort itself, but that she thought it was concealed from him.

Her self-satisfaction at the small deception almost consumed her spirit. She was absorbed in it.

"I can't help you if you refuse to help yourself." She sat back into her chair, crossed her legs, making sure her skirt covered all that was necessary.

Good fucking thing he hadn't come here for help; if so he'd be pissed. At present he was actually in relatively good humor—Her behavior was the most entertaining he'd seen in weeks. It's funny how people act when they think they're more intelligent than you, what they let slip, the airs they put on when they think no one will notice.

This self-absorbed bitch would likely put me on drugs if I let her. That's what they do for people with problems they can't understand: Take this and you'll stop worrying about your problems, never mind I have no God damn idea what they are.

"I thought my coming here was an attempt to help myself."

"That is the first step, but now I need you to talk to me, so I can understand and help you deal with whatever is troubling you."

In a way he *was* here for help, but certainly not for her clinical opinion of his psychological state, nor for her help in discovering and ousting the various demons tormenting his soul. He was here for an accidental burst of information, the kind you can only get from people who have no idea what they're talking about; he'd come to speak to someone he was absolutely sure had no understanding of what she was saying, someone who *knew* she was clueless, regardless of whatever falsity she told herself in the light of day.

He'd come to a psychologist.

He slouched forward in his chair. "I've told you about my dream. It's always the same. I thought you people specialize in the interpretations of these things."

Of course that was a lie; he knew quite well these assholes couldn't interpret or even analyze a dream if their lives depended on it. To produce such an interpretation she'd have to actually enter into a relationship with him; she'd have to share in his emotions, understand the nature of his beliefs, *know him*. But that would never happen, not in this lifetime, not with someone like her. For that you need a friend, not a business woman.

Removing her glasses she looked him in the eyes, attempting with all her well-learned falseness to seem concerned. "The only person who can interpret your dream is you;" she glanced at her pad. "All I can tell you is you're exhibiting insecurity and a resultant distrust, which is why you seem unable to share your problems with me now."

She thought she was clever there—Tell the person who apparently came for help he's exhibiting signs he feels he needs help, but you're unable to help him because the help he needs is with the asking for help itself.

All that education and you merely speak in meaningless circularities. You're a fucking gem of the modern dialectic.

Maybe he was being unfair; he *was* refusing to play her game, the only one she knew.

Is it then wrong to denounce her as false?

No. Not really, anyway.

Her falseness stemmed from more than simply being unable to help someone who had no desire to be helped by her. Her deceit was that she was still pretending she was trying to understand his problem, that she could somehow give an answer if only he'd cooperate. She was trying to blame her ineptitude and lack of commitment on his silence.

The fucking hypocrite. Whore.

If indeed he had deep-rooted psychological problems and a paralyzing complex of insecurities she'd only be reinforcing them. The least she could do was *pretend* to delve into his psyche; perhaps then something would emerge.

Presently their conversation had the flow of a clogged toilet. Neither of them had the desire to plunge into it. At all.

The sidewalk outside the office sparkled in the sun, a product of new and inventive ways to recycle glass, and as he walked down the street away from this most recent failure the glancing blows pierced his eyes in a most uncomfortable way. It was different at night though; he'd often thought the effect beautiful.

That's how it always is in The City, I guess. Most everything seems more beautiful when poorly illuminated, when illuminated just right. Enough light in this place and you see just a little too much, the faded stain of a squashed rat at every turn.

He needed to put some distance between himself and the psychologist; the dreary realities of mental actualities were beginning to drag him down. Turning sharply, he descended eighteen steps to the subway platform, swiped his metro card, walking toward its center.

God the air fucking sucks down here.

A friend had recently told him the air in New York was the worst in the entire United States, and being down here he could believe it. It felt thick, the reek of subway stench infecting his pores.

I need to get the fuck out of Manhattan.

Where to go was an uninteresting question to say the least. The trains here only took you to more city. Different types of city to be sure, but nonetheless New York.

Maybe I'll go to the beach.

Before his mind flashed an image, a shore of pure white set beside a placid expanse, there broken by an ill-defined figure, rising from the waters.

He banished the scene, an inward laugh.

From wherever, whatever recess of his mind, the image had sprung, *that* was certainly not anywhere to which *he* had access.

The back-to-back row of seats, five to a side, were all taken; the remaining fifty-odd people were forced to stand and wait. He leaned against a filthy column, gazing down the track in the direction of the hopefully soon to come train. Thankfully there was an old man banging on a steel drum a little ways down the platform: tum-tum-tee-tum-tum. Under the Boardwalk, a good tune, grimly fitting here beneath the greyest of cities.

He at least was feeling bored.

Maybe if I knew more people…

Fuck.

The company of people was more boring than even his own. Only way to squeeze entertainment out of them was in the manner of extreme cynicism, and of that he was most tired today.

No; the thing to now do is get out, away. The beach it is.

Perhaps he'd go take a nap under a real boardwalk, and not merely sleep his way though the series of gestures known as walking.

That was something at which the denizens of The City had become great experts: the bored walk. They did so much walking the practice was the only way to retain a grip on sanity. Or perhaps sanity was in the walking itself. If you were to linger at every occurrence you crossed in this dreadful place the horror of it would likely engross your consciousness completely. If unable to simply keep moving there's no telling to what depths you'd sink. Jesus, the continuity of walking itself a seeming miracle, he really must be bored.

He could hear the screech of a train approaching the platform, could see lights shining along the floor of the tunnel as it curved away into the distance. Those waiting craned their necks in an attempt to peer around the corner.

About fucking time.

The old man was at the peak of his performance, mallets flashing to and fro as he bleated out the final refrain, moving into the closing melody: tum-tee-tum-tum.

Shit.

It was the express, now moving swiftly along the middle track, bypassing the unimportant local stop on its course downtown. He could see the backs of people, their heads reclined against the windows, comfortable in their repose. It looked almost empty, no one standing at all really, save the occasional lone man hanging loosely onto the vertical bars of the car.

The racket of the train passed, and again there was the familiar void of the subway platform in waiting. Apparently the musician, having completed his song in the noise between, had entered into another. Sounded like Flight of the Bumblebee, although in the echoey acoustics of the underground amphitheater the fast pace and small spaces of the tune blended together, sounding more like a high-pitched racket than a complex melody: clangity-clang-clang.

Daniel re-reclined himself against the column, would've lit a cigarette had he not been in Manhattan. These folk wouldn't put up with that. Even if they didn't really mind the smell itself, the simple disregard of the rules would prompt at least one of them to confront him, an encounter with which he at present did not wish to deal. He wanted out, not in. Fuck that whole scene.

The mole-like mentality of modern courtesy had evolved to an extreme form in the close quarters of The City, the almost infinite permutations of man avoiding man infecting its entirety with a deliberate separatism that mirrored the way these people lived: entirely close together but completely removed from one-another. Usually by thin yet sound-proof walls, floors, and ceilings.

Freedom through confinement, autonomy through the law.

Never mind that he himself *seemed* to be exhibiting these same symptoms. *He* was aware of his self-inflicted separatism. The reason for his smokeless environment wasn't neurotic isolation and social fear, not reliance on principles of cooperation and affected harmony, but instead a calculated decision to stay the fuck away from the whole of a world he found odious, from those intolerable souls who called it home. At the very least this made him feel superior in his own head; being aware of this as well only added to the effect.

Slouching forward now, hands on knees. Bide your time; that's the ticket. When walking was out of the question, when waters had to be crossed—continuity through suspension.

Lights.

The collected biders moved slowly toward the edge of the platform.

AN INNOCUOUS POSITION

The image of the subterranean musician remained long after he'd departed the terminal. His single-mindeness in producing the tumult of sound amidst the general apathy and hurry of the New York underground was veritably inspiring, or depressing, depending on the trajectory of apprehension. In any case the musician, thin and aged, wearing tattered jeans and a denim sport-cap, stayed with him on the journey out of The City, as did the strange resonance of his tunes.

Must have an interesting sense of humor, that one. Any mind that could juxtapose those two is sure to have a fascinating commentary on the present situation.

But alas, the platform was in the past and the musician with it, probably still beating his heart out for a few dollars an hour. In the space there, lodged between the street and the sewer, the air was his to manipulate. For him it would remain so unto the end of time.

Maybe I should've stayed a little longer. Maybe even put in a request. Then the air would in some small part be mine as well. The ears that move with it.

Where'd he been going again? Couldn't remember. Somewhere nice though. He'd been going to go somewhere nice…

Shit.

The train had reached Rockaway Parkway, the last stop in Brooklyn. He'd drifted the entire trip and was now about to journey back to Manhattan.

Maybe I'll go back to the platform, request that song.

Quickly now, very quickly, he jumped out of the car.

Most likely for the best.

The station was equally as filthy as had been Union, if in fact a little less oppressive. No musicians here though, just the bustle of those returning home after a day's work. Most of these would now transfer to a bus for the remainder of their journey, the hour-long subway ride apparently not enough to reach their particular monetary valance from The City.

I can't even imagine what that would be like, to move from city to home five, or even seven days a week.

An hour and a half by train, nearly half that again by bus. Nigh an eighth of the day gone in transit; four times that lost to wage labor, embedment in the cogs of The City. When one accounted for a decent night's sleep, the remaining free time seemed fragile, almost ethereal. Considering most of these people had families to take care of, house work to do, many simply had no explicit existence at all. It was all to service The City.

It was like some great experiment, behavioral science on a massive scale. The great mass of warrens and ways had for the most part completely consumed all who'd entered, had bred for a single purpose an entire stratification of labor and energy. These castes each had their designated places of habitation, from the outskirts of Brooklyn to the landfills of Staten Island, culminating in Manhattan. The top of Manhattan to be precise. The multimillion dollar penthouses overlooking the park were reserved for the crème of the world's wealthy and affluent.

Here at Rockaway Parkway the scene was a little different. These were the base laborers, street sweepers, transit workers and the like. True, the food service crowd generally stayed close to home, along with the local merchants. But all-in-all to get a good job, enough hours, with benefits, you had to go downtown.

That's what these people are doing; they're on the last leg of a repeating system, going home to live a little and prepare for the morrow.

I don't even know why I'm here.

But I should hope for a better reason than that.

The whole notion of procreation and labor, like a motif from some old parody of communist propaganda, seemed grossly overemphasized.

That's how they getcha. Forsake your freedom for a dollar and a dream, an American euphemism for the new power of feudal capital.

Nineteen steps to the top, he paused, lit a cigarette. It was late, maybe 6:30, yet the sun still hung surprisingly high, visible yet midst a blue-yellow sky. The humidity in the air gave it a supranatural, larger-than-life appearance.

He stood for a short duration, pulled a few drags from his smoke, taking in the sticky warmth before flicking its half-burnt length to lie amid the refuse and clutter that filled the crease between sidewalk and roadway.

There was a corner deli to the right. He entered, emerging a few minutes later with a hot toasted bagel, extra cream cheese, and a fresh pack of Mediums.

Likely the best thing about New York; the availability of fresh, tasty bagels is truly unsurpassed anywhere else in the world.

Or so he'd been told.

He took a seat at the bench there before the barbershop adjacent to the deli, polished off the bagel with a few quick bites.

Sparked another cigarette.

From this far out he couldn't see the Center of the New World Trade, just as he'd not been able to see it from Midtown. But he knew it was there.

Dressed in mirror-like clarity, the towers reflected perfectly the hue of the great dome above, and at night stood black as black above the Manhattan skyline. That is if you could crawl high enough to catch a glimpse.

The site had been completed over three decades earlier amidst the trailing ends of last depression, striking a hollow cord in a nation concerned more about paying the rent than reclaiming some ambiguous vestige of lost honor.

Now, as the golden anniversary of the September 11th attacks drew near, Daniel contemplated the significance of having lived the sum of his life in the shadow of buildings he'd never enter, buildings that marked the restoration of an ideal he'd never known to begin with.

The need to escape New York pressed upon him, had for what seemed a long time. Somehow he knew he couldn't stay.

I don't belong here, not anymore at least. This place took her from me.

He'd had similar thoughts before, had dismissed them, chased them away, yet then, sitting on the bench in Brooklyn, having come from nowhere, on his way to the same, he felt the final tumbler slip into position, could feel the formerly secured door to his future swinging blithely open to the unknown.

I have to leave The City.

Fuck. What a pain in the ass.

He'd grown accustomed to the ease with which he could disappear into the crowds of the place, the anonymity of a polo shirt and khakis, and above all the readily available women and entertainment that filled its nights.

Where to go, what to do…

And with this moment of contemplation, of openness to the unfolding future, he began his inexorable journey to The Centre.

IN THE SHADOW OF THE IDSC

Daniel of course was unaware of this new beginning, as are all who, in the midst of irony and impotence, sally forth blindly from the origin. This very blindness accounts for the new beginning. For the blind know no limits, not really. When there's no necessity of perspective, lines merely draw boundaries.

Now if only the world could see that sometimes a distinct perspective is necessary.

The people of this world have lost something.

The ancients had dubbed it Telos, and this understanding, although certainly not lost on The Party or its instrument the IDSC, had slowly been purged from the national and indeed world consciousness. Centuries of science and machine, a deluge of mechanism and sense, had finally achieved their end—the elimination of purpose as an active force in the psychological being of mankind itself. If then everything had a cause, if all could be explained by overlapping power structures and innocuous systems, the entire operation of willful instantiation seemed very small indeed, held against the blunt realities of field and necessity.

And in this listlessness, in this very same hole in the fabric of man's being, Daniel unknowingly found himself finally ready to have no plan whatsoever. He was prepared to leave his home, forsaking his divisive and objective bonds, his position, and even himself. The lines of the sighted had dissolved in the faceless solvent of The New World Order, leaving him, as a babe, with nowhere to go and nothing to do.

Apathy and impotence seemed mere dim realities of a world too far gone to be called home any longer.

The Party's platform, the system that allowed it to perpetuate its rule, was founded of the dual and irreconcilable position into which had been thrust the totality of the world's peoples. To have position but no effect, to have a future but no possibility of choice, to be a mere cog… no wonder the masses had long since forsaken and forgotten their role in the unfolding of domestic and global politics. There no time for such concerns, no possibility of influence. Sit, watch. Live. No matter that they themselves would never reach the promised land, the land dictated theirs by their god. Enough to merely be a part of the journey.

Adept at the systems of human psychology, The Party knew well how to exploit their oppositional nature, and if left involved long enough a man could not but become a part of their web, prey and spider met as one, while those watching scratched their heads and wondered aloud how indeed a pig could bring forth such a magnificent design.

For Daniel, long since silently slipped from the machine of New York, the system had been an uncomfortable sanctuary, had allowed him to slide undetected amidst the mechanism and function of the place, free from necessity and thus free to recognize himself and the ridiculousness of the entire project.

As for the friends who'd sheltered him these past few years he could only be grateful, but gratitude itself does not engender loyalty, at least not to the point of sticking around to see how this all turned out. No. The face of the new New York was just a little too blatant, unable to be forgotten or dismissed, even if he could have otherwise done so. To live in the shadow of Their earthly triumph wasn't the thing to do. Not at all.

So I suppose, even here, there's yet a teleological directive: Let's get going.

As to where he should go, he did have some sort of direction in mind: north, to the wilderness of Canada. It was simply a shorter trip than was the long journey to the South. The US, secured in the tight grip of the IDSC, was itself entirely too locked-down, a place where travel was restricted and identities were carefully monitored and verified at every major crossing. In Canada, there at least, security was fairly lax, and the harsher realities of economy, aside from the mines and fields of the north, were for the most part absent. Merely another consumer base for the smooth operation of the *free* market.

It was in this way as well, the differentiation of laborer and consumer into distinct geopolitical zones, that the oppositional thinking of The Party sought to perpetuate systems of control. Due to strict regulations on transmigration and data flow, it had so far been fairly successful, and here indeed was found his present dilemma.

Canada lay nearly three-hundred miles away, across a mountain range and at the far end of roads watched by innumerable state and federal authorities, let alone the omnipresent gaze of the IDSC. And he had no travel pass, no identification… no documentation of his existence at all. Technically speaking he was an illegal person. His very existence balked the order of things.

To escape New York was itself an undertaking. The tunnels and bridges were strictly monitored, and all vehicles entering or leaving the area were subject to a complete sonographic scan, able to detect even the minute disturbances created by the circulatory system. All transit out of the area was strictly monitored; the only way to avoid confrontation with the authorities was to travel the old fashioned way.

If I want to leave this fucking place I'll have to do it on foot.

Glancing at his shoes with a grimace he lit another cigarette, exhaled upwards.

Fuck. I'm gonna have to get back on the god damn subway, take it uptown.

There was still the dilemma of actually leaving, easier on foot than in a vehicle, yet still no simple matter. The entire island could be locked down in under fifteen minutes, and even when open pedestrian traffic was restricted to merely a few bridges. The way he was going, north, there was really only one crossing to be made, Broadway. Unless he wanted to find himself in the Bronx, the prospects of which he did not find appealing.

At the very least he was now moving with purpose. His plan of escape was clear: First get out of New York… as for the rest it remained to be seen.

AS LITTLE FUSS AS POSSIBLE

At this time of day the subway was less crowded, not that it was empty or anything, but he was able to get a seat, without the guilt of forcing some elderly or pretty woman to stand. Reclined against the window, the subterranean cut of the tunnel flashing along outside, he considered his next move.

He didn't have much money to speak of, a couple hundred dollars remaining from what he'd been able to finagle for his bike a while back.

Should be enough to at least get me into Upstate, barring any unforeseen complications.

Yet, that was the thing: There were always complications. Life was nothing more than a series of complications, and any given moment of it was no less complicated than another for its brevity or superfluousness. He'd come to be acutely aware of this, observing those around him, and did what he could to minimize his own entanglements. This did nothing to make his particular movements and interactions less complicated, however, although it did keep him aloof from the more onerous realities of karma. If anything each movement he did make was made even more tedious than it otherwise would've been.

The key now is to slip out of The City with as little fuss as possible.

Emerging from the recess of the subway, Daniel was presented with a bustling motif, the living mural of uptown New York. People hurried passed, vendors wafted enticing signals of greasy smoke into the air, a few bums slept in archways and deserted stoops. Down the street a young boy, no more than twelve years, was breaking to music emanating from a small yet surprisingly loud digital music projector.

Here, even just a short distance from downtown, the smells and sights of people took on a more human feel, less forced, perhaps more natural. Although what counted as natural these days was a question better left to philosophers than to an alienated man, in his mid twenties and on the run, who was fleeing New York for no better reason than that he didn't feel quite comfortable in the place. Looking around, he saw many people, hundreds maybe, who seemed quite comfortable. Even the bums, supine in their small nooks, seemed content.

How the fuck do they do it?

That anyone could contort his soul to the point at which sleeping in a vacant doorway was acceptable, let alone desired, was simply beyond Daniel.

For Christ's sake, I cant even sleep comfortably in a bed in this place. What the fuck is wrong with me?

But he knew, in the way he knew the answer to all of his reflexive rhetorical questions, that there was nothing wrong with him, at least not anything relevant to his not being able to sleep comfortably in New York, surrounded by millions of people he didn't know or care to know and watched by eyes he couldn't see nor would want to see if he could. There was something wrong with The City. There was something wrong with the world. There was even something wrong with the kabobs being burnt a few meters away, the acrid smoke pouring from them smelling of dirty socks and toasted anus.

He retched, acid burning the back of his throat, held a hand to his mouth and hurriedly turned away.

He ran smack into a beautiful girl, knocking a coffee from her hand and splashing the lukewarm liquid into the air and onto her jacket, a well-used thing looking to be cut from suede.

Before he could utter an apology, the girl, wet and uncomfortably pressed against him, smashed coffee cup wedged between her breasts and his upraised arm, kicked him sharply in the shin.

"You mother *fucker*! Watch where the fuck you're going." She stepped back, brushing droplets of brown liquid off herself even as they soaked into the soft leather.

He managed a weak response, "Sorry," the pain in his leg nearly enough to break his composure. "I was just…"

"I couldn't give a shit about what the fuck you were doing."

"Oh."

"What the fuck *were* you doing?"

He began to turn and point to the vendor and his funky, spoiled kabobs, to explain his nausea and maybe even his aversion to people and their various grotesquitudes in general, yet realized he too couldn't give a shit about what he'd been doing.

This girl was more beautiful than any he'd before seen, aside from maybe those whose images constantly beckoned from behind the glass veil of computer monitors and televisions, and of course aside from Hannah.

Yet This girl wasn't a plastic construct, carefully marketed and produced. She wasn't a memory, haunting him. She was a real person, angry to be sure, demure in a loose pony tail, without makeup or adornment. She seemed more real than had anyone in recent memory. He recalled the psychologist with whom he'd talked earlier that day, how he'd momentarily thought about fucking her.

He nearly gagged again.

This girl before him, in all seriousness, shed a light that illuminated some fairly distasteful and all-in-all gross aspects of his life and attitude in general. His cynicism faded in the presence of what could only be said was the closest thing to an angel he could then have conceived.

Now if only he hadn't despoiled her with lukewarm brewed bean juice.

"I was distracted by something," he spoke quickly, reaching down to rub his shin. The pain seemed distant, irrelevant.

"Well, pay the fuck attention." She crossed her arms, appraising him as one would observe a strange animal found rummaging through the garbage.

He observed her as well.

A brunette, slightly shorter than he, she wore the traditional uniform of a middle class New York woman: blue jeans, brown, calf-high boots, a light-grey mock turtleneck sweater, the suede jacket. Now that the shock of smashing into her and being kicked had worn off, he realized she wasn't actually angry—She looked more amused than anything. Her pony tail hung to the side as she stood with head cocked, waiting for him to do something besides gawk at her and mutter excuses.

Her breasts had seemed quite well formed, in the short time he'd been in contact with them.

He had nothing to say. The events of the day, or rather his thoughts on this day, had left him ill-prepared to actually interact with anyone, and as he stood pondering the impossibility of simply talking to the girl she began to turn from him, inspection over, and continue on her way.

"I'm sorry," he said. "Let me help you clean that up." He reached behind himself, snaking a few napkins off the kabob vendor's stand.

Laughter in her eyes, she moved to walk around him. "Don't worry about it."

Having successfully circumvented both him and the vendor, she was gone, lost amid the swirl of people on the street. For a moment he could see the back of her head weaving along the sidewalk.

Daniel exhaled heavily, relief washing over him, strength returning to his knees.

"Thank God," he thought aloud.

That had very nearly caused a fuss.

He walked away from the vendor, away from the girl, and again began brooding on how to escape The City.

A COURTYARD AT TWILIGHT

As Daniel worked his way northward, the streets that had just under an hour earlier seemed rather busy for 8:00 on a Thursday began to clear, as people found their ways home or out, depending on the particulars of their respective social, biological, and economic realities.

The buildings in this part of Manhattan were decidedly smaller than their southern counterparts, although even the most diminutive towered nearly thirty stories above the cement walk upon which he moved. Light still, the dusky Autumn sky was cut in jagged form by the irregular and severe silhouettes of buildings, their edges tracing lines that encompassed the lives of thousands of people, now hidden within.

Walking along the street, Daniel couldn't help but feel small and slightly outnumbered.

Street lamps began to awaken before him, casting the scene into stark relief; previously absent shadows sprang up behind every tree and bush, the smaller side-streets disappearing into wells of darkness.

It was getting a little late to travel.

The streets of Uptown were unsafe after dark, both for the occasional miscreant or thug and, for Daniel particularly, for the watchful eyes of the IDSC, which never slept and could readily identify a lone man. He knew well the ever present cameras, hidden now behind the glare of the street lamps, could capture an image of his face, identify him as an unauthorized person, and have security forces in the area within minutes. It was different in midtown, where restaurants, clubs, and bars kept people out until dawn, where even at this hour he could readily blend in with the crowds and move with anonymity. Here, he was quickly finding himself one of only a handful still out and about.

He made a left onto Amsterdam Avenue, moving into the upscale Washington Heights, two kilometers beyond which lay the Broadway bridge, his first challenge.

In the face of this challenge he'd decided to exit the subway further south, giving himself time to consider a clear line of escape while allowing him to keep moving. Yet now, with the bridge no more than an hour away, he still had no idea how to cross without being detected, detained.

Manhattan was a place strictly delineated by lines of water, traced blue in maps, in actuality a pallid brownish-grey. For Daniel the finitude of The City marked the edges of a vaguely sinister and utterly complex and meaningless maze. Interestingly though, as far as he knew Daniel himself was the only one of its rodential denizens searching for a way out, ironic as he was also the only one of whom he knew who couldn't simply leave if he so desired. People in The City weren't looking for a way out; they were looking for a way in, a way up.

That I'm leaving is perhaps an advantage here. Traveling light too. Maybe I can talk my way through the checkpoint. If I attempt a crossing at the right time of day…

That's not gonna fucking work. Fuck.

Spotting an archway to the left ahead, he ducked through its carved, rough marble aperture, finding himself in a quiet courtyard, flanked on the other three sides by the sheer brick faces of buildings whose tops where lost in the hazy twilight above. No mere vacant lot, the courtyard was perhaps two-hundred meters square, landscaped. Vines of ivy met well pruned lilacs; a few statues reclined in seemingly gently embraces. One of these, a life-size likeness of John Maccabeus, he could easily identify, however strange it was to find such a thing in The City. The others bore no resemblance to anyone he could place.

A path wound its way through the courtyard in an anfractuous loop, the trailing tails of which led to the archway through which he'd just come and another arched portal, this one sealed with an oak door bound in wrought iron.

I suppose that's what realtors call quaint.

The courtyard was illuminated by the soft light of a wrought iron lamp beside the doorway, and at its center, encircled by the cobbled walk, stood a moderately sized Japanese maple, delicate leaves spreading as a flutter of red, somber and poised in the quiet of the place. Beneath the venous boughs sat a granite bench, also roughly cut.

Daniel walked slowly about the tree, paused to study the surface of the bench. An inscription there read:

当我放下現在的自我 我便
可以成為那個理想的我

He looked to the door, only a few meters away, openly curious. What is this place?

The strangeness of the courtyard lay not so much in the oddness of its contents but rather in its sharp contrast to the world outside.

He moved back to the archway, leaning his head through to glance up and down the street, eyes cut by the sharp light of the street lamps above. Temporarily blinded, he leaned against the exterior of the arch, swiping tears from his eyes, reached within his pocket for a cigarette. A stale breeze bustled down the street.

Down an empty street, to be precise.

Vision returned, Daniel found himself the only one in sight, not the position he wanted to find himself in. He lit his cigarette.

No big deal, really. Just another guy come outside for a smoke. Don't mind me.

He turned with measured speed and nonchalantly strolled back into the courtyard. Once again inside, he dodged immediately to the right, ducking behind a tangle of ivy.

He knew he was being paranoid. He knew the chances of his having been spotted were slim. Yet he also knew what would happen were he caught, at least the first part of what would happen. He settled back against the wall of the courtyard, stubbing his smoke against the cool red bricks.

Fuck. What the fuck am I doing?

Perhaps his decision to leave The City had been premature; the move itself now certainly seemed to be. He was stranded uptown, the nearest friendly place at least a forty-five minute walk away, with no one else on the street to lend cover. He was stuck in a queer garden courtyard in Washington Heights with only five cigarettes left and nearly ten hours till daylight.

The sound of footsteps approaching from the south caught his breath. He strained his ears, marking the steady and undeniable rhythm of two sets of feet nearing the archway.

The courtyard, serene as it was, offered little in the way of concealment.

If anyone enters and looks around, I'll be spotted for sure.

The dull clack of hard-soled boots grew louder. Daniel, losing some of his hard-earned composure, felt a moment of panic. He knew quite well the standard uniform of IDSC agents.

He hurried across the courtyard, treading on a flower bed planted there on the far side of the maple, to the left of the iron-bound door, and knocked.

To his surprise it opened easily, softly almost, under the impact of his closed fist, revealing an interior filled with warm light, laughter, and a bunch of momentarily surprised people.

THE PUB ON AMSTERDAM AVENUE

This gave him pause, yet he quickly traversed the threshold, slipping slightly to the side, closed the door behind him. He knew this place, if only abstractly. It was a bar, a pub really.

Tall benches surrounded a large bar and well to the left; beyond this a small stage was set on a riser. The rest of the room was dotted with tables of various configurations, circular, square, triangular, hexagonal, large and small. High-backed booths skirted the walls before, to the right, and behind him. A fireplace, blazing comfortably, was tucked among them into the wall to the right, opposite the bar.

The patrons turned back to their drinks and conversations, nonplused by his sudden entrance. He took a seat at the near side of the bar, slouching forward to rest his elbows on its polished, cherry surface.

Interesting place for a pub like this.

Moving to rub his furrowed brow, Daniel glanced to his right. The bartender, a healthy-looking man of perhaps fifty years, wearing small, wire-framed glasses and a full, well-trimmed beard, approached, polishing a pint glass with a small, white towel.

"What can I get for you, stranger?" He set down the glass and leaned against the inside of the bar, arms fully extended, a slight smile upon his lips and an expectant look on his face.

"What's on tap?"

"Well, lots of stuff." He looked down the line of the bar, at the taps set thereupon and in the wall behind. "All the usual domestics, some microbrews from upstate; even have a few of our own."

"What's good?"

"Depends." The bartender sat back against rear well of the bar; grinned, "Are you a pussy?"

Daniel, never one to be unduly offended, laughed aloud. Not in his presence for more than ten seconds and already the guy had him pegged.

Tenting his fingers, elbows still resting on the bar, "Not at all. Not in terms of my taste in alcohol at least." He raised his cap, resettling it slightly higher on his head. "What do y'all make?"

"An oatmeal stout, a pale ale, an amber, and we just barreled the first batch of our winter ale, brewed with juniper tips; the oatmeal is hand-drawn and served at room temperature."

"Word. The oatmeal sounds just right"

The bartender nodded in agreement, turned, and walked down the bar to draw a pint. Daniel ducked his head, searching for his wallet in the generous confines of the left front pocket of his coat. Resting it on the bar, he raised his eyes, finding himself face to face with the girl from earlier that day, whom he'd despoiled with lukewarm brewed bean juice.

The bartender returned.

Without looking away, "And for my friend…"

"A martini, two olives."

"Make that a Sapphire martini."

She smiled. "Don't think I will be so easily persuaded to forgive you," sitting down on the stool beside him. "Although I do appreciate the thought."

Her suede jacket was nowhere to be seen. Her sweater had been replaced by a thinly strapped tank top, black, which left most of her shoulders and the top of her ample breasts bare. Her hair, down now, spilled over her shoulders and across the top of her chest in rich brown waves, behind reaching near the middle of her exposed back.

Holy shit, Daniel thought, and said "I appreciate your being here," immediately regretting the statement.

What the fuck is that supposed to mean, anyway?

"I know exactly what you mean; I appreciate my being here too."

He couldn't help but laugh. Her presence, the warmth of the pub, the solid taste of stout now running down his suddenly parched throat, it was all enough, just enough, to make him forget how shitty everything actually was.

"Are things really that bad?" she asked, accepting her martini from the bartender with a nod and a smile. Sipping it, swirling the olives around its edge.

Shit.

He must've let his thoughts slip through his eyes, the hang of his head.

Even in forgetting there is an aspect of recollection, a faded few moments of wispy consciousness clung like webs in high-vaulted chambers, moving ever so lightly with the draft.

The last time he'd had the opportunity to drink a hand drawn stout was before the incident that had freed him from The Machine, before Hannah had left him.

"What's your name?" he asked suddenly, brushing old thoughts from his mind. Blushed, "I never got your name."

"Alena."

"Earlier, did I destroy your jacket?"

She smiled, "Basically." Took another sip of her martini; "I'll probably never wear it again, if that's what you mean."

He hid his face in his pint.

"Coffee stains don't really come out of light suede, you know."

She was teasing him, and he, so far gone from his game that he didn't even know the score, was left to squirm. Which he literally did, backing off the bar and turning to face her directly.

"All I had to change into were these rags."

He again laughed aloud. For the third time in just the past few minutes impressed with another's ability to be legitimately humorous.

"They look alright to me," he said, crimson again staining his cheeks. "Err... I mean," swallowed; "You look quite lovely."

The understatement of the year.

This time it was she who blushed, a warm glow spilling into her cheeks, a giggle rippling its way through her chest, just not quite contained by her delicate lips.

"You think so, do you?"

Where the fuck am I? This has got to be the corniest shit I've ever been a party to.

Yet still, he had no inclination to leave, as he normally would've. A simple, "Sorry again. Gotta run," and out the door—his usual modus operandi. Presently he had no desire to exit the pub, and not even for fear of the IDSC agents who very well may have been in the courtyard outside. Concerns of these had completely fled his mind.

He simply was quite content where he was. It was a strange feeling.

And at that moment, the only time he could clearly recall when he was actually comfortable, happy, she stood up, turning toward the oaken door.

"I'm gonna have a smoke. You wanna come?"

He looked at her martini glass, now sitting empty on the bar, glanced down at his pint, also empty. A few brown suds trailed down its near side to collect into a thimbleful of dark liquid.

How long have we been talking? It can't have been too long; we barely said anything.

Alena was nearing the door, the round protrusion of her ass beckoning him to follow, the gentle curve of her back swaying ever so slightly as she moved to pull it ajar.

He set his empty glass on the bar, nodded to the bartender, who raised his hand in acknowledgement, and quickly, but not too quickly, followed her outside.

The sky was dark now, encapsulating the courtyard in a bubble defined by the glow of the lamp behind him. His shadow, cast large by his proximity to the source, lay across half the garden, hiding the flower bed he'd recently trampled, touched the granite bench.

Alena, stopped a few feet away, lighting a cigarette, gazed at him with an odd scrutiny, different from that to which he'd been subjected earlier on the street.

"With that light behind you, I can't see your face." She squinted into the void of his shadow.

He smiled, enjoying the momentary advantage, taking in the beauty of her body, eyes caressing the soft angles of her face, made perhaps more beautiful in the soft penumbra cast thereupon.

When illuminated just right...

The moment stretched as long as possible, he moved to the side, leaned against the wall to the right of the door, directly opposite the archway, whose open mouth yawned eerily through the branches of the maple. He was struck by the realization of why he'd entered the pub in the first place, started, barely maintaining his poise.

She watched the entire progression with open amusement. Laughing softly as she hit her cigarette, she exhaled upward through pursed lips, the cloud at first bright in the lighted envelope of the garden, then slipped away, into the unknowable ether beyond.

"You sure laugh a lot."

"Well, many things are funny."

"You seem to laugh a lot at me."

"You are funny most of all."

She moved from before him to begin a lazy stroll along the path, moving passed his position to stop in front of the statue of Maccabeus. He followed suit, bringing his body behind hers, close enough to touch.

"You know what this is?" She traced the knotted lines of the statue's folded arms with an outstretched finger.

"Of course I do. That's John Maccabeus."

"Maccabeus is the name of a man, the man of whom this statue is a representation. That is who he was." She let her hand fall to her side. "But this does not tell us *what* he was," turning to face him directly, "and even less does it have anything to say about what the statue *is*."

"You seem rather serious all of a sudden."

"When have I ever not been serious, Daniel?" She demurred, bringing her chin slightly down and to the left.

"How do you kn..."

"This statue is a reminder of the man, of what he was. Who he was... This changes with perspective, many definitions of the same name. Yet the man himself cannot be encompassed in a name, which simply serves to mark the occurrence of a character in a story, just as what you are cannot be held in your name."

Alena backed away from the statue, sitting down on the granite bench. Framed by a crimson lattice of leaves, illuminated in clear, unimpeded light, she looked him directly in the eyes.

His breath caught in his throat.

"This statue is a reminder that a man must be what he is, that what a man is is irrevocably tied to what he will be, to what he has been. Maccabeus was his name, yet this name poses to draw an identity through the entirety of his life. Tell me, when you evoke someone's name, what is it you realize? The entirety of what he is?"

Shit. She actually wanted an answer.

He cleared his throat.

"Generally, I evoke a concept defined by how he relates to me. Like, Joe's the guy who sells me cigarettes at the stand around the corner from Grand Central, middle aged and slightly cranky; Maccabeus was the man who led the last revolt against The Party." He sat down beside her; "Alena's the girl I just met, who takes my breath away."

Grinning mischievously, he pulled one last time on his cigarette, stubbed it against the granite underside of the bench. Her cigarette was nowhere in sight.

"Exactly. That which you evoke is purely incidental, often anecdotal. The sum of these things falls far short of what the thing itself *is*. At any given moment everything is much more than what it presents, much more than can be seen." She looked off, "Seeing is more a function of contrast than of reality."

"Do you know what these characters on the bench mean?"

"Yes," she shivered.

"Would you..." halted, "like to wear my coat?" He smiled awkwardly. "It's the least I can do, considering."

She gazed over her shoulder at him, hair blocking the lower portion of her face as it fell to rest on the pebbled skin of her right clavicle below.

"That's OK, Daniel." She began to rummage through her purse. "But, again, I do appreciate the thought."

He cringed inwardly.

I suppose that was a little much.

Sitting close to her now in the crisp Autumn air, away from the smells of the street and hubbub of the bar, he could catch her scent. Not a perfume, too subtle for that, but instead a muted muskiness, sweet on the finish, full. She almost smelled like...

"Hey. What do you have there?"

...The headiest ganja he'd ever seen.

"Just some Kind I got from a Friend," she replied, her hand disappearing into her purse once again to reemerge with a pack of papers.

Who is this girl.

"Tell me, Daniel, how is it you came to the pub tonight?" She began crumbling resin-coated morsels onto a paper held in her left hand. "I've gotta tell you, most of the people in there were surprised to see you. The pub is… not well known; I mean, there isn't even a sign, in here or out on the street."

"I was walking up Amsterdam; it was getting late then. I remember the street lamps had just come on."

He watched, not quite amazed but nonetheless severely impressed, as Alena twisted, in one smooth motion, a nice-sized joint.

"At any rate, I was walking when I saw the archway there," he pointed across her, over her left shoulder, toward the portal, "and decided to see where it led."

"It led you here," sparking the joint with a few quick puffs, "yet what caused you to open the door?" She reclined backwards onto her left arm, elbow locked.

He again recalled why he'd knocked on the door of the pub. His head jerked toward the archway, uneasiness palpable upon his countenance.

"Jesus, what's wrong?

"Maybe you should put that joint out."

"That's *not* gonna happen."

He quickly looked at her, glanced back at the archway; "I'd really feel more comfortable if you put it out," adjusted his position on the bench, bringing both her and the archway into his field of vision.

She looked up at him, laughter again touching the corners of her eyes, making a slight appearance at the periphery of her pursed lips. "And why is that, Daniel?"

"I, uh…" eyes darting from her upturned face to the portal beyond. "You just never know who might be out there."

"I wouldn't worry about them." Holding the joint out to him, she exhaled, the cloud deep with textures and tastes no tongue could know, ethereal and subtle.

"Sure, but still…"

"They don't come in here," still extending the joint for him to take.

"How can you be sure?"

"Well, *no one* comes in here, really." She brought the joint back to her lips, inhaling deeply. "Not very often anyway." She shifted her weight to her right arm, bringing herself closer, and again offered him a hit.

"But *I* just came here, not an hour ago."

"But you're special."

He had to chuckle at that, reflecting on the many ways in which he was "special."

"Honestly. I mean, most people don't even see the arch. Too busy, too much in a rush."

"The IDSC sees everything," he said, feeling a furtiveness he was barely able to keep from his eyes, the small of his back tensing involuntarily.

At this she giggled, bringing to her mouth the hand on which she'd been leaning. He gawked, openly, as the change in her position brought her cleavage directly before him.

"They don't see it at all." She looked up at him. "Take the fucking joint. It's OK; I swear."

And so he took her advice. Something in her eyes, the knowing humor that lay therein, apparently enough to overcome the fear and learned discomfort he'd been developing since childhood.

The aromatic smoke filled his lungs, tingling and expanding, instantly changing his head. He felt... comfortable.

There in the courtyard, suspended in a moment of soft light and strangely friendly company, he again pulled deeply, flavours and feelings like nothing he'd ever smoked or tasted before.

Alena leaned into him, her head resting on his left shoulder.

"Better?"

"Much better."

And so they sat together on the bench, silent, close, the joint passing between them.

He gazed at the statue of Maccabeus, pondering the import of what she'd said.

A man must be what he is.

THE DEFINITION OF CENTER

It was later that night, the other patrons since departed, as he and Alena, the bartender whose name he'd learned was Thorin, were sitting at a table to the right of the door, fire crackling nearby and mugs of ale on the table, that he realized he really didn't know what he was.

This scene certainly didn't seem to fit him, and yet here he was, content and weirdly compatible with it.

The strangest thing.

Did he not know himself better than he did Joe the cigarette-stand guy, Maccabeus? He didn't know them at all, really, yet when he reflected on himself the image projected was of no finer definition than those he had of them, or anyone else for that matter.

Daniel's a guy who should be dead, a guy who generally shuns the company of others and when with them is reserved at best, quiet generally. He doesn't feel comfortable; he's angry, awkward. One time long ago he was happy.

All stories, movements of a character on a stage poorly set, a mere player himself of a script poorly written. That character certainly wasn't special, the one who played him even less so. They were detestable, pathetic.

Irrevocably tied to what he has been, what he will be.

The smallish rectangular table at which they sat, standing at a crooked angle to the fire, was close enough that the warmth of the flames was felt by all, even Daniel, who occupied a seat away from the fire, down the opposing long side. Alena reclined in a chair, back to the fire, somewhat facing him, and Thorin encompassed them both from the short end near her.

They'd been talking about, well, quite a lot, for what seemed quite a long time. Daniel thought the entire thing odd; they really had nothing in common. This, however, merely served to keep the conversation abstract, which to a mind quite sick of mundane actuality was a welcomed respite from conversation with itself.

"You seem lost in thought, Daniel." Thorin looked at him through his spectacles, wiping a froth of ale from the hair on his upper lip.

"Not so much lost. My thoughts are not deep or wild enough for that."

Alena laughed.

He blushed.

Thorin picked up the pipe, a delicate, elaborately blown, side-sloped sherlock, taking a puff that soon came streaming back out his nostrils, sweet-smelling vapor blending with the smell of hearth, fire.

"Perhaps so." He set the pipe back on the table, its crystal protrusions magnifying here and there the light from the flames. "But the thoughts, nonetheless, are there."

"I was thinking about what I should do next." He corrected himself: "I was thinking about what *I* would do next."

"And there's some sort of doubt there?" asked Alena, legs tucked under her as she lounged before the fire, a glass of red wine held lazily in one hand.

"In a way, I'd been leaving The City, when I somehow ended up here. I," he paused, taking in the woman across from him as she resettled herself, knees now drawn to her chest, both feet sharing the seat with her... "I don't know how I'm gonna cross off The Island though." He hurriedly took a sip of crisp winter ale, setting it down and resting his head on his right hand, propped up by table and elbow. "I don't have a travel pass."

"A simple ID should be enough to get you out of Manhattan, I'd think," Thorin mused. "Unless there's some kind of heightened security level right now."

"I don't have ID either."

Met with a broad smile, "What are you, some kind of deviant?"

"In a way. I'm definitely off the curve, if that's what you mean."

"You too, eh?" Alena grinned, took a sip of wine.

The conversation paused then, long enough for the pipe to pass among them.

"To be honest," he said, biting off a chewy hit and coughing it lightly into the slowly circling ceiling fan above, "I can't believe I randomly found this place, with you two here, and ganja like this."

"I've a hard time believing that as well," Alena chirped in.

"What is that supposed to mean?"

"What do you suppose it means?"

"If I didn't know better, I'd say you're questioning my motives."

Thorin leaned forward. "Should they be questioned?"

He had to think about this for a second, started reflecting on who he was again, stopped, reached over his head, lifting his cap and brushing his hair back, tossed the cap on the table beside his mug of ale.

"No, they shouldn't. I can't expect you to know that or believe me though." He looked down at the table. "I barely believe myself."

"I believe you," Alena said, set her empty glass on the table.

"And I put much stock in this young lady's opinion," Thorin rejoined, glancing at Alena with a broad, paternal smile.

He looked at Alena, the angel; asked, "Why?"

"Because I see you, Daniel the Dreamer."

Startled, he sat upright. "How do you know about my dreams?"

"Dreams?" she mused, gazing beyond him to the door, he imagined, he hoped, peering into the past, to the short time they'd spent alone in the courtyard. "I was just referring to the look of your eyes, the…"

He looked at her then, saw for a moment something more than a beautiful, incredibly warm and chill girl.

She broke off, paused. "…how you're looking at me now, like you see things that aren't there, like I'm more than I am."

"But I see you too."

For a moment they sat there, the room silent except for the crackle of fire, eyes meeting for more than a moment, more than that.

Pale aquamarine and darkened amber.

First to break contact, always first in that, Daniel snuck a glance at Thorin, who sat with arms crossed, looking not at them but the fire, apparently engrossed by something *he* saw *there*.

The older man's gaze returned to the table, pausing for a moment on Alena, moving swiftly to Daniel. "You too are leaving The City then. Where will you go?"

"I'm not sure, really. I'd been thinking about Canada."

"Interesting." He shared a look with Alena, who slipped a cigarette from her purse, lit it.

"You're leaving The City too?" he asked, looking from Alena to Thorin, back again.

Thorin responded quickly, "I'm leaving within the week, possibly in the next few days. Alena… has matters here to attend to."

"Where are *you* going"

"I'm going to The Centre."

"What the hell is The Centre?"

Alena laughed, "It's where he's going, Daniel. At least try to keep up."

"Err... and where is It located?"

"Could be anywhere, really, things being as they are. Not here though. New York is, well, not what it used to be.".

"And I thought I was the only one who'd noticed;" Daniel smiled, laughed gruffly to himself, polishing off the rest of his mug.

"Would you like to come with me? Otherwise I'll be traveling alone, and I could use the company."

Alena, sitting quietly in her chair, feet again tucked under herself, was staring into the fire.

"She has to stay, Daniel."

"How can I come with you when I can't even cross the bridge?" he asked, in a way now looking for excuses to stay, knowing he couldn't.

"I am... familiar with the captain of the morning watch on the Broadway crossing. He is a friend."

"A strange friend to have."

Gazing over the table at Daniel, "Well, these are strange times. Strange times indeed."

CHAPTER 2
ACROSS THE NATION

TO LEAVE THE BAY

The three young men made their way across the broiling black expanse of asphalt, here having to pick their way around a parked
car, there between a large truck and a minivan. Andrew led the way,
with Peter behind him and Thorin bringing up the rear. They carried
among themselves several bags, plastic stretched thin by the weight
of their contents.

Peter, bearing two heavy loads, was glad to see the vehicle they,
well *he*, really, had purchased earlier that morning, an old Jeep Cherokee, green, with nearly three-hundred thousand miles on it, air conditioning that no longer worked, and seat belts that had the annoying
habit of retracting just a little too much and then refusing to loosen.
He'd bought it from an old man outside of San Mateo for eight-hun-
dred cash, no paper work; the plates would be good through the end
of the year.

A little expensive for a 2001

Not the first time the thought had occurred to him that afternoon.

Reaching the jeep, Andrew opened the trunk, placed his burdens
within. Thorin and Peter followed suit, the former pausing momentarily to retrieve a bottle of water and a package of beef jerky before
drawing the hatch closed and taking his place in the front passenger
seat.

Peter was more than content to lounge, legs stretched in front
of him, shoes off, in the back. He'd brought along a pillow expressly
for the purpose, having long ago determined the best way to spend

a long car ride was comfortable, preferably asleep. Not that he could spend the entire journey lying in the back seat. Eventually, of course, he'd have to take his turn at the wheel. Yet one of the conditions of his buying the Cherokee was that he wouldn't have to drive until they reached Salt Lake City, giving him a solid twelve hours of no real responsibilities at all.

Andrew, slightly taller than Peter and in far better shape, boasting a rough, dirty blond mane that fell in not-quite-stark contrast to Peter's semi-rumpled brown, put the jeep in drive, bringing the vehicle in a broad turn around the column of cars and toward the exit of the parking lot.

From his position in the back seat, Peter watched the blue and white sign, an icon of the American landscape, disappear as they turned the corner, heading north toward San Francisco.

Live Better.

He mused on the familiar subscript, wondered how many others across the nation were also then leaving the domain of Wal-Mart, how many of these were set on the same destination as they.

"I wonder what's happening on campus," he stated to no one in particular, shimmying his way into the pillow propped behind him. "Hey Thor, lemmy get some of that jerky."

Thorin, broad of shoulder, sporting a short-cut, full beard, handed the pouch over his shoulder without turning, catching Peter's eyes in the mirror set into the visor before him.

Andrew laughed as he turned the wheel, bringing his cigarette from his mouth to his left hand. He merged onto 101, which would take them to I-80 and the greater world beyond The Bay.

Peter grinned, dug into the bag of jerky.

Thorin hated being called Thor, said it made him seem like a dimwit or a second-rate porn star, both of which were clearly unacceptable. Peter and Andrew, however, persisted in teasing him about it, his disapproval merely more impetus for their mockery.

Thorin had long ago given up attempting to make them stop; letting it simply slide served to dispel the situation best.

Taking back the bag of jerky; "I dunno if too much has changed since it closed, honestly."

"I suppose so," he stared at his grey-socked toes, chewing thoughtfully.

Andrew broke in, "If things had gotten better they'd have re-opened campus. If things have gotten worse we'd have heard about it." Pulling on his cigarette, he exhaled through an open mouth, attempting the impossible feat of blowing smoke rings in a speeding car with its windows down. "I'm sure campus is fine; the National Guard has been posted outside of Oakland all week. That place is locked down."

The three roommates, all enrolled at Berkeley, sharing an apartment in Elmwood, had been forced to find lodging elsewhere following the explosive onset of riots in Oakland the week before.

The school administration had said the situation was too uncertain for the university to continue as usual, canceling class for the rest of the quarter. The friends had then settled into their apartment for an extended summer of dedicated chilling, but a fire in nearby Rockridge, which consumed an entire block before firefighters were able to put it out, had given them second thoughts. Thorin, who hailed from Brooklyn, and Peter, who'd grown up in Ithaca, NY, had been lucky enough to stay with Andrew at his parents' house in Belmont, just south of San Mateo.

"That shit's crazy," Thorin muttered, bringing a hand from his scruff-lined jaw to open the glove box. The clear stoner of the group, he pulled a pre-rolled spliff of Humboldt's finest from a tin held therein, running it under his nose with an approving sniff before sparking it behind a curved hand.

"Seriously," Andrew accepted the joint, taking a few puffs, handed it to Peter. Exhaling, "It's hard to believe it's gone on for this long."

Reclined in his own world, Peter closed his lids against the sun's brightness, chiefing the spliff as they cruised into South San Francisco.

The scene was replaced by one arguably just as brilliant, perhaps with more depth of image and hue. The flat colors that drew the planes of three dimensional space seemed somehow dull compared to the vast chasm created by his closed lids. Cosmos of red and green danced in opening space, repeating patterns conglomerating to form intricate and vaguely articulate images of things far too sensitive, far too absorbing, to be illuminated by the sun's radiation.

Slowly but much too quickly his eyes adjusted, dilated—all that remained a bright magenta devoid of detail and interest.

That's the way of things, I suppose. It's in the transition, the change, where lie the more engrossing elements of experience. The rest just seems filler. I guess that's where I differ from most people. They seek the end of the rainbow, whereas I seek... rain?

It's a difference of perspective. And of actuality. Rainbows are formed as circles; there is no end, only repetition, much like the great Wheel itself. Yet still, pointlessly still, perspective seeks termination, a golden land spun by pure wistfulness. This is the nature of perspective and should rightly be acknowledged as such.

Really, how can it be otherwise? There is of necessity a counterpoint to be sought, a balance to be struck; otherwise what would there be to experience? Without balance can there be perspective at all? Just as the eye seeks the end of things, so too does light rejoice in refracted estrangement from itself, to this end generates in perception a counter-perspective to its separatism.

The necessity of perspective thwarts itself in its object, the two circling each other, an endless game of limits and completion.

"What the fuck, man." Thorin glared at him through the space between the seat and headrest. Hazel eyes, greens and browns, a touch of gold, met Peter's dark gaze.

He'd been spacing out. The joint looked to be nearly half gone.

I must've been hitting it pretty hard.

Handing it to Thorin around the left side of the seat, Peter again lay back; smiling contently, "Wisdom falls as rain."

A purposeful tinge of scorn in his voice, "Whatever, you fucking hippie;" Thorin laughed. He wasn't one to get very upset at another's indulgence in fine organic herb, at Peter's not at all.

The three of them were likely as close as three friends could be, and Peter counted the years they'd thus far spent together among the best in his life. Never before had he been so able to simply and thoroughly be himself. He imagined, well hoped really, that the others felt the same.

They were coming up on San Francisco itself now, the skyscrapers of downtown shining brilliantly ahead as rush-hour traffic pulled them to a near stop.

Andrew sighed, "I wonder if traffic will be bad all the way to Richmond."

"Likely;" Thorin passed him the joint.

Taking a pull, "I suppose we aren't in any real hurry though;" exhaling, "The protest isn't for three days."

Peter roused himself from his fancy, sitting up to examine the road ahead. "You have to wonder how this thing in Oakland will affect the protest. I do at any rate."

Andrew passed before Peter the spliff to Thorin, who accepted it easily, sitting back into his seat.

Peter also sat back, rolled down the window, bringing the sounds of San Francisco in gridlock closer, lit a cigarette.

What will happen in Philadelphia? Anything?

In the lane beside him a gorgeous woman in a metallic-sliver BMW Roadster convertible, top down, slowly passed. Catching Peter staring at her, she smiled broadly, raising an inquisitive brow.

He nodded, offering his most winning grin.

"Why are you in the fucking left lane?" Thorin admonished Andrew. "Get in the middle. These people are toasting us."

Looking at him sideways, steel-grey blue, flat and unforgiving, "You wanna drive, Thor?"

"Not particularly."

Andrew put on his right blinker, insinuating the jeep between the BMW and the SUV behind it.

What seemed like hours later found the jeep crossing the Bay Bridge, I-80 bringing them close to Oakland before veering north passed Berkley and Richmond and into Solano county. An hour of Gridlock had drained any enthusiasm they may have had, and their approach to the city found curiosity replaced with impatience.

As they neared the end of the bridge, though, none of them could forestall a slight intake of breath, a peak of interest.

Visible from even such a great distance, National Guard troops occupied the streets on the outskirts of the city. There appeared to be quite an encampment, sprawling through most of Campbell Village and Prescott. Large transports and military vehicles huddled in sporadic groups; entire villages of tents, here and there an imposing pavilion-style canvas structure, a large medical area noticeable for the red cross found on the top of each of its component tents, could be seen

Several clouds of dark smoke rose from Cypress, just west of downtown, fairly close to the encampment.

The riots were far from being cooled or quelled.

"God damn;" Thorin breathed.

"Fucking crazy;" Peter gaped out his still open window.

Andrew, hands tight on the wheel, remained silent with thoughts apparently too dark, too much, to articulate.

There was silence in the car for a seemingly long, likely fairly brief, duration.

"What the fuck did they expect would happen?" Andrew asked angrily, gazing at the scene, close enough to witness yet for this still remote, untouchable. The steel in his countenance spoke volumes, a story lurid with deep-seated grievances and unfinished business.

"I don't know they expected anything to happen," Thorin turned his attention from Oakland to his friend, "honestly;" he glanced at Peter, seemingly in need of some sort of support or commentary.

"I, uh..."

"Gimmie a fucking break;" Andrew signaled a left-hand turn, jerked the jeep into the passing lane, swiftly circumventing a car that had been slowly approaching a quite intolerable speed. "What would you do if it were *your* city, or *your* sister?"

Thorin looked at him with measured cautiousness; "I don't know what I'd do."

"It was the fifth one just this month."

Again silence owned the car. The dull roar of wind rushing across partially cracked windows filled their ears.

"Something needs to change," Andrew spoke. Mainly to himself.

Sitting up, taking a position directly between the two front seats, Peter brought his hand to Andrew's right arm. "Isn't that why we're going to Philadelphia?"

"You think a protest will change anything?" Andrew scoffed. "Nothing ever changes."

"Fuck that, man. Things don't change until someone changes them, until the people decide they *will* change, until people change themselves."

Andrew turned from the road, from the siege of Oakland before them, met Peter's eyes. "People don't change."

Steel and dark void, there opposed across the small extension of the car.

Sitting back in his seat, Peter broke contact, lit another cigarette, its rising smoke testament to the truth of his friend's words. Gazed out the window, unfocused; "Let's hope you're wrong."

Thorin, quietly observing them, hunkered down in the crux of his seat and the door beside, absently stroking the scruff of his beard. He pulled another spliff from his tin, hoping earnestly that his friends, these two men he knew and loved like brothers, wouldn't change.

As the road brought them north, away from Oakland and one step closer to their destination, the sweet smell of ganja again filled the cabin of the Cherokee, mixing first with the flat smoke of Peter's cig, later, long after they'd journeyed beyond the provenance of The Bay, to find itself entwined with the acrid fumes of burning tires and car upholstery.

A DESERT HIGHWAY AT MIDNIGHT

The drive out of California was a muted affair at best, the highlight a single stop at a gas station outside of Sacramento, after which Peter, who desired to see neither the beauty of the Sierra Nevadas nor the austerity of the desert beyond, signed out for an extended nap.

He awoke to find the jeep speeding down the deserted highway, its lights pitifully unable to penetrate the dark expanse ahead.

Andrew, no longer driving, was engaged in a somewhat heated discussion with Thorin, who slouched in the driver's seat, a half-burnt joint held loosely between the middle and ring fingers of his right hand as he gestured authoritatively, obviously making some sort of resounding point.

Must have switched somewhere outside Reno.

Peter, squinting the sleep from his eyes, drew a cigarette from his pack, sparked it, attempting to orient himself with the direction things had taken while he was asleep.

"That's bullshit, man, and you know it;" Andrew turned from Thorin, tracing the shadowy limits of the road ahead. "What was it Mao said? 'The party commands the gun; the gun must never command the party'?"

Yawning, "And why again should we listen to Chairman Mao?" Peter stretched his back, arching diagonally, slid to the left.

Thorin, wearing a grin Peter couldn't see but nonetheless knew was there, cut it; "Were you listening to The Dude's story, Peter?"

"The Chinaman is not the issue," Andrew added.

At this Peter couldn't help but smile. For his part Thorin laughed aloud, lighting the previously dormant joint.

"We'd been saving the rest of this for after your lazy ass woke up."

"Much appreciated." He accepted his friends offering. Looking at Andrew, "But seriously, why should anything Mao said be relevant to anything at all?"

"Because there's much to learn from him."

"Like what?"

"Like how to break party rule;" Andrew turned toward him.

Thorin chimed in; "We were arguing about whether protest is an effective vehicle for political change. I was saying that in today's world affecting the popular will through protest and grassroots movement is one of the few forms, if not the only form, of actual political power regular people can exercise."

'Which is absurd," Andrew rejoined.

Peter, handing the joint forward to Andrew, "Then why are you coming to Philly?"

"Because I have to do something;" he smiled. "And I have nothing better to do than drive across the country with you fucks."

"Then you admit the protest is worthwhile;" Thorin concluded.

"I never said it wasn't."

"But you just sa..."

"Peter, see if *you* can understand what I'm saying." Andrew hastily passed the joint off to Thorin, faced Peter. "In modern American politics we see two parties vying for control. These parties lay claim to vastly different ideologies, yet queerly enough display nearly identical policies on all but the most topical concerns." He paused, gathering his thoughts. "We all agree this is no accident, that the two party system is charade, yes?"

Thorin and Peter nodded their agreement.

"And I'm sure we also all agree the subterfuge is working quite well, generally. So, I've gotta ask: What good is protest when there's only recourse to one power? Such a system is not responsive to the people." He paused, lit a cigarette. "That we have the freedom to protest, that we do protest, is then meaningless."

Peter adopted a mask of confusion. "But I thought you were *not* saying that going to Philly is a waste of time."

"Exactly;" Andrew sat back in his seat, tapping the ashes from his smoke out the cracked window.

"And somehow the wisdom of Mao brings sense to this?"

"Yes;" he paused. "Well, in a way. What we can learn from him makes sense of it."

"Enlighten me."

"'Political power comes from the barrel of a gun' is the statement in question, or rather its corollary 'The party commands the gun; the gun must never command the party'." He pulled quickly on his cigarette, a habit he had when his thoughts were most animated. "Mao's thinking here is transparent, honest, unashamed: The party holds power, holds it as a single party, because it holds the military, the police; it makes the policies and laws these agents enforce, and these agents owe their allegiance to the party, to the state actually, and not to the people."

"And so long as there's only a single party the people have no way to effect change in these laws and policies, and so live by the party's dictate." Peter turned from the window to face Andrew directly; "I see nothing new here. This is all pretty obvious."

"Indeed. Which is why it's strange no one has exploited the opportunities these statements reveal."

"And these opportunities would be..?"

"To effect fundamental change in a nation one must control the gun."

Peter laughed, turned from Andrew to flick his cigarette out the window. "Yeah. I'm sure no one has ever thought of staging a coup d'état before."

"Thought about it, maybe, but actually attempted it? Not that I'm aware."

"And you want to... stage a military overthrow of the United States Federal Government?" Peter asked dryly. The dark of his eyes did not reflect the humor that otherwise could have been inferred from the question.

"Of course not," said shortly. "Every coup I can think of involved the military itself turning on the government. That's not the answer; I mean, who the hell would want that?" He again drew a cigarette, sparked it, turning to exhale out the window. "Besides, the US military is this government's favorite pet, and even a pet such as it wouldn't turn on such a loving master."

Thorin, who'd during the intervening exchange managed to single-handedly chief the joint to extinction, grinned broadly, teeth glinting in the darkness, bounded by a scruffy frame. "You have such a way with words," began to laugh, "Maybe you should be a politician."

"Fuck off, Thor."

Turning back to Peter, "The only way, the only real way to achieve anything here, is to remove the military and police, the executive mechanism itself, from the hands of the state, or rather *from the hands of those who control the state*. Now, in the US the executive apparatus is entirely loyal, through and through, to the state. However," he paused for dramatic effect, "this is precisely where the opportunity presents itself."

Slightly interested now, Peter nodded for Andrew to continue.

"In remolding our democracy into this charade, these assholes have left themselves, not the state, vulnerable." Pulled on his cigarette, "They've created a situation in which whoever controls the state apparatus can act with impunity; any action of the state is made out to be the will of the people. In setting up their oligarchy they've cast themselves as disposable figures. What I've come to realize is the state itself is the gun; the military and the police, or any other of its agents, are merely ammunition, that which strikes where it is aimed and serves as the actual potency of the state's will. What needs to be done is for the gun to be taken out of the hands of the party. Not the military, the state itself."

"Brilliant," Peter sighed.

"Astounding," Thorin interjected, grinned.

"Yet how do you plan to turn the state on the party?" Peter asked innocently, reaching quickly to gaffel Andrew's smoke.

"I'm still working on that part." No hint of jest touched his voice.

Laughing, Thorin brought his full attention back to the dark expanse ahead. "You're so full of shit man."

Peter, looking hard at Andrew, wasn't so sure he agreed. Not that he thought in any way Andrew was capable of doing what he suggested, no, but still he couldn't ignore the conviction in his friends voice.

"So why, again, do you not think going to Philly is a waste of time?" Thorin glanced at Andrew from the corner of his eyes.

"Because a protest is more than a bunch of people voicing their malcontent," Andrew replied, reclaiming the last vestiges of his smoke from Peter. "It is a meeting of people, where we are going hundreds of thousands of people, people with whom to talk, people with a will to effect change." He looked at Peter questioningly; "The protest is set to last all week, yes?"

"That's the plan, as far as I know." He looked out the window at the passing emptiness; "But I suppose it all depends on whether anyone actually shows up." He laughed, "I'd hate to spend all week standing around with only you dipshits."

THE GIRL FROM SALT LAKE CITY

"What's your name again?" Andrew swayed over his Crown and Coke, likely his sixth of the night, leaning toward the buxom blond seated beside him at the bar.

Taking the question as flirtation, she giggled slightly, sliding back on her stool, bringing her arms together to rest on the bar and arching her back, managing to make her breasts seem even larger than they had before. "Gloria."

"Gloria from Salt Lake City," he appraised her with open appreciation; "I didn't know they had girls like you here." Finishing his drink, he set it down firmly on the bar, the ice cubes within responding with a satisfying clink. He motioned to the bartender for another cocktail.

Seated at a table a bit away, Thorin and Peter, kicked back in their chairs with drinks of their own, a smoked porter for Thorin and a scotch, straight, for Peter, watched the scene.

"I think she's a prostitute," Thorin grinned at Peter. "I mean, why else would *she* be into *him*?"

"Jealous?"

Thorin turned, "Definitely not." Glancing toward Andrew and his companion at the bar, "Though Andrew does seem to pull an inordinate amount of ass, generally."

"He's more charismatic than you or I;" Peter also turned from the bar. "Besides, what the fuck would you do if she did want to... flirt with you?"

"Nothing, obviously. But that's not the point." Thorin laughed; "Let a guy fantasize. It's not like I'm married."

"I'll be sure to tell her as much when we meet her in Philly," grinned sinisterly. "If anyone should be jealous it's my lonely ass."

"So why don't you go talk to her? Andrew won't mind."

Peter's smile broadened, "Cause I'm not into prostitutes."

The bar in which they found themselves hummed with the conversations of what could be called a comfortable number of people.

Too few people in a bar and it feels awkward, too many and it feels crowded, a microcosm of society, a manifestation of human psychology, alienation and fellowship together. People go to the bar to be around people they don't know.

"Hey man, I'm gonna go outside for a smoke;" Peter rose from his seat.

Thorin looked up at him, "You smoke way too much."

"You gonna fucking come or not?"

"Of course I'm coming." Thorin rose as well; "Just saying."

The two of them wound their way among the tables, heading for the front door. They'd just crossed the threshold, Peter bringing a Camel to his mouth, when Andrew burst through behind them, blue eyes bright with laughter and a full smile upon his face.

"What the fuck guys!" He stumbled slightly as he skirted behind and around Thorin to bring himself opposite the door, back to the street, Peter to his left and Thorin to his right. "I'm not invited?" He motioned for Peter to give him a cigarette, sparked it with a lighter from his front shirt pocket.

Peter, a quizzical look on his brow, "We thought you were busy in there with the blonde." He glanced shortly at Thorin then back to Andrew, "To be honest I didn't know you were so insecure."

"I had an inkling." Thorin's smile showed a crack of ivory, nearly luminescent in the light of the almost full moon.

"Meh," Andrew quickly exhaled upward. "I think she might be a prostitute."

Peter burst into laughter, Thorin and Andrew soon following.

Peter caught his breath; "We were thinking the same thing."

Andrew stopped laughing.

"I think I'm gonna run to the jeep real quick," Thorin dismissed himself.

"She's fucking hot though, no?" Andrew looked to Peter.

"Quite."

They puffed their cigs for a silent duration, broken by Thorin's triumphant return from the jeep, his smoldering prize held loosely between his lips.

Andrew, sentimentality in his eyes and mirth on his lips, brought his hand to Thorin's shoulder. "I love you, man. You never change."

They passed the spliff among themselves, in deep and perhaps too loud conversation about the various merits of marijuana, particularly as found in the social aspects of its use.

"Excuse me," a small voice, feminine, interjected itself from behind Peter, who presently faced away from the bar's door.

The three friends turned to address the interloper. Peter stepped to the side, making her a de facto fourth member of the cypher.

"I couldn't help but notice you guys aren't from here;" she accepted the joint from Thorin with a shy smile, pulled it, approval clear on her face.

Peter accepted the joint from her, "Just here for the night."

"You guys are from California?" She pointed to the Cherokee, its plates clearly visible in the moonlit parking lot.

"Indeed we are," Andrew received the joint from Peter.

Waving the ganja away, to the girl, Thorin added, "We're on our way to Philadelphia."

The girl, a petite brunette who looked to be about an age with them, held the spliff, murmured, "It's a small world."

"How is that?" Peter asked.

"It's just, well, everyone in the bar is simply out on a Wednesday night, here to drink and hook up and..." she trailed off. "You know, do whatever people out at a bar on a Wednesday night do."

"Your powers of observation are truly astounding," Andrew commented dryly, gaze intent on the young woman's face.

Thorin snickered, rocking back on his heels.

Peter grinned, finding humor not in the girl nor in Andrew's sardony, but instead in the still he perceived in his friend. Only Peter would be able to see it; only he knew Andrew well enough. Hidden behind the dry humor, the somewhat mocking demeanor, lay an interest Peter hadn't seen in Andrew for quite some time.

"What I'm saying is you three stick out in there. You're not here just to go out; you're different from the others. It's obvious in the way you hold yourselves."

"And this makes the world small how?"

"Well, you see, I also don't belong here."

It was then Peter noticed the backpack she wore, the Columbia jacket gracing her shoulders where should have been found the straps of a dress or tank top, the jeans that weren't skin-tight, more comfortable than fashionable.

"And you're also going to Philly," Andrew surmised.

"Indeed I am," she blushed, holding out the joint, which had gone out, to Thorin, who moved quickly to relight it. She took a hit.

"And you want a ride."

"If I did," exhaling, "would that be a bad thing?"

"Not at all."

Peter groaned.

She looked from Andrew to him, asked, "What?" Turning to face him squarely, "You not like girls or something?"

"I like my leg room," he replied; smiled, "But I suppose sacrifices have to be made."

"In the name of the cause." Thorin giggled.

The three of them looked at him, back to each other, shared a moment of communal humor.

"What the fuck's your problem?" Thorin addressed the group.

Peter laughed; Andrew giggled. The girl took them all in with a smile.

Drawing two cigarettes from his pack, "Don't worry about it, Thor." He handed a Camel to Andrew, lit it for him before sparking his own.

The girl looked from Peter to Thorin. "Thor?" she asked, a slight look of incredulousness on her face.

"Thorin."

"I see."

Andrew broke in; "And this is Peter, and I'm Andrew." He paused to hit his smoke; "What's your name again?"

"Edith."

"Edith from Salt Lake City…"

"Outside of the city, actually"

"…who somehow happens to be at a bar on a Wednesday night, packed and ready to go to Philadelphia?" Andrew raised an eyebrow.

"And what of it?"

"Simply a little odd is all." He brought his cigarette to hang idly between his lips.

"It's not odd in the slightest. I was meeting a friend here; we were gonna drive to Philly together."

"What happened?" Peter asked from the sidelines.

"I just found out her car broke down north of Farmington."

"And now you're stuck in Salt Lake at two in the morning, with no ride and nowhere to stay," Andrew concluded. "Quite the damsel in distress, eh?"

"Would you be prince charming?"

"It's a part I wouldn't mind playing;" he pulled on his cigarette, held between the tips of his thumb and middle finger.

"So you're a player then?"

Peter guffawed; Thorin grinned.

Andrew, unfazed, "The world's a stage," flicked his cigarette, "or so The Bard says."

Recovering his composure, Peter looked to the door of the bar.

We're done with this place.

He looked to Andrew and Thorin, who'd seemingly come to the same conclusion.

"I'll get the tab," Andrew filled the void, walked into the bar.

Edith, still in possession of the spliff, marveled at them. "You guys are somewhat spontaneous, eh?"

"Not so much," Peter replied. "We just have an acute understanding of when it's time to move on."

"And what would this understanding be based on?"

"Things are done when The Spirit is whole."

"What he means," Thorin interjected, "is you've made our group complete."

"What I mean is there's nothing more to do here."

"Exactly," Thorin grinned.

Edith glanced from one to the other, brown eyes creeping slightly to the corners, away from them, looked down, face screwed in seeming perplexity, or perhaps concern.

Thorin's smile broadened; "Don't worry. We're not weird at all."

A DIALOGUE AT DAWN

Nearly four hours later found the jeep hurtling through the barren hills of southern Wyoming, the lighted dawn finally bringing some relief to a formerly black and featureless scene. Thorin and Andrew lay in the back, each reclined against his respective door, Thorin on the passenger side, taking full advantage of Peter's pillow, Andrew wedged in an uncomfortable looking position in the seat behind Peter, neck kinked at a sharp angle.

"What did you mean earlier by The Spirit, Peter?" Edith asked across the space separating the two front seats.

Peter took a sip of the now lukecold coffee he'd gotten over an hour earlier at a twenty-four hour Starbucks in Rock Springs. "Strange you'd wait until now to ask," he remarked mildly.

"I wasn't waiting," she rejoined; "The sunrise reminded me."

"How's that?"

"I don't know, really. It just seems... I dunno." She lay back in her seat, putting her knees up on the dash before her. "Sunrise has just always seemed like a spiritual time to me, I guess."

"I suppose it does;" he flicked open his pack of Camels, drew one for himself, offered the pack to Edith.

She hesitated momentarily, then quickly accepted. He retrieved the lighter from the dash, a new Bic he'd also gotten in Rock Springs, the image of a bear catching a fish upon its surface, lit her smoke and then his own.

"Why do you think that is though?" He studied her for a moment before turning back to the road.

"I dunno. I never really thought about it"

He laughed, "That sounds nice."

Leveling a look at him, "And you're making fun of me again?"

"Not at all. I'm just saying: It would be nice to simply appreciate something, even know something, *think* something without having to think about it." He grinned; "It must be nice to be a girl." Finishing quickly, "Not that I'm thinking about a change or anything."

"And *you* think girls *don't* think?"

He leaned into his seat, "Trust me, it's not the same," hitting his smoke, flicking its ashes out the window.

"Really." Not a question.

"I think about *everything*." He cocked his head, glancing at her as she gazed out the windshield.

"So tell me, then: What did you mean by The Spirit... what was it again? 'Things are done when The Spirit is complete'?"

"Indeed. Basically." He smiled.

"I've just never heard 'spirit' used like that before."

"Well, let me ask you a question."

She nodded for him to continue, hitting her Camel.

"Is sunset any less spiritual than sunrise?"

"No."

"And what about noon, when the sun is high in the sky, when shadows are smallest. Is noon also a spiritual time?"

"Sure."

"And a few hours ago, before we stopped to get gas, in the middle of the night, the darkest hour, as we sped down the highway, all awake, would we also say this was a spiritual time?"

"Perhaps."

"And the time between then and now?"

"OK. I get your point. Every time could be called spiritual."

"Indeed."

"But doesn't that just water down the concept of spirituality itself? If every time of the day is spiritual, if then ever action could be spiritual, what does the word even mean?"

"See," he tapped his smoke out the window, "now we're thinking," grinned.

Edith rolled her eyes at him, resettled herself, knees still on the dash.

"OK," he continued quickly; "The point there, I suppose, is that such an understanding does not dilute the concept of spirituality at all—It raises our awareness and our understanding of Spirit itself. Forcing a preconceived notion of spirit onto the world merely robs each moment of that which it rightly is."

She pondered this for a moment, knocking the coal of her cigarette out the window, placing the butt in her empty coffee cup.

He turned to look at her; "What does 'spiritual' mean to you?"

"I guess it means there's more to something than is actually there," she paused, "or rather that what is actually there is more than what can be seen."

"But, on some level, you must 'see' the spirituality in things," he posed; "Otherwise you'd never think to use the word."

"Touché." She gazed out the windshield at the now fully risen sun. "I suppose I *feel* the spirituality in things."

"And this feeling is somehow different from other feelings you have, from the sensuous, the aesthetic?"

"If I just say I'm *aware* of the spirituality in things, will you still have an inane question?"

"No."

"Then," quickly sneaking another cigarette from the pack, "I'm *aware* of the spirituality in things."

"But what is it then you're aware of, exactly?" Innocence framed purely, his dark eyes veritably glinted in the retreating dim of the car.

She gave a small shriek, disturbing Thorin, who grumbled something inaudible and snuggled deeper into his pillow. "You said you wouldn't have a fucking question!"

"I said I wouldn't have an *inane* question, which is true;" he offered a toothy smile. "None of my questions are inane."

Sparking the cigarette, taking a hit before turning her body to face him, "I suppose I'm aware the thing is part of something greater, something more, even though I can't say what this greater reality is." She hit her cigarette again, thinking for a moment. "Why don't you just tell me what 'spiritual' means to you?"

He laughed, "You learn quickly," extended his hand, index and middle fingers held open in the manner of a peace sign.

She placed the burning cigarette between his outstretched fingers; "Really."

Nodding thanks, he transferred the Camel from his right hand to his mouth, took a hit, retrieved it with his left hand, bringing his right to rest on the top of the steering wheel.

"Sure. Be a part of the conversation, don't merely respond; react, create, compete and cooperate." He hit the cigarette again; "Some people never get to that point. They simply answer questions forever, and even when they question they do so only because they were asked to do so. If you never ask your own questions, if you don't pursue those you've asked, you live by others' answers, which are always implicit in any questions they may pose."

Looking at him queerly, "What is your fucking deal, dude?" She motioned for him to return the smoke, "Honestly."

"Meh;" he yawned. "'Spiritual' refers to a way things can be, to a formal relationship among things." He handed back the smoke. "Spirit is itself abstract, and only its instantiations may be witnessed." Paused; "Speaking empirically. Now, we feel a thing like sunrise is spiritual, not because the rising of the sun itself is especially significant but because when we witness the rising of the sun *we* manifest a spiritual moment."

"So you're saying spiritual realities lie in us."

"No. I'm saying 'spiritual' applies not to things or actions, nor to set times and holidays, but to moments of personal relationship with the world." He glanced to the left, at the clouds visible there to the north. "'Spiritual' is what we call situations that come to be more significant than the parts of which they're constituted."

"So something is spiritual when the sum is greater than the whole of its parts."

"Yes, but also more than that. A thing becomes spiritual only when the spiritual aspect is of greater importance than the instantiations." Paused; "Speaking ontologically."

Slouched in her seat, she looked at him; frowned, "Yeah... You lost me there."

"A thing is spiritual when that which is not particular is the animating force... or rather, when the animating force is itself not confined to particular things," broke off, glanced quickly to the cigarette in her hand, little more than a filter and a coal, "when the force with which we animate things acknowledges the spiritual in that which it admits." Gathering his thoughts, he drew a new smoke from the pack, "Like, the sunrise we just witnessed was spiritual not in that we were driving east toward the rising sun, not because the Earth spins on its axis causing night to turn to day," paused momentarily, with a flick of a lighter took a hit, looking to her, "but because it was a moment of being," exhaling, "a great moment of fully realized animating potential whose form and heart weren't the individual players but instead the truth expressed among them, truth to which they all conform and bear witness, a building truth of which they all are a part."

Errr, basically…

Hit his smoke, grimaced.

She looked thoughtful, gently pulled a final drag. "But sunrise is eternal, for all intents and purposes. It probably hasn't even hit Salt Lake yet, and will be here again tomorrow."

"Precisely."

"…So, what the fuck did you mean outside the bar last night?"

He smiled; "I meant *that* moment had realized its potential; it was time to move on. The Spirit had realized its purpose." He looked her over, noting the set of her eyes, the angle of her jaw. "There's always purpose where and when The Spirit is concerned."

They both turned to fully address the coming highway.

"That is something people tend to forget."

A MUCH NEEDED BREAK

The next day of hard driving, broken only by a brief stop at a rest area outside of Cheyenne that found all four pilgrims sleeping uncomfortably in their seats, and by a few unremarkable stops to get gas, use the bathroom, and switch drivers, saw the Cherokee skirt the Rockies, journey the interminable expanse of Nebraska and Iowa, consume six healthy spliffs of fine organic herb, and cross the Mississippi into Illinois.

Tired from nearly twenty-four hours of straight driving, the three companions had assented to Edith's taking a turn at the wheel, and as they pulled into the parking lot of a gas station in Gary, Indiana, all four were quite ready for a break from driving and the general discomfiture of travel.

"I'm not even tired," Thorin groaned as he slid out of the rear passenger seat, attempting to stretch the stiffness from his limbs. "I'm just fucking worn out."

Peter, who could not but agree, exited the front passenger seat. Arching his back with a shiver, he ran a weary hand through his hair, attempting to bring some sort of order to the ragged brown, road-rumpled mop. "Don't be such a puss, Thor."

Edith excused herself, disappearing into the gas station.

Andrew, filling the tank as per the financial agreement of the venture, called to them from the far side of the jeep. "Yo. Come check this out."

Peter looked to Thorin.

What the fuck does he want?

Beats me.

They circumnavigated the jeep, Peter walking around the front, Thorin around the back, flanking Andrew and taking positions at either bumper.

"Look," he said, pointing across the street to where a number of people spilled from the large doors of what appeared to be a musical venue of some kind. "Seems like we missed the show." His smile bared a full set of teeth, framed by miraculously untousled golden extensions.

"Indeed," Peter looked across the expanse.

More people were exiting the broad doors now, filling the sidewalk before the venue and spilling into the street. An eclectic blend of persons both exotic and nondescript, those exiting the hall and milling about the sidewalk looked to have had a not negligible measure of fun.

Thorin observed the spectacle with interest. "Those people look fucked up;" he grinned at his friends.

"We *could* use a break," Peter commented, watching as two inebriated concert-goers attempted to cross the street.

The young couple, both looking to be in their early twenties, ungracefully ran across the four lanes of asphalt. Laughing and stumbling, they reached the far side just down from the station.

Thorin, wearing a roguish grin, sauntered over to them. Soon, fingers were pointed, in more than one direction; questions were asked, answered with laughs, slurred words. Diagrams were drawn in air.

Thorin, seeming satisfied, gave the boyfriend a hearty pat on the shoulder, sending them into the store and returning to the jeep with a spring in his step and an even broader grin than he'd had a moment before. "You guys up for an afterparty?"

"Up for a what now?" Edith appeared beside Peter.

Andrew, a shimmer of interest behind his eyes, "An afterparty."

"An afterparty for what?"

Grinning, Thorin pointed across the street, drawing her gaze to the throng of people there gathered.

"I see;" she turned back to the small area between the jeep and gas pump around which somehow they still were gathered, even though Andrew had finished filling the tank some time before.

The four of them stared at the concrete, in silent contemplation.

"Yeah," she broke the odd quiet. "We definitely need to do something, get off the road for a while at least."

Andrew voiced his agreement, followed quickly by Peter.

"Where is it?" Peter reached into his pocket for a cigarette, remembered where he was, tucked its bicolored length behind his ear.

"Just south of the city, in Ross."

"And you know how to get there?" Edith asked.

"Well... kinda. That guy was a little unclear on some of the specifics, but we'll find it." He grinned, looking devious if not quite wicked.

"What?" Peter gave an inward sigh. He knew well the look on his friend's face.

Andrew, also alert to Thorin's mischief, "*How* are we gonna find it?"

Thorin's grin became a full-fledged smile; "Cause we're gonna give those two a ride."

THE AFTERPARTY

The company arrived at the house in Ross not quite a half hour later. Driving down the dead-end road, they passed a large number of vehicles parked along its side, only to find the driveway completely full of not only cars but men and women as well.

"Damn," Thorin said as they pulled to the side to turn around and find a place to park; "This looks like it's gonna be fun."

Peter, crammed in the back with Edith on his lap and their two guides beside him, had to agree. Just in passing the place he'd seen several active cyphers and two or three barbecues throwing tasty looking white smoke into the air. In turning they had to wait as two men lugged what looked like a large tank of nitrous across the road from the back of their van.

Andrew, impatient behind the wheel, broke into a broad smile.

They finally found a place to park a couple hundred meters down the road, and as they disembarked their two drunken guides ran off toward the festivities without a word, laughing.

Thorin, apparently anticipating some extended politicking, riffled through his bag, emerging with an entire tin of spliffs, one of only five he'd brought. For his part, Peter grabbed a bottle of water from the trunk; it was his turn to drive next, and he didn't plan on drinking. Edith donned a hooded sweatshirt. Andrew waited patiently for them a little down the street, sparked a cigarette.

The house, a large, ranch-style affair, was amazingly secluded for being so close to Gary; in fact, it was one of only three houses on the entire street, and the neighbors didn't appear to be home. Set alone on what must have been at least two acres, it backed up to a veritable forest of hardwoods.

The party, having spread throughout the house and spilled into the yard around, was indeed in full swing, or at least was getting there fairly quickly, the sounds of laughter and conversation growing loud as they approached.

Andrew, who'd taken the lead, paused long enough for them to catch up. Looking to Edith, he smiled, "You might wanna stick close, chica." He brought his cigarette to his mouth; "These people look like they party pretty hard."

"I'm sure I'll manage," she replied dryly. "But thanks for the thought."

Peter watched as a group of surprisingly attractive girls, all carrying beverages of some kind, made their way around the right side of the house, disappearing behind, toward what he assumed was a large bonfire—if the flickers of light that escaped therefrom were to be trusted.

"Hippies." Thorin, taking in the scene, grinned broadly.

Andrew offered his arm to Edith, "Would you care to join me for a drink?" Graciously, he drew her with him through the front door, passed a thin man with a handlebar mustache who, reclined on a swinging chair set on the porch, tipped his cowboy hat as they passed.

She looked back with a smile before disappearing within.

Thorin turned to Peter, smiling wolfishly. "Let's go see what's happening around back."

Apparently he'd seen the pack of girls as well.

They threaded their way among parked cars and people, between the barbecues and the right side of the house. Peter began to suspect that these people, many of them at least, were likely a lot more than drunk and stoned.

The backyard could only be said to resemble a Turkish bazaar, one in which you'd find magic lamps and enchanted monkey hands, exotic fabrics and spices, *if*, that is, you were to remove from this image the vendors themselves.

People, in multicolored array, filled the yard, engaged in conversation and spectacle.

Attached to the back of the house was a large patio completely covered by an angled glass awning, under which was found a comfortable-looking arraignment of couches and lounge-chairs, centered around a large table crafted from a single cross-section of some great tree, left irregular at the edges yet finished to a glowing sheen. Upon its surface sat a large, many-armed hookah, the sweet smell of shisha and hash mingling with the sharper notes wafting from the fire beyond. This had been the destination of the girls—Peter could spot one of them, a shapely blonde with light, cream-colored skin and slightly curled locks, lazily lifting an arm of the hookah to her mouth, laughing softly as her friend, a darker-skinned brunette, whispered something in her ear.

The fire, set perhaps ten meters away from the patio, slightly to the right, was indeed large, its flames forking nearly three meters into the air. Around it sat people of all descriptions, including a young man with a great, full beard and hair to match playing a guitar. A large spliff dangled from his mouth as he caressed the neck of the instrument, hands peeking from beneath a faded poncho to journey its length with deceptive ease.

As Peter and Thorin stood gaping at the menagerie before them, a tall, strong looking man, clean shaven and seeming to be in his late thirties, approached.

"Welcome to my home!" He greeted them with a mirthful laugh. "I am Jonathan."

Peter, dumbstruck by the entirety of the place, turned to gaze at him.

Thorin was first to react, stepping forward to clasp the man's outstretched hand. "How's it going?"

Peter shook himself into action, added, "This is some party, man."

"Indeed it is, indeed it is;" he glanced over his shoulder, gaze following the arc of a girl as she skirted the fire, moving toward the house. "And who might you be?"

A little awkwardly, "I'm Peter, and this is Thorin;" he placed his hand on his friend's shoulder.

"You were at the show?"

"No," Thorin reached into his pocket, retrieved the tin, removing a spliff; "We're just passing through town." He sparked its not insubstantial length; "Needed a break."

Their host's eyes lit up as the deep funk reached his nose; he accepted the joint with a smile. "And how..." pulling deeply "...did you end up here?" He coughed, eyes immediately fading as the Kind did its work. "If you don't..." coughed again "...mind my asking."

He passed the joint to Peter, who puffed it before responding; "Actually, we just happened to be getting gas across from the venue, and this couple told us about an afterparty." Casting about the yard, "I don't see them now;" he laughed, "I don't even think we got their names."

"Oh, I got their names," Thorin interjected, taking the joint from Peter and smiling broadly. "I just forgot them already."

Jonathan laughed, bringing a flask from the back pocket of his jeans to his lips. "No worries;" he offered it to them. "All are welcome here."

Peter accepted, taking a healthy pull, not wanting to seem antisocial. Tasted like cognac.

One drink won't hurt.

Thorin declined the flask, instead handing the spliff back to Jonathan.

"To be honest," Peter broke the silence, "We don't even know who was playing."

"Doesn't matter," Jonathan replied. "That you're here now is enough." He gestured toward the fire, to a space there roughly across from the guitarist, "Why don't you make yourselves comfortable." He passed the joint back to Thorin. "I have to go inside and make sure no one is having sex on my bed..."

Thorin laughed aloud.

"...without me;" Jonathan finished with a grin.

Peter nodded thanks; Thorin laughed even more loudly. Jonathan smiled mischievously at them both before moving through the crowd toward the back door of the house, stopping once to greet and tightly embrace a passer-by in a great bear of a hug.

They stood for a duration, finished the spliff, contemplating his departure.

Before they could move to the fire, Andrew and Edith emerged from the door Jonathan had entered minutes before, each holding a beverage, looking like they'd had an interesting time within, the unusual hat gracing Andrew's head, curiously made of straw, bearing testament.

Edith already seemed a little tipsy; she clung loosely to Andrew's elbow as they made their way toward Peter and Thorin.

Andrew grinned broadly, "Some party, eh?"

"Quite;" Peter replied, eying Edith with a smile.

"We just met our host on the way out," Andrew continued. "Seems like a decent fellow; chilling with a flask of incredible cognac."

The four of them sat down beside the fire, Andrew to the left, Peter to the right, Edith with her back to the flames and Thorin facing her, listening to the ethereal melody being realized by the anonymous musician.

Thorin giggled as he snuggled up against Andrew, leaning his head back to rest on his friend's right flank. "Fucking hell guys," he addressed them all, resting a hand on Edith's leg; "This is exactly what we needed."

To this no one objected. Nor did anyone object when Thorin sparked another spliff, handing it first to Edith.

"You know," she took a pull; "I'd say you guys are cooler than I'd initially thought," handing the spliff to Andrew, looking from him to Peter to Thorin, back to Peter, "but I thought you were pretty cool from the beginning."

"Awwwe," Thorin crooned, waving the joint away, indicating to Andrew it should be passed around the fire.

"Seriously." She moved a little away from the flames; "I mean, for all I know I'd still be in Salt Lake if it weren't for you."

Her statement hung in the air; apparently none of the friends felt like addressing what would clearly have been, what was for some reason, an awkward topic.

They sat back, listening to the hum of conversation around them, seemingly one sound, the melody of guitar touching in places, highlighting and intertwining.

Sound is itself a dimension... it moves through matter, expands in time, yet its space is different, of a different nature, from that which it moves. It is there music exists, in the space of sound that is neither the vibration of its instantiation nor the form of its wave.

Space, as it is truly, is an affect of a meeting of things, whatever these things may be. Space may be great; it may be close, yet always implicit in the thing is distinction, harmony. This sound that surrounds me speaks. It moves with me, following me, even when I do not move. This space is... spiritual.

"Hey," Andrew started; "I know this song."

Peter, turning his attention from... whatever it was he'd been thinking about... to the music, suddenly realized he too was familiar with the tune. It was an old song, one his parents had played often when he was young.

The guitarist, glasses slid down his nose to rest atop the dark puff of his beard, was now singing softly, adding his own voice to the chorus of the surrounds.

"Strange shadows, from the flames will grow..."

Andrew murmured softly, loud enough yet for the others to hear, "Till things we've never seen, will seem familiar."

He and Peter met eyes.

You are the sailor, my friend.

Andrew raised his eyes to the sky, deep azure into the rising smoke.

Would you then be a solder?

Peter delved, darkness into flames.

Looking from Andrew to Peter, wondering what exactly she wasn't privy to, Edith decided to mind her own business, snuck a cigarette from Andrew's pack of Camels, which peeked from his front shirt pocket.

That's a good idea.

Both Andrew and Peter also lit smokes. Thorin, still reclined against Andrew, lay with his eyes shut and legs fully extended, quite comfortable and content, oblivious to his friends' silent exchange.

The four of them, three smokers and one stoner, sat, lay, beside the fire, absorbing the energy of the place, losing themselves in the strange harmony.

Feeling an acute need to be alone with some bushes, Peter flicked his cigarette into the fire, stood up, dusting off his pants. "I'll be right back."

Thorin, head resting on Andrew's leg, opened his eyes; grinned, "Famous last words."

Peter moved hastily toward the edge of the firelight, aiming for the tree line beyond.

A TRIP IN THE WOODS

Moving among the knots of party-goers, Peter stumbled slightly; his balance wasn't quite right. Not that he was dizzy or light-headed, but instead the ground seemed to swell slightly as he moved, making it difficult to walk a straight line. However, as he broke from the circle of the fire the effect seemed to lessen, cool moonlight bringing stability to his sight and confidence to his step.

He reached the edge of the yard, looked back at the fire from which he'd come, perhaps thirty meters away.

I really shouldn't piss this close to the party.

He cut among the trees, bringing himself around the far side of a large maple, relieved himself thereupon.

He held his cigarette, somehow he again had one, lit, between his lips, staring upward as its smoke disappeared into the darkness of the spreading limbs above. He shivered, zipped his pants, turning from the tree to gaze into the woods beyond. Audible somehow even from this distance, subdued among the more mundane chatter of the party, the soft resonance of the guitar crept around the tree, a light bird, song set aloft in the maple.

He brought the Camel from his mouth, managing to produce a satisfying ring of smoke that wafted away from him, rotating in on itself as it expanded into the space between the trees. In its wispy form, lit by moonlight cracking through the canopy above, he could see the intricate patterns of its eddy, fractal arms meeting in lace looped around itself, into itself.

A slight breeze carried the thing away, tearing it into evanescence.

Peter stubbed his smoke against the maple, slowly began to move into the dim embrace of the woods, flowing among the trees, stopped to rest a hand on a thin ash, its young bark soft under his hand.

He brought the bottle of water from the pocket of his hoody, took a sip, recapped it, noticed himself noticing himself doing these things.

Yeah.

I'm definitely fucked up.

Fuck.

A grin split his face; he giggled aloud.

Jonathan, their particularly gracious and ostensibly cool host, had dosed him.

Now alert to what was happening, he became aware that all was very quickly becoming more than it was a moment ago. His smile became even larger.

Andrew tried the cognac too. I wonder, did Edith?

The thrill of an incoming trip, a train set to carry him away, rushed through his body. He felt like dancing, like lying amid the undergrowth, beside a fern, leaning against the uprooted tree on its side before him.

What he did was sit on its broad length, spark another cigarette.

Pausing, he slid his body down, lying on the trunk, face to a patch of sky visible through a gap in the foliage left by the tree's passing.

The moon, half obscured by a maple to his right, peeked down on him, vivid amidst an otherwise black stain.

She is looking at me, but why does she cover her face? Is she shy? Hiding something?

He could feel the rough touch of bark beneath him, extended a hand over his head to caress its rutted face.

A sharp pain in his other hand jerked him upright. He flung the cigarette, burnt down to the filter, from himself, blowing on the space between his index and middle fingers, attempting to ease the burn.

Time was moving more quickly than he.

Hopping off the downed tree, he moved further away from the party, journeying a seemingly great distance through maple and ash. A stand of birch, white trunks glistening in the moonlight, looked at him through the woods, columns of light in an otherwise dark milieu.

Not so much ignoring them, but instead simply choosing another path, Peter passed by, eventually emerging into a large, lighted space, a pond, he realized, once he adjusted his perspective to allow for the existence of two shining moons, one above, steady and magnificent, the other below, luminescent and rippling in the breeze that moved its surface. The clarity of the scene, its intensity and crispness, was such that Peter's jaw literally dropped.

He fell to his knees beside the still waters, grasped a stone he found there, flung it at the shimmering visage of the moon.

Such perfection is too much to bear.

Striking the water of the pond, the stone slipped beneath with an easy thlump, impelling ripples to expand in concentric rings across the face of the dark liquid and through the moon reflected upon its surface.

The effect was more perfect than that which it disturbed. He kneeled, mesmerized, as the vibration spent itself, a semblance of still reasserting itself, mirror images again opposed, Earth meeting satellite before Peter's dilated vision.

Backing himself up, he propped his head against a log there found, bringing his hands to rest together on his chest.

Why are you here?

Where am I?

You have come to this place… to lie in the ground?

The derision in the question was clear.

I have come to this place to find peace.

And what is peace?

Laughter in the recesses of his mind.

This is peace.

Perhaps it is.

I don't know.

A pause.

Talking to yourself, eh?

There is no one else around.

That is the beginning of wisdom.

And what of it?

Who are you?

I am Peter.

What are you?

I... I am that which says I.

Clever.

Sometimes.

He sparked a cigarette, nicotine bringing a touch of stability to his otherwise entirely too excited cognitions.

What is I?

I am.

That is all?

I don't know.

Where is I?

Where am I?

I am between this and that.

This is again wisdom.

He laughed aloud now, pulling deeply on his smoke, exhaling through clenched teeth.

I am space.

Of a sort.

I am a character in a story.

Sometimes.

Nothing more?

A page of your life turns. Do you see it?

Sometimes.

The blank of the page, the openness of its margins, do you see?

Yes.

This is the void of your unfolding imagination.

Indeed.

Would you fill it with your own story?

I am void. I am between. I am neither this nor that. I am an idea of a between.

What story would you have?

Whatever I can. I am nothing.

That is enough?

No.

What would you be?

A man.

This is also wisdom.

And so he continued, time stretched to meaninglessness, in conversation with himself, the mirror image of the moon before him, voyaging the recesses of his mind, all that was not and all that was there.

A COMMON DESTINATION

What should have been hours later, could have been minutes for all Peter knew, found him reentering the clearing of the party. Appearing suddenly from around the same maple behind which he'd originally taken refuge, he startled a couple leaned up against it, or rather he startled the guy leaned up against a girl there. She didn't seem to notice at all.

Peter muttered an apology, quickly moving away from the somewhat nauseating scene that was a man literally drooling all over a woman, while she liked it.

The fire had died down a bit, although still it blazed with warmth he could feel from several meters away. His friends were gone, as was the strange musician.

Moving with the calculated ease of one passed the peak of his trip, comfortable and assured, Peter cast his gaze around the yard, spotted Edith lounging on a couch, pulling gently on an arm of the hookah. He altered his trajectory, bringing himself around the far side of the fire, toward the waiting comforts of the patio.

Before he could reach the cushy-looking lounge chair he'd had his eye on, however, he was nearly tackled by Andrew, who threw his arms around Peter in an exuberant embrace.

"Thought we'd lost you, man;" Andrew grinned at him, the black of his eyes plainly visible, deep wells. "Thorin suggested you might also be... energized." He left his hand on Peter's shoulder as together they walked toward where Edith waited.

"Looks like you had a... singular time;" she was also grinning broadly, cracked from ear to ear, as she examined him. "Did you wrestle an alligator or something?"

Peter looked down at himself then, noticed the dirt and mud that stained his clothes from ankle to shoulder, filthy hands more appropriate for a migrant farm worker than a spun college kid. He could not help but smile.

"No gators in Indiana," he said, attempting to dust off his hands. "There's an amazing pond somewhere back there, though;" he pointed passed the fire towards the woods.

"And that's what you've been doing?" Andrew's smile could've devoured him whole. "Mucking about in a pond?" He giggled, took a seat to the right of Edith.

"Not really," bringing himself to rest across from Andrew, "Mostly I was lying about the pond. Quite peaceful really."

"Why would you lie about a pond?" Edith asked innocently, taking a pull from the hookah.

"Because I didn't want to stand." Peter ignored her attempted irony. "You guys have been out here this whole time?"

Edith looked to Andrew, who looked to Edith, both of them turning to Peter wearing suspicious smiles.

"We've been here and there," Andrew replied mildly

"Where's Thor?"

Edith glanced over her shoulder toward door to the house, "Last I saw him he was in the living room taking bong hits with some kids out of Chicago."

Peter looked in through a window set to his right. It was still fairly crowded.

Definitely not going in there right now.

He stretched himself out, reached for one of the hookah's hoses, studying it before taking a pull. The woven length was capped by a well worn wooden piece whose face was carved with an intricate Celtic knot.

"It's just shisha," Andrew commented across the table.

"But it tastes great," Edith added, pulling her legs onto the seat with her, curled up in the manner of a cat.

"You know," Peter puffed a few, "I've never seen a hookah with this many hoses before."

"That's because it's custom made;" a familiar voice, deep with warm notes of humor. A great big smile, Cheshire, sat down on the couch opposite Edith. "Having fun, Peter?"

The sight of Jonathan didn't actually faze Peter, as he would've expected it to, if that is he'd thought on it at all, which he'd not. Instead, he brought himself upright, looked at his host. "You know, there's the most amazing pond set back in the woods behind your house."

"Again with the pond!" Andrew guffawed. "Seriously man, you could have been out here partying." He paused to pull deeply from the hookah; "I mean, Thor's already scared half the girls away."

Jonathan took a sip from his flask, setting it atop the table. To Peter, "I'm glad you appreciate what my home has to offer;" he glanced over his shoulder toward the tree line. "You like the pond, eh? Did you happen to see the stand of young birch, before the pond and a little to the west?"

"Of course," Peter replied, kicking back into his seat, slouching slightly.

"Did you go to them?"

"No," rubbing the thumb and index of his right hand together, feeling the grit of soil on them, "I went a different way."

Jonathan appraised him and, apparently satisfied by whatever it was he perceived, turned to glance at Edith and Andrew; "Your friends have told me," he brought his gaze back to Peter, "that you're traveling to Philadelphia for the big protest."

"Indeed;" Peter took a final pull from the hookah, set the hose on the table.

"It's interesting," Jonathan mused; "In a sense the protest is why I threw this party."

"I thought it was an afterparty." Peter looked genuinely confused.

"It is; it is." He stroked his bare chin; "But that was mainly coincidental. Really, the party is a goodbye to my friends here." He laughed; "Most of them were at the concert though."

"So you're also going to Philly?"

"Indeed." Jonathan smiled.

"It's a small world," Edith murmured, caught herself, laughed gently.

"Smaller than you know." Jonathan spared a look at Andrew, who sat in his chair, chiefing the hookah, lost in some thought or another. He offered her a friendly smile. "Or maybe you do know."

She blushed.

"Motherfuckers!" Thorin burst through the door, swaying slightly as he came to a stop, one hand supporting him as he leaned against the back of Andrew's chair. "These pussies from 'the big city' are all smoked out." He paused, taking in the four figures seated around the table, the singular smile tugging at the corners of all their lips. "Spun ass motherfuckers," he muttered, falling into a papasan there between Andrew and Jonathan.

"You could have come too," Andrew chided him.

"I was too tired."

"Which is why you're still up at..." Peter glanced over his shoulder to the east, where the rim of the horizon, mostly obscured by trees but nonetheless visible, cracked a touch of light. "...four-thirty in the morning?" He gazed serenely at his friend across the table, tilting his head minutely to the left to peer around the hookah.

"Whatever, man;" Thorin grumbled, searching his pockets. "I seemed too tired at the time. Besides," he withdrew the tin, "it isn't 4:30 yet." Smiling, "It's 4:20."

Jonathan laughed, bringing his hand to rest of Thorin's shoulders. "A friend such as you is hard to come by, Thor."

Thorin's head whipped sharply to look at him; Andrew hid a smile behind an upraised hand, shooting Peter a mirthful look.

"Appreciate what you have," Jonathan continued. "Nothing lasts forever."

They passed the joint among themselves as dawn began to grow on the horizon.

THE FINAL LEG

Nigh four hours later, after much conversation and pleasantry, they said their farewells to their host—Peter and he exchanged phone numbers—and by noon the jeep had passed Cleveland, a mere seven hours or so distant from its destination.

Long before they'd left, Peter, Andrew, and Edith had all come to realize they'd not be sleeping until at least they reached Philly, if then, and so had shot for driving order, splitting the day's work among themselves, letting Thorin, who now seemed quite tired indeed, sleep undisturbed on the passenger-side of the back seat. Peter had prevailed, paper covering rock, rock breaking scissors, and had chosen to take the first shift behind the wheel. Thereafter Andrew had lost to Edith, scissors cutting paper, who opted for the second shift, taking them from outside Cleveland into the middle of Pennsylvania.

It was now nearing nine o'clock, and as Andrew brought the car down the final stretch of I-76 all four were awake, peering curiously through their windows at this place they'd journeyed so far to reach.

It looked like a city. Tall skyscrapers rose before them into a dusky sky, the pale blue of their mirrored surfaces shining still above the smaller buildings of the old city.

"I've never been to Philadelphia;" Edith stared out the window from the front passenger seat.

"Philly's cool," Thorin commented from behind her. "You can feel the history," rolling down his window. "And there's always something to do." He grinned; "The late-night munchies are amazing."

Pulling a cigarette from his pack, "I think it's a good place for the protest;" Andrew exited the highway.

Peter, who above all other places loathed D.C. most, silently agreed.

Philly is the perfect place.

"Where are we staying?" he asked Andrew, who'd supposedly made reservations somewhere in the surrounds.

"The Alexander Inn," Andrew puffed his smoke out the window, "Right in Center City. That way we wont have to drive."

Edith, concern showing in her voice, "Shit. I...uh," she snuck a smoke from Andrew's pack; "...I didn't think that far in advance." Sparking it, "Do you think they'll have any vacancy?"

They were now pulling into Center Philadelphia, whose streets were unusually busy for so late on a Sunday, or so it seemed, none of them being in a position to authoritatively say what was usual for the streets of Philadelphia. Many of the people they passed had the distinct look of travelers, wearing large backpacks, looking tired and road-weary. Peter thought he'd seen some setting up for the night in Logan Square when they'd exited the highway.

"Gonna be a cramped week for the homeless in Philly," Andrew grinned.

"Kinda in poor taste, man," Peter chided him from behind. "Nothing funny about homelessness."

"Tell me that after this chick spends a few nights in the park." Andrew laughed over his cigarette. "Honestly though, I don't think there will be any vacancies in the entire city." He looked to Edith; "I made our reservations over a month ago, and even then I think I called twenty hotels."

She looked out the window as they stopped at a traffic light, at a man there napping on a public bench, "Err…"

"Don't worry though," Andrew continued; "We have a suite. Plenty of room for you."

She sighed.

"Only two beds though," grinning wickedly.

Thorin sat upright at this. "What the fuck you talkin about."

"You have to share with Peter."

Glancing at Thorin through lowered lashes, Peter reached out, caressed his leg.

Thorin groaned; "Fucking likely. Aleta is meeting us later tonight."

"Then Peter will have to sleep on the couch."

"And I suppose the plan is that *I* will share with *you*?" Edith's brows climbed her face.

"Pretty much."

"I suppose it's better than sleeping on the street." She gave Andrew a once-over, puffing her cigarette in contemplation, "I guess."

"We're here." Andrew pulled the jeep up beside a large SUV, sliding into the spot behind with practiced ease.

Unloading his belongings from the trunk, Peter lit a smoke, glancing up and down the narrow street, marred down the middle still by iron tracks made for trolleys that hadn't been seen in Philly for… well, as long as he'd been alive. He turned to look at the aged red brick building, perhaps twenty meters up the street, that would be their home for the next week.

Looks unassuming enough.

The four compatriots crossed the street, walking up the sidewalk. Arriving at the covered doorway, they entered. Peter, however, held back.

"Just gonna finish my smoke," he excused himself, leaning back against the brick, bringing his right foot to rest flush against its vertical surface.

There he stayed, finishing his smoke and sparking another, taking in the smell of the city, nodding to passers-by.

We are here, and we are not leaving until we have been heard.

CHAPTER 3
WE WILL BE HEARD

MONDAY MORNING

Peter gazed upward at the bronze likeness of George Washington, seated atop a bronze horse, seeming about to leap off, gallop away from, the pedestal upon which he'd been placed.

I wonder what he'd think of all this. Probably nothing good.

Washington's visage was fixed on the distant form of City Hall. Most of those gathered around, the great mass of people assembled there in Eakin's Oval and the surrounds, those stacked down the length of Ben Franklin Parkway, before the steps of the Museum of Art, were set in the opposite direction. There, on the steps ascending the museum's perch, was set a podium, bristling with microphones and flanked by a number of quite serious looking men and women.

It was the first day of the protest, the first hour really, if the preceding hours of milling and gathering could be discounted, and the protesters, from parts near and far, of means great and small, seemed ready to exercise some real political power.

Andrew, apparently sensing the same thing, turned to grin at him. "It's funny, isn't it?"

Peter shrugged.

"What's funny?" Aleta seemed annoyed. "You two are always having conversations no one else can follow;" she looked to her fiancé, "Thorin, do you know what they're talking about?"

"Back off yo," Peter shot her a look of transparently affected affrontery; "I didn't say anything," teeth flashing.

He'd known Aleta as long as he had Thorin; he'd met them together. Aleta, however, attended Georgetown, and so he'd not seen
her so much over the interceding years. He'd always been amazed at
how well Thorin managed the long distance relationship, although
he suspected the nature of Thorin's relationship with Aleta—or more
precisely that Thorin had to operate as does one in a relationship despite Aleta's absence—was the main impetus for his friend's raging
marijuana habit.

"Andrew's a cynic," Thorin put his arm around her, "but you already knew that."

She looked from him to Andrew, who, maintaining his grin, was
now leaning up against the bronze figure of a sixteen-point buck,
which graced the northeastern corner of the monument.

Andrew drew a cigarette from his pack, lit it behind a curved
hand, offering it to Edith, who stood before him patiently watching
the empty podium. "Just an inside joke, Al."

Peter burst out laughing, quickly silencing himself as Aleta
turned a cold gaze on him, eyebrow raised in question.

Edith jabbed Andrew in the ribs; "Don't be a dick." She snapped
the smoke from his hand, turning back to the podium with a smile
only Peter, standing to the left, could see.

Andrew sparked another, leaning back again against the bronze.

Just then a tall man, strong looking and clean shaven, approached
the podium from the far side, descending twenty-four steps to the
fourth tier where he paused a moment, surveying the crowd.

Motherfucker.

Thorin echoed his thought, turning to whisper into Aleta's ear.

Jonathan, wearing a plaid button-down flannel tucked into jeans,
stepped behind the podium, motioning for silence, which took more
than a few moments to be realized.

Leveling his gaze over the crowd, he began to speak. "My
friends," Peter could have sworn he paused slightly he passed their
position, "We have come here together, in fellowship and in protest,
because for too long our voices have not been heard." His voice, amplified a hundred times, a thousand, projected into the crowd, over
them and through, likely reaching the object of Washington's gaze
itself, rebounding.

"We have come here, to this place that saw the genesis of our nation, because for too long this country has been ruled without care
for her people, without thought for our rights or well being. On Saturday we will celebrate the two-hundred and fiftieth anniversary of
our independence, and on that day, a day of remembrance, a day of
attention, of consideration and reflection, we will be *here*." He paused.
"We will be here, in Philadelphia, while throughout the nation our
countrymen will be in their hometowns, their backyards and public

parks, watching the spectacle of fire rain down upon them like so many phosphorescent tears, testament to the continuing existence of a republic founded on not just liberty but violence, sustained not only by laws but by sweat and blood, remembered by all yet defended by a vanishing few."

Peter looked around himself, studying the faces of those in the crowd. All eyes were fixed on Jonathan. Even Andrew, no longer re-clining but standing stock still, at attention, had dropped his mask of irony and humor.

Jonathan continued. "Here we make our stand. Here we find our-selves surrounded by others with a will to effect change, by those who refuse to sit and watch as our democracy becomes a fiction, a ruse that merely distracts from a single inescapable truth. This truth, as painful and *inconvenient* as it may be, is impressed upon our nation, known to all with eyes to see." He leaned forward onto the podium, both arms extended. "*I* see before myself tens of thousands of people. I know there are tens of thousands more beyond my sight. By Inde-pendence Day we will have gathered hundreds of thousands, a great multitude. We will fill this city to bursting, overflowing its streets and public spaces. The air will resound with words spoken by free men and women; the streets will pound with our steps.

"It is not enough, however, to simply be heard, not enough to merely raise voices in anger, to march the streets and make demands. This is the manner of the mob, and we are no mob. It is not enough to craft a simple fiction and stand behind it, beside it, to hold it be-fore ourselves and proclaim 'This is what we are,' as such is an il-lusion. We, as Americans, are more than can be comprehended in a slogan; we are more than can be stated in a sentence or conveyed by a sound-byte." He gestured with an outstretched arm; "Look around yourselves. This gathering is not limited to a single idea. It is not con-stituted of a single demographic. We have come here as representa-tives of America. Our elected leaders, the parties to which they belong, have forsaken this role, seeking only to further their own ends and increase their own shares of power and wealth. We represent the uni-fied self of a thousand cultures, a thousand colors of humanity. We seek to push no agenda other than that the will of the people be heard and acknowledged. We fight not for a single idea, law, or policy, not for the rights of a single group, nor for any particular right. We are not protesting war; we are not gathered in the condemnation or praise of any ideology. Our message is simple. It is clear. It is universal."

The crowd gave forth a mighty bellow, more than eighty-thou-sand people speaking as one, as many.

Jonathan waited for the cheer to subside. "I'm sure most of you know of the situation in California presently, of the riots and siege of Oakland that have stretched now for nearly two weeks. The people

of Oakland, presented with an impossible situation and facing injustice at every turn, have turned to violence, to burning and rioting,
to physical confrontation with first the police and now the national
guard." His gaze turned to the statue of Washington, or perhaps to
downtown Philly beyond. "I wish I could say I condemn their actions,
but I cannot." Silence. "I am not one to dictate the actions of others. I
cannot say which action is right and which is foolhardy. I cannot say
what *I* would do if my community were being brutalized by a police
force that cares neither for the people's well being nor for the laws it
is charged with upholding. I do not know how I would respond to the
beating death of a young girl whose only mistake was to ask the simple question 'Why are you doing this?'." He moved away from the podium for a moment, brushed back the sweat from his brow, through
his hair. Speaking more softly, perhaps, Peter thought, venturing off
script, "I do know, however, that if it had been my daughter, my sister,
my granddaughter or friend, the man responsible would be dead."

At this, many in the crowd fidgeted uneasily, eying those around
themselves to see if they were alone in their discomfort.

"I say this not because I have disregard for the law; I have great
respect for the law. I say this not because I do not value life; I value
life above all else. I say this because the laws in this country are unjust.
They have been crafted by a political machine that has no connection
whatsoever to the people of the nation, that creates laws not for the
benefit of the people but for the perpetuation of their bondage and
for the advancement of the few. I say this because the executors and
makers of these laws are held apart, unbound by the strictures they
enforce and create, and conduct themselves in ways that are an af-
front to human decency and liberty itself. I say this because the courts
are rotten to the core, caring more about filling prisons than bringing
justice to the people.

"This situation is unacceptable. It is a disgrace, and we who have
witnessed its fruition are as much to blame as are those who have
endeavored in its realization. We have sat, docile, as the government
of this country fell into the hands of two bickering parties, as behind
this charade the brokers of power made deals and agreements that
stripped the rights of the people and fattened these brokers' pockets.
We have assented to an unconscionable expansion of executive power,
ignoring and neglecting that those who make the laws in this country
are the same as those who enforce them, a situation our forbearers
knew well was a path to tyranny and the slow death of the republic."

Jonathan paused, shuffling his papers atop the podium. "If you
will indulge me for just a moment, I will quote one of the great fathers
of this nation, a man who toiled in this very city over two centuries
ago to bring lasting liberty to the people of this nation and indeed the
world."

He glanced from his papers, making sure the crowd was still there, still with him. It was.

"'If the law-makers, who ever have the supreme power, should be also the constant administrators and dispensers of law and justice, then, by consequence, the people will be left without remedy in case of injustice, since no appeal can lie under heaven against such supremacy... In all kingdoms and states whatsoever, where they have had any thing of freedom among them, the legislative and executive powers have been managed in distinct hands; that is to say, the law-makers have set down laws as rules of government, and *then put power into the hands of others*, not their own, to govern by those rules; by which means the people were happy. Kings and standing states never became absolute over the people, till they brought both the making and execution of laws into their own hands; and as this usurpation of theirs took place by degrees, so did unlimited, arbitrary power creep up, there to domineer over the world, and defy the liberties of the people'

"These words were written by John Adams, the second president of this nation. Here he cautions us about the danger of allowing the same power to both create and enforce laws. Ostensibly the solution to this problem lies in the creation of three distinct branches of government; however, as we today have witnessed, this formal distinction is inconsequential so long as the people do not keep vigil to preserve it. Adams addresses this as well. 'The interest of absolute rule,' he writes, 'has been visible and fatal under all forms of government and may reside in the hands of many as well as of a single person. Though it hath often been disguised by sophisters in policy, so as it hath lost its own name by shifting forms, yet the thing in itself hath been discovered under the artificial covers of every form of government... One would think that there is no shelter for a monarchal interest under a popular form. But alas! The people not keeping a strict watch over themselves, according to the rules of a free state, but being won by specious pretences, and deluded by created necessities to entrust the management of affairs into some particular hands, such an occasion is given thereby to those men to frame parties of their own, that by this means they in a short time will become able to do what they list without the people's consent; and, in the end, not only discontinue, but utterly extirpate their assemblies.'"

Jonathan brought his full attention back to the multitudes before him. "I apologize for lingering here too long. I apologize for the archaic language, that I cannot speak these truths as well as did one who died two hundred years ago *to the day* from this coming Saturday. I apologize, but I make no excuses. These words are as true today as they were when The Constitution of this nation was being drafted. They speak the truth, and it is imperative, as we proceed with our demonstrations and speeches in the coming week, as we fight to be heard, that we keep in mind not only the nation for which we fight, not only the people whom we represent, but also the nature of the enemy we face. This enemy is not a single man, not a king; it is not a single ideology nor even the greed and lust of the powerful. A single man can be defeated easily; an ideology can be shown to be misguided, immoral; the threats of greed and lust exist only so long as their objects are present. Our enemy, our true enemy, is the lie behind which these men move, the fiction that allows them to pursue their greed, the veil behind which shadowy hands act to strip this nation's people of their rights not only to equitable treatment under the law but also to life, to liberty, itself."

He seemed to be coming to some sort of conclusion.

"I thank you for listening to me today, for allowing me the honor of initiating this historic week of protest. My name is Jonathan, and I have come here as you have come here." Gathering his thoughts, "We here today have come not to push our personal agendas, whatever these may be, but instead to fight for the rights of all men to work toward a future they deem best. We fight for our democracy itself."

He stopped, stepped back from the podium. The crowd, unsure if he'd indeed finished, hesitated a moment, the void filling with the distinct sound of more than eighty-thousand people's absolute silence. And then a crush of sound, a deluge of applause and whistles. Thousands of faces turned to the sky seeking purchase for their voices, the cacophony rising, fighting with itself, emerging melded and fused into one horrific force.

Peter, himself not one to scream for anything, really, again surveyed the crowd, perceived the anger and conviction there, the energy, the hope.

Holy shit.

He looked to his friends. Andrew had reached his arms around Edith, holding her in a loose embrace from behind; both looked somber. Thorin and Aleta were also in the midst of an embrace, more intimate, passionate.

And I'm alone.

He sparked a cigarette, inhaling deeply and reflecting himself within.

What would you be?

The question haunted him.

AN AFTER DINNER CONVERSATION

"You know," Andrew sat back in his seat, "I honestly have a hard time believing this thing's actually happening."

From across the table Edith eyed him over a glass of Bordeaux; "What do you mean?"

"Well, I mean, just think about what Jonathan said earlier: Oakland is still under siege; the people there show no sign of giving in. It's very likely something rather bad is going to happen there this week, and we are all here, thousand and thousands of frustrated people."

"Seems to me the situation in Oakland gives people even more reason to come here," Aleta interjected from beside Thorin, at the end of the table, to the right of and perpendicular to Andrew.

"Exactly. Which is part of the reason this thing's happening is so incredible."

Aleta turned from Andrew to Edith, "Does that make sense to you?"

"There's a lot said in this company that doesn't make sense to me."

"Look," Andrew sounded slightly exasperated, "it's not that hard to understand." He pushed his empty plate away from the edge of the table, sitting forward to there rest his elbows. "What I'm saying is I can't believe They are letting this thing happen"

"They can't very well stop it," Aleta rejoined.

Andrew brought his hands to his forehead, eyes set on the grain of the wood below, snuck a glance to the left, to where Peter sat quietly nursing a scotch.

"I think what Andrew's saying is they could stop it if they wanted, but for some reason haven't." Peter had for the most part stayed out of the conversation, content to sip his drink and fiddle with the trailing end of his dessert.

Aleta flashed an irritated look between them. "Who in God's name are 'they' again?

Peter smiled from across the table, "You know, Them."

Andrew drew his pack from his pocket, removing a cigarette, "No one knows who They are, exactly, but we know They are there. Really though, it doesn't matter. Let's just say it's incredible *the government* is letting this happen." He looked around, replaced the cigarette and tossed the pack on the table.

"And you think the government should want to prevent this gathering? Because of what we are here to protest, what the speakers are saying?" The smile on Edith's lips quirked slightly as she eyed Andrew.

Thorin laughed, sharing a look with Peter that spilled onto Andrew.

Peter grinned.

Andrew simply looked tired.

"Obviously not. The show here is meaningless."

Aleta gave a dry laugh; "Then why?"

"Because by tomorrow there will be over a hundred thousand people in Philly who don't live here, with more coming every day, every hour. Because we are all here with, honestly, nothing to actually do... Just thousands of people, talking and walking around."

"And..."

"And what happens if something goes wrong? We all saw the police presence at the rally this morning;" looking to Aleta, "You must have seen them later at the rally in Washington Square as well."

"Sure. Nothing unusual there though."

"Of course not. There's likely a noticeable police presence in every city in this whole damned country right now, and they've made a strong showing at every rally or protest I've ever been to. The unusual thing here is the sheer number of people who are, or rather who will be here." He turned to face her; "Do you think the police you saw today would be able to handle two-hundred thousand people, if these people decided to not play by the rules?"

"I suppose not."

"And do you think, given the situation in Oakland, the government would let us all come here without having adequate security ready?"

Looking unsure, "I don't know."

"Well, I do know, and I'll tell you now they definitely *do* have more security forces available, national guard likely, stashed somewhere close by." He again sat back from the table, taking in his four friends, "And what I want to know is: Why let us come here at all if doing so admits the risk of *another* catastrophic situation."

"Perhaps they're just trying to draw us all out into the open," Thorin's smirk testified to the conviction in his words, "to like, smoke us out or whatever."

"Perhaps so"

Aleta laughed aloud; "Come off it, Andrew. You think we, or rather you, are that important?"

"It all depends;" he gazed across the room, unfocusing on something on the far wall. "Maybe."

"Bu..."

He cut her off; "Actually, yeah: I do think we are that important. Think about it;" he caught the eyes of Peter, Edith, Thorin, finally resting on his interlocutress. "Everywhere we go we stick out; we don't fit in." To Edith, "You said it yourself back in Salt Lake."

She nodded agreement.

"And I'm willing to bet the same goes for a lot of people here. We *are* different, drawn here in an ambiguous purpose to protest a situation most in this nation do not even acknowledge."

"We are here," Aleta rejoined, "to protest the fact that this government is no longer responsive to the people's will."

Andrew laughed, "That is indeed why most of us think we're here, but I've been thinking since this morning and have come to conclude the problem is *not* that the government is not responsive to the will of the people, but instead that the people themselves have no will."

Peter here felt the need to say something. "What the fuck are you talking about, man? The people cry out. The situation in The Bay bears witness to this."

"Crying out and having a will are not the same"

"And what is the difference?" Aleta asked, voice tilted high.

"The difference," patience clear across his countenance, "is that will has effect whereas weeping is just noise."

"Seems a little cold, man." Peter eyed him from behind his scotch.

"Perhaps cold, but nonetheless truth."

"Perhaps it is," Thorin joined the conversation, "but to say the people have no will is silly."

"Is it?" He again poked about his pack of Camels; "If the people have a will, where has it been?"

Edith broke in, "You talk like you're so above it." She seemed rather irritated, angry perhaps. "Where has *your* will been, if you're so different?"

"Just as Jonathan pointed out earlier, I too have been derelict. We all have."

She set her glass down on the table, sat forward; "Yet somehow we here are 'different'."

"In a way." He paused; "Look, those gathered here *feel* their will is potent. We believe we can change things."

"Seems to me," Peter chastised him, "that you don't feel we can change anything."

"Not true at all."

"But you just said that this... what did you call it?.. this 'show' is meaningless." Aleta was also getting riled by Andrew's discourse.

"This show *is* meaningless"

"Then what can we change?" Peter was actually now enjoying the conversation, the girls' irritation as well.

"We can begin by changing the way we think about the entire thing, to realize simply raising our voices is not enough, that even when accompanied by violence voices are moot so long as there's no will behind them." He pulled a smoke from his pack, twiddling it between his fingers before jamming it behind his left ear. "You see, exercising will, true will, is more than demanding to be heard, and it is more than lashing out when one is not. True will accepts things as they are, comprehends their actuality, and moves to effect a change in this actuality. The problem with the rioters in Oakland, or even with the protest here, is that both are, generally at least, expressions of people's inability to accept the truth."

The four of them waited for him to continue.

"The reality is no amount of complaining or protesting or rioting is capable of affecting the way things are done in this country. Jonathan hinted at this in his speech. 'We are no mob,' he said. Such actions are only effective means of applying will in a *functioning* democracy. What we have, what we have to address without myopia, is we don't have representatives in this country anymore. We have rulers, rulers given to us by masters. In the guise of candidates these rulers appear in couples from which we must select. In reality there's no choice, and so those who win elections don't represent those who vote for them, at least no more than in the façade of the ballot itself."

For his part, Peter could not argue with this. Given the silence enveloping the table, he guessed the others had no response either.

"Jonathan seems to understand this as well," Andrew broke the silence. "Behind his words, in the margins of his speech, I saw a will to actually deal with things, beyond simple talk. Even if he seems hesitant to voice such thoughts aloud." He stood up. "Honestly, making such a will public would only be detrimental anyway."

Edith, inferring his present purpose, also stood up. Andrew looked at Peter questioningly.

I'm cool, man.

With a nod Andrew circumnavigated the table, heading for the door, Edith in tow.

As soon as he was through the door, Aleta turned to Peter. "What's his deal?" She moved to take the seat Edith had vacated, looking from him to Thorin; "He seems a lot more than just pessimistic."

Thorin, taking a bite of cheesecake, "I think the thing in Oakland has affected him more than we or even he would like to admit."

"Agreed," Peter finished his scotch, "but it's more than just that. I think he's come to some sort of conclusion." He shivered, "Even if he himself isn't quite yet aware of what it is." He shifted his chair slightly, a smile on his face. "I've been meaning to ask you something;" his eyes flickered from Aleta to Thorin, back to Aleta.

"Yes?"

"I couldn't help but notice you aren't drinking;" his smile widened.

Aleta blushed, looking to Thorin who sat with a stupid grin on his face.

"How far along are you?"

"About six weeks... that's what the doctor says at least, give or take a week."

He looked to Thorin, "And why didn't you tell me?"

A little flummoxed, Thorin stammered; "Well... err," looking to Aleta, "She didn't want me to tell anyone."

He looked at her with a quizzical brow.

Cheeks flushed, "I'm sorry Peter. I... I haven't told anyone but Thorin yet, not even my parents."

"Indeed." He broke into a mirthful grin. "This is good news?"

"Yes;" Thorin answered nearly before he'd finished asking the question.

Aleta looked at him, warmth flooding her face.

"You know, you may have to actually grow up now."

"The thought had crossed my mind;" He grinned, sucking down the final dregs of his porter. "But not for a while at least."

Still smiling broadly, Peter excused himself, moving to join the nicotine crew outside.

Aleta and Thorin remained within.

NOT WHAT WAS EXPECTED

The following afternoon found the five of them in JFK Plaza contemplating the fountain, the fall of its water, found there in the shadow of City Hall. Really, this is all they *could* do. It had become abundantly clear earlier in the day that the sheer number of people who'd descended on the city *were* quickly swelling its streets and public spaces to near bursting. There were then being held numerous individual events, in Franklin Square, Washington Square, before Independence Hall, and even back at the steps of the museum, yet these might as well have been happening in another city entirely, for all that they could be reached.

Perhaps Philly isn't the best place to have this thing after all.

"I bet *Jonathan* isn't having this much trouble getting around," Andrew caught Peter's eye over the collective shoulders of Thorin, Edith, a couple attempting to take a picture of the fountain.

"WHAT?"

"I said..." Andrew noticed the mischief on Peter's face. "Fuck you;" he grinned.

Thorin turned his back to the fountain, creating a small space between himself and Aleta that found Andrew and Edith on one end, Peter on the other. "This is retarded."

The five of them turned into the circle, observed each other.

"Let's get the fuck out of here."

They made their way through the crowd, which spilled from the square into the street, toward City Hall and to the sidewalk on the other side, also found completely crowded with people. The police, having apparently given up on keeping the mass of people out of traffic, had instead set themselves to keeping traffic out of the crowd.

I wonder how long it will be before they simply close these streets to vehicles completely.

They moved around City Hall, turning south onto Broad Street, more or less as a group putting some distance between themselves and the milling horde. Slowly but surely the street began to thin, and six blocks from the square, not too far from the hotel, they found themselves in a parking lot crowded with cars but more or less devoid of people. A large mural, an amalgam of cultural icons and scenes, was painted across the entire side of the building that flanked the east side of the lot.

Without a word Peter opened his pack of smokes, offering them to Andrew and Edith before drawing one himself.

"This is not what I thought it would be;" Edith spoke around her cigarette, accepting a light from Andrew with a quite smile.

"Isn't it?" The voice came from behind her.

Five sets of eyes turned as one to appraise the interloper. Of course it was Jonathan, wearing a grey herringbone flat cap.

"That was some speech you gave yesterday," Edith was surprisingly unstartled by his sudden appearance directly behind her.

Andrew, almost nearly on top of her, "How the fuck did you end up *here*, exactly when we got here?"

Jonathan grinned; "To be honest, I was wondering the same about you." He eyed them carefully; "You aren't following me, are you?" Looking to Peter, "I thought I saw you watching me yesterday as well," grin broadened.

For his part Peter remained silent, unsure what to make of the unexpected meeting.

Turning from Peter, "And you must be Aleta, about whom I've heard so much."

Aleta blushed, bobbed her head. Beside her Thorin wore a stupid smile.

Perhaps Jonathan knows more about that than do others.

"So you're saying you just happened to be here, in this parking lot, at the exact time we decided to stop for a smoke?" Incredulity colored Andrew's voice.

"More walking passed to be honest, but, I mean," he gestured toward the building on the far side of the lot, "the mural kinda draws the eye. You guys just happened to be there when I looked down."

Edith, bringing the conversation back to where it had started to begin, "And you expected this to be as it is?"

"Sure. Think about what I said yesterday: We are here as representatives of America." He paused to take a sip from his flask, quickly slipping it back into his pocket. "Is there anything more American than having to deal with the fact that there are *many* fucking people here who all want the same thing, the same space, as you? Than letting that reality get right up in your face?"

"But what's the point of coming here," Aleta rejoined, "if we can't even approach the actual demonstrations?"

"And you need someone else to tell you what to think, what is happening?" He laughed, casting his gaze over them. "If our time together back in Ross taught me anything it's that these four definitely do *not* need someone to tell them what to think." He gave her a most winning grin; "I can only assume you're equally well on top of the situation."

Andrew chortled, receiving a cutting glare from both of the girls.

Jonathan continued, "So let those who need to hear the truth listen. The point of your being here is not to listen to people speak, but to speak yourselves, to be seen, to meet others with whom to speak"

"Speaking of speaking ourselves, how did you end up giving the opening address?" Peter was genuinely curious.

"Ah yes, well…" he lost himself to the north for a moment, "*someone* had to give it."

"But how did that someone end up being you?"

"Let's just say I know a guy who knows a guy who knows me, and no one else wanted to do it."

"Are you affiliated with the organizers?"

"You could say that;" he broke off. "Honestly though this really isn't important." Looking back to Edith, from her to Aleta and back again, "What's important is determining what you do now."

"What are you doing now?" Andrew interposed.

"I'm talking to you, obviously."

"Let me rephrase;" he hit his smoke. "What are you doing later today?"

"I had been considering hanging out with you guys for a while;" he looked from Andrew to Peter, moving to Thorin. "You have any more of that marvelous herb?"

Thorin grinned, "Back at the hotel;" turning to nod at Aleta, "She convinced me not to bring it."

"It's just a couple blocks over," Peter quickly added. If there was one thing he was sure of it was that he wanted time to talk with Jonathan, even if the explicit nature of the desire was slightly opaque.

"Shall we?" Jonathan's smile encompassed them all.

THE SUITE AT THE ALEXANDER INN

A short time later found them taking their ease back at the hotel. The suite was fairly large for an older establishment, comprised of two rooms, three if the bathroom were counted. They occupied the main room.

Two couches, set against the long walls, opposed each other, and Peter had brought chairs from the bedroom to complete the cypher. Backs to the open windows, Thorin and Aleta sat in one couch facing Andrew and Edith. This left Peter and Jonathan to sit in the higher stiff-backed chairs, there to gaze at each other on a plane slightly above that of the main interaction.

Presently a fat spliff made its way around the circle.

Peering through a billow of swirling smoke, "How many people do you think are here now?" Edith handed the spliff to Jonathan.

He pulled a hit, "Last I heard, over a hundred and thirty thousand," leaned forward to tap ashes into a tray that lay on the coffee table before her; "But truthfully it could be more than that, or it could be less." Handing the spliff to Thorin, "We really have no way to be sure." He looked passed Thorin to Aleta, face tinged with a hint of concern. "Are you sure you should be in here?" His eyes flicked to the smoke filled expanse of the room.

"Why shouldn't she?" Edith sounded genuinely confused, looked to Aleta, who blushed beside her fiancé.

Thorin, arm around her and the joint in his mouth, quickly passed it off to Peter. He sat back and considered the woman beside him, with whom he shared a look before turning to face those on the other couch.

Peter shared a grin with Jonathan.

"Aleta is pregnant."

Andrew nearly choked on his scotch, smile splitting his face in two. "Holy shit, man." He set down his glass; "Congratulations!" He started to rise, thought again, resettled himself beside Edith.

"When are you due?" she asked.

"Most likely the last week of February."

"Holy shit," Andrew seemed genuinely astonished; looked to Thorin, "You're gonna be a father."

Thorin wore a dumb smile, unable to articulate a response, perhaps merely content to make none.

Peter looked to the spliff in his hand, to Aleta and Thorin, glanced at Jonathan, unable to discern exactly what he should do with it.

Rising from her seat, Aleta shared a somewhat awkward kiss with Thorin, the entire room observing them; "I'll just step out and get some air," moving toward the door.

Edith sprang from her seat; "I'll come with."

And thus they left the room, leaving Andrew, still gaping at Thorin, Jonathan, smiling to himself, Thorin, still looking stupid, and Peter, now chiefing the joint heartily, to chill in the room without the pleasure of feminine company.

"To be honest," Jonathan spoke into the silence, "I don't think her being in here is necessarily bad for the baby, although I suppose it's best to be on the safe side." He grinned, "Really though I just wanted to speak with you guys alone."

"About what?" Peter was still chiefing the spliff.

"About what happens next."

"What do you mean," Andrew gaffled the joint, puffed it.

"Well," Jonathan began, "I've been pretty busy today, last night too, feeling out those who have come for the protest;" he accepted the joint from Andrew. "And I've got to tell you, as people I know to be level headed and thoughtful," he flicked a look at Peter, "some of them are none too happy with our government."

Andrew laughed, "No shit."

Jonathan turned to address him; "Indeed. Yet, this is not the simple malcontent we would expect to find in political activists." Hitting the joint, "Many of these people are genuinely, dangerously, ready to *act.*"

Thorin broke from his reverie, "What do you mean?" He craned his neck, looking out the window at the street below.

"Well," Jonathan took a final hit, stubbed the joint into the ashtray, "I have the feeling things may get… hectic… before the week is out."

Andrew adopted a front of gravity, looked to Pete, back to Jonathan; "We'd been speaking about just that last night."

"Had you now."

The room grew quiet.

"Thing is," he continued, "with all the crowding, things are only going to get worse." Paused. "This is why I decided to come find you today, before anything happens."

Peter sparked a cigarette, "Why search *us* out? We're just a few people, come here for the protest, sure, but no different from anyone else."

He contemplated his answer before responding; "Sure enough, yet out of all the thousands upon thousands of people here, to me there are two types: those I've known for a great while and those I don't know at all. You are neither," looking around at the setting of their parlay, "and I can't ignore our meeting back in Ross." He drew his flask from his pocket, set it on the table before him. "Nor can I ignore that you," again he glanced toward Peter momentarily, set themselves on the table, "were able to drink with me then, without reservations and without holding back." He looked to Thorin, "Nor that you decided not to drink, without a second thought and without being out of place or uncomfortable." He smiled, "This speaks well of your constitution;" smile warming, "I *think* you will be a good father."

"More like *how* did you search us out?" Andrew broke in, focusing a steely look on Jonathan.

"Like I said," he leveled a gaze back at Andrew, "I was walking around, feeling out the protesters and the general vibe of the city. All I did was also keep an eye out for you. You're not very hard to spot, you know."

"How's that."

"You guys are different."

Andrew chuckled, sharing a look with Peter before turning back to Jonathan, "We were just talking about that last night."

Peter looked to Jonathan, "Yet *you* are saying we're different from others now in the city, somehow easier to spot."

"Indeed."

"In what way?"

"*You* seem to be at home, moving as if you're doing what you're meant to do. You clearly aren't natives, yet you don't present as tourists."

Peter laughed aloud, leaning forward to tap his cigarette into the tray. "To be honest, Jonathan, I have no idea who I am, let alone where I am... beyond that I'm in a hotel in Philly... Even less so do I know what I'm meant to do."

"There's a difference between being and doing something, and knowing something."

This is also wisdom.

"What was that?" Andrew turned from his examination of Jonathan, brow furrowed, to look at Peter.

"Huh?"

"You mumbled something."

"Oh..." hit his smoke, "just thinking."

"Do you think something dangerous may happen?" Thorin posed, worrying a hand along the scruff of his beard..

"I'm not sure," he stifled a small smile as he turned from Peter to Thorin. "I just know I felt compelled to seek you boys out."

"Yet you..."

He cut Thorin off; "You must understand that... well, it's not clear who can be trusted. Especially here, now." He broke off. "No, that's not right. Rather, it's not entirely clear who can be relied on." He nonchalantly reached for Thorin's tin, which lay on the table beside the ashtray, looked to Thorin in question, opened it and withdrew one of the smaller joints, sparking it quickly with a lighter from his front shirt pocket. "You guys showed up at my party, the only people there I didn't already know, three men somehow journeying to the same location as I." He puffed on the joint, "So you were tested, opening yourselves." He passed the joint to Thorin. "And what I saw was good."

"But you're dodging my question," Thorin would not be dissuaded.

"I just know that, whatever happens, I want to stay in touch with you guys."

Thorin's gaze remained intent.

"As I said," he smiled, "I'm afraid things might get hectic before we see the sun set on The Fourth. Beyond that I can't say... It's just a feeling."

"I suppose we'll see," Andrew stated, drawing a cigarette. He waved away the joint.

'Why did you come here, Andrew?" Jonathan resettled himself in his seat.

"Because something needs to be done."

"And you would do it?"

"If given the opportunity... Yes. Absolutely."

Jonathan accepted the joint from Peter, twiddling it between the thumb and index fingers of his left hand. "What is it you would do?"

"Whatever it takes," conviction steel in his voice.

"I believe you would." Jonathan bent to gaze out the window, handed the spliff to Thorin and moved to rest his hands on the sill, leaning his head out to glance up and down the street; he took a deep breath, inhaling the semisweet, humid and dry smells of summer in center Philly. "It looks like the girls are coming back in."

Thorin also peeking his head out the window, confirming that Edith and Aleta were indeed waiting for the front desk to buzz them in.

"I wanted to talk about this without them because I didn't want to worry them unnecessarily," Jonathan turned from the window to address them; "Call me old fashioned if you must." He moved back to his chair, shorted the half-burnt joint in the tray. "However, I expect," he looked at Thorin and Andrew in turn, "that you will take due responsibility for them as things progress."

They nodded in agreement, even Peter, who was not sure exactly whom he was claiming responsibility for.

The girls reentered the room to find all four engaged in a deep conversation about the various merits of marijuana, shared a look and shook their heads. Boys, thought with a slight laugh and a longer sigh.

OUTSIDE CARPENTER'S HALL

"You know," Andrew turned from his contemplation of the building before them, "they say the original group of rebels had their first meetings in the attic." He peered over Peter's head toward the reconstructed site of Benjamin Franklin's house, from which they'd just come; "It makes you wonder what role he actually played in the initial development of the rebellion."

The sun, set high in the sky, cast small the shadows of early Friday afternoon. Thorin and Aleta had retired to the hotel, claiming fatigue from the morning's activities; Edith had excused herself as well, leaving Andrew and Peter to walk about the Old City alone.

Peter suspected she'd simply wanted a bed to herself. Not that he saw a rift opening between her and Andrew, nothing like that... She'd just seemed legitimately exhausted. They all were, in a way. Five days of navigating crowds, of early mornings and late nights, arguments and conversations, of cigarettes and ganja, had taken their toll.

"I'd always imagined he played a rather large role," Peter replied, raising an arm to mop the sweat, an errant brown strand, from his forehead. "No one ever talks about it though."

"It's interesting, isn't it?"

"What's interesting?"

"That his role on that level is downplayed to such an extent. We hear of Franklin the scientist, the inventor, the statesman and diplomat, yet we never really hear of Franklin the rebel... He's always cast as some sort of grand public figure." Andrew drew a smoke, offered one to Peter. "I mean, the whole history of that time is completely opaque. Just imagine though, a small group of men in the attic of that building," he gestured over his shoulder, "plotting treason against the most powerful empire on Earth..." He paused to spark Peter's smoke, then his own. "It's just fucking crazy."

"Uh huh."

"Fuck you." He looked legitimately hurt. "I'm just saying."

"Right."

"Look man, I..."

What the fuck was *that*?

He met eyes with Andrew for a split second before both of them were knocked off their feet by a sudden swell in the crowd. A couple, who'd just moments before stood beside them, now stood over them, on them to be precise. Peter felt the hard sole of the woman's shoe press into his right calf.

Andrew attempted to raise himself, was knocked down as the crowd surged again. There, faces pressed against the red brick of the sidewalk, they again met eyes, sharing an unspoken moment of understanding, friends through and through.

You're OK?

Yes.

There's somewhere I need to be.

I understand.

Take care of yourself.

You too.

And with that, Andrew rose from the ground, fighting against the press of people who were even then being inexorably pushed back, over him. He regained his feet, swimming to the right, toward Independence Hall, into the crowd and away from Peter.

Watching as his friend vanished among a tapestry of tangled legs and bodies, Peter was overcome with an unexpected wave of sorrow whose origin he could not quite place.

What story would you have?

He scrambled in the opposite direction, moving with the crowd on hands and knees. Finding his feet, he made a dash for the far side of Carpenter's Hall, hoping he'd there find space to breathe.

Behind himself he heard a woman shriek, cut off suddenly.

He kept moving, neither wanting nor being in a position to know.

BREAKING AND ENTERING THE WALLED GARDEN

He was over fourteen blocks from the hotel, and already Andrew knew realizing his objective would be difficult, if not impossible. Having successfully made it to Walnut Street, which ran along the south side of the historic district, he'd run into a wall of people extending as far as he could see, filling the street and the park set on its north side. Unlike the chaos he'd just fled, this end of the crowd was set as a single mass of bodies, stock still, dominoes waiting to be toppled.

I need to get the fuck out of here before this crowd consumes me, locks me in.

He slid through the sea of people, not caring on whose feet he stepped or passed which breasts he brushed. His mind was set on a single unswerving purpose.

Funny she has such power over me after such a short amount of time.

But he knew, knew to the depths of his heart, that she was the only thing that then actually mattered to him. Even before his pledge to Jonathan he'd known Edith was his responsibility, regardless of how much she'd likely object.

He had, several days ago in fact, begun to realize he loved her.

Making his way west on the southern margins of Walnut, he became aware of a dull roar, a reverberation ripping through the crowd, growing louder as he inched toward Washington Square.

Suddenly the gridlock of men and women oozed back like some viscous liquid, back to breast to shoulder to back. Andrew made a quick move toward the extreme edge of the street, hugging the building he found there, snaking west against the movement of the crowd until he found himself beside its stoop. He ducked down, taking refuge behind its four concrete steps, realizing a moment of release from the press of bodies, caught his breath.

He peeked through the iron bars of the railing, standing up to get a better view.

What he saw stole any measure of breath he'd recently recovered.

The crowd ended abruptly at a dark line of shield and club, glossy helmets with lowered visors set against the people, marching inexorably east, driving back the great mass of bodies, seemingly unaware there was simply nowhere to which the people could retreat fast enough.

A eerie still held the crowd, for the most part silent, unmoving, unable *to* move.

And then, before Andrew's eyes, the dominoes began to tumble.

Mother of God.

The people did not quite fall, and in this way were very much unlike dominoes, yet the motion that rippled through the crowd was definitely a chain reaction, horrendous and inescapable. Those directly in front of the police, attempting to stop themselves, were beaten with dark batons, falling away from the advancing line and into their fellows. These then were pushed back a few steps, the effect compounding until, at a point slightly west of Andrew's position, there was simply no more room. He could see clearly the panicked faces of those trapped in the crowd, the hopeless, mute cries of women whose chests were compressed until they could not draw air. He watched from the sidelines as people began to scream, tearing into one another in an attempt to escape. Yet, as was painfully obvious from Andrew's vantage, there was nowhere to escape to.

He knew then he was witnessing death on a scale he'd never fully imagined, that couldn't *be* imagined. Powerless, he watched as those in the center of the crowd began to fall among the shifting feet of the horde.

The police continued their advance.

Having realized what was happening behind them, the front lines of people surged forward with a building roar, breaking through shields and smashing the thin, dark line.

Andrew, dumbstruck, watched as armored figures fell, as the line was itself trampled beneath thousands of feet.

Beyond, near the intersection of 6th Street, from the direction of Washington Square, another brigade of riot police appeared, setting themselves against the oncoming rush of frenzied and desperate people. Many in the crowd had availed themselves of clubs and shields, helmets, taken from fallen cops. The people, now a mob in truth, broke the second line on contact, a chain of ants attempting to hold back an avalanche.

This is not good.

Even then, in the rush and sheer unreality of what he beheld, Andrew felt the hollowness of his thoughts. He simply had no way to express the multitude of emotions and half-realized cognitions flooding through him.

As he watched, he was frightened to realize one of the strongest was satisfaction.

On the sidewalk down a ways from him, perhaps halfway to Washington Square, an unmasked policeman, blood staining his face as it poured from a gash somewhere above his right eye, crawled out of the stampede, searching for respite there along the side of the same building against which Andrew hunkered. A man wielding a baton emerged from the crowd and bludgeoned him across the face, sending blood flying against the brick of the building, again on the backside of his head.

I've never seen someone murdered before.

Nausea, but also a kind of nervous anticipation, the crunch of the cops skull, audible yet above the great din of the mob, crept through Andrew's guts.

But still, he felt no sympathy. The police had shown no mercy to the crowd; why should they be given any of their own?

The streets before Andrew had thinned enough for the bodies lying there to be visible, and to his horror he realized there were more than he would've guessed. Hundreds littered Walnut and the surrounds, civilian and police, some moving feebly, fractured limbs scratching pavement, others eerily still.

And throughout the gruesome scene the companions and loved ones of the fallen stared in dumb bewilderment, unbelieving, not yet moved to action, unable to do so.

What the fuck do I do now?

Slowly, Andrew turned, casting about, unable to escape the broken forms of what had just minutes before been living, breathing people.

Backtracking, he turned down 5th Street, broke into a run, attempting to put as much distance as possible between himself and what had transpired.

He heard then a sharp and unmistakable crack, quickly followed by several others, echoing down the street from somewhere before him. Turning sharply into a brick-paved alley to his right, sprinting for his life down its narrow, tree-lined length, he spotted a low wall, hoisted himself over it and dropped into the garden behind, heart pounding, lungs raggedly gasping for air.

With shaking hands he pulled a cigarette from his pack, realized its smoke would give away his position to anyone walking the alley on the other side of the wall, sparked it anyway. He moved deeper into the garden. Passing beneath the boughs of a tall maple and among hanging vines of ivy, Andrew set his back against its trunk, inhaling deeply, attempting to slow his pulse, regularize his breath.

I wonder if this is also going down elsewhere in the city.

He sat, eyes closed, smoking his cigarette, a measure of calm returning.

"Hello," a voice spoke from before him.

Andrew's lids jerked open; he jerked upright.

There was a man in the garden with him, reclined against the far wall, smoking a pipe of all things.

Andrew gazed at him warily, ready to at any moment either flee the way he'd come or rush the interloper.

"You needn't be frightened," the man said calmly, "I'm here seeking refuge, the same as you."

He wore a dark navy suit, nearly black, a red tie draped over a white collared shirt, buttoned to the top. Perhaps twenty years Andrew's elder, the man was amazingly calm, considering the mayhem that ruled the world just outside the sheltered confines of the garden.

"My name is Michael;" he puffed his pipe, appraising Andrew.

"I..." he paused, reasserting a semblance of composure, "I am Andrew."

"Andrew," Michael grinned, "what brings you to my garden this fine afternoon?"

He could not but goggle. "What... I... Bu..." Words had failed him.

"Take it easy, young man. I'm simply making a poor attempt at humor."

Andrew found words, grasped them, threw them toward this anomaly of space and time; "This is *your* garden?"

"Is there anyone present to say otherwise?" The man grinned again, leaning back against the wall.

"I suppose not." Andrew cocked an inquisitive eye.

"You've come here to escape the riots?"

"If that's what you call what is happening out there, then yes;" he shuddered. "I've never seen... I... I don't know what I just escaped from;" he swallowed hard, "It was terrible though."

"I suggest you stay here until things have cooled down," bluish smoke swirled from the bowl of his pipe. "There's nothing out there but trouble."

"Who are you?"

"I may be a friend."

"I don't need any more friends."

"Don't you?" He held a finger to his ear, seeming to be listening to something.

It was then Andrew noticed the small ear bug Michael wore, a realization that completely changed his impression of the man.

"You're a Fed."

Michael laughed quietly, bringing the pipe from his mouth to bare a full set of glossy white teeth. "Well, that's a fairly broad term, isn't it."

"Are you somehow involved in what's happening out there?"

"No," sounding sincerely offended. "That is the work of the police, who take orders from the mayor, who is himself a creature of The Party."

"'The Party,' eh?" Andrew didn't know whether to take the man seriously.

"Yes."

"And from whom do *you* take orders?"

"I take orders from no one."

Andrew laughed aloud; "And now I *know* you're full of shit." He leaned back against the maple. "Everyone takes orders from someone."

"Well," he brought his hand to his chin, stroked his jaw with the back of his hand; "There is someone," he looked out, over the wall, back to Andrew. "But he isn't here right now," smiled.

What a creepy fucking dude.

"Look, man, if it's all the same to you I'd like to just chill here quietly until we both can leave."

"But it's not all the same to me, Andrew;" he stepped forward. "I think we should talk."

"What the fuck is there to talk about?"

He continued to advance, now only a meter away. "We could talk about your friends, if you like, Peter and Thorin, Aleta, Edith… Jonathan."

Oh Christ, what the fuck has that hippy gotten me into.

His eyes darted to the left and right, judging the height of the wall, planning an escape. His ears, however, had made an unpleasant discovery; the sound of footsteps marching in double time, clearly not belonging to regular citizens, was discernible on the far side. Really though, none of this mattered, as his feet had reached a firm decision to remain as they were.

"Don't be alarmed;" Michael stopped, brought his pipe from his mouth, puffed a swirl into the air, there coiling to rest among the branches above. "We've been watching you for some time."

"To what end?"

He laughed, looking at Andrew with a crooked gaze; "I've already told you: To my own ends"

"And what would these be?"

"The defense of liberty and the salvation of the republic."

"Those sound like noble ends."

"Quite an astute observation." He smiled wryly. "You're presently on your way to the hotel? On twelfth street was it?"

Realizing any attempt to lie to this man would be more dangerous than useful, Andrew nodded.

The secret is to not lie, but to also not give him any more information than he already has.

"You're going to ensure the safety of the girl, Edith?"

He nodded again.

"Then let me assure you she is not in any danger. She's in the hotel right now, with your friend Thorin and his woman." He set his feet apart, standing at ease. "The riots are all far from there anyway."

"So it is more than just here then."

"Yes."

"Is it as bad elsewhere?"

Michael hesitated before responding; "Yes."

"And you know why this is happening?"

"Look, Andrew," he said plainly with a shrug, "You can keep asking me if I know things and keep getting the same response, or you can assume I'm *quite* well informed and fully appraised of the situation."

"Then why have you brought me here? What purpose is there in that?"

He laughed, perhaps more of a chuckle; "I didn't bring you here; you brought yourself here. I'm sure you remember that."

"But you know so much about me, about my friends."

Again met with laughter, "To be frank, all you know is I know your names and where you're staying."

It was Andrew's turn to laugh; "But you surely know more than that."

"That would be a good assumption;" he grinned.

What the fuck?

Somehow the conversation had taken on the cast of old friendship. A lingering humor hung in the air, in marked contrast to the world around. There in the confines of the garden passed a moment of simple, inexplicable familiarity.

Banished with an inward shake of his head.

"So you want to talk to me just to reassure me Edith's safe?" He executed a skeptical arch of his eyebrow; "Thanks. I truly feel assured," dripped with sardony.

"Of course that's not all I wish to speak with you about—simply the information required to ensure you don't do anything rash."

"If that's true, perhaps I should go see to her anyway. How can I trust you aren't simply telling me what I want to hear?"

"Sometimes, Andrew," he tapped his pipe out onto the well-trimmed grass of the garden, "Sometimes the truth and what we want to hear coincide."

For some reason Andrew believed him. Standing there in the shadow of the maple's broad leaves, secure in the walled garden, he simply accepted the stranger's words, for he *knew* they were the truth. He sparked a cigarette, somehow already held between his fingers. "So what do you want to talk about?"

CONCERNS

Edith poked her head out the window for the third time in as many minutes, glancing up and down the street before sliding back onto the couch.

"Don't worry," Thorin attempted to reassure her, which would've been more effective had his voice not betrayed his own anxiety. "Peter and Andrew are big boys who know when to duck, and when to run." He rose from his position beside Aleta and snuck a glance out the window; "Besides, it's not like they're alone out there—They have each other."

Aleta glowered at him from across the room. "I still say we should go try to find them; they could need our help."

"For the last fucking time, we're *not* leaving the hotel to wander the city in hopes of finding two men among two hundred thousand." He angrily tore a joint from the tin on the coffee table, moving to stand by the window where its smoke could readily pass out of the room, sparked it. "It was a stupid fucking idea an hour ago, and it's a stupid fucking idea now."

She looked momentarily to Edith, back to Thorin, "Then maybe just one of us could go, just to see what's happening."

"And who would that be? *You're* certainly not leaving the hotel, and neither is Edith. If it were just me here, *maybe* I'd go... But there's just no way in hell I'm leaving you two alone;" he puffed roughly on the joint, pulling it too hard, causing it's burn to become uneven. "I don't even trust that if I left you nitwits wouldn't be out trying to find *me* within the hour."

"He's right, Aleta. Peter and Andrew will be here as soon as it's safe." Edith sounded far less sure than her words indicated. "Right now they know exactly where we are; if we leave no one will know where anyone is." She smiled; "besides, you're definitely not going anywhere, Thorin's certainly not gonna leave you, and I can't leave either."

"You could leave if you wanted, if you weren't so scared. Your friends need you, perhaps desperately, and you sit on a couch playing the helpless woman."

Steel rose in Edith's countenance as she turned to face Aleta directly. "You don't know me; you don't know where I've been or what I can do. You certainly don't know my reasons for wanting to stay."

"Sure I do; you just told me." She met Edith's eyes; "You and Thorin don't think they can be found. You don't think it's safe to walk the streets. You have a convenient excuse, that they will come here, which allows you rationalize doing nothing."

"It's NOT safe to walk the streets!" Thorin thundered at her. "Just let it go, for Christ's sake. They're my best friends, and I can't do a thing to help them." He abused the joint further. "Don't you think I would if there were any way?"

The three of them had been disturbed earlier, woken in their beds by what seemed a thousand police and fire sirens screaming north on Broad, loud still even from four blocks away. When the spectacle was repeated, this time east on Locust, reappearing a moment later going north on 11th, they knew something terrible had happened. Thorin had immediately tried to call Peter's cell, then Andrew's, yet both had been busy. Perhaps thirty minutes later, when a policeman stumbled passed on Spruce, collapsing just below their window, they'd realized just how bad terrible could be. The man had looked like he'd been through hell, or perhaps just run-over repeatedly by a large truck. The doorman had rushed out to help, but it had soon become clear the man was beyond the help of non-professionals. That no ambulance had come, even for a wounded cop, had been perhaps the most foreboding and disquieting aspect of the entire scene. Presently the guy was laid out in the lobby downstairs, attended by a partially hysterical cleaning woman. Thorin had helped carry him in, returning with blood-stained clothes and hands, vague and troubling news that some sort of large-scale riot was in progress somewhere in the city.

He flicked the remainder of the mangled joint out the window, returning to his place beside Aleta.

"I understand," she said, working her way into his side.

He draped an arm over her, drawing her close.

"I'm just worried about them."

"We all are."

"I'm pregnant too," Edith blurted out, eyes wide, feet nervously tapping the floor.

"What?" Thorin gaped at her.

"I'm pregnant, with Andrew's baby."

"How can you be sure?" He looked from her to his fiancé. "Can she even know this soon?" Returning to Edith, "You've only known him for a week."

"I know, Thorin."

"They have tests now that can tell you after just three days," Aleta added, giving Edith a queer look. "Why did you even think to check though?"

"Well," she began, "after we found out about you, I got to thinking Andrew and I hadn't used protection, so I went to the pharmacy the next day before everyone woke up."

Thorin, thoroughly befuddled, "When the hell did you guys even have time to have sex? I didn't know you were having sex." He looked to Aleta; "Did *you* know they were having sex?"

"I had an inkling." A smile touched the corners of her mouth for a brief moment.

"In the bed next to us?" he asked the room incredulously. "I'm pretty sure I'd have woken for that." He stopped for a brief duration. "Wait a minute," head whipping toward Edith; "Jonathan's party?"

The red staining Edith's cheeks was answer enough.

"While you were spun?!"

She nodded.

"Holy shit." He sat back into the couch.

Aleta studied Edith. "Does Andrew know?"

"No, and I can't tell him. Not right now anyway."

"Why not? Are you planning to have it terminated?"

"Of course not."

"Then why?" She looked genuinely concerned.

"Because I have to tell him in my own time, in my own way. I'd like to be able to get to know him better first." She turned toward the window, then away and down to the floor, hair falling to partially obscure her face; "If I scare him off now this will never work."

Thorin marched over to the micro-fridge, pulling out a ten dollar bottle of domestic beer that would be charged to Andrew's card. "Motherfucker." He looked from Edith to Aleta. "I suppose I'll have to drink by myself." Sitting on the arm of the couch by the window, peering briefly to the east and west, seeing nothing, he brought a hand to his chin, absently thumbed his beard. "So I guess even on a day like today good news is possible." He caught and held Edith's gaze for a moment. "We'll be seeing them momentarily; I'm sure of it." Breaking into a broad grin, "After all, it's not like Andrew to leave his child without a father."

THE IDSC

Peter hunkered behind the tall Corinthian columns that fronted The First Bank of the United States, chain smoking cigarettes and apprehensively watching the deserted length of 3rd Street before him. With the solid structure to his rear he enjoyed a modicum of security; however, the columns themselves offered very little actual cover. When last the riot police had passed his position he'd lain prone, hoping they'd take him for a casualty of the mob, or even better simply overlook his presence altogether. The ruse had apparently been successful, and he'd not seen anyone on the street for what seemed a fairly long time.

The question now was how he should proceed.

Having escaped from the chaos that had earlier enveloped the historic district, he'd not since had to make any actual decisions, perfectly content to remain where he was, the sound of gunshots echoing through the streets perhaps twenty minutes earlier serving only to emphasize the wisdom of staying put. Yet now, with the streets deserted, remaining seemed simple cowardice rather than prudence.

He rose from his position behind the southernmost column, flicked his cigarette onto the steps of the building, and cautiously ventured away from his sanctuary, moving South on 3rd, avoiding the street and hugging the bricked walk that traced its western side.

As he emerged from the shadow of the building, his head turned slightly right, making a brief survey of the park he'd fled nearly an hour before. The back side of Carpenter's hall, or rather the lawn there, had missed the majority of the afternoon's action. It lay eerily empty.

He continued down the street.

What the fuck am I doing? What the fuck is going on?

The realities of the afternoon seemed entirely incommensurable with those of the morning, and now, walking a deserted street in Philly that before would've been bustling with people, Philadelphia natives and protesters, Peter felt as though he journeyed a post apocalyptic world, locked in a safe while all around was destroyed.

I don't wear glasses though....

Laughed.

He jerked his thoughts from random irrelevance to acute necessity.

What I need to do is get back to the hotel. Andrew's probably already been there for at least a half hour. If I don't get my shit in gear they may do something stupid like come look for me.

He passed by Walnut, continuing south. Given the odd peacefulness of the street, he decided to take 3rd all the way to Lombard, and from there to approach the hotel on 12th from the south, giving both the historic district and Washington Square a wide berth. If there was one thing he'd learned at school it was that the best policy is to go with what you know until it is demonstrated to be erroneous, and he *knew* the area directly to the west had not to long ago been home to chaos and riot.

It's strange how the postulates of empiricism play out in the real world. In class, in study, they serve to keep one on the path toward knowledge. Here, now, they serve to keep me safe from God knows what... injury, imprisonment, perhaps even death. Yet, is it truly possible to maintain such skepticism while also acting? Can one refuse to accept fully what seems to be the case when this case must be interacted with from moment to moment? I act *as if* what I'm doing is correct, knowing I very well may be marching toward danger. Can I do otherwise? Assuredly not... Still though, sound process is harder to maintain when each step measures not an abstract investigation but instead an acute movement that brings the unknown intimately, uncomfortably close.

There wasn't a car driving on the street for as far as he could see, nor any pedestrians. He looked up suddenly, examining the edifices of the buildings he passed, half expecting to see faces observing him disapprovingly from high windows, but there were none.

As he approached Spruce Street, which marked the median of his journey to Lombard, he began to hear the first creeping sounds of footsteps, approaching from the unknown expanse of Spruce and the western vicinity to which it was a gateway. They sounded hurried, although definitely not marking the pace of a run.

He quickly hopped the low wrought iron fencing running between the two stoops of the building to his right, crouching in the recess there among waste containers and recycling bins. Not even wanting to look at whomever it was who approached, he ducked his head.

The footsteps came to a stop at the intersection of Spruce and 3rd, perhaps four meters from Peter's hiding place. The man—the fall of his steps and deepness of his breaths clearly indicating he was such— was taking his time in the intersection, which Peter thought strange given the clear hurry in which he'd been just moments before and that intersections were perhaps the most vulnerable places to be.

What the fuck is this guy doing?

"Peter?" The man's voice was familiar. "Peter, come out from wherever you're hiding. We don't have time for this."

What the fuck is *he* doing *here*?

Peter's sense of incredulity was so strong he could actually hear its high tones marking the recesses of his mind.

"Seriously, man: We have to be going. Now."

This is beyond believable.

He cast about, looking for the hidden cameras, the snide yet somehow likable host... perhaps a rumpled screenwriter, too pressed to be more creative and too lazy to hide his presence. What he found was an empty street cast in shadows by the late afternoon sun, and Jonathan standing in the intersection, quite aware he was hiding somewhere nearby.

He stood up without a sound, watching as Jonathan surveyed the other side of the street, turned toward him.

"There you are." He looked relieved.

"How in the hell did you know where I was?" He paused, continued, "What the fuck are you doing running around the fucking streets?" Thought again, "Why are yo..."

Cutting him off, "Look: We'll have plenty of time to discuss all of this later;" he glanced over his shoulder, down 3rd, to where Peter had been journeying. "But right now we should really be leaving."

"I'd like to know how and why you found me, before I go anywhere." He stepped over the fence and onto the sidewalk, "I mean, you can't just blow this off like you did the other day. I *know* you didn't just happen upon me." He reappraised the man before him. "Who the *fuck* are you, really?"

Jonathan met him with a steady gaze. "I'm someone who is here to save your ass;" moving to stand beside him on the sidewalk, "Right now that's all you need know."

He grasped Peter's elbow, gently turning him west and impelling him down Spruce Street.

Against his better judgment, he allowed himself to be guided away from the intersection. "Why must we go this way?"

Moving them along more briskly, "Because this is the shortest way to your hotel."

"What about the riots?"

"They've been put down." Looked over his shoulder, down the street before them, "At least in this part of the city."

Jonathan was clearly ambivalent. For himself, Peter didn't really know how he felt about it, although the momentary feeling of relief that rushed through his body seemed to suggest the idea was favorable.

"Then why must we hurry? Shouldn't the streets be safe now?"

Jonathan laughed aloud, picking up the pace.

Of a sudden a sound grew behind them, coming from the southern extension of 3rd Street. Footsteps, many footsteps, loud enough to be heard from a distance and falling in unison.

Not cops. Troops.

Peter added a little speed to their progress, which suddenly and at Jonathan's discretion made a sharp turn down an alley to the left, Saint Joseph's Way.

The brick-paved alley was close with trees and bushes; quaint, short streetlamps intended solely for pedestrian use marked its length at regular intervals.

They paused there, maybe ten meters from Spruce, between a tall forsythia and one of the lamps, against the brick face of a building on the east side of the alley.

"It's the way in which the 'riot' was put down that's dangerous," Jonathan spoke quietly. "The police were woefully inept;" he hesitated. "Actually, they caused this whole mess to begin with... but that's another discussion altogether, and one that can be had later."

Peter nodded, pulling a cigarette from his pack, sparking it behind a curved hand. Jonathan was much more well appraised of the situation than he.

"The steps we heard weren't made by the police," Jonathan resumed.

"I could tell."

"Indeed," giving him a queer look, "you're powers of perception are truly remarkable," grinned wryly. "But what you couldn't tell, what you'd never think, is they weren't made by the National Guard either."

Peter, cigarette poised between his lips, was now listening quite intently.

"I'm sure you're aware the majority of the Guard has been assumed into the regular army because of the wars."

"But only the Guard can operate within the country." Any school child knew that.

Jonathan's smile was... something quite distant from anything resembling or communicating mirth. "Yeah, well, given the whole situation in Oakland and the fact that more than half of the Guard is in either Pakistan or Venezuela, what we have operating here is something altogether different."

"So... from whom are we hiding?" He pulled on his smoke, exhaling into the knit branches of the forsythia. "The army?" He could barely believe he was asking the question, so absurd did it seem.

"No. Not the army."

"Then who?"

"A specialized security force, initially formed as part of the Department of Homeland Security, trained in internal security, counterinsurgency and the suppression of civil unrest."

"And this 'security force' is under the purview of the executive?"

Jonathan hesitated for a moment. "Basically..." He reached out, snapped Peter's cigarette from his mouth, took a hit, and stubbed it against the brick of the building. "IDSC is technically an *independent* agency."

"Independent." Peter had to form the word himself, feeling its significance when used in this context. "That's just lovely."

Jonathan laughed, "Isn't it though?"

"What does 'IDSC' stand for?"

"Why, the Internal Defense Security Council, of course."

"And how do *you* know so much about this IDSC, when I've never even heard of it?" He sparked another smoke, looked at Jonathan, head cocked to the side.

"I think they've continued up 3rd," Jonathan strained his ears. He began to walk back up the alley toward Spruce.

Peter caught up with him, skirted a streetlamp and planted himself between Jonathan and the mouth of the alley. "What the fuck, man?"

For the first time since Peter had met him Jonathan seemed unsure of himself, glanced at the ground before meeting Peter's searching gaze. "Well," he began, "technically I'm an IDSC operative."

Peter's cigarette, of its own accord, fell from his mouth.

Jonathan cast his eyes about the alley, discomfort palatable upon his face.

"Then why are we hiding from them?"

"It's…" he trailed off, searching for the proper words, found none. "It's complicated."

"Enlighten me."

"Let's get you back to the hotel first; then perhaps we can have a more thorough discussion."

Having no recourse, no other option and no idea as to how he could fabricate one, Peter simply raised his eyebrows, allowing Jonathan to pass onto Spruce, following close behind.

JULY 4TH

With Andrew and Edith sharing one bed, Thorin and Aleta in the other, Peter and Jonathan had been relegated to the couches in the sitting room, Peter near the windows and Jonathan on the other. That Jonathan had decided to spend the night at the hotel had seemed rather odd yet understandable, to everyone except Peter, to whom it seemed rather creepy.

They'd arrived at the Alexander Inn having had no further encounters, with police, regular people, or even obscure and vaguely sinister government agencies.

The entire journey of eight and a half blocks, a straight-shot down Spruce, had traced in Peter's mind an eerie feeling of disquiet, and as he'd crossed the threshold of the darkened lobby, he'd had to consciously refrain from simply shutting Jonathan out of the hotel entirely. Not that he hadn't trusted the man, he had, still did. After all, why should his feelings toward Jonathan change simply because he'd told Peter he was part of an organization Peter wouldn't even know about had Jonathan not told him about it? The revelation would've been senseless if Jonathan's motives had been part of some sinister plot to… do some ambiguous and likely quite horrible thing to… someone, either Peter himself or another of the group.

No, he wasn't scared of Jonathan. He was just in no way presently prepared to actually deal with any large shift in paradigm.

Thankfully, Jonathan hadn't attempted to bring the matter up in open company; Peter had steered clear of anything that would've remotely touched on the issue, simply relating the basics of his journey. Surprisingly, there'd been no questions as to how Jonathan and Peter had come to be united. The day's happenings had apparently been sufficiently engaging and/or terrifying already, and no one had seemed to desire anything new with which to deal.

Andrew's ordeal by far had been the most engrossing. His description of the crowd's encounter with the police had been terrifying even when simply related from the safety of a couch, set close to Edith and unwinding with a large spliff. That he'd managed to escape unscathed, realizing the safety of a private garden, had seemed a remarkable stroke of luck, given what Andrew had reported about the happenings on Walnut. He had, actually, managed to arrive at the hotel before Peter and Jonathan, greeting them with the others as they entered the suite.

Now, as the full light of morning cast its warmth across his uncovered face, Peter could hardly believe the events of the previous day had happened at all.

Independence Day.

The irony was so strong Peter could almost taste the pungent reek of its bitter dregs.

He lay on the couch, wondering just exactly what the day would hold, what its illumination would reveal. He switched on the television. Finding a twenty-four hour news channel, he reclined against the cushion he'd used as a pillow.

Yesterday's riots in Philly were the top story, followed closely by the new developments coming out of Oakland.

As Peter watched, Jonathan squinted his way to wakefulness. Sitting upright and giving his back a mighty stretch, he glanced at Peter, snagged the remainder of a spliff from the coffee table. Moving to the end of the couch away from the TV, near Peter's head, he opened the window and sparked it, gaze also set toward the talking heads on the screen.

Interestingly enough, there was little actual footage of what had actually transpired. They were told the protesters had become violent for reasons unknown, that the police had been forced to break up the protest, detain a large number of its participants. Casualties among the police and civilians were said to have been light. No mention of the IDSC or the use of unconventional tactics whatsoever.

The others, having been sleeping lightly enough to be disturbed even by the low drone of the television, entered the sitting room in staggered order throughout the report, first Thorin, followed closely by Edith and Andrew. Aleta entered last.

Jonathan tossed the roach out the window; "Ya gotta love the news, eh?" He grinned, "Always the epitome of objectivity and completeness."

"Shit," Thorin took a seat on the couch opposite Peter, "you'd think what happened was no big deal at all."

The news moved on to the situation in Oakland, which had apparently also been pacified the previous day, details even more sketchy than had been those of Philly.

I suppose the celebrations may now proceed without distraction.

"Not exactly how I pictured this 4th going;" Edith lowered herself into one of the chairs. "What are we supposed to do now? Is it even safe to leave the hotel?"

Andrew sat beside Thorin on the couch, at the end near Edith. "I can't imagine why not;" he paused, stood back up, moving toward the window on the far side of the room. "Although I can pretty much guarantee we will *not* be allowed to gather for the final rally." He lit a cigarette, leaning slightly out the window.

From his dry tone it was unclear how he felt about this fact.

Peter, rising from his seat to join him, was also ambivalent. Although he'd journeyed nearly five-thousand kilometers to be there, to participate in an unprecedented show of nonpartisan political expression, he had no desire whatsoever to repeat the past day's horrors. He accepted the already burning smoke from his friend; "I wonder if they'll have fireworks tonight."

Andrew guffawed.

Edith looked at him, expression blank.

Jonathan snickered quietly; beside him Aleta wore an expression of anger.

Thorin, ever a bastion of centered good-humor, simply reclined further into the couch, closing his eyes. "I imagine, if they're held at all, the fireworks will be quite spectacular, given this *is* the 250th anniversary of independence, and we *are* in Philadelphia."

Regaining his composure as well as the cigarette from Peter, "Shit," Andrew took a puff, "They'll probably be even more grand than they otherwise would've been, to like blow the memory of yesterday from our minds."

No one said anything.

That night they stood, having passed the day in bored confinement and frustrated designs, atop the Alexander, which the management had been kind enough to allow.

Thorin, perhaps because he'd sat out Friday's excitement, had ventured out earlier and purchased a magnum of Champagne. Now all six of them—Jonathan had chosen to remain with them at the hotel—shared a toast to friendship, with even Edith and Aleta joining in.

There was no display of fireworks, official or otherwise, yet as they stood there together in the bright luminosity of the moon, the lights of the city themselves seemed to sparkle and crack, hundreds of thousands of points, each significant of life, crawling beneath the surface of every building, every home.

Peter looked to the face of the moon, that fateful mistress he felt must somehow be responsible for all that had happened since the time he'd spent with her by the lake in Ross.

You have come to this place... to lie in the ground?

Yet I stand. We stand here together.

And what is peace?

I have not yet found it.

What story would you have?

WE WILL BE HEARD

The question hung in space, sinking in, resettling among the fragments of self he called memories.

No answer was forthcoming.

CHAPTER 4
UPSTATE

AGAINST A CEDAR

"You ready for this?" Thorin asked over his shoulder as they began a rather steep climb up a ridge, parting with the road and valley they'd followed the first couple kilometers out of town.

Daniel, already slightly winded, responded with a rough grunt.

As ready as I'll ever fucking be.

Shit.

He was caught between wishing this Centre was closer than it seemed It must be and hoping It was quite far away indeed.

Even here, as free as I've ever been, I'm trapped in irreconcilabilities.

The morning of the third day of their journey away from New York and still Daniel was amazed at how easily they'd been able to exit The City. It had been so simple, laughably simple.

He'd stayed with Alena and Thorin through the weekend, sleeping in an actual bed, not a couch for once, and spending late nights in the pub drinking and generally being unhingingly happy with a woman he found both incredibly attractive and human.

Thorin had yet to be more forthcoming about the nature of his journey. When Daniel had again questioned him about his leaving The City, the answer had been equally as obscure as his stated reason that first night. "There are things to be done," he'd said, offering no further elucidation. Daniel had begun to suspect Thorin himself didn't really comprehend the full significance of the journey, although it was abundantly clear that, for whatever reason, he felt compelled to travel to this place called The Centre, wherever It was.

The late morning sun slipped behind tall maples as they wound their way up the incline, following an unmarked yet well established path whose cutbacks provided a regular if drawn-out ascent. Interspersed stood balsam firs, dark needles contrasting markedly with the broad, five-pointed leaves of their hardwood peers.

Here, far from The City, away from even rudimentary human habitation, the smells of the forest filled Daniel with a sense of stability, of belonging, even though he'd never before *been* in a forest. Having spent his entire life in The City, he was amazed to discover the scent of musky leaves and fresh pine spoke to him more of home than had anything he could recall of New York.

When they'd set out the past Monday, Daniel had been filled with a hopeful anticipation, alien in its own way, quite different from the simple apprehensiveness that traditionally colored his mind, marred only by a touch of confusion when they'd begun to pack their belongings... that is, when they'd begun to pack Thorin's belongings and provisions; Daniel had nothing of his own except the clothes on his back and the money in his wallet... into large backpacks, antiquated, designed for extended trips away from civilization and the human world in general. When he'd asked why they were preparing for such a journey, Thorin had responded simply that the trip to The Centre would likely be long, that they'd be avoiding the main roads and larger towns and cities, traveling cross-country whenever possible

Thorin, quite generously Daniel thought, had purchased more appropriate footwear for him, and as he walked behind the man he was acutely aware the leather boots, now properly broken in, had already saved him from several falls and more than a few blisters.

His feet were comfortable, at least as comfortable as feet can be when a man is walking thirty kilometers a day with over thirty kilograms on his back, yet this simple and critical reality barely touched his thoughts. These were focused, had been since he and Alena had parted ways, on the girl he might never see again.

The space she had, in a few short days, forged in his heart lay barren. Now, as he and Thorin breached the edge of civilization and moved into the relative wilderness of the southern foothills of the Catskills, the void at the center of his being, rather than filling with warm thoughts and memories, crept outward, permeating his soul, infecting his mind with a longing for completeness he knew wouldn't be fulfilled for a long time, if ever.

He'd last seen her when she'd dropped them off just west of Sloatsburg, about seventy kilometers northwest of The City. Thorin's ability to travel freely, even with one such as Daniel, wasn't limited to merely crossing the Broadway Bridge; he'd also successfully gotten them across the Tappan Zee, a feat Daniel would've thought impossible. They'd crossed both without the question of Daniel's identity coming up at all.

Quite strange, really.

The journey had been fairly rough, even over the flat terrain they'd thus far covered. Daniel had never before walked more than a kilometer or two, let alone heavily laden—his legs and back had begun to ache just a few hours into the first day of travel. Now, with over sixty kilometers behind him, he could feel strength creeping into his limbs, solidity returning to his back. The ridge they currently ascended, however, seemed intent on beating from him any vestige of new-found stamina. Even so, as they reached the end of the incline, moving onto more level ground, he could feel his strength building, finally awakened after long years of slumber.

Thorin shrugged off his pack, resting it against a slender beech to the right of the trail, sat upon the downed length of a cedar. Grateful for a break after the thirty minute climb, Daniel did the same, retrieving a bottle of water and sitting down beside him.

"Not too bad?"

Daniel smiled, "Nothing I can't handle," sipping his water.

Amusement in his eyes, "Good;" he searched the side pocket of pack, "The next one will be a little more challenging," grinned. Having found the object of his search, Thorin lowered himself from the trunk, resting his back against its grey bulk, let out a long sigh. "To be honest, I haven't worked this hard since I was your age," gave Daniel a broad smile, began to crumble ganja onto a wide rolling paper.

"For an old man," Daniel looked down on Thorin from his perch, "you certainly smoke a lot."

"She and I have always been close," Thorin responded without looking away from his work. "Have seen a lot of strange and difficult times together;" he finished rolling the joint, bringing it to his mouth, sparked it. "A lot of good times too."

"I'd be interested in hearing about them," accepted the spliff from his new friend, took a long pull.

"Perhaps someday I'll have the opportunity to tell you;" he took in the forest before them, "but now is not the time for old tales." He reached within his jacket pocket, pulled out a pouch of beef jerky, offering it to Daniel.

Trading joint for smoked meat, he slid down beside Thorin, observing an inchworm, bright green and incredibly tiny, which dangled from a thin thread perhaps half a meter to his left. "In your own time, then."

The inchworm, descended from the heights of the beech above, swayed gently in the breeze, lowering itself slowly, searching for solid ground. Daniel sat forward, extending his hand so it would settle thereupon. When it had done so he sat back, observing the queer creature as it scooted along the back of his upraised hand.

He again traded with Thorin, and with a mischievous grin blew a cloud of smoke, engulfing the inchworm in heady fog. Still grinning, he turned as Thorin chuckled beside him.

"The young never change."

Ganja having brought a sense of peace, comfortable and familial, gravity took hold of Daniel. "What happened to Alena's mother?" Paused. "If you don't mind my asking." He set his hand against the cedar trunk, allowing the inchworm to climb from his hand and back into the greater world of the ridge-top.

I am simply passing through.

Thorin sat silently for a moment, perhaps contemplating a response, perhaps simply spacing out. Of a sudden he began to speak. "Not at all, Daniel;" waving away the joint Daniel offered him, "There really isn't that much to say. She left us when Alena was still very young." He laughed ruefully; "I suppose this world was not her place."

Daniel puffed the joint, lay back, watching the light filter through the oblong leaves of the beech. "When did she die?"

Thorin tucked his legs beneath himself, Indian style; "Oh," he laughed, "she didn't die," paused; "Not that I know of anyway. She just had to leave."

"Had to leave?"

"Indeed," he snagged the joint from Daniels hand. "Just as I have to go on this journey now;" puffed, "There's little we can do to prevent having to do what we must."

"Sounds a little tautological to me."

"Perhaps," broke into a wide grin, "but it is true nonetheless."

Daniel laughed aloud, "You're a funny fucking guy."

Thorin rose, sitting on the cedar as he tightened the laces of his boots. "I've been told something similar before." He stood, hoisted his pack onto his back.

Daniel groaned.

"Let's get going;" Thorin started a little down the trail. "I'd like to make Joseph's before dark."

"A friend of yours?" Daniel was incredulous.

This is the gateway to the middle of nowhere. No way someone lives out here.

It was Thorin's turn to laugh. "You need to expand your horizons, my young friend. We aren't in The City anymore."

SAINT JOSEPH'S LAKE

One steep climb, another sizeable spliff, and perhaps fifteen kilometers later found the two men unburdening themselves beside the still waters of Saint Joseph's Lake. The sun sat low on the opposite bank, lighting the sky in refracted colors, oranges and pinks.

The lake was surrounded by an eclectic mix of trees: pine, cedar, maple; a little to the north Daniel could see an oak, broad and proud amidst its less bold neighbors. Beyond the lake, to the west, set beneath the setting sun, ran an old road, fallen into disrepair, long unused and forgotten.

This was their first night away from the amenities of civilization, and Daniel, who'd previously never spent so much as a day away from The City, found he was woefully inept at erecting a tent, so much so that Thorin eventually asked him to exit the project altogether, sending him on a mission to collect firewood, another novel task. This latter, however, was nonetheless within the domain of his powers, at least much more so than had been the arraigning of tent poles and stakes.

By nightfall they were sitting beside a comfortable blaze, finishing off the remains of a stew Thorin had made from bullion, beef jerky, freeze-dried potatoes, and a little lake water.

Daniel lay on his back, lit a cigarette, staring upward at stars he'd never really known existed.

"There are so many," he said, quietly puffing his smoke; looked to Thorin, "This is the first I've been far enough away from the lights of man to see them."

'We grew up in different worlds, you and I;" Thorin turned from the fire to also gaze at the heavens above. "My father used to take us camping for a couple weeks every summer, further north, up in Vermont, in the mountains."

"I've always wondered what it would be like to go camping," Daniel's followed the path of a satellite as it crossed the sky. "Never had the opportunity though;" hit his smoke, "The IDSC took my parents when I was still very young, you understand, and by the time I was old enough to leave The System, to live by myself, New York had become a different place entirely." He sat up, turning toward the fire, toward Thorin, who sat on its opposite side. "The City had become more than just the place where I lived; it was my *home*." Flicked his cigarette into the flames, "I never really thought to leave until much later, recently, maybe a year or so ago."

Lacking a real home, a man owns what he's given; failing to be adopted, he adopts himself.

Thorin spoke quietly, "And what precipitated this change?"

Daniel took a deep breath, reached into his pocket, drawing another cigarette; "I don't know," sparked it, "a lot of things, I guess."

He leaned back on his left arm, palm against the earth, "I guess there was just a point at which I no longer belonged, when I didn't care anymore to belong."

Thorin, thankfully, didn't press him further on the subject, instead moving silently to roll a spliff, eyes downcast in the flickering light of the fire. "I'm sorry, Daniel," he said without looking up.

"Why are you sorry? It's not like it was your fault."

He licked the paper, twisted it into unity; "Perhaps, yet still I'm sorry."

"That's… very sweet of you."

"I'm serious. I'm sorry they took your parents from you. I'm sorry you had to grow up in a world like this." He paused long enough to light the joint, puff a few. "There was a time, you know, a long time ago, when I was a young man such as yourself, when I thought I could change things, thought that by simply speaking my mind the world would somehow reform." He looked to Daniel over the flames, caught his eyes, tossing the spliff over the blaze and onto the ground to Daniel's right.

Daniel picked it up, depositing his half-burnt cigarette in its place. "And what happened?"

"I was shown the naïveté of my belief, in stark, glaring clarity."

"Sounds like an 'old tale' worth hearing."

Thorin chuckled, breaking free of whatever darkness had prompted him to offer apology for something for which he was in no way responsible, "I'm sure you're not alone in desiring knowledge of those days. I myself still don't fully know what happened." He held his hand up, motioned for Daniel to toss back the spliff, catching it in an open palm before quickly lifting it to his lips.

Retrieving his smoke, Daniel pondered these words, allowing the formality of their construction to sink into his mind.

Something tells me there's more to this guy's story than one would suspect.

He remained silent though, again lying back to observe the delicate lace of the cosmos.

That night, as he lay sleeping beside Thorin in the close confines of the tent, Daniel was visited once more by the dream, its haunting images and dreary realities once more jerking him awake, covered in sweat and filled with a despair he could not banish from his mind, even after lucidity returned.

The soft sound of rain falling on the thin skin above brought a little comfort, a gentle reminder he wasn't in the cell, that the wretched figure wasn't him. Yet still, bringing his hands to his face, wiping off the perspiration and tear there found, he could not shake the feeling that he *had* actually been there, that it was more than a mere dream.

He lay in the tent, the muted percussion filling his ears, awake, as the day awoke to dawn.

THE MIDDLE OF NOWHERE

They broke camp early in the morning, continuing more or less on a northwestern bearing.

The trail they'd followed out of Westbrookville had terminated at the lake, and they now traveled roads patently designed for the passage of vehicles. Clearly, however, they'd not served this function for some time.

Walking along the cracked asphalt, occasionally passing an abandoned house set to its side, Daniel considered the reality of a world whose function and nature actually changed, quite unlike the fundamentally static existence to which he'd grown accustomed in The City.

Here roads become something else altogether; houses become aviaries, warrens and dens. I wonder: Will I also experience change? I too was formed in the presence of people, their movements and activities surrounding me, filling me.

Yet already he could sense a change in himself, feel that his learned apathy and derision here had no place, no object upon which to center. He'd grown so used to loathing others he found he didn't know himself otherwise.

I guess that all really started changing back when I met Alena. I'd been so focused on her the actuality of the change was lost to me.

They followed an irregular path, Thorin in the lead, turning from time to time, from one road to another, intersections marked by lonely stop signs. Forest had been replaced by sweeping fields, corn and grain, literally extending as far as the eye could see, broken only by the narrow cuts of the roads along which they travelled.

As they passed yet another group of abandoned houses, Daniel moved to catch up with his guide, matching his pace, walking beside him.

"I never really thought about people's actually living so far away from cities."

"Indeed," looking around himself, the clear of the sky revealing a scene devoid of any movement but their own, "Not too long ago this whole area was home to hundreds of people, had been for thousands of years."

Daniel looked at the nearest house, turned to Thorin questioningly.

"Well," he grinned, "they weren't always the *same* people, and they certainly didn't all live in the same manner, but the point stands."

"What point is that?"

"That the world you know is not absolute; in fact, that it is quite arbitrary."

He set his eyes ahead, to where the road vanished over the rise of a distant hill, "I'm not sure if I follow."

Thorin paused, shifting the weight on his back, turned to Daniel; "The place we came from, where we met..."

"Your pub?" asked innocently.

"The City," Thorin continued, "places like that haven't existed for very long, in the grand scheme of things."

"I'd been under the impression New York has existed for hundreds of years."

"Sure. *Hundreds* of years, and before New York there was London, Vienna, Rome, Bangkok, Babylon, Timbuktu." He began to move forward again, dragging Daniel along by the ear. "But still, even looking at the entirety of their existence, these things we call cities have only exited for a fraction of human history, a place like New York, New York as it is now, this has *never* existed before."

Thorin had picked up speed as he spoke; Daniel missed a beat as he tried to match the new pace. "And... what... is so special about New York?"

"First off, there are *a lot* of people living there, nearly one-hundred-fifty million in the area, twenty-five million in Manhattan alone." He paused, "And then there's the nature of the place itself..." looked to Daniel. "Do you know why we're traveling cross-country right now?"

"To avoid confrontation with the authorities, I'd imagine."

"To avoid confrontation with the IDSC," Thorin corrected him; "Regular authorities I can handle."

"I've noticed."

Giving Daniel a sidelong glance, "I'm sure you have. But I've gotta ask: Why were we able to travel more conventionally before?" He continued without waiting for an answer, "Because within the greater metropolitan area security, in terms of transmigration enforcement, is fairly lax. If we were to drive a car out here, the IDSC would be on us within the hour."

Daniel looked down at the road quizzically, back to Thorin.

"Well," he sighed, "not *here* precisely, but *out here*. Some of these roads, actually one perhaps only twenty kilometers to the north, which we are shadowing, are still operational." Thorin slowed. "Security is lax downstate because the IDSC generally doesn't have to worry about people's attempting to leave. The City is an end unto itself."

Daniel, grateful for the return to a more reasonable pace, smiled. "I've thought the same thing myself."

Thorin stopped, turned toward Daniel; "Certainly you're any-thing but inattentive," paused; "Tell me, then: When you were in The City, what was real to you?"

"'What was *real*?'"

"What did you deal with when you acted? What defined the do-main of your movements?"

Daniel's brow furrowed. He'd touched on similar ground himself only hours before. "The movements of others, those whom I moved about and who moved about me."

Strange that this man can so easily speak to me of that which I already think, have thought.

"Exactly!" Thorin's smile was vicious; "And that is *precisely* how people become convinced all is normal, when in fact it is anything but." He looked around; "You wanna take a break?" shrugged his pack from his shoulders, set it down beside the road.

Daniel nearly beat him to it, his pack finding itself strewn against Thorin's almost before the older man had set it down. He stretched his back, twisting his torso and raising his hands above his head. He'd gotten used to the weight of the pack, yet it felt good still to move without the burden, unstrapped from its buckled confines.

Thorin sat down beside the packs, leaning his back against them, pulled a spliff he'd pre-rolled back at the lake, from a tin in the front pocket. "If you took a bunch of people and forced them into a rel-atively small place like The City, say in the manner of the German ghettos we saw in the earlier half of last century, they'd all know the situation wasn't right, that they should be elsewhere, because this is what they *feel*, what they feel from each other." He paused to light the joint, taking a long pull that seemed to calm his thoughts a bit. "However, if you took only a few, and forced them into the same place, already populated by a great many others, these few would, instead of *knowing* that being in The City was wrong, infer there was some-thing wrong with themselves, that The City was perfectly normal, that living in a ghetto is what people naturally do." He again took a puff, handing the spliff to Daniel who remained standing. "Given that peo-ple in The City, nowadays at least, have lived most if not all of their lives therein, we can see how most never even consider leaving, and why security is lax."

"Yet still, travel out of The City, among its different sections, is restricted; they don't simply let people wander."

"This is more a function of keeping people among their peers than anything else. When people wander too much, when they break from routine and interact with those who reflect different images of the world, they are more apt to discover the truth of themselves in the difference, whether they belong or not."

"You're referring to me, I take it."

"Of course." He accepted the joint back from Daniel, "*You* were aware you didn't belong there;" taking a hit, "That was clear from the moment we met in the pub."

"So what you're saying is you knew right away I was a weirdo."

"More that *you* knew you were a weirdo. We all, in our interactions with others, tell the truth of how we feel about ourselves and the world."

Accepting the joint Thorin held extended, "What is your point again?"

"That the world you come from is artificial, that you should now be able to see it for what it is since you've left it behind."

Daniel looked back down the road, at the houses they'd passed earlier, still visible in the distance. "If that world is artificial, if it is not right for people to live there, why have the houses we've passed been deserted?"

"Deserted? Not quite. And I never said The City itself is artificial, nor that it is wrong for people to live there. I'd simply said that people who are forced to live in such a place, whatever the manner of the compulsion, should feel it is wrong, that *your* world there was artificial, forced upon you before you even knew who you were." His voice grew dark. "At any rate, a more apt term to describe these houses would be *vacated*."

"But why? Where have the people gone? To The City?"

"Some."

"The others?"

He paused before responding; "It is unclear."

Daniel, filling the silence left by his companion's vague response, lowered himself, also reclining against the packs, not quite on the opposite side from Thorin. "Why did you live in The City?"

"Me?" He paused in thought, "I..." reached over the packs, beckoning for the remainder of the spliff, "I had matters there to attend to."

"Just as Alena has matters to attend to now?" He could not tell if bitterness or wistfulness colored his voice. Regardless, the feeling was far from pleasant.

"Perhaps." He finished off the joint, flicking it to the side of the road.

"And why do you have to journey to this Centre now? Why not a year from now, or five years ago?"

"Well, to be quite frank, *you* showed up at my door, unannounced, having already met my daughter."

"And somehow my arriving at the pub last week, that I'd met Alena, forced you to leave?"

Thorin sat up a little, turned to face Daniel, who'd himself turned to face Thorin. "I certainly couldn't have had you and her running around the Upper West Side together, and besides, you were already set on leaving."

Somehow anger had entered Daniel, a biting venom he could not keep from his words, "You left The City *just so we couldn't be together?*"

Thorin was unfazed; "Of course not. You and I had to leave regardless, as it was time to do so. Alena *stayed behind* just so you and she couldn't be together."

Daniel scrambled to his feet, glaring down at the old man before him. "*What?*"

"Look, Daniel, there's no point in getting all upset." He slowly stood up, surveying the surrounding miles upon miles of amber grain, rippling in the wind; "It's not like you can do anything about it. She's in Manhattan, and you're here. Without me to guide you, to turn away the authorities, you'd be imprisoned within the week." He grinned, "Try going back to Manhattan without me, and I can *guarantee* you an extended stay in a dark, dank place. *I* brought you out of the city; you'd never have made it without my help. You cannot return, not now."

Daniel gathered his fist, striking the old man square in the jaw with all the strength he had. "You old fucking bastard," spit into the wind.

All the strength he had, however, seemed to have been pitifully impotent, as Thorin, still unfazed, punched him *hard*, on the upper portion of his left flank, literally knocking the wind from his lungs. "Save your rage for someone else," he spoke quietly, watching with somber eyes as Daniel attempted to draw air. "I did nothing but save your life;" he gazed into the distance, unfocused. "Don't judge me because I chose to also safeguard the life of my daughter."

Daniel found air and with it tears. "I didn't *have* to leave!" nearly a sob; "I was happy with her, happy for the only time I can clearly remember." Drew a breath, calming himself, "I'd only been leaving because I didn't belong there."

"You don't belong there."

"I belong with her!" he cried, taking a few steps away from the old man, putting some distance between them before he was compelled to strike him again.

"Perhaps you do."

He turned on Thorin, fury in his eyes, scorn upon his lips; "Again with that word. Do you know no other?"

Thorin broke into a smile, more gentle than before, almost mirthful; "Perhaps."

Daniel paused, took another breath, reevaluating both himself and the man before him. "You don't give up, do you."

"Not usually," Thorin's grin broadened. "I've found giving up is… without merit."

It was Daniel's turn to smile, a quite different form from that which graced his companion's face. "Then *why*," he met Thorin's eyes; "Why did you force us apart?"

"Because this is the way it must be. She no more belongs out here, on the road, than you do in the confines of The City."

"How can you be so sure?"

He laughed, closing the distance between them, "Because I've been alive a lot longer than you. Because I've seen more than you could imagine." He now stood directly in front of Daniel. "Because I love my daughter, would not see any harm come to her, and because I *know* who you are."

Strength had fled Daniel, who stood as a limp flag, flaccid in a stale breeze. "I could've stayed with her," nearly a whisper.

"No, Daniel, you couldn't have." Thorin set a hand on the young man's shoulder, forcing him to meet face to face. "As soon as you met my daughter, in finding us at the pub that night, you sealed this fate."

"But why?"

"That is something I cannot tell you, my friend." Holding Daniel's gaze with his own, "But you tell me, when you look at me now, as you've come to know me this past week, is there anything in what you see, in what you've experienced, that speaks of malice or ill intent?"

Daniel looked, both within himself and at his companion, and knew, in a way so striking he'd nearly overlooked it for its blatancy, that the man before him wasn't an enemy, that he was a friend, a true friend.

The only friend I have.

Met there on the road in the middle of nowhere, the two men, one young and one old, knew the truth of each other, at least as much truth as is given men to know of anything, embraced one another.

Tears streamed down Daniel's cheeks as a strong yet gentle wind found its way across the road, surrounding their huddled forms, stirring the unfastened plackets of his jacket.

CONSIDERATIONS

Still though, as they traversed the hills of southern New York, moving into the Southern Tier, Daniel couldn't shake an awkward distance, or at least the feeling of an awkward distance, between himself and Thorin. There was simply too much Daniel didn't understand, couldn't understand, of what had been said.

They'd spent the night after their skirmish in the small town of Bethel, finding lodging in the town's only inn, a smallish thing with a cozy bar and grill on its ground floor, its rooms apparently having been vacant for some time, judging by the stale smell of the bedding and towels.

Set between two lakes, the smaller Amber to the west and White, much larger, to the east, Bethel was a town of farmers and agriculture. Those who lived there, the only town for at least fifty kilometers in any direction, worked the entirety of the fields in that part of the state, including those through which Daniel and Thorin had just travelled, providing grain and produce to The City. It was a life Daniel could almost have envied, far as it was from the bustle of men, if not for the fact that every single one of the people they'd encountered, in the bar mainly, had given the clear impression his life was anything but enviable.

Now, more than three days out of Bethel, Daniel's thoughts returned to the men he'd there seen, those few with whom he'd spoken.

Although each had had a different stated reason for living there, working the fields, maintaining irrigation and controlling pests, cultivating and harvesting, there'd been among them a single continuity that had only later, over a hundred kilometers distant, hit Daniel.

To a man those he'd met had been content with their existence, as hard as it seemed this existence must be, and to a man they'd never actually been to The City they serviced. To them The City existed as foreign soil, those who lived there more alien than even the insects they battled in the fields. Not twenty years since the IDSC had imposed itself on the movements of people, selecting who would live where and who could move between one area and another, and already the nation was divided into urban and agrarian cultures. Just as City dwellers had no will to leave their designated area, so too had the farmers in Bethel been purged of any desire to see, let alone live in, The City.

Daniel wondered if the phenomenon were common to all of the cities in the nation. Was Chicago just as insular, its satellites also worlds unto themselves? Los Angeles? Did the people there also refer to *their* city as *The* City?

Is this a nation at all anymore, or have we degraded into city-states, our common identity lying merely in the memories of the old, the pages of dusty books, only read when one is forced to do so? How much longer before these memories fade, before the books themselves disappear and are replaced with less... informative... histories?

He paused, thoughts having come close enough to the surface to halt him in his tracks, bringing the reality of his position before his eyes and mind.

Just a few days ago I'd never even really considered the existence of other cities myself; the existence of The United States, the nation, had been merely an assumption, vague and ill-defined. Are my beliefs about the rest of the world equally as unreal?

He laughed.

I'd been set on *Canada*. Does this place even exist? Could I truly go there if I wished?

Ahead Thorin walked, setting a steady, brisk pace. Both men had by now grown accustomed to the exertions of travel and had been making remarkably good time. Daniel's back no longer ached. His legs felt strong.

He stood, still, considering the implications of his thoughts, their nature and origin.

Thorin's right. When people don't travel to places different from those they inhabit in their routines they become habituated to the actualities of their worlds. They see things as one, knowing what they see is true. Nothing in their experience has the possibility of exposing the frailty of their illusions, of self, of world, of morality and each other. I've been out of The City only a week and already my thoughts have ventured far beyond anything with which they'd before been occupied.

He looked around himself, at the low hills there covered in a thick fur of wheat. A passing breeze marked the textured surface, a ghostly hand stroking a beloved pet.

I'd been going crazy back there, lost in myself amidst a world of people. I'd thought something was wrong with me, that somehow, if only I could be normal, I could have learned to live there, to live like them.

But why wasn't I *already* like them?

I didn't want to be like them.

He realized now, lost in the country with only Thorin as his guide, that his whole life he'd felt different, from the others at the orphanage, from his parents before them… however vague his memory of them now was, he still recalled that… from his friends and acquaintances in The City. Perhaps the loss of Hannah had brought this difference to the forefront of his mind, yet now when he thought of her he didn't recall happiness or love; he didn't remember her beauty or the contentedness he'd felt in her arms. Looking back at the time he'd spent with her, before the accident, he saw himself *acting* like he was happy, playing a part so convincingly the illusion had been indistinguishable from reality.

Nothing of his former life now seemed real.

Something is happening to me, out here on the road, the path. I'm losing myself in myself. Finding myself in myself, now illuminated by the actual dark of night, the un-smogged light of day.

There must have been something, even back then, something that had caused him to know, unconsciously yet undeniably, that his life in The City was false.

Daniel set himself on determining exactly what this thing was, had been. Further, he set himself on determining who exactly Thorin was and how he knew the things he did.

Reanimating his legs, Daniel moved to catch up with his guide, a distant figure, just now cresting the hill before him.

ON A HILL TOP

They reached the outskirts of Binghamton, a lone city set at the intersection of three great roads and as many rivers minus one, just after nightfall.

Why they ventured so close to such a large inhabitation was beyond Daniel. This place, quite different from the isolated simplicity of Bethel or the vast singularity of The City, exuded a dull dread he could feel even from their present distance.

Thus far they'd steered clear of major roadways, had travelled a fairly rough path to avoid them, yet here they blithely approached what seemed to Daniel a major junction. From their vantage on a hill just south of the city, he could see clearly a steady flow of traffic, trucks and smaller vehicles, entering and leaving, moving about the city.

Binghamton lay seemingly as a sentry post, guarding the crossroads of southern New York. All who wished to travel this part of the state, whether north to Syracuse or Albany, east to The City, south into Pennsylvania, or west to the greater country, had to pass there through.

To Daniel it seemed precisely the sort of place they should avoid. Thorin, however, had brought them directly to it.

"Why the fuck have we come here?" He asked, sparked a cigarette, shading it from the wind that stirred on the hilltop. "This place has to be *crawling* with IDSC."

Thorin looked at him, a rueful smile on his face; "Indeed it is, my ever-observant friend;" turned toward the city, "Yet nonetheless I here have a task that cannot be avoided."

"*You* have a task?" Daniel could not keep the apprehension out of his voice. "Am I to accompany you?"

"No." He again faced Daniel; "You must stay here. There are those in the city below who'd do you harm, I fear."

"But not you?"

"Alone, they cannot do anything to me," steel in his voice.

For Daniel, this was the last straw. He brought himself before Thorin, between him and the city. "I think it's time, man, for you to tell me more about who you are," he looked the older man up and down, "and to explain how exactly you move with such freedom."

Thorin raised an eyebrow; smiled, "That's what you think, eh?"

Daniel was unmoved.

"I think it is time for me to be about my business, and for you to settle in for the night here;" he cast his about the hilltop. "Or rather over there," pointing to the tree line on the distant side of the clearing from the city.

"Do you seriously expect me to stay here while you do God only knows what, in a nest of IDSC?"

"I expect you to do what you must." He grinned, "You can erect a tent by yourself at this point..?"

"I believe so."

"Then I suggest you do just that, and let me do what must be done."

"You won't tell me what this is?"

"If you *must* know, there's a man in Binghamton with whom I have to speak," he paused, "an old friend I haven't seen in a long time."

"Speak with him about what?"

"Something that is none of your concern."

Daniel flicked his cigarette angrily to the side, "How is it not my concern, when you've brought me with you all this way to see him?" He looked down on the city; "Is *this* The Centre?"

Thorin chuckled, quickly suppressing his mirth as Daniel rounded on him. "No. *This* is Binghamton." His smile quirked at the corners, "Not our destination, just a stop on the journey." He looked passed Daniel at the lights below, smile become a hard line, set. "Hopefully a short stop, devoid of complications and without trouble."

A GOLD SEAL

Thorin picked his way down the hill, cutting west as he descended, making sure to mark his progress in his head.

Would do no good to lose the kid up here, after all I've done to get him this far.

He shook his head as he passed among the thin growth of the hillside.

The best laid plans…

In all honesty he could barely believe things had progressed this far without any serious derailment. After so long no plan should still be viable; then again, this was really the first time *he'd* had to play a significant role in its unfolding. There were still plenty of opportunities for him to fuck it all up.

Reaching the base of the incline, he turned left onto the street he found there, moving west into the outer extensions of the city. At this hour most citizens were either at home, comfortable, perhaps settled in with their families, or out on the town, at a bar, a show, maybe getting closer to intimacies with others they'd found who also were out. Regardless, none walked the street along which he moved, its length marked at regular intervals by halide lights, bright, almost blue in their intensity, illuminating so brightly the street from before and behind that he cast no shadow as he made his way toward downtown and away from the lonely clearing where he'd left Daniel.

Poor kid. Doesn't even know why he must travel, yet knows still that he must.

Thorin would never have been able to operate like that, in the dark, with only instinct and intuition to guide him. Then again, Thorin came from a different world entirely. In the past quarter century much had changed about America, none of it as yet for the better. Most striking was the fundamental shift in the American psyche itself. Thorin, for all intents and purposes a passive observer of this change, had at first found it fascinating. Recently he'd begun to be rather disgusted. People's ability to accept the world around them, regardless of how intolerable or inhuman this world actually was, was at times simply too much.

Now, with Daniel waiting...

He'd better be fucking waiting.

...with Daniel waiting alone on the hilltop, accompanying him to The Centre, Thorin had to be sure, and thus he had to visit a man he'd not seen in over twenty years, not since Aleta had left, since before New York and the other Great Cities had been Reformed.

The risk involved could not be overstated. Bad timing could spell disaster for them all, and as Thorin moved north, nearing the southern bank of the Susquehanna, his heart filled with doubt, barely held at bay by a faith he'd held onto for many years, now seeming elusive, ethereal.

He'd never really believed in God, certainly not the caricature of human fear and hope most labeled as such, yet he found himself silently praying all would here go well, that he'd again see his daughter, *that* at least, even if the greater ends for which he'd prepared these long years, toward which he'd worked his entire adult life, were lost.

Nearing the Exchange Street Bridge, he adjusted his cap, a houndstooth flat he'd retrieved from his pack before descending the hill, straightened his coat.

They will see me coming as soon as I round the corner.

Even here, at what could rightfully be called the heart of IDSC activity in the region, a conspicuous place where outgoing trucks were as likely to hold troops as they were to contain grain, travel across bridges, through every exit and entrance, along all the main roads, was restricted, monitored, identities checked and rechecked. Perhaps here even more than in The City a man had to be careful where he stepped and whom he crossed. Binghamton was the nerve center for a security establishment whose influence and purview extended from the streets of New York City, the alleys of Philadelphia and the slums of Pittsburgh, to the halls of Cambridge.

Walking now toward the bridge, Thorin felt his discomfort vanish, confidence returning to his steps.

Perhaps I'm in danger here. Perhaps this *is* folly. These guards, these functionaries, however, are no threat to me.

As he stepped onto Exchange, moving toward the checkpoint, two young men, IDSC troops proper, high-collared uniforms, black on black, testifying to this truth, approached. Each had an mp-45 slung across his back, standard IDSC light arms, and as they moved to meet Thorin, who displayed no sign of stopping to wait for them, one took the lead, the other hanging back approximately ten meters, bringing his weapon to rest easily in his hands, safety still on, yet certainly, clearly, at the ready.

The guard, one red knot of rank identifying him as a lieutenant, appraised Thorin as the distance between them closed. Having seen nothing worthy of his respect, he brought himself directly into Thorin's path, condescension clear on his face. "What is your business here, old man?"

Thorin continued to approach, bringing himself within a meter of the lieutenant, stopped; smiled, "My business, *young man*, is my own," a purposeful tinge of scorn.

This certainly got his attention. He signaled to his companion, who leveled his weapon on Thorin, clicked off the safety, waiting for the order to fire. "What purpose do you have downtown at this time of night?" He moved to grasp Thorin by the upper arm.

Thorin stepped back and to the side, easily evading the guard's reach, causing the other to tighten his grip on his weapon.

I'd better settle this before that one does something rash.

On closer inspection, the guard who now stood with a submachine gun aimed straight at Thorin's chest was perhaps only nineteen years old, green and likely twitchy on the trigger.

"Take it easy, lieutenant," he smiled again. "You wouldn't want to do anything you'll regret."

"The only thing I regret is having to speak to a worthless old man like you," the lieutenant spat; "Now be on your way before you irritate me further and I decide to have you detained for *questioning*."

The vicious grin he displayed upon pronouncing this last word literally turned Thorin's stomach. "I see." He slowly, and with a nod to the guard providing cover, drew his wallet from the confines of his jacket, flipping it open to reveal the identification held therein. The official seal of the IDSC, three intersecting rings on a field of black, wrought in pure gold, was unmistakable on its surface.

The lieutenant's face nearly slid from his skull. He looked at Thorin, back again to the Gold Seal, then to his companion, motioning for him to drop the muzzle of his weapon, backed up a step and quickly lowered his eyes. "Sir, I apologize, sir!" waiting for whatever Thorin would do, anticipating something quite horrible from the look of him.

Thorin, feeling humor he didn't let touch his face, walked passed the man, bringing himself before the young guard, turned halfway toward the now thoroughly frightened lieutenant. "*You* will remain at your post here until dawn, after which you will present yourself to the Captain of the Watch for disciplinary action."

Poor fool. Likely has never before even seen a Gold Seal.

"And you, soldier, will escort me to The Commander."

The guard hesitated momentarily, shooting a look to his superior, who still stood facing the location where Thorin had been moments before. "Yes sir!" He brought his right fist to his chest in salute. Turning sharply, he began an overly formal march across the bridge. Thorin followed unhurriedly behind, leaving the lieutenant to stare into the now vacant space of the street beyond, at attention.

A FRIEND

Daniel watched as Thorin disappeared down through the trees on the north end of the clearing, momentarily considered following behind, thought better, made his way to where the packs were lying together, far back on the east side.

What the fuck is that stoner doing down there? Who is this "old friend" he has to see?

Fuck.

What am I supposed to do on this god damn hill? Will he even be back before daybreak?

Realizing he was likely to get very few answers to these questions at present, his own being fairly sarcastic and unhelpful, Daniel began the procedure for erecting the tent, joining segments to form long poles, slipping them through the appropriate fasteners and sleeves. He'd found once you get used to it setting up a tent is actually pretty easy.

He made no fire though; Thorin had been very clear. Although the hill top was out of sight of the city, flames could possibly bring attention, as could smoke. This close to Binghamton one had to be careful, even at night.

He sat down before the tent, gazing into the emptiness of the hillside as darkness came.

He brought his body from the cold stone of the floor. His head ached, as did his limbs, his back. His eyes, fully dilated in the dank twilight of the cell, traced readily the limits of his confines, a hard, windowless cube, a little wider across than necessary for him to lie down. The floor, inlaid with rough-cut stone, kept him up at night... not completely, for he certainly slept, but enough still to ward off true rest. Its irregular surface and jagged angles marked pieces of his life, come now to confine him. No need for chains; he'd forged no chains in life. The fragments so completely encapsulated him, edges meeting so perfectly, that not even a sound of the world outside could be heard.

In his long duration here he'd named them all: regret, sorrow, cowardice, misplaced courage and broken faith. That none had found the name of love was to him no concern. Love must be given, received, freely, and here there was no freedom. His love had become a thing of legend, spoken of yet, never known in truth by the many who populated his mind.

In the dark one tends to speak to oneselves.

These spaces fill with darkness... hidden. Nothing to believe in.

He tore the skin of his arm slightly with a jagged nail, bringing a dark rivulet to gather thereupon, drip onto the floor.

The sharp reality brought him back. He dabbed a finger in the black liquid, tasted its sweetness.

Still some life in me yet.

He knew they would come for him soon. If nothing else he knew that.

What would you be?

Echoed in silence.

He broke from the dream at the sound of something moving outside the tent. To one used to the solidity of city walls, the thin film seemed more threatening than secure, surrounding him in flimsy blindness.

He'd never awoken so early from it; had never been able to recall clearly its beginnings. Now he sat upright in the tent, shivering, bringing his hand to feel for the gash he knew could not be there. That anything could seem so real, when even the world in which he now found himself seemed muted and out of focus...

He shivered again.

The sound returned, from the other end of the tent, near where the packs lay against a maple, on the east side.

There was silence for a time.

"You'd better just come out now. Would make this whole thing much easier."

The voice was that of an older man.

Daniel sat still, mind dumb in the confines of the tent.

They have come for me. I will not go back.

"Come out, Daniel. No one is going to harm you."

Sent by Thorin then? Could this be his friend?

There was a rustling as the man outside rummaged through one of the packs, a zip as he opened the other, a clank as a tin was opened. A spark of a lighter as a joint was lit.

What the fuck?

Daniel opened the tent, crawling out, quickly raising himself, turned toward the man, now sitting quietly on one of the packs puffing one of Thorin's spliffs. He was tall, clean shaven yet old, certainly older than Thorin. Daniel felt as though he'd seen him before.

He set his hand against the tree on which he and the packs rested. "I've always loved red maples;" he looked upwards through its branches. "They have a presence other trees lack. All maples really."

Daniel, not knowing how to approach the situation, at all, decided to simply accept it as it was. "How is that?"

"It's really hard to say… Just a feeling I've always had."

"And you've come here to smoke my friend's ganja and fondle a tree?"

The man laughed.

Daniel gazed at him over the dome of the tent.

"Well, Thorin's smoke was always good, so perhaps that just a little."

"So you do know him then?'

He smiled. "I know you too, young man, although you wouldn't remember me."

This set Daniel off base, just a little.

He glanced quickly around the clearing, searching for other interlopers, found none. "And for the rest?"

He sat back against the tree, hit the joint, retrieving it with his left hand, between his middle and index finger. "I've come here to meet with you, obviously." He smiled; "What else would find me here, now?"

He drew a cigarette from the front pocket of his hooded sweatshirt, lit it, surveying his strange companion.

That the man had come specifically to meet him came as no surprise; this had been clear since he'd revealed he knew Daniel's name. His half-answer only served to set Daniel more ill at ease.

He'd never really trusted anyone, not really. And even Thorin, whom he'd trusted as he hadn't anyone for a long time, had betrayed him.

Thoughts of Alena flashed through his mind, images and half remembered laughter.

Now this guy is here, talking to me like it's no big deal for him to just show up in the middle of the night and start smoking our ganja.

"You've come from Binghamton?"

"I have not."

Daniel lost himself in thought then, gazing above the man to the blood-red foliage, venous magenta, that dripped from the maple, suspended in air, pulsating lightly in a breeze he couldn't feel but knew must be there.

"I've come from the north, from Ithaca. Do you know it?"

"No."

"It lies perhaps eighty kilometers from here." He stood, stretching a kink from his back.

Daniel looked at the man, noted his light shoes, the distinct lack of travel wear to his clothing, arched an eyebrow; "A long way to walk."

The man grinned, seeming aware of Daniel's cynicism. "Oh, I didn't walk;" turned to the left, nodded, "I have a vehicle, parked on the road that skirts the southern slope of this hill."

"You can drive then? What of the IDSC?"

"It's part of my job to make trips down here from Ithaca. Come down a couple times a week."

"And what do you do?"

He grinned again; "Generally I sing songs and try to stay between the lines," extending the joint for Daniel to take.

Yeah, I don't think so man.

"What's your point, and why have you sought me out?"

"Well," he straightened his jacket upon his shoulders, "a Friend told me you needed a lift."

"A Friend?" He recalled Alena's use of the term like that, back in the courtyard now seemingly so long ago. "Do you mean Thorin?"

"No, but he's a Friend of Thorin as well." He laughed; "I think you'll find Thorin has many friends, of all types." He began to break down the tent, sliding poles from their positions, unfastening ties.

"What the fuck are you doing, man?"

"Getting ready to leave." He began to disconnect the poles. "We have somewhere to be in not too long."

"I'm not going anywhere with you. I don't know you." He paused, "I don't even know your name."

The man, bent down, slipping the rolled-up tent into its sack, looked at him; "Suit yourself. Just know Thorin will not be returning here, and I'm taking the tent and both of these packs."

Daniel moved toward him; anger in his voice, "The hell you are." He grasped the tent, trying and failing to rip it from the man's hands.

He was rewarded with a swift elbow to the chest, breaking his grip on the tent, causing him to stagger back a few paces.

"I am, Daniel, and there's not much you can do to stop me."

Daniel knew the truth of his words. Even as old as the man was, at least in his late fifties, maybe older, he was solidly built. Perhaps ten centimeters taller than Daniel, he looked to be used to hard labor, shoulders strong, arms thick with muscle. Daniel, perhaps now in the best shape of his life, was still no match for him. He'd never even been in a fight before, not a real fight. Judging by the power conveyed by his elbow just a moment ago, the man had obviously been in a not inconsiderable number of physical engagements.

"How do you know Thorin isn't coming back?"

He placed the tent within Thorin's pack, closed the zip. "A Friend told me."

"Has something happened to him?"

"Nothing that wasn't expected." He paused, looked up from the packs, hand lowered, ready to lift one onto his back; "Look, as I said, we don't have time to stand here and talk for hours." He hoisted Thorin's pack, settling it on his back. "Are you coming with me or not?"

Seeing very few options, Daniel nodded his assent, flicked his cigarette to smolder beneath the trees beyond.

"Good." He grinned, "To tell you the truth I wasn't looking forward to carrying both of these fucking things anyway." He lifted Daniel's pack easily with his left hand, tossed it to him.

Daniel caught it with a grunt, resting its mass upon his shoulders, now used to the pressure of its straps.

"You know," turning from Daniel to begin walking south, along the tree line, "Thorin's burden is greater than yours."

"And how would you know anything about my burdens?"

The man chuckled, glanced at Daniel, who followed closely behind; "I was referring to the weight of the packs, my young Friend." He turned to face once again the direction they traveled, laughed more loudly; "Perhaps it's all the fucking ganja."

Daniel couldn't help but laugh with him.

THE COMMANDER

"You realize I'll have to confine that kid to quarters, send him to Bismarck or something, before the sun rises;" The Commander brought his steel-blue eyes to the portal that led to the greater bulk of the compound, a sour expression on his face.

"It couldn't be avoided;" Thorin sat against the arm of one of the ten straight-backed seats, all formed of dark mahogany, which encompassed a rectangular mahogany table found at the center of the room. "The other as well."

Andrew broke into a grin; "I never liked him anyway." He moved around the table, resting against its dark mass, slightly to Thorin's left. "It's good to see you. These days I hardly see anyone to whom I'm not giving orders. Everyone here is," he paused, looking Thorin over, grin widening, "shall we say a *true believer*."

Thorin laughed, "And you've not, after all these years, fallen into conviction as well?"

"My conviction is as strong as it's ever been." He pushed the chair before him back from the table, sitting down, shifted it and himself to face Thorin directly. He ran a hand through his now grey hair, bringing it to rest against his left temple, elbow on the table; "This is not a good time."

"It couldn't be avoided."

"Couldn't it have?' Andrew reached within his black jacket, retrieving a silver cigarette case from the front breast pocket, drew a dark length therefrom. "I can't imagine what lunacy impelled you to come here," sparked his cigarette, a long thing wrapped in brown, almost black, paper. "We're preparing to enter the next phase of Reformation, and I tell you truthfully Michael himself will be here within the week to go over the final preparations." Drew on his cigarette, "It would be best if you left as soon as possible, now even. I miss you, but this isn't the time to catch up." He glanced around the room, searching for ears he knew weren't there. "We're close," voice lowered, "closer than we've ever been."

Thorin ducked his chin, peered over his glasses at Andrew, The Commander. "You think so? And what exactly is involved in the 'next phase of Reformation'?"

"Well," he leaned forward onto his knees, "now that the military and police, the rest of the executive, are within the compass of IDSC, and the population redistribution is complete..."

Thorin interrupted, "Both of which were implemented nearly two decades ago."

"Implemented, sure, yet they weren't perfected, either one, until recently." Andrew turned slightly, tapping the ash from his cigarette into a silver ashtray.

"And now that they've been perfected?"

"We don't need the politicians anymore. We need not heed the ignorant masses. The Party is now nearly completely superfluous." He laughed; "They're so blinded by their riches and perceived power they don't even notice. Safe in the protection of their laws and police, *their* security establishment." A dark grin graced Andrew's face. "They don't even acknowledge the beast they've unleashed."

"The IDSC will provide, eh?" Thorin looked... unconvinced, to say the least.

"Do you understand the power *I* have now, Thor? I'm not sure if you could." He snubbed his cigarette into the ashtray. "I could have any town or city in this entire sector locked down within minutes, all of Manhattan, just Washington Heights. *Within minutes.* We know everything that goes on in this country, everything that's spoken, written, transmitted or voiced. I know Alena's still in New York, tending the bar. I knew when you left, that you didn't leave alone."

"But still, you didn't expect me to come here."

"Of course not. We had no warning, so I assume you traveled cross-country, a smart move, yet I still don't understand why you're here, nor whom this young man is who travels with you."

"Is this your way of avoiding my question, Andrew?"

"It's my way of asking one of my own."

"The boy is none of your concern. Simply one who has interests in my daughter, who agreed to accompany me on my journey."

"Alena," Andrew stood from his seat, moving to retrieve a short glass from a smaller table along the wall before Thorin, to the left, "How is she?" He began to return to where Thorin sat, paused, returned to the table, retrieving also another glass and a crystal decanter of what appeared to be whisky.

"She's good, Andrew. Beautiful, like her mother."

"Aye, beautiful she may be, yet always that woman and I chafed each other." He poured a dram into each glass; "I should hope your daughter is," sliding one toward Thorin, "a little more chill?"

Thorin accepted the drink, spinning it slowly on the table with his thumb and forefinger. "My daughter is my concern, not yours."

"Sure, sure," he lifted his glass from the table, "I'd just hate to see her get into any trouble." He raised it to Thorin in toast. "To peace and freedom."

Thorin matched his gesture, sipping the amber liquid, eyes, reflecting its golden light, steady on Andrew over the rim. "To liberty."

Andrew eyed him back.

"As for you and the boy, you must leave tonight. Michael would want to know *why* you have come to me, after so long." Paused. "I'd like to know as well."

Thorin sat forward slightly in his chair, bringing the glass of whiskey to rest between his hands, an elbow on each knee. "I've come to ask you if you know where *he* is."

Between them there was no confusion as to whom Thorin referred.

"I believe he's currently in Ithaca, although it is notoriously hard to keep tabs on him." Andrew poured himself another dram, forestalled Thorin's attempt to interject. "That is where The Centre can be found currently, if that's your next question."

"Indeed." He finished his glass, declining Andrew's offer of more. "You track all of Them then?"

Andrew laughed; "He tracks Them for us. Keeps us well apprised of any significant movements. That way we can avoid any serious problems." He sat against the table, looking down on Thorin. "You must understand our intentions are only good. I personally hold no ill will toward any of your *Friends*."

"So you don't regret giving me the Gold Seal?"

Andrew seemed genuinely offended. "You are my friend, and I trust you to do what you feel is right." He finished off his second dram, poured another; "If at some point your interests and ours should come into conflict, which I sincerely hope they never do, I will do what I must." He rose from the table, walking a little away, "But presently I can see only good coming from good people acting according to their consciences and convictions." Faced Thorin directly, "You and your Friends are worthy of respect, and you will have a place in the new order. It is for the strong in spirit that we have done what we have. That you disagree is immaterial, as this merely proves you are worthy of your... *liberty.*"

"So you simply let Them be?"

Andrew nodded, sipping his whiskey.

"And I take it you don't care if I tell Them what you've told me?"

"It is immaterial, Thor, as I've said." He chuckled, "There's nothing they can do to stop what is to come, just as there was nothing they could've done do to stop what has already passed."

"You always have been sure of yourself."

"I'm sure that if you do not leave, if Michael discovers you've been here, you'll regret not having heeded my words. I don't care why you want to find *him*, or what your business with Them is. Leave now: Godspeed. Be about your business and leave me to mine."

Even now, after all that has passed, Andrew wouldn't lie to me.

Thorin rose from his seat, meeting eyes with The Commander, one whom now only Thorin, he alone, knew as Andrew.

"We are old men." Andrew broke contact, looking at his hands as he turned them over before himself. "How has it been so long that we haven't talked? That we've not simply *been* together?"

"I don't know, Andrew." Thorin felt a knot form at the base of his throat.

"You know..." he returned to the table, resting once more against its dark grain, "in another time we could have raised our children together, gone to the park and played guitar, smoke some weed on the weekends." He paused.

"In another time."

"Do you miss her?"

"Dearly."

Andrew sighed. "Sometimes I think... and I can't even remember what Edith looked like. You at least have your daughter. Tell me: Is it easier or harder for you?"

Thorin was quiet for a moment; spoke into the void, "It is... better." Looked to his friend, "I couldn't imagine life without her."

"All I have left is what I can imagine, and this too is slowly leaving me."

Feeling no need to coddle anyone, "We all make our own beds," Thorin rose from his seat.

"I make not a bed but a vaunted tomb, a place of weary rest and lonely shadows;" he rose from the table, "But I tell you this: My strength has never been greater, my control so acute. With only memories to stir my attention, purpose looms large, vivid, nearly at hand. All else is moot." He laughed, "In truth I sleep on a flat board, a shelf really. Sets a good example for the troops."

Thorin grinned. "We will meet again."

Andrew moved to embrace him; "Of that I have no doubt. That day we still meet as friends, regardless of what transpires."

EVEN BETTER IN THE RAIN

Daniel gazed out the window as the large truck pulled up to the south end of the Exchange Street Bridge, coming to a stop just short of the intersection. His companion left the vehicle running, sprinting through the now pouring rain to the guard post there on the near side of the bridge, entered for a few moments before sprinting back to the truck.

Brushing water from his brow, "It'll just be a few minutes."

Daniel was both relieved and anxious about being reunited with Thorin. There was simply too much he didn't know about the man; this other's recent appearance merely punctuated the point. However, Thorin was also the only person within maybe two hundred kilometers whom Daniel knew at all.

With ambivalence he peered through the rain, yet on seeing the older man appear on the bridge, move toward the truck, the only feeling he had for certain was curiosity. The guard on the bridge seemed to be almost afraid of him.

Thorin tore open the door of the truck, roughly sliding into the front passenger seat, nodded to Daniel, who sat in the back seat on the opposite side. He turned then to the driver, broke into a wide grin. "Motherfucker;" moving to face the man more fully. "I had no idea *you* were giving us a lift."

The man smiled broadly back; "It's good to see you, Thorin."

Thorin hesitated, setting his eyes on first Daniel and then the driver; "You guys smoking my ganja?" His grin consumed his face. He turned to Daniel, pointing at the man, "Jonathan here has helped himself to my herb more times than I can count."

Daniel glanced before himself, "Jonathan..." he paused, looking to Thorin and back the driver, "Your friend here certainly did help himself. While I was still in the tent," turned back to Thorin.

Jonathan merely shrugged, putting the truck into gear and pulling away from the bridge, headed west.

"You're not taking 81?" Thorin asked as they pulled onto the road.

"I'd rather not have to deal with the hassle of traveling through the city;" he brought the car onto a broad, four-lane parkway that traced the southern bank of the river. "Besides, for us the back way is better."

"The information I have says that road is shut down;" Thorin squinted at him over his glasses.

"Shut down to conventional traffic;" he grinned, "The road is certainly a little fucked up, but I assure you the truck is up to the challenge."

"Even in the rain?"

Jonathan picked up speed, quickly leaving downtown behind; "Especially in the rain."

A half an hour later they sped north along a road Daniel could tell had once been a relatively major thoroughfare; aside from a few bumpy turns it was still in fairly good condition. Jonathan's confidence at the wheel had thus far brought them without incident as far as it would've taken them nearly two days to walk.

The two old men had been talking for some time, of Alena, her mother Aleta, some mysterious "he," whom Thorin had apparently met in Binghamton, as well as several other things Daniel had no context for whatsoever.

Ahead he could see an abandoned town, Candor, by the sign guarding the former boundary of its southern limit. It had never really been anything but a simple stop at a three-way intersection, at the bend of a minor river, yet now its quaintness had turned gaunt; abandoned gas stations and dark houses huddled together, marking nothing, home to vermin and other squatters of the region. As they drove through the town's remnants, continuing north, Daniel couldn't help but wonder what it would've been like to live in such a place.

The more he spent away from the city, the more aware he became of how things must have been long ago, before he was born, the more he felt the wrongness of the change. Daniel found the idea of living in a small town, in which everyone knew each other's name, where strangers were only encountered infrequently and thus were welcomed, idyllic.

A lost utopia, rotting now, abandoned.

Did those who lived here appreciate what they had?

"Toward the end of things," Jonathan broke in, "it was made impossible for them to appreciate it at all, so heavy were the weights of life and economy."

Shit. He must have spoken that last out loud.

"So their leaving was a blessing?"

Jonathan looked to Thorin, back to the road; "Some see it that way."

"And others?"

"You'd have to ask them, if you can find them."

Thorin gave Jonathan a slanted look, shifted in his seat to face Daniel. "You'll have a chance to do so in just a few minutes, if you like.

Many of those we will meet about The Centre used to live in areas such as this."

Daniel perked up in his seat, "We will be there so soon?"

"The Centre can presently be found in Ithaca."

"It... moves?"

Jonathan broke in, "Generally not, but sometimes, when the situation calls for it."

Feeling that perhaps Jonathan wasn't as reticent to share information as was Thorin, Daniel pressed him further. "And what exactly *is* The Centre?"

"On the most basic level It is a place around which people meet, where you will find welcome. If It is to be anything more, you must Judge."

Fucking hell. Again with these people's strange intonations.

"Am I supposed to know what that means?"

"Do you?" Jonathan caught his reflection in the rear view mirror.

"No."

"Then I suppose not."

Even in the narrow reflection Daniel could see the grin that touched the older man's eyes.

Thorin returned to the conversation; "You have to understand, Daniel, this is your journey. None can make it for you."

"*My* journey?" He frowned; "Then what are you doing here?"

"I told you a long time ago: I'm going to The Centre."

"With me."

"I suppose we shall see;" Thorin broke into a wide smile, "*perhaps we will. That is not for me to decide."

"You guys are fucking impossible." He lit a cigarette, turning away from Thorin to crack the window to his left.

It was then that they crested a hill, bringing into view the lights of a decently sized city. As they descended, moving into and slowly through the proper of what Daniel had to assume was Ithaca, he was struck by the people he saw there, their apparent contentment, the lack of hard toil around their eyes; most of all he was struck by the fact that no security checkpoint had interrupted the road before them.

"There's no checkpoint because this is the back way?" Daniel asked their driver.

"There's no checkpoint because Ithaca has no security."

Daniel was nearly speechless. "You can't be serious."

Jonathan again caught him in the mirror; "I'm quite serious, Daniel. The function of this place demands its people be let do as they please." He brought his gaze back to the road; "There are checkpoints on all the other roads that lead here, but they are kept far away. No need to have them any closer."

"Sounds like an interesting place." Daniel returned to staring out the window.

Thorin laughed, "The last time Jonathan and I were both here it was very interesting indeed."

CHAPTER 5
APART

ASHES IN GLASS

Peter sat alone on the couch in the living room, staring out the window across from him. The blank red brick of the building found there, just far enough away from the window to allow for the fire escape, stared back at him, as devoid of comment and spirit as he.

It had been two months since the events in Philadelphia, and this day found him back in the apartment in Elmwood, for the first time left alone with his thoughts, without even the distraction of travel to turn them from the grim realities with which they were occupied. That neither of his friends had returned with him had come as no surprise, not really. Thorin had decided to take a break from school, indefinitely, to stay with Aleta in D.C.. Andrew…

Peter wasn't quite sure what Andrew was doing. He'd simply told Peter he wouldn't be going back to school, that he had "more important" matters to attend to.

The entire thing weighed on Peter's mind heavily. Now, with only the silence of the once incredibly chill apartment to keep him company, he contemplated his present situation.

Yesterday had been the first day of classes, the beginning of a new semester. Ordinarily he would've been somewhat excited, perhaps getting ahead on his reading, thinking about hanging out with his friends and a nice spliff, plotting with Andrew how best to hit on the new batch of freshmen.

He could almost hear Thorin's commentary from the sidelines. "Freshmen girls like to drink more than they like to smoke. But not anything good; they like cheap mixed drinks, cocktails and sweet tasting shots. You gotta remember: Never offer to smoke-out a freshmen until she's already drunk." "And you would know, Thor?" Andrew would say mockingly, gazing over the coffee table, around the tube set thereupon. "Just because I have a girlfriend doesn't mean I don't know how to hit on girls," grinned. He'd of course have been reaching for the tube to pull a large, chunky hit.

Peter rose from his seat, moved to the closet, retrieving the tube from its confines. Filling it at the sink, he turned toward the living room, thoughts turning to the one of their group who *had* journeyed west with him.

Clearly Edith had wanted to stay with Andrew. Yet Andrew's demeanor, the conviction in his voice when stating his intention to stay in New York, had silenced her before she'd even spoken.

I wonder why he didn't ask her to stay as well.

The spirit she'd exuded on the trip east, during their stay in Philly and even later during the remainder of the summer they'd passed in New York, had been notably lacking when he'd dropped her off back in Salt Lake. For the life of him he couldn't place what had occurred to make her take parting with Andrew in such an incredibly grim way.

Perhaps she knows more of what he's up to than even I.

Peter didn't trust Michael; even less did he trust the bond Michael and Andrew had formed in the weeks after the riots. To be honest, he didn't know anything about the man, just a name, that Andrew was entirely taken with him and that he had no desire or intention to know the others in the group. This latter had been made abundantly clear during their second week in New York, when Peter had asked if he could accompany Andrew on a trip into Manhattan.

"I don't think it's a good idea," Andrew had said. "He's... rather isolated, antisocial at any rate."

"But he can't take offense to your simply bringing a friend. I mean, it's not like it's a date or anything." Peter remembered having displayed a broad grin.

Andrew had been unmoved. "Trust me, man: It's not a good idea."

And that had been that. Never again had anyone asked to accompany Andrew on his trips into Manhattan, not in public anyway; even Edith had apparently been proscribed the pleasure of an audience with the man. Andrew himself had never broached the subject, and he'd grown increasingly isolated from the group as the weeks had passed. When the time had come for them to return to The Bay... weeks after Thorin and Aleta had said their goodbyes and left for Georgetown... by then Andrew had put so much distance between Peter and himself that Peter had no longer had a read on him at all.

He'd attempted to discuss the matter with Edith on the drive west, but she'd simply deflected his question, turning it to talk of what had happened in Philly, vague commentary on present political realities, a discussion she could've had with anyone, devoid of interest and the close knowledge that existed among friends.

Having returned to the couch, Peter placed the tube on the table before him. Pinching a measure of ganja from a jar set beside it, he sparked the bowl and pulled a hit, water churning violently as he pulled free the slide. With no one to whom to pass it he quickly drew another, settled back into the couch, leaving the tube on the table, a wisp of smoke rising from the mostly cashed ashes.

The ganja was left over from the stash Thorin had used to roll the joints for the trip to Philly; of the original four ounces there remained less than an eighth, plenty with only one person smoking.

He didn't refill the bowl.

ANSWERING A SUMMONS

He strode the halls of the great building, noting the simple yet precise construction of its corridors, the cleanness of their lines. Even here, deep within its confines, it shone with a unique light, bright and clean, filled with vitality and purpose. Never would Andrew have considered he'd be welcome in such a place, let alone allowed to travel its ways at his own discretion. Now, more than two months since his first visit, he made his way toward the elevator with confidence.

In fact, the nature of today's meeting filled him with something more than confidence, an anticipation bordering on excitement, animating his spirit, bringing speed and precision to his steps enough to match the shining passages he traveled.

Today he'd receive his first assignment, from Michael himself.

He wondered what it would entail, what sort of job Michael deemed appropriate for him.

I don't even know what the fuck these people do, really, aside from occasionally suppressing urban unrest and paving the road to a bright and glorious future.

Somehow the connection of the two, although Michael assured him it was there, eluded Andrew. Still, he *knew* the IDSC was up to more than mere riot control, yet beyond a feeling there was no substance to the belief. While Michael had made it abundantly clear he had a special interest in Andrew, for whatever reason, there was nothing with which to fix a perspective on IDSC itself. Nonetheless, The Council was if anything an institution of security and social control, a thing that would've frightened Andrew not three months earlier, now an accepted fact, to be dealt with as anything else: with an eye for reality and an end in mind.

What Michael's end was Andrew couldn't say, yet in the months Andrew had known him one thing had proven true: None Andrew had met or seen commanded the man.

Never before had he been summoned to Michael's office. Aside from their initial encounter in the garden, Andrew had never seen Michael outside of the building, yet never had he been invited into its inner, or rather upper, chambers.

Pushing the button for the elevator, which opened easily before him, apparently already at ground level, he stepped within, surveyed the panel to the right of the door.

Eighty-Eight floors. Goddamn.

He pushed the button for the eighty-sixth, settling in for what he assumed would be a lengthy journey to the top of the world. There was no music to keep him company.

Momentarily his thoughts touched on Edith, whom he'd not seen in nearly two weeks. The look of abandonment on her face when he'd informed her he'd be staying in New York, that it would be best if she didn't remain, had haunted him ever since.

Perhaps it's just as well she's gone. I haven't the time she deserves. Best to end things now, before anything too serious happens.

Still though, regret tugged at his mind, a lonely remembrance that accompanied him on his journey to the sky.

I wonder why his office is on the eighty-sixth floor. Why not the eighty-eighth?

Is there someone here with even more authority than Michael?

The thought seemed silly to him, even though he had no basis for discounting it. There was simply something about the way Michael carried himself that belied the possibility of anyone's having authority over him.

He did say there was one...

He chuckled under his breath at the perceived connection between authority and simple height, images of precariously balanced turtles touching his mind.

Exiting the elevator and stepping into what he thought would be a corridor like that from which he'd entered, he was presented with a stark yet fairly imposing antechamber, fronted on one side by the elevator he'd just disembarked, opposite a large desk set before a single door, hewn of ornately carved mahogany. The only portal to break the sheer sterility of the wall, the door gave the room a sense of focus perhaps even greater than that of the parts of the building he'd thus far encountered.

Behind the desk sat a man in a dark suit, looking at him expectantly.

Andrew stepped forward. "I am here to see Michael."

AMIN

Flipping open his wallet for the fourth time in as many minutes, Andrew gazed at the odd emblem now found therein, three intersecting rings, blooded crimson, set on a black field. This apparently was enough to identify him as an official IDSC agent, although what good the thing would be he had yet to see. Certainly it would be of little use in any practical matter, unknown and obscure as The Council was. Still, having it on his person did serve one very important function: It made Andrew feel like a certified badass. He almost welcomed the opportunity to employ, to test, its unknown powers.

Maybe I should go fuck with a cop.

Michael had told him he'd have no trouble securing compliance from any government agency or official, whether from simple policemen or the secret service itself, representatives or senators. Even the CIA, the proverbial boogieman of the executive apparatus, was within the compass of IDSC, which seemed to exist as a sort of superstructure, connected to every, yet not a part of any, particular governmental body.

When first he'd spoken with Michael in the garden, Andrew had thought The Council was a new creature, in its infancy and without established legality or precedented history. What he'd come to learn these past weeks, however, told a different story altogether. The Council, for this was how those of whom it was constituted referred to it, had been existent and operational for the entirety of Andrew's life, longer, since shortly after the catastrophe that had befallen New York back in 2001. And all that time, throughout the whole of The Council's development and implementation, Michael had been there at its head, constructing the most pervasive national security structure ever to grace the Earth.

He laughed to himself, reflecting on the queerness of a world that would find him, of all people, set to work in the service of such a thing.

Michael himself was still somewhat of an enigma to Andrew. Sure, he trusted the man; there was something about him that denied the possibility of doing otherwise, yet at the same time he evoked a sense of unreality, as if he weren't exactly what he posed to be, a frightening prospect considering that to which he did admit. That he was certainly older than he looked was doubtless, unless one were to believe a man could be given control of such a powerful entity at the shy age of twenty. Andrew believed no such thing, and so the reality that the man with whom he'd spoken earlier that day must at least be in his late fifties, if not older, despite the fact that he presented as a man of little more than forty years, was undeniable.

Andrew opened the window of the car that presently conducted him out of Manhattan, sparked a cigarette. The small tiles of the Holland Tunnel slid passed, an infinitude of gridded planes stretching as far as he could see. The thick air of the tunnel battled with the stale smoke of processed tobacco, reaching a draw that left the inside of the car smelling of slightly burnt, old tennis shoes.

He glanced for a moment at the driver, presently occupied with the various intricacies of keeping a car between two dotted lines at less than one mile per hour. Several years older than he, the driver comported himself with the utmost respect, assured and calm, without coming across as overly formal or stiff. Being that this was the first time he'd ever had a "driver," he was unsure what to expect, yet he was fairly certain the man now sitting before him was a good driver. His name was Amin, and as far as Andrew could tell he was Middle Eastern, although no accent touched his voice.

"You want a smoke, Amin?"

Without turning from the road, "No sir; thank you, sir. I don't smoke."

"I don't know if I could live like that;" Andrew laughed. "Life is just too stressful."

Amin turned slightly, catching Andrew out of the corner of his right eye. "Stress is in the mind, sir." He turned back to the road; "Besides, it is forbidden."

Definitely Middle Eastern then... Muslim at any rate.

Tapping his smoke out the window, "Have you long worked for The Council?"

"For the past five years or so, sir." He moved the car into the leftmost lane as they exited the tunnel, aiming for the south-reaching stretch of I-78, which would take them through the less palatable parts of New Jersey and onto I-95. "Ever since construction on the main complex was finished."

"What did you do before, if you don't mind my asking?"

"Not at all, sir. I was in the Service, before that the marines, sir."

Andrew turned from the window to more fully address his companion, reevaluating his read on the man, unable to mask the incredulity in his voice, "And now you drive a car?"

The smile that marked his face, unseen by Andrew, could nonetheless be heard in his response. "I serve at the pleasure of the Chairman, sir."

Andrew could only assume he referred to Michael. "Can I take that to mean that you do more than drive this car?"

"Indeed, sir. From time to time."

"You were in Pakistan?"

"Yes, sir."

"May I ask in what capacity?"

"You may ask whatever you wish, sir. I was a covert operative, sir, counterinsurgency and strategic ops."

"And you followed that up with a tour in the Secret Service."

"Yes, sir."

Andrew finished his cigarette, flicked it out the window. "I can see why Michael wanted you."

Amin stiffened slightly, nearly coming to attention in his seat. The phenomena wasn't new; the same had occurred earlier that day when he'd entered the building on Greenwich, the week before when he'd been measured for his suit. Yet still Andrew could not quite place the nature of the discomfort his use of Michael's name evoked.

Amin called him The Chairman, not Michael...

The thought tickled Andrew's memory; he reflected on the time he'd thus far spent in the company of IDSC familiars.

Has anyone else ever called him by his Christian name?

He wasn't sure, yet he decided then and there to stop doing so himself. He wanted to become one of these people, know who and what they truly were, and to accomplish this he first had to ensure they didn't see him as different. Respect and obedience were nice, if somewhat awkward at times, but the fear that seemed to manifest when he uttered Michael's given name was something else altogether, something alienating.

When I speak with the man it is as old friends, set on a new purpose. That I'm not his friend, that I don't really know him at all, seems moot. Yet discussing him as such when among others... Perhaps this is beyond the bounds of propriety.

The question of why Michael himself dealt with Andrew in such a way was one for further study, to be understood in its entirety before any conclusions were reached.

I'm just some kid from The Bay.

"It should take us approximately four hours to reach The Capital, sir." Amin caught his eyes in the rearview mirror; "Would you like me to turn on the radio?"

Andrew thought for but a moment on this. "No thank you, Amin." He had quite a lot to consider before then.

He sparked another cigarette, turning his thoughts to the matter before him, opened the dossier set on his lap.

A PLAN OF APPROACH

That which he had to consider was at once straightforwardly simple and utterly complex. Then again, perhaps he was over-thinking things.

At the very least the task itself was clear-cut: He was to meet with a man named Mark, a political activist and self-proclaimed enemy of the state who worked in the D.C. area. Andrew's job was to convince him to scale back his rhetoric, to lessen the entirety of the political force he focused on the government generally.

The question of how to achieve this end was a matter of debate, or rather it would've been had Andrew had anyone with whom to debate its various intricacies.

He looked toward Amin, dismissed thoughts of conferring with him.

Michael gave this to me. How would it look if I were to defer to another before even attempting a solution of my own?

It was just as likely Amin had been sent along to observe Andrew as it was he'd been sent to drive and help Andrew in his task. In fact, the former was more likely, given what he now knew of the man.

I must here determine a course on my own.

His instincts told him honesty was the best avenue. Michael had proscribed him nothing in his purpose and had actually chuckled when Andrew had inquired if he could reveal the nature of IDSC in the course of the assignment.

"Do what you feel is best, my young friend," he'd said, pinching a portion of tobacco into his pipe. "This job is yours, to execute as you see fit."

At the time Michael's apparent confidence in his abilities had been empowering; now, however, Andrew felt inadequate, unsure.

That Jonathan worked for The Council, a fact Michael had revealed to him back in Philadelphia, made the matter all the more convoluted. Why The Council would wish to in one place, at one time, foment dissent as they had in Philly only later to do the exact opposite in D.C. was simply beyond him. That Jonathan had been sincere in his speech before the steps of the museum, that he honestly had a will toward change in the nation, Andrew could not deny, and so he could also not deny that Michael too had such a will, or at least that he desired to further such a will in the people, whatever his true motives were.

Perhaps the events in Philly were acute enough to affect even the policies of The Council.

On the other hand, perhaps Michael's playing a more complex game than I care to acknowledge.

And so he considered his options, held them against the realities of the nation as he knew them, against the facts he'd been given about the man he must confront.

Not three months ago he'd likely have found himself on the other side. The man's primary agenda was one of socioeconomic equity, of forcing the government to acknowledge its responsibility to provide for the working class and the poor, to expand the social safety net. These were things to which Andrew would've otherwise been sympathetic, had he not been explicitly sent to dissuade the man, had he not in the time since he'd left The Bay come to conclusions of his own that argued strongly against not only the efficacy of such actions but also the soundness their ideological bases.

It wasn't that he no longer cared for the plight of the poor, far from it; he'd simply come to the unequivocal determination there were much bigger problems in the country than poverty, which itself was merely a symptom of a greater disease.

The people, however inhuman their treatment or iniquitous their circumstances, seemed perfectly willing to accept their lots in life. Not that they didn't struggle to lift themselves from their particular bondages; many did... Yet for the most part the people of the nation seemed to have accepted the rules as they were, and worked within these confines to effect change in their lives, if they did so at all.

He sat back in his seat.

It is this mentality that has to be broken, reshaped. To perpetuate the present system, to induce the people to spend just one more month, one more day, year, in impotence and waste is unacceptable.

His economics professor back at Berkeley, a now aging, formerly young idealist whose dreams had never been realized yet who nonetheless continued to preach the gospel of dedication and struggle, would've disagreed, pointing out the symbiotic relationship between the affluent and lower classes, their mutual dependence.

Andrew focused on the leather before him, jaw set in a hard line below eyes flat as slate.

Puffed.

No longer do the powerful need masses of the weak to plow their fields, as fields are now plowed by but a few with many machines. No longer do the rich require the exploitation of the poor to maintain themselves. The fiction of capital economy remains, yet only as a cover, a distraction.

Gazed out the window.

Money is but a reification of an agreement among men. Why should such an agreement be maintained when there's no choice to begin with?

Ashed his smoke.

Puffed. Thought.

The mass of people are being groomed for an existence of mere subsistence, conditioned with the cold brand of reality to accept survival, continuation of whatever state is present. Transferring wealth down the economic ladder in the form of aid so it can sent back up in the form of purchases is an instrument of subjugation, nothing more.

The system of capital economy has realized its final movement: complete and total inefficiency.

He laughed to himself at the irony, flicking the now spent cigarette out the window, lit another.

Just as the German predicted.

Yet these people will never rise up and seize the means of production. They're habituated to a vanishing share of wealth and power, grown accustomed to living with fewer and fewer material resources. The goods available to them distract from the fact that things themselves are mere tethers.

These people are weak, placated.

He knew he was exaggerating, yet he also knew social phenomena had to be understood in terms of systemic trends, that there was nothing he'd witnessed in his life to make him believe the present trends wouldn't continue.

The car slowed as they approached Baltimore, the traffic of early evening growing thick as they neared the mouth of the tunnel that would take them under the befouled waters of the northern Chesapeake.

That I agree with the particulars of the course on which I've been directed to set this man is irrelevant. I have a task; that is all.

Yet, Michael's claims that The Council, far from being a mere instrument of security and control as its name would suggest, would in fact enable the restoration of liberty and the survival of the republic, as he'd put it, had to be taken on faith, and Andrew, who was short on faith, always had been, took some small comfort in his ability to rationalize his present assignment.

Let Michael scheme all he wants. My purpose here is clear: Do what I must to further know what The Council is about. Work to realize my own ends as such opportunity may arise.

I will be honest with the man.

YOU AGAIN

When Peter ran into Jonathan at the weekend public market in San Francisco, he wasn't surprised, a little startled perhaps by the man's unexpected appearance from behind a tall pyramid of blood oranges, but unmoved in any real sense of the word. His experiences the past summer had taught him that coincidence, at least, no, *especially* where Jonathan was concerned, was anything but accidental.

He'd never had the opportunity to discuss with him the nature of the IDSC or his role in it—Jonathan had left Philly shortly after The Fourth—and so his sudden and obviously planned appearance in The Bay, just days after Peter had himself returned, filled Peter with subtle dread, as though hands were working to shape his destiny, behind the scenes and with ambiguous, insidious purpose.

"So we meet again," Jonathan smiled, moved from behind the fruit stand to confront Peter, bringing himself before him, turned momentarily to study the stack of fruit, vermilion flesh hidden within their soft, semi-glossy skins. Without turning from his observation, "Surprised to see me?"

"Not really." Peter couldn't hide the tinge of resignation, touched with a splash of curiosity, from his voice. "Although to be honest I hadn't expected us to meet quite so soon after my return." He also turned to examine the fruit; "Did you just get in, then?"

"Oh, no;" Jonathan laughed, picking an orange from near the base of the pile without disturbing the structure. "I've been here for quite some time."

"I'd have thought you'd returned to Ross."

He laughed again, signaling to the vendor his intent to purchase the fruit, handed a dollar across the makeshift counter. "Sadly, no." Turned to once again face Peter directly, "I fear my time in Ross has come to an end."

Feeling no need to press the question further, knowing any answer he'd receive if he did would be at best ambiguous, most likely confusing, Peter moved away from the stand, drawing Jonathan with him. "And what brings you to The Bay?"

"This and that," he paused, letting an old woman pass between them, began to peel the fruit, digging into it with a sharp thrust of his right thumb. "Visiting with old friends, meeting new ones, catching up with acquaintances."

Peter refrained from asking which of the three categories he fell into, feeling it was the last.

He'd come to San Francisco mainly to get away from the apartment, the memories and distinct lack of activity there found. Having had nothing better to do, he'd thought a walk through the market, which sprang up near the intersection of Haight and Central on Sundays, just to the northwest of Buena Vista Park, would provide the distraction he needed. Now, with Jonathan walking beside him, thoughts of his friends came to him unbidden; memories of the summer past mingled with those of earlier times, before they'd ever considered or even heard of the protest in Philly.

It had been here, or rather near here, at a brew pub just to the west, on Masonic, where he'd first met Andrew, a strange thing considering they'd both then been attending the same school, many miles away and on the other side of the bay.

"What's your problem, man?" Andrew had asked, sidling up to him at the bar where Peter had been quietly nursing a pint of hand-crafted microbrew, a broad and slightly mischievous grin on his face.

Peter had turned to him, shrugged, turned back to his drink; "Just chilling out."

Andrew had sat back, appraising him slyly; arched an eyebrow, "It looks like you're pretty intent on sitting here alone, eh?"

"Not really," he'd replied. Leaning slightly on his glass, he'd tilted his head to face the interloper. "Just chilling out."

He'd smiled.

Peter turned them toward the park, away from the center of the market. The street was close with people come to pass the time and perhaps find a trinket or two, some fruit, maybe a homemade pie or fresh-baked loaf of bread. Jonathan was forced to take up a position behind him.

Not seeming to mind being relegated to the rear, he continued to peel his orange, now intently removing the bitter, white inner skin, which came off in small pieces to be dropped unceremoniously on the pavement.

As they emerged from the relative chaos of the market, moving east, up and into Buena Vista, Jonathan brought himself beside Peter, offered him a slice. "You seem contemplative, Peter."

Accepting the offer, Peter popped the juicy morsel into his mouth, leaned up against the wooden rail of the stairs they'd begun to ascend. "It's been that kind of week."

I am void, the idea of a between.

"I know the feeling." He smiled, took a bite of the red fruit.

"In all fairness, it's been that kind of summer."

"And you look to me for some sort of resolution?"

Peter dug into the pocket of his jeans, drew a cigarette, sparked it, speaking around its smoldering length, "More like perspective, I suppose." He took a hit, bringing the cigarette from his mouth with his left hand. "You are, after all, here for *some* reason, I imagine."

"Indeed, indeed;" he turned to face the incline of the hill. "Shall we walk?"

They ascended the stairs, Peter quietly smoking his cigarette, Jonathan quietly finishing his orange.

At the top they paused momentarily before Peter, feeling that for some reason he was in charge of the expedition, chose the rightmost branch of the path they found there, continuing into the wooded expanse of the hill.

Jonathan broke the silence, keeping abreast of Peter, whose steps measured a slow, veritably somber pace through the woods. "I'm here because I have something to ask of you."

"Of me." The question wasn't a question.

"Yes." Jonathan eyed him cautiously without turning his head.

"I think," he pulled the last of his smoke, pocketing the butt, "that first I have a few questions for you."

"I thought you might."

He sparked another cigarette, paused again before choosing the left fork of the path, which as best as he could tell would take them toward the summit of the hill. "You say you work for this IDSC... the people who suppressed the riots in Philadelphia."

"Yes."

"And this is how you found us, how you found me?"

Jonathan nodded his assent.

Peter hit his smoke, gathering his thoughts. "You know what Andrew's presently doing?"

"I know what all of you are doing;" he corrected himself, "Rather, I know where all of you are," paused, "although I *do* know what Andrew is about."

He stopped. "You know this because this Michael, with whom Andrew's so obsessed, is also affiliated with the IDSC?"

Jonathan chuckled wryly; "You could say that."

"So, I've gotta ask: Why are you people so interested in us? Are we that special?"

He brought his hand to his chin, stroked the line of his jaw, forehead wrinkling in what Peter could only assume was thought. "Well, that's a hard question to answer, Peter."

"Hard because you don't know the answer, or hard because you don't know how to tell me the answer?"

Grinned, "Perhaps a little of both." He brought himself around, before Peter and slightly uphill, so that he had a slight vantage. "Look: Before we met in Ross I'd never heard of any of you, not you, not Andrew, not Thorin. Nor Edith nor Aleta. Yet afterward I had the feeling that you, all of you, would play vital roles in what is about to unfold, a feeling confirmed by the events in Philadelphia."

"And what is that?"

He looked at Peter solemnly for a moment, meeting his eyes, quickly looked away; "I cant say right now, Peter, but you must trust me it is for the greater good."

"OK…" Peter was unsure what to make of that, the answer or Jonathan's strange behavior. "Then how did you know, how *do* you know, that we are 'important'?"

"Because when I look withi…" Jonathan broke off, following the path they'd followed to where it disappeared to the right behind a stand of firs, just shy of Daniels last decision.

Laughed.

"I just know. I did then, and I do now." He brought his eyes back to Daniel's befuddled face. "For now you must accept that as it is." He turned from Peter, starting a slow advance up the hill Peter was forced to match.

Peter pulled on his smoke, the slight burn on his mucous membrane comforting, familiar. "I knew then, also, that my story was starting in truth."

"How?" Jonathan studied him as they walked.

"I… I just did. It was clear, painfully, acutely clear. I was an empty vessel, open."

The dual image of the moon, one bright above, the other luminous below, came before his mind. He dismissed it, chasing it away as he'd been so unable to do back at the lake, when actually confronted with its utter perfection, the completeness of its presence.

"Why did you people instigate the gathering in Philly?"

"So we could get the ball rolling, so to speak. You yourself stand as testament to that."

"And the riots?"

"The riots were an unfortunate consequence, unintended yet not entirely unexpected." Jonathan kept his gaze studiously before him, set upon the dirt of the path. "We were ready though, as you saw for yourself, perhaps not quick enough, but ready still."

They'd reached the summit of the hill, the center of the park from which they could see both the majesty of the Golden Gate and the awesome expanse of downtown San Francisco.

Peter had never before ventured this deep into Buena Vista, yet now, presented with what had to be the best view in The Bay, he wished something had brought him to this spot sooner, even though he knew that before now he'd had no reason, let alone will or opportunity, to see things from such an elevated perspective. He didn't intend to waste the opportunity.

"Where's Thorin when we need him?" Jonathan asked in jest, also absorbed in the presence of the scene.

Peter, understanding his meaning and wholeheartedly agreeing, thankful to have someone with whom to share the moment, even if it was a somewhat disconcerting and ambiguously creepy man he hardly knew, not really, dug into his pocket once more, drawing from the pack therein not a cigarette but a nice-sized joint, sparked it before handing it to Jonathan.

"So then: What would you ask of me?

A PROPOSAL CONSIDERED

"And that's the sum of it," Jonathan finished, pulled the last of the joint, flicking it among the undergrowth that framed the clearing in which they stood.

Peter didn't know what to say, so ludicrous was that which he'd just heard.

Unreal.

That they'd ask this of me... Me, who is no one, introspected and awkward... This is beyond the bounds of reason.

"What makes you think I could do this, even if I were so inclined, which of course I'm not?"

Who the hell would want this task? A would-be hero? A madman?

"What you're asking is sheer folly."

Madness.

The unfolding page, do you see?

Perhaps I am mad.

"What I think is that you'll do what you feel is right;" Jonathan looked on him with eyes slightly faded, perhaps from the ganja, perhaps from the gravity of his thoughts, his words. "The will is there, all around. You know this better than most. The people are ready"

"Bu…"

"And you would have the support of The Council." He glanced away momentarily, tracing the flight of a bird that alighted atop a tree on the far side of the clearing. "Not open support. That would be impossible. But I can guarantee we will do everything in our power to ensure this end is seen through;" his eyes once again flicked toward the bird, now hopping from branch to branch.

"You're serious."

Jonathan grinned, "Have you ever known me to be otherwise?"

Irony dripped from every word.

The bird located a victim, knocked its head back, and with a flutter of wings departed the scene.

"I can't see the point in this;" Peter stared off, looking vacantly toward the skyscrapers of downtown without really seeing them. "It is destined to fail."

"Are you one to give up before you even begin?"

"It is not giving up to rationally decide not to do something."

Jonathan cut towards him, "Yet you have already set yourself on this path." He looked away. "Your coming to Philadelphia, what was the point?"

Peter laughed, a dry, dead thing that lurched out of his throat and into the air of the hilltop; "I'm not sure there ever was a point to my going to Philly."

"Of course there was. You are not a trifling or superfluous man, unless I'm completely mistaken."

He sighed, exasperation moving him to respond. "I went to Philly because I had the opportunity to do so, because I could see no other recourse, because I knew then as I know now that something has to change in the country."

"Well," Jonathan smiled, "all I'm asking is that you seize another opportunity, one with a much greater chance of success than simply walking the streets of a decaying city, hoping someone hears when you yell."

There is truth to that.

Leave me alone. I have no business here; this is not me.

What am I, again?

I do not know.

Jonathan studied him from across the void.

Does he know?

"This is madness, Jonathan."

"Perhaps it is. Perhaps…. Yet, what good is sanity in a world with no freedom?"

"Sanity is peace."

"Is peace enough?"

Peter sparked a cigarette, inhaling deeply, exhaling a billow of smoke and pent-up thought. "I don't know what peace is, Jonathan, yet you're asking me to start a war."

Madness.

"I'm asking you to do what you can to fight for your country."

"Who am I to do this?"

"You're one who can do this, one who's been asked to do this. The one who will do this."

"I'm just a kid from Ithaca, a student at Berkeley, a part-time philosopher and full-time coward."

Jonathan chuckled. "What we think of ourselves is often less important than we'd like to believe; even less so does it have a bearing on what we're capable of doing." A soft smile remained, embracing the corners of his mouth.

"And you think I'm capable of doing what you ask?"

His smiled dissolved. "I think you're capable of doing what needs to be done."

THE TUG OF FATE

Jonathan, never one to overstay his welcome, parted ways with Peter later that afternoon, leaving for God knows where, a smile upon his face and the last of Peter's ganja making its way through his veins.

Peter was left with the uncomfortable task of wrestling his self doubt and general incredulity, alone once more at the apartment in Elmwood. He felt… Well, he felt someone somewhere must be making fun of him, giggling perhaps at the grand joke that was Jonathan's asking him to foment a rebellion, an actual, physical uprising.

He again looked around, out the window to the alley, for the rumpled screenwriter, the lazy, incompetent wretch who would concoct such a thing.

He found no one but himself, caught in blurred reflection on the pane, brought to life by the darkness outside's failing to bring transparency against the illumination within.

Darkness surrounded by light, encased in twilight. I sit as one with no recourse.

The man hadn't even discussed how Peter would actually go about the thing, let alone where he should start. Yet, sitting there in the empty apartment, alone, he felt the tug of fate pulling him, toward himself and the unknown, away from emptiness. This at least brought hope of a sort, enough to get him thinking, the rudiments of plan forming.

What story would you have?

I would have my own.

Laughter.

Who are you to write the future?

One who would see it realized.

This is wisdom.

This is madness.

Perhaps.

The question remained: Was this his story or one merely given to him.

Is there a difference?

I am free. My story is thus the same.

What is the difference between choice and creation?

There is none.

Options are given.

Assuredly.

You make, you are, the choice.

I am…

I am what I am.

Yet what would I be.

Pangs of hunger struck him, breaking his reverie. The single section of orange from earlier that afternoon returned, acid touching the base of his throat. Nausea moved him upward, off the couch and toward the door.

He struck out from the apartment, heading down Telegraph toward Alcatraz Ave, to a bar there he and the others used to frequent, The White Horse Inn. The White Horse made the best reuben sandwich north of 24, which was to say they made the only reuben north of 24, and for some reason he had a particular hankering for corned beef and rye.

It was also a gay and lesbian bar, which always made for an interesting time, sandwich or no.

Making his way down the street, he reflected on the city to the south. He'd not been to Oakland since his return—travel there was still restricted—although he'd heard rumors of what had happened.

The national guard, perhaps simply tired of standing its post, perhaps on explicit orders from the governor, had entered the city in force, subduing resistance with an iron hand that was hard to fathom. No one seemed to know specifics, as the rioters themselves had been either killed or rendered to parties unknown, yet the city itself bore testament enough to the brutality of the action.

The fires had continued to burn for several days after the rioting was put down, as hard as that was to believe, and supposedly, though none he'd met had themselves seen or knew anyone who had, several hundred people, at least, had been killed in the process. No one had made any mention of any exotic actors. *Apparently* the IDSC hadn't made an appearance.

Strange they weren't here when they played such a prominent role in Philly. Perhaps they simply don't have the manpower.

Yet he knew it was more than just that.

They simply *chose* to not intervene here.

The implications of this possibility were too vague for him to grasp; something told him the fact was significant.

He shivered in the growing evening chill, still dressed in jeans and a t-shirt, which had been appropriate for the warmth day; goose bumps pebbled his arms. No streetlights here illuminated his journey, and by the light of the almost full moon he made his way down the sidewalk, now crossing Telegraph, The Horse ahead to his left.

He nodded hello to the bouncer, a man named Bruce Peter had known for years, since he and Andrew had first ventured here a freshmen. That the White Horse had not only granted them entrance but served them as well had ensured they'd return. Peter had always secretly wondered if it had been simple conviviality or Andrew's studly good looks that had been the key to their welcome.

He grinned.

Regardless, he now thought of the bar as friendly ground, a place in which he'd not be bothered, which the weirdness of Jonathan and his ill-conceived plans wouldn't be able to penetrate.

The bar was arranged more for drinking and partying than for dining. A relatively large stage set with turntables and towering speakers, now idle, dominated the far wall; most of the space before it was open for dancing and general merriment. Still though, there were several booths to the left, a scattering of couches and love seats to the right, fronted by low tables upon which to place drinks while one flirted with members of whatever sex one was into. A bar occupied the front of the establishment, to the left of the door, set behind with a selection of liquors that would make even the most stolid of alcoholics catch his, or her, breath.

He sat down at a booth, sliding down its wooden length to rest his back against the wall, observed the happenings before him.

Fairly empty on a Tuesday evening, the bar nonetheless contained an eclectic blend of persons, queer, straight, and other.

Across the room a butch lesbian couple, absorbed in animated conversation, occupied a plush couch. To their left, closer to the stage and more toward the center of the room, a heterogeneous mix of people stood in a rough group, laughing and seemingly having a good time doing… It was unclear what exactly they were doing, but whatever it was seemed incredibly engaging.

The rest of the booths and seats were empty.

Peter smiled as the server, a girl named Mandy, approached.

"Haven't seen you in a while," she said, grinning slyly. "I'd thought maybe you and your boyfriend had eloped, left the state for somewhere more homofriendly."

He guffawed at this, the familiarity of old jokes bringing him back from the truly queer land he'd occupied since last he'd last patronized The Horse.

"Sadly, he left me for another man." His grin faded as jocularity met reality in an uncomfortable way.

Unsure how to take his sudden change in mood, Mandy laughed. "Can I assume you want the usual?"

"Indeed;" his smile returned. "And whatever micro is on tap."

The bar's selection of brew was meager—most of its patrons preferred something harder, or sweeter—but it was always good.

"Be back in a jiff;" she turned, making her way passed the group, now dancing awkwardly to Flowers on the Wall, which someone had selected from the internet jukebox in the back corner of the room, opposite the bar.

Peter lit a cigarette, a thing now forbidden in any "regular" bar, accepted here as was most anything else.

Here, among the outcasts of what is generally counted as society, freedom thrives.

Mandy soon returned, bearing a pint of pale ale and an ashtray, set both upon the table before moving toward the bar, there to lean against its polished oak surface, chatting with the bartender, a new face Peter didn't recognize.

Change is everywhere, slight yet ever encroaching.

He sat, silently puffing his smoke, observing the denizens of the bar, now and again losing himself in the smoke rising before him. The pale ale, an india now that he'd tasted it, quite good, ran down his throat, cool and fresh.

Just then, as he opened his eyes—he then realized he'd closed them some time before—a man approached, dark skinned yet not black, brought himself before Peter's table.

He looked up at the man, who appeared to be older than he, somewhere in his thirties.

Another new face?

"Mandy already took my order;" he smiled congenially.

Unmoved, the man brought his hands from behind his back, where they'd apparently been clasped, placing his right upon the back of the bench opposite Peter.

"You're not here to take my order, are you?"

Fuck.

A smile tugged at the left corner of the man's mouth, "May I sit down, Peter?"

FUCK.

Not saying anything, Peter gestured to the seat opposite himself. The man sat down.

Peter offered him a weak grin; "I don't suppose you just want to like dance, or something…"

The man didn't smile back. Instead he slid further into the booth, set his elbows on the table.

Mandy returned with the reuben and, seeing Peter had company, quirked a smile at the man. "And for you, sir?"

He glanced away from Peter, meeting her eyes. It was then that a smile, for all anyone could tell good-natured, cracked onto his face. "Just some water, please. No ice."

She snuck a look at Peter, who sat, a rumpled sack, slouched back in his seat, gave the man a grin and nodded herself away.

He turned his attention to Peter.

"My name is Amin, Peter. I'm here to help you in your task."

Peter looked at him over his steaming sandwich, now forgotten.

Fuck.

SEEDS IN THE WIND

Thorin walked south on Georgia Ave, moving passed the baseball diamond, heading to the apartment he shared with Aleta.

That was damn fucking odd.

He couldn't shake the feeling something strange was at work, and as he made his way south from Howard, toward Georgetown, the events of the meeting from which he'd just departed rose before him, still unreal, disconcerting. Memory, fresh and unobscured as yet by reflection, gave his progress a halting, meandering feel.

Not knowing exactly what he should do, yet feeling an immediate return to the apartment where Aleta waited, absorbed in study and of no use to his troubled mind, would be at best awkward, likely boring, he turned sharply to his right, breaching the outskirts of the field.

He looked up at the now full moon, which stared down at him from an angle, behind and slightly to the south, casting small and ethereal shadows from the trees toward the infield.

Thankfully, Aleta knew some pretty kind people in the area, and he was not deprived recourse to ganja in the settling-down of his thoughts.

He sat beside a moderately sized maple, back to both the tree and the greater world of D.C. beyond, moon hidden by the tree's branches, himself hidden in the darkness of its embrace.

He set himself about the rolling of a small joint.

Since departing New York he'd fought the entropy of idleness, working to maintain some semblance of political and personal vigor.

Now, with Fall on the horizon, he was nearly devastated by the realization that the efforts to which he'd applied himself, both in the trip to Philly and here in D.C., had all come to nothing.

I just can't believe Mark would abandon us like this.

It seemed so unlike him. In the time Thorin had known him he'd been nearly always first to voice his opinion, to take the steps toward making his vision reality. Not easily dissuaded by political frustrations or setbacks, always with a plan, Mark was one to whom Thorin had come to look for direction, as sad and pathetic as this now seemed.

If I were more like Andrew, perhaps I wouldn't *need* someone to look to.

Twisting the finishing touches to the joint, he brought it to his lips, sparking the blunt end, inhaled deeply.

Not three hours ago he'd walked passed this same field, full of excitement, anticipation. The group, The People's Movement for Democratic Change, had been in line to conduct a televised protest, and not just on local T.V.—Mark had been set to give a speech that would've been broadcast throughout the nation, blasting the administration for its continued support of the wars in Venezuela and Pakistan in the face of deteriorating domestic social and economic conditions.

It had been going to be epic, not just bringing attention to The Movement itself but also giving voice to a charismatic man who Thorin believed, or rather who he *had* believed, could one day bring some real change to the country, perhaps even ascend to high office.

He pulled a hit, puffing a perfect circle into the still air before him that, leaving the confines of the tree's shadow, burst bright and thick into the moonlit space beyond.

He'd first met Mark at a rally at Georgetown when Aleta and he had been freshmen, on his first visit to the campus that held his girlfriend nearly five-thousand kilometers away from Berkeley.

I wonder if my coming here was a good idea.

He knew it had been the right decision, the idea of leaving Aleta alone to deal with both school and pregnancy was simply unconscionable. Yet for a while, until just a couple hours ago, he'd also known it had been a wise decision for other reasons. He'd been involved in important things of his own.

Now, the prospect of being a stay-at-home stoner dad, without even a daughter to yet look after, seemed unacceptable.

What the fuck made him so suddenly change his mind?

If he didn't know better, he'd have thought Mark had been frightened. The idea itself was ludicrous. How could a man who'd spoken before countless congregations, who'd stood not a year and a half ago before the Wailing Wall in Jerusalem and demanded recognition of the State of Palestine, how could he be frightened of a simple, if important, televised speech?

Thorin hadn't been alone in his incredulity upon Mark's pronouncement that he wouldn't be speaking at next week's rally. That the remaining leaders of The Movement had thereafter eventually decided to cancel the rally altogether had come as no surprise to anyone. How could it proceed without the man who'd imagined it to begin with?

Thorin now saw that The Movement, as influential locally as it had become, had had a fatal weakness, a weakness he'd mistaken for strength.

Such a thing cannot be centered around a single man, however charismatic he may be.

He puffed thoughtfully on the now almost consumed joint.

For a political movement to have real power, true effect, it must be generalized, not in ambition or purpose, not in organization or strategy, but in will. It was Mark's will that moved us, set our ends and the nature of our actions.

A single man, easily identified and rallied around, is also too easily broken, too easily diverted.

He saw this now that it was too late.

The joint in his hand was spent, the sticky stump left brown with resin, unwilling to give up even one more good hit.

He rose, balancing himself with his right hand against the solid trunk of the maple, leaving the roach to lie on the ground where moments before he'd lain.

A gentle breeze now crossed the field, stirring the hairs on his arm, bringing a shiver that ran down his spine as he stretched the tension from his back.

Leaving the shadow in which he'd been hiding, he crossed the track encircling the outfield, kicked the fluffy protrusion of a seeded dandelion, watched as its tiny puffs rose into the air to disperse and fall into the well manicured lawn.

So too is The Movement, spent, unable to hold itself against the wind.

Where will we fall, now that our leader had forsaken us?

CHAPTER 6
EDITH

MOVING ON

That she'd not had the time to know him well had been perhaps the most disillusioning part of the whole thing.

That she'd again found herself at her lonely house in West Jordan, set to resume her duties back at the bar, had come in a close second.

Not that it had lasted long or anything. After her second day back, during her shift actually, she'd quit her job at The Liberty, finding herself empowered and unemployed on the streets of Liberty Wells, just southeast of downtown Salt Lake. She'd loved her job—both the clientele and the management were incredibly chill—yet nonetheless she'd been compelled to leave.

Her mostly quiet life, mostly comfortable and fulfilling, no longer satisfied her soul.

I need to find the truth of myself.

This truth could not be found in the patterns of her old warren, set and established, routine. A simple labyrinth of self stamped in brittle pewter, no longer worth her time.

That night, the first of her second week back in Utah, had set softly, the hush of falling leaves casting shadows on the houses through the trees. She'd sat in her living room, attempting to come back to the book she'd begun before the trip, unable to focus on its lines, the light from a streetlamp painting queer patterns on her wall. The green tea set before her in a small, black, cast iron pot, in a small and handless ceramic cup, had done nothing to bring inner calm or focus.

The next day she'd set herself to selling the place, which apparently wouldn't be, hadn't been, difficult. As close to Salt Lake as the house was, demand had been high, and her home, which had been in her family for three generations, had found itself sold and vacated not three weeks later.

To be honest, she'd never really felt it was *her* house to begin with. It was the house of her father, his father before him, whom she'd never known.

The house had come to her over four years ago, after her father had been killed in a car accident. At the time she'd been staying with her mother on the Washington Coast, maybe 30 kilometers north of Ocean Shores, who'd been perhaps a little more than encouraging when the prospect of Edith's moving to Salt Lake had arisen. Edith too had been eager to leave the isolation of The Peninsula, and although she'd hardly known her father, having visited him a scant few times since he and her mother had split, she'd accepted the responsibility of taking over the family stead, the freedom that had accompanied her doing so.

The trip to Philadelphia, however, had drawn her gaze beyond simple freedom and stability to a place where freedom itself wasn't enough, where will required an object, herself a purpose. If nothing else, the failure that was this past summer had taught her that much.

The house had become a tether, one that had now been liquidated, consolidated into something useful, a swollen bank account and a brand-new vehicle.

As she drove south on I-15, which would take her to the lesser highways that ran to Albuquerque, she was exhilarated, yet also disconcerted to a great degree.

This might not be the smartest thing to do with a baby coming.

Already she was showing. Though most would overlook the slight protrusion of her abdomen—even with the added girth she could not have been said to be anything but slim—she could see a marked difference it its contours, a new fullness that realized a constant reminder of new responsibilities to come, present precautions to be taken.

All the more reason to leave Jordan before it's too late.

She had to consciously refrain from peering back, to where already neither Salt Lake itself nor its southern extensions and suburbs could be seen.

The fact remained that there was more to providing for a child than simply having a place to live and a job. There was more to her than simply providing for her child, even if she didn't quite know what.

She opened the aperture of the moonroof. Cool Autumn air feathered her hair, sent a thrill of goose bumps down her arms; the subtle light of the waning moon, little more than half obscured, met her eyes as she tilted back her head. Her new car, a 2025 Subaru Outback, was assuredly awesome, and as she caressed the bulbous length of the stick-shift in the recess beside her, a smile touched her lips. Her father, dead now a long time, had finally provided her something beyond the simple grace of his absence, in her life and in the house she'd come to call his.

Her destination was New Orleans, a place wrapped in exotic history, set at the mouth of the Mississippi, a trading town couched in Creole, a culture born of European adventurers and emancipated slaves, subjugated natives, where Jesus Christ and Papa Legba were equally welcome and in which the dead were acknowledged along-side the living.

She'd always wanted to visit the place, and since she had no need to be anywhere, that is no need to be anywhere specific, Edith, having found herself already driving south, had simply and silently deter-mined to go.

Perhaps her enthusiasm in the face of the unfolding unknown had made her a little romantic, for she knew the reality of New Or-leans was for the most part one of poverty and desperation, that the rich spiritual life of which she'd read likely would not live up to the descriptions in the books she'd loved to read growing up.

Still though, she couldn't hold back a soft giggle as she sped down the highway toward the first stop of her new life, couldn't hold back the smile that blossomed on her face as she held a hand to her belly.

Andrew had chosen his path, one that involved a new job in New York of which she was apparently not privileged enough to know the details, which for now didn't involve her.

She didn't know if he'd be a part of her life or of their unborn child's, yet she did know he loved her, that she loved him. Perhaps that would be enough to bring them together again.

For now she travelled a darkened highway, with no one to talk to but herself, yet not alone.

Her hand moved once more to cover the slight curve of her stom-ach.

She'd never be alone again.

SOMETHING GIVEN

Hours later as she crossed into New Mexico, moving toward Al-buquerque, dawn cracking the horizon to the east, she realized Peter was mistaken.

As random as the thought seemed, there was a weird symmetry, reciprocity perhaps, between her conversation with him so long ago and her present silent contemplation. She surveyed the empty vehicle, held it against the experience of that first night on the road; pieces fell together, a sense of completeness. Perspective.

What had truly changed since then? Merely herself.

He said *we* manifest the spiritual moment, that we realize it through that with which we animate the world, in the relationship of self and world.

This is partially true.

The moment itself is something given. Awareness of this moment is of course key to realizing The Spiritual, yet awareness, consciousness, is itself also something given.

She wasn't one to deny the reality of will. And surely she acknowledged the practical reality of the will's freedom. But that consciousness, generally or particularly, was something entirely given was also an undeniable conclusion.

One can not simply decide to be aware of a thing, for without awareness judgment has no object. The best we can do is navigate the appropriate series of moments, progressive contexts, that will allow us to develop an awareness of a thing.

The problem was in such a system one never quite knew what one was looking for, if indeed one was looking for anything. Blind movement in the dark, decisions based not on purpose or end but on feeling and… faith, that was the nature of the explorer, much different from the behaviors of the businessman or laborer, even distant from the creative movements of the artist and craftsman. The philosopher and theologian, the natural philosopher and scientist, the explorer and pioneer moved with the infinite steps of faith, regardless of how much many to whom the designations applied would object to the characterization.

If spiritual awareness is awareness of something greater than the simple base constituents of experience, if it is consciousness of an emerging unity, then the path toward this consciousness extends through the entirety of our antecedent movements, tracing a path defined by a near infinitude of individual moments of awareness and being, the totality of a life.

The emergence of a thing, its realization and actuality in experience, is a gift predicated on countless other gifts, each one a measure of not only one's relationship with the world but also the relationship of the world with itself aside from perspective.

The spiritual moment is something given. We express our gratitude by allowing ourselves to acknowledge its truth.

So I suppose he wasn't exactly *wrong*. He was simply assuming an unfounded independence. Even if only in his language, he'd reserved for himself the power of realization.

She laughed slightly.

Men.

Everything that had happened to her in the past months had led to this understanding. She could only hope Peter would realize his error before he got himself into trouble.

She'd set herself on the trip to Philly, had gone there to fight for her country and the rights of the people; she'd decided to journey with Peter and Andrew, Thorin, because they seemed like people who would help her in this task, who themselves were also set there on. Yet in the end everything she'd decided to do had come to nothing. Instead she'd found herself right back where she'd started, except for the small fact that she was now three months pregnant.

I went to fight and instead was given a great gift.

A gift that will change everything about my life, where it's headed and what's important in it.

She'd also been given the gift of perspective.

Her entire attitude and agenda had been terribly misguided.

Having come to redefine the world of which she was a part, through which she moved, which she created and shared, now alone in the car but for the tiny life who grew inside her, she'd finally been given a clear, if rudimentary, understanding of her relationship with the world.

The fully acknowledged moment of oneness filled her, impelled her along the path on which she was set. She skirted the line of the rising sun, racing along its edge and into its embrace.

Edith had found faith in the disillusion of her soul.

MARGARITA ON THE ROCKS

After over fifteen hours on the road Edith finally reached her destination, parked the Outback before room 168, at the far end of the motel from the office. Gathering her belongings, really just the same backpack she'd taken to Philadelphia, plus a nice down pillow, she locked the vehicle, jimmied the key into the door, and lay on the bed, pillow forgotten on the floor.

She awoke some hours later as the sun slowly retreated from the sky, having passed both night and day on the bed, clothed still.

Slipping a cigarette from the pack in her bag, she ducked her head out the door.

No one around.

Stepped outside, breathing in the cooler air of approaching evening, sparked her smoke.

She knew she shouldn't be smoking, and really she didn't, yet she did keep a pack around for emergencies, which of course this wasn't. But then, standing before a shitty motel room in the city of El Paso, not knowing really what had drawn her there, a cigarette was nonetheless *needed*.

Fuck it.

While she was at it she might as well have a drink.
One won't hurt.

She journeyed a quiet sidewalk in Chihuahuita, Oregon St., near
the train depot, southwest of downtown and her hotel. The sun was
set low in the sky, colors of evening flooding the western horizon,
over the dry bed of the Rio Grande.

Edith could not truly say what had made her continue south on
I-25 instead of turning east for New Orleans; she'd done so in a semi-
catatonic stupor, the result of too many hours in the car with no cigarettes to keep her company.

Looking around now she could not help but think the decision
had been poor, so washed-out and plain was El Paso, in no better condition and actually far more desolate than its sister to the south. Low
buildings fronted with dusty signs spoke of poverty, disuse. Most
here were empty, some for sale while others sat abandoned, doors
ajar in their settings, bent and hanging by rusted hinges.

No one lived in this quarter anymore, not really, hadn't for a
while. Even the seedy bars, gentlemen's clubs and card rooms, were
for the most part vacant.

So much for some authentic Mexican and a well-made margarita.

As she was about to retreat, back toward downtown where she'd
at least seen *some* evidence of functioning hospitality, she paused,
catching sight of a vivid red awning a few blocks further south. Its
hanging fabric was gathered up, loose yet pulled underneath at the
edges, falling from its support in rich, voluptuous folds. Clearly in
good condition, it lay as a silent sign of life, somewhere within the
aperture it shielded from the sun.

Without really realizing it, Edith had begun to move toward the
crimson flag, squinting the sun from her eyes enough to read the
hanging plaque that graced its undercarriage. There, branded on the
wood in a dark char, read The Rose.

As she neared the place warm scents of roasting meat, spices,
reached her nose, as did the slow melody of country-blues, pedal-
steel, reach her ears. The windows were formed of clouded glass, yellowed and opaque; still though she could see within the shadows of
movement. There was no bouncer at the door.

Striding through the entrance, she nearly collided with a dark-
skinned waitress, clearly possessing a strong portion of native blood,
who carried a broad circular tray set with several drinks and more
than a few quesadillas. The woman ducked a smile at her, continuing
on her way toward a table to the right, near the windows fronting
the cantina, to a group of men there, Caucasian and Hispanic, who
Edith could now see had been the figures behind the shadows she'd
moments before observed.

She brought herself into the cantina, navigating the spread of tables, mostly empty, taking a seat at a small table at its rear, opposite the group of men and near the bar.

Ordering some roast pork enchiladas de mole and a margarita on the rocks, she sat back, watching the musician perched on a simple stool behind the horizontal plane of his instrument, right hand moving deftly to pluck strings, his left alive and fluid on the slide, feet active yet calm on the pedals.

His song was slow for country, more blues, yet there was an eeriness to the tones as they bent and blended together that bespoke a different style altogether. A halting beat, set aloft in the air between the notes, one-drop.

It was mesmerizing.

Her reverie was broken as she became aware of a man seated at the bar, who was staring at her rather intently; she didn't know for how long.

She looked up, smiled.

Just then the waitress returned with her margarita, slipping a small napkin onto the table underneath. The iced liquid within had drawn beads of perspiration that slid from the bell to the stem, slipping into the fibers bellow.

She looked up from her drink to see if the man was still watching her.

He was not.

In the interim he'd closed the distance and now stood directly before her, holding of all things a tall walking stick.

This guy doesn't quite belong here.

"You have come seeking answers." The man had brought no smile with him to the table. He stood there, in a white polo and grey khaki shorts, dreads pulled back, tied with a beaded length of leather.

Edith gave him a queer look around her margarita; "I don't suppose I've come seeking anything."

"Then perhaps they are seeking you."

"And why would you say that?" She was curious now, for she'd recognized the man's strange accent.

"Because you have come here."

Some sort of East African, Sudanese. Maybe Ethiopian.

His dark skin, nearly black in truth, certainly lent credence to her surmise.

She paused for a moment, attempting to place the man into a frame that could bring some semblance of rectitude to the oddness of his presence and strangeness of his questions, posed: "Why have *you* come here?"

Again Peter has taught me well.

"I am always here," he replied, leaning slightly to the side, back and on the staff, whose long length was intricately carved, totems and strange characters, as tall as was the man.

Shit.

What the fuck kind of answer is that?

She didn't quite know what to say.

"I see you are not alone." His face betrayed nothing.

Edith fidgeted slightly in her chair.

"I come from across The River," he spoke, sitting up against the back of the chair opposite Edith.

"I thought you said you were always here;" she cocked her head at him.

"A figure of speech;" he paused, "then again, *here* is a curious sign."

The man seemed remarkably well spoken for a non-native speaker, the depth of his expression belying the accent in his voice.

"My name is Gabriel."

"And you have answers for me, Gabriel?"

He rotated the staff slowly with his right hand. "Perhaps;" he gazed at the musician. Turning, he repositioned himself against the seatback, brought the staff to rest on his right shoulder; "What is your name?"

Seeing no need for subterfuge, "Edith."

"Edith, if you will allow me I will tell you a story."

She nodded her assent. There was something about his voice, the deep and fluid tones of his accent, that carried with his words comfort, assurance.

GABRIEL

"I came to live on the slopes of the mountains south of here, to the southwest of Chihuahua, many years ago, decades ago. I picked this place because it reminds me of my home.

"I fled Ethiopia, where I had lived my whole life, when the civil war in Sudan crossed into our land, consuming my village, taking with it the lives of my wife and children.

"I had been away, far afield with our flocks, grazing them in the highlands of Amhara, west of the sacred lake that feeds the blue river Gihon.

"When I returned to find my village destroyed and my home burned to the ground, my family dead or abducted and sold into slavery or worse, I took my flocks to the market at Bahir Dar to sell them.

"There was no way for me to pursue those who had murdered my family; Sudan was then a place of chaos, madness. I could not stay in Ethiopia, so close to their deaths did I feel there. I needed to leave that place, the ancient homeland of my ancestors, for it had become a place of pain, war and despair. Yet even with the money from my flocks I did not have enough to buy a ticket to take me away."

He paused momentarily, "May I sit down properly?"

She nodded, thoroughly intrigued by not only the oddness of the man's sudden appearance, his desire to talk to her and the exotic accent with which he did so, but also the story he told. It was a thing of far-off places, a reality with which she'd never come into contact, let alone had to experience herself.

The practicality of his tone belied the horrors he related.

Surreal.

He lowered himself onto the seat, now on her level; she saw more clearly the lines that chiseled his features, the grey and white that highlighted the folds of his dreadlocks, which she could now see were not just pulled back but also gathered in a fairly large bun just below the base of his skull.

If they were let down they would likely trail on the ground.

"So I made my way to Djibouti," he continued, "spending nearly a third of my money on a bus ticket to reach the port, where I arranged transport to Yemen.

"I passed nearly a month in Yemen, exhausting the remainder of my money, before I secured a job as a scullion aboard an oil tanker bound for New Orleans, a trip of just a little under a month.

"New Orleans, however, was... not the place for me. I had some money I had earned on the journey, and in the wake of the hurricane that made landfall there later that summer I traveled to Tampico, eventually finding my way to San Miguel de Allende.

"It was there I met Maria, Dasta as I came to call her. She was a young woman, untouched and beautiful. She worked at her father's bakery, where one morning I stopped in for a pastry. She was setting upon the shelves behind the counter the morning's efforts, still steaming from the oven. Her hair was held back by a red ribbon; I remember a few strands had come loose, which she had to brush back from her face, as she bent down to lift a loaf onto the shelf."

He paused then again, to move the length of his staff from the path of the waitress as she passed carrying a large circular tray, set with several empty glasses and more than a few grease-stained plates.

"I took a job with the city, keeping the main square, the park there, clean, just so I could be near her. I lived in San Miguel for two years, visiting the bakery every morning on my way to work, before, one summer morning, I was comfortable enough with myself and my Spanish to speak with her.

"The next spring I walked the bounds of the square, not looking for trash or a trampled flower bed, but instead at the head of my own wedding march, Dasta by my side. Early that summer we said good-bye to San Miguel, searching for a place to call our own.

"Her father had given us one of his trucks as a wedding present, and we simply drove, first east to the ocean at Punta Mita, then following the coastal highway north to Culiacan.

"Following our hearts, we crossed the Sierra Madre, finding our home in an abandoned cabin set there, overlooking the Great Plateau, where we live today."

He grinned.

"After a too-long absence, I tend the flocks once more."

PERSPECTIVE

"This story, brief in its telling, spans nearly four years of my life."

Shaken into action by the abruptness of his conclusion, Edith lifted her drink to her lips, only to discover that the margarita, the salt that had crusted its rim, was entirely gone.

"It is a good story," she said, setting the glass back down on the table. "You've done more in your life than I ever will."

Who am I to comment on such a thing.

She made an attempt to back away from the table, recenter herself upon him, movement denied by the presence of his eyes. There, crow's feet stretched themselves, supine forms tucked into the face of epoch itself.

"Perhaps that is true;" he smiled. "Yet I also lost very much, gained very much. The two seem to always travel hand-in-hand."

He stared then, out into the space of the cantina.

"The sum of an experience is always so much more than can be told in a story, no matter how detailed or colorful. The story of those four years is vivid to me, clear, yet the story of any four years since, or any four before, is no less real, no less full of life and depth, no less important. The summary of those times... my time of hardship and journey... I could tell it for hours, days, without repeating anything. I could spend an afternoon discussing the sunsets from the hill in San Miguel, or the single sunset that greeted me when I returned to my home so long ago to find all I loved gone."

Edith didn't quite know what to say.

"We are all but characters in our own stories, and it is up to us if these tales are to be told."

"Why do you tell me your story?"

"We tell ourselves stories about what we have seen, what we witness, to bring some sense of continuity to the paths of our lives, to the confusion of Being that is life. The threads of our lives, moments of self, are clear, made so by the simple structure that is the telling."

She wasn't sure if he'd been answering her question or simply continuing.

"And what answers would you have for me?"

He hesitated a moment, bringing his gaze back to her. "None of which you cannot tell the story yourself." He glanced at her abdomen, back to meet her eyes; "Why have you come here?"

It was her turn to hesitate. "I don't know."

"This is no place for a woman with child."

Momentarily without a response, she seized on the first excuse she had to avoid his statement. "*You* still haven't told me why you've come here," a slight smile of satisfaction...

"I come here, as I do often, to trade my wool. The buyers here pay much more than do those across the border, so I am always here."

...gone as soon as it blossomed.

What the hell am *I* doing here?

"I'm here because I had nowhere to go." She blushed; "El Paso was just the last stop on the road I was already on."

He laughed then, loudly and with the taste of actual mirth. She couldn't help but feel he was laughing at her, which of course he was.

"The road you traveled here, did you choose it yourself?"

Giving the matter a serious contemplation, "Partly."

A broad grin remained, "But you do not live just part of a life. You live a whole life, a full life. Why do you not choose it all?"

She had no response.

"Edith," the way he spoke her name sounded more like *Edeh*, the exotic notes bringing a softness to the end of its vocalization, "Your life runs short; your time with the child you carry will be brief. This world knows not the sanctity of such things, for sanctity is what *we* bring."

She watched him, not sure if she was holding her breath but pretty sure she was, waiting for him to continue.

"You must choose what is important. Some things you can replace; others you cannot. Time... Time is irreplaceable, and every moment lost is a story that will never be told."

He stood up then, apparently having accomplished whatever he'd intended.

"For your sake, for the sake of the child, do not merely accept the path you are on. Choose it, whatever path it may be or wherever it may lead. A path we have not chosen ourselves is a thread of another's story. You must write your own."

"Thank you, Gabriel." Eloquence of speech and sharpness of wit had fled her long ago, all that was left a simple gratitude for the strange man, a true appreciation of all her short time with him had been.

He smiled broadly, bringing his staff to his right hand. "Goodbye, Edith"

It was then that the waitress returned with her enchiladas.

Glancing at her empty glass, "Another?"

Edith smiled, watching as Gabriel exited the cantina, headed south.

Back to his Dasta.

"Just a sparkling water please."

CHAPTER 7
SAMAEL

A MONTH'S ACCOUNTING

Samael sat quietly at his desk. The month's accounting lay spread before him, lists of lists, numbers representing entire worlds of economy and intrigue.

Foremost among these were the summations accounting for the trending of public discontent and dissent and the projections of the expected glean for the coming quarter.

Both numbers were on the rise from the last accounting.

All Samael truly cared about was the glean. So long as that number was large, better yet increasing, things were good with the world. The former was of only incidental, if undeniable, importance, predicated on the possibility of successfully effecting the object of the latter.

The crisp white cuffs of his shirt, French, protruded from the dark pinstripe of his suit, bound with links of white gold, as he held before himself the report.

The past month had seen a three percent rise in the incidence of noncompliance with law enforcement. All areas, curiously excepting D.C., had seen increases in inflammatory public speech and expressed anti-government sentiment.

He glanced shortly to the general economic prospectus. Unemployment had again increased, the numbers bringing a new steepness to the curve, whose points denoted the decaying material reality of the nation, each a summation of idleness, waste and desperation. Production had increased; surpluses were up.

That the economic prospectus was grim came as no surprise—How can an economy be stable and healthy, let alone strong and virile, when value is siphoned in direct proportion to any gains that are made? The game of capital in a fully integrated market is one of manipulation, inflation and deflation, timing... easy when you know the patterns and trends better than anyone, when you write the rules yourself.

He set the papers aside, satisfied the present demanded no significant change in policy; he made a mental note to inform the Secretary of Commerce to make available a few hundred thousand jobs in some of the more troubled areas, to direct IDSC to keep a tight watch on organization and promulgation of dissent.

He leaned forward, tenting his fingers, elbows on his desk and papers pinned between.

Things had been a little rough since the events of the summer past. First Oakland and then Philadelphia had spiraled out of control, none of which was his fault but which nonetheless was his problem.

Damn Michael. I should never have heeded his advice.

He wouldn't make the same mistake again. IDSC was after all an instrument of The Party, to be used, not followed.

He'd learned though in the years of their acquaintance that IDSC, Michael at its head, was unsurpassed in its intelligence, deft in its purpose. That Michael had made a mistake, two mistakes, of such magnitude was almost beyond reason. It was beyond reason.

Still, his confidence in Michael was unshaken. In the past the man had acted with seemingly poor judgment, perhaps a touch of madness, yet in the end things had progressed exactly as Samael had wanted, better even.

Michael's surely loyal. If he'd simply share his plans with me, these minor inconveniences would be of no matter.

He stood, bringing himself before the large window set in the south wall of his office, looked out, overtop his smaller neighbor, to where he could glimpse the white rotunda of The Capital, some five-hundred meters distant.

Matters outside the nation were progressing as planned. The resistance in Venezuela wouldn't be able to maintain itself much longer, and the occupation of Pakistan, now entering its sixth year, had finally begun to bear fruit.

When last he'd spoken with Beijing the word had been the Uighur rebellion was in full retreat.

With South America thoroughly quelled—aside from Venezuela economic forecasts from the region were quite favorable—and central Asia nearly pacified, the nationalist threat, in both its social and religious expressions, would soon be a thing of the past.

Samael smiled.

The final stages of globalization, in progress for decades, had been long and wearisome. That now on the horizon loomed an economic landscape that could be properly and efficiently fashioned, terraced as it were, free from the tethers of border and identity, he could scarcely believe. Even the vastness of Africa, so long a splintered boondoggle, had been effectively reined in under the purview of the Global Mining Corporation, whose board assured him output of both precious metals and crude would see a steady rise for the foreseeable future.

The only thing left with which to deal was the domestic security situation. In addition to the growing unrest punctuated by the events of the summer, there were now rumors of a man from Oakland, although some reported he was from Chicago, who was organizing support for some sort of action. Whether his intents were political or guerilla, Samael didn't know. The limited information he'd received from his own sources was sketchy at best, apocryphal. IDSC had reported nothing on the matter.

Again he cursed Michael.

If there was one thing Samael couldn't abide it was remaining in the dark.

Turning from the window, he walked back to his desk, tapped the intercom.

"Contact IDSC. Tell them I want a meeting."

ANSWERING A SUMMONS

It had been some time since he'd been to D.C., longer still since he'd been obliged to meet Samael at his office.

Michael nearly cringed at his name. Even voiced silently in the finitude of his mind, Samael, what he represented and who he was, called forth slimy revulsion. That one such as he could wield the power he did was testament enough to the necessity of the course Michael had set.

Not that he didn't respect the man's skill, for failure to do so would preempt any possibility of effectively handling him. In his long duration in the margins of government Michael had learned many things, foremost of which was that any enemy worth having was one worth respecting.

There is, however, a difference between respect and deference.

This was something Michael sincerely hoped Samael would eventually come to know, in due time. Presently appearances had to be kept, and for now he was at the man's beck and call.

Samael's office was set on the top floor of Party Headquarters, a large yet innocuous brick building just west of Columbus Circle, on whose ground floor Michael presently waited, in a grand, columned hall dominated by a broad staircase ascending to a landing against the far wall, there splitting in two, branches rising to either side.

He shrugged the rain from his coat, a dark charcoal length that fell to just below his knees, grinned to himself.

He'd known The Party nearly his entire life, had worked for it, or rather had done work for it. He knew for just how long they'd been entrenched, which congressmen and senators were members. He knew the president, now two years into his second term, was merely a middling member who owed not just his job but his life to the man Michael had come to see.

In fact, Michael knew full well the president was proscribed the pleasure of Samael's company.

Neither puppets nor parrots were accorded such respect or honor.

These of course were the words of Samael himself, reported to Michael by the man's secretary.

He wondered what had caused Samael to demand his presence. Certainly there was no pressing issue requiring such a meeting.

At a gesture from the front desk clerk, Michael, settling his coat, the suit beneath, square on his shoulders, turned from his silent contemplation of the columns to climb the stairs, taking the left set at the landing.

He probably wants to talk about Philadelphia again.

HALF TRUTHS

Samael had a few questions to ask, one of which he'd asked before, to which he'd received less than satisfactory answers.

Perhaps a face-to-face meeting will serve to clear things up.

He walked to the case set against the wall on the far side from his desk, opposite the windows. The slight tapping of rain thereupon could be heard in the still of the office.

Michael stood, reclined slightly against a bookshelf at the west end of the room, tamped a plug of tobacco into his pipe.

Samael glanced over his shoulder, "Straight?"

Michael nodded, flared a match to the bowl, pulling a sharp puff and again a long pull.

Samael contained a grin as he dropped a dram of fine Islay into two short glasses each. Michael's pipe, its archaic quality, was a trademark of the man, legendary in its own right. He'd known its scent for many years.

He moved from the bar, crossing the thick expanse of the square Persian rug that graced the center of the room, handed Michael his drink. "How long have you worked for Us, Michael?"

Michael took a sip of scotch, "Officially or unofficially?"

"Either."

Placing the glass atop the bookshelf, "Over thirty years."

"And in thirty years have you ever known me, or any of my associates, to interfere with what you do?"

He puffed his pipe before answering. "Not to the best of my knowledge," smiled.

"In all our years of acquaintance, whether we knew your explicit purpose or not, we have never disrupted your organization?"

Moving to the desk, leaned slightly back thereon, he nodded.

"Then I must ask why you keep secrets from Us, from me."

Michael pulled again on his pipe, smoke coiling into the open air above; "Why don't you just tell me what you want to know, Samael, and forgo the rhetoric."

"I want you to tell me your full reasons for allowing the events of this past summer. I want to know what you're doing to ensure it doesn't happen again."

"Surely you must know I can't control the police forces of the entire nation, Samael. What happened in Oakland resulted from the individual actions of a single officer, others before him; the disaster in Philadelphia also was caused by the police, ordered in by your man, I believe." A bluish swirl danced in the air.

Samael finished his scotch, setting it on the table beside Michael, gaze set out the window, into the rain. "That is not what I'm concerned about."

Michael turned slightly toward him, grinned; "Don't be so serious."

Softening slightly, "Then tell me truthfully: Why didn't your people intervene? Why let the National Guard botch things so badly? *Why* allow the action in Philadelphia to happen at all?"

Michael sighed, brought the pipe to rest in his lap, held lightly in his left hand. "Sure, we could have preempted the action in Philadelphia, obfuscated awareness thereof and minimized the impact, yet I feel the lesson learned is worth any collateral damage that may have been incurred."

Samael laughed, actual humor touching his voice; "And what, Michael, did we learn from Philadelphia?"

Holding a straight expression, "It was not *we* who did the learning," paused, a slight touch of smile brushing the corners of his eyes, considered Samael for a moment. "People, from all over the nation, learned they are impotent, that no matter how great their numbers or how loud their protests, how powerful they may be, in the end they're at the whim of others." He paused, sipped his scotch. "Think about it, Samael." Resettled himself on the edge of the desk, "If we'd prevented the gathering no one would've known we'd done so; we'd be faced with another such situation again next summer, or this winter, or any number of times, as public dissatisfaction grows. Eventually we'd face an action that couldn't be forestalled, the sentiments of which would

Beside him strode Lilith Matthias, the Undersecretary of Homeland Security, a ranking Party member and Samael's personal intelligence officer and whore.

He smiled, considering what he'd subject her to later that night, if matters of state allowed.

It has been too long.

She pleads very well when properly motivated.

A blond more than thirty years his younger, the product of meticulous breeding, her well proportioned features and body belied a cold, surgical mind, cruel in its rationality, dispassionate in judgment.

Samael half suspected her throes of ecstasy and despair, delivered so forcefully in the close of his bedroom, were nothing more than a façade. In fact, he knew they were. Yet the performance was convincing, real, the visceral reaction of body completely removed from whatever dark recess of inner being she inhabited in truth.

She would've scared him, had he not known, been an intimate part, of her conditioning. Samael had broken her himself long ago, when she was just an adolescent, had forced her into what she now was: a cold-blooded, detached and calculating, agent of his will.

That she had no true emotions of her own to speak of, Samael had no doubt. These had all been made long ago too painful to admit or acknowledge.

He smiled, eyes caressing the fall of her hair, touched slightly with flecks of snow, as it curved closely around the soft angle of her jaw...

Another time, another place.

Presently he'd come to The Basin, to trace its bounds in the cold of early December, not to admire and abuse his whore, but to speak of pressing matters with his devotee, a woman of power and discernment, matters too sensitive to be spoken of in his home or even Party Headquarters.

Not two weeks ago they'd discovered working in his own office, the very place in which for decades the path of the world had largely been decided, of the nation long before that, a mole. Samael didn't know who the mole was, but they'd definitely found his murine droppings, recording devices, in the walls. That the devices had no broadcast capabilities, presumably to reduce the probability of their being detected, entailed rather clearly there was someone with access to the building in a position to directly download their data. That security had also been breached on other levels was a strong possibility.

And so he found himself walking with Ms. Matthias in the crisp air of late afternoon.

For a moment Samael had suspected Michael of keeping an eye on him, yet the relatively primitive nature of the devices, not only their bulkiness but also the quality of the recording apparatus itself, bespoke someone who lacked basic technologies IDSC had employed for decades. IDSC would never have been so sloppy as to be detected in the first place.

The mole is definitely working with an outside element.

This was at once relieving and disquieting. The simple possibility Michael may have been directly observing him opened up innumerable questions skirting the line between the surreal and the sinister, and Samael was glad to be able to discount it. That there was a third party though, with enough influence to have swayed one or more of his own... This touched somewhat his worldview, rattled it slightly in ways in which it should not, at this point, have been able to.

Since it had been one of Samael's own, there was no use questioning Michael; the man wouldn't, couldn't, admit it even if he did know something. IDSC was proscribed the observation of all High Party members, and although Samael knew very well many ranking members had been observed, likely were still observed to this day, Lilith among them, he knew Michael would never admit to investigating members of Samael's or another High Party member's office.

When Samael had mentioned the discovery to him in their last virtual conference, Michael, a smug smile on his face, had offered to lend him a few of his agents, "For security," he'd said.

Samael had pressed him on this point, asked "Do you believe I'm in danger?"

To which Michael had responded, "Anyone with knowledge enough to bug your office surely knows who you are. Anyone who needs to do so is surely an enemy. Anyone who can do so is surely a threat."

He had no doubt that were Michael put to a polygraph, the very idea of which was laughable itself, the statements would prove to be completely true.

Keeping the conversation abstract, Samael had asked whether Michael knew of any group that *could* have perpetrated the act and had a will to do so, to which Michael had responded. "IDSC is currently tracking a few organizations that meet the criteria, yet none seem to have a direct connection to D.C.;" Michael had then paused to hit his pipe, which Samael had thought he could almost smell through the image on his wall, distant yet as New York was from The Capital. "We are currently looking into the matter," he'd said; "For now take my advice and accept my help."

And so he'd done just that, the IDSC agent presently trailing them, one of three who Michael assured him were among his best, a cold reminder of his reliance on the man.

I can't trust my own staff, but I can, have to, trust Michael.

He laughed aloud, drawing a sidelong glance from his companion.

He'd ordered the listening devices placed back where they'd been found, hoping the mole would reveal himself when he surfaced to collect their data. The possibility existed though that this wouldn't happen for weeks, months, who knew how long, as did the possibility there were other devices, in other places, which hadn't been found, that perhaps the mole was aware he'd been sniffed out.

Lilith was informing him of the current happenings in DHS, also of other events of interest in the cabinet generally, none of which was news to Samael. All was proceeding as planned, including the current president's scheduled decline in approval, which would help facilitate the installation of a candidate from the "other" party, who'd sound different, propose new initiatives and a better vision for the nation, but who'd nonetheless take orders from The Party as had all such men for nearly a century.

Presently they were just clearing the bridge over the west inlet, coming up on the Jefferson Monument.

He paused then beneath the leafless lattice of a cherry tree, turned toward her, eyes set on the monument in the near distance over her shoulder. "And what of this man from Oakland, Maccabeus was it? What news is there of him?"

She paused, expressionless, gathering her thoughts.

The IDSC man took a position on the opposite side of the tree, a respectful four meters away. Samael was fairly certain the man couldn't hear them from that distance, not without some sort of amplificatory device, yet regardless the point was of little concern. Samael's first assumption when dealing with IDSC was that they knew as much about what was going on as he, if not more, the way it should be, the way he'd envisioned it when first having its charter drafted, way back when he'd simply been First Secretary to The Party... long before his ascension to his present, unnamed position, the manner of which was a mystery to most and a frequent matter of speculation, yet not to Michael and certainly not to Lilith, who'd been... instrumental in its realization.

The warmth of her breath puffed condensation into the air; "News of him is very sparse. In truth we don't know very much at all, not even a decent description, although his existence has been verified by a number of reliable sources."

Bringing his gaze from the monument, "How in God's name can your people confirm his existence without having even seen him?" The touch of irritation in his voice would've been enough to make another flinch.

Lilith was unfazed; "That the activities we attribute to Maccabeus are actually the work of a single man is unclear, yet certainly they're the product of a single organization." She paused, sparing a look passed Samael at the IDSC man, presently with his back to them. "Our current thinking is he doesn't attend to all of his business personally, so as not to be tied directly to multiple incidents. But that there's a man called Maccabeus at the heart of this thing seems undeniable, so similar are the objectives and rhetoric of the cells we've discovered and infiltrated, so sure of his identity are the people who constitute them."

"And his goal is definitely guerilla in nature?"

She nodded, considering the surrounds; "That fact has been materially corroborated by a number of sources who have been approach by several disparate and for the most part anonymous agents seeking everything from small arms to elaborate communication equipment." Having finished her assessment, she turned back to him. "We were able to locate and detain three such agents, two men and one woman, all of whom informed us, 'The Maccabean Revolution was nigh upon us,' to quote one of them directly."

Samael returned to his contemplation of the monument; "How were these people dealt with?"

"After interrogation they were released," she paused, "Of course we conducted thorough reconnaissance of their homes and investigated their known associates. One of the men was found to have large stockpiles of white vinegar in his garage, another operates a fairly large greenhouse."

And now they've bugged my office, likely have sympathizers in other key locations as well.

Lilith continued, "We've been keeping close tabs on them; however, nothing has come up, and it's likely the Maccabean group is aware of their exposure."

The only organization I can trust to be completely untouched by these people is IDSC, and this only because Michael's so fastidious in the security and solidarity of his little empire, so skilled in the ways of intelligence and counterintelligence.

Samael began to walk once more, toward Jefferson's monument, Lilith keeping abreast, the IDSC man trailing behind.

If what Michael says is true there's really nothing to worry about.

That the so-called Maccabeans represented a real threat was hard to believe, and so Michael's summation *was* likely accurate. Yet the prospect of a public that would willingly accept, cheer, the imposition of IDSC security was almost too good to be true, and Samael had learned long ago to be wary of such things.

He halted his progress just as they neared the great white dome, turned to the IDSC agent. "Andrew, is it?"

The man gave a single nod.

"Wait here with Ms. Matthias. I will tour the monument alone."

AGENT IN CHARGE OF OPERATIONS

Andrew smiled in spite of himself, sat forward in his chair and leaned his head upon his hand,

It was amusing to have people think he was some sort of cold-blooded, complete badass, understandable as well. The others who'd accompanied him to D.C., like Amin, were experienced solders, former government agents. Fatik was from India where he'd been an agent of the Intelligence Bureau, and also like Amin he carried no accent; he was tall and lithe. Cooley, who hailed from Woodlawn in the Bronx, was a former Seal, as tall as Andrew yet nearly fifteen kilograms heavier, all muscle; he was powerful, impassive.

And then there was Andrew, at twenty-two years the youngest of the trio, who hailed from The Bay where he'd spent most of his time smoking weed with his friends and studying political science, with no military training and no real experience in counter insurgency or intelligence.

And he was in charge.

The impression this gave others was ironically about as far from the truth as could be imagined. His relative physical weakness was attributed to the nature of the command function, his youth to the obvious intelligence and skill he must surely posses. It was simply assumed he was, even at his young age, a veteran of several unknown, certainly dangerous and covert, operations and engagements. Michael chose only the best to be IDSC agents and operatives. Ranking agents, who had the power to detain and question even cabinet members, military officials, certainly anyone with whom Andrew would come in contact, must therefore be even more formidable, one as young as Andrew dangerous as a pit viper, around whom one stepped quickly and lightly.

He'd found the secret was to speak as little as possible. Imaginations ever more colorful than reality, never satisfied with the mundane, people filled the void with images and expectation that thankfully, hopefully, he'd never have to live up to, for he knew the threat against which they'd been sent to guard was immaterial.

In the intervening weeks since he'd initially come to D.C. with Michael, he'd been briefed in full about the man he was to guard, and eventually whom he was to kill.

What he'd learned filled him with disdain bordering revulsion, perhaps a touch of hate, but more than this it had impressed upon him the nature of The Party, Samael's role it its character and by extension the present state of the nation and world.

The necessity of what he'd been sent to do was quite clear, as was the line he now walked, a delicate balance between powers the likes of which he could barely comprehend, let alone rationally deal with.

Perhaps most importantly his new knowledge shed a good deal of light on the true nature of IDSC and its enigmatic chairman.

Beyond feeling inadequate to his task, out of place in his company, and generally overwhelmed, Andrew had found new assurance of the path he'd accepted.

This is exactly the kind of man who needs to die.

That he could utter this with such calm certainty, even to himself, knowing it wasn't empty talk, that he'd be the one to execute the order, spoke even more of the ways in which he'd changed in just a few months than did the company he now kept or his daily regimen.

Fatik and Cooley had actually, contrary to his initial summary, turned out to be quite good company.

Fatik's keen wit, clever and sharp, invoked a discourse strikingly similar to the play of language and concept to which he'd become accustomed hanging out with Peter and Thorin. Sure, the subject matter was... different, the humor more cold and severe, yet Andrew felt at ease with the man, although still he made all efforts to keep conversation concise, limited to the immediacies of their shared purpose and situation.

Cooley, Andrew had determined after much deliberation, actually *was* quite cool and likeable, a fact belied by the general form of his presence and the curt solemnity of his interactions.

They too seemed to take Andrew for a sort of prodigy, so young was he relative to both of the men currently under his command. Appearances, however, were everything, and Andrew had learned from watching Michael that people expected those in charge to be severe and aloof, distinct. He had no compunction against embodying any and all of these qualities, for the exact opposite reasons from those others were likely to infer.

Their stated purpose presently was the protection of Samael, his own security and staff unable to be trusted due to recent discoveries at Party Headquarters, discoveries Andrew knew had been entirely fabricated by IDSC.

The ruse had been his idea, developed back in New York in the lighted confines of his office on the thirty-third floor of the building on Greenwich Street. That he even had an office in such a place was perhaps just as surprising to Andrew as was his present position of authority. Sometimes it all seemed a little too surreal, as if at any moment he'd wake to the rude sound of his alarm back in Elmwood, just in time to make it to class before the beginning of lecture.

But his plan had worked, his presence in D.C., again in his own office, in Party Headquarters itself, proof.

Perhaps I *am* cut out for this.

Then again, if this were a dream I most certainly would be.

He made a mental note to keep an eye out for sudden and inexplicable knowledge of kung fu or an odd ability to fly.

You must learn how to throw yourself at the ground and miss.

He laughed then aloud, Adams' line bringing him a soft and secure vantage on the firmament, still solid, below in the distance.

I fell, tripped, long ago and have neglected to remember I forgot about the ground.

Edith...

Interrupted by a knock on the door.

"Yes?"

Fatik entered, bearing his report on the day's events, having apparently returned from Samael's home, where Andrew assumed Samael and Cooley were now, closed the door behind himself.

He stopped just inside the portal, studying Andrew's visage. "Is something wrong, sir?"

Andrew, lost in his thoughts, had neglected to hide them from his face.

Sitting up slightly, he drew a smoke from the pack that lay to his left, beyond the small pile of dossiers he'd been examining; "Nothing that can't be dealt with," sparked his cigarette, extending his hand for Fatik's report, which he'd later scan and forward to Michael's office in New York.

One thing Andrew had learned fairly quickly was that the reports, as they were intended not only for his eyes, were invariably overly formal, proper. Much of the information he required could not be determined from the detached accounts they contained.

Glancing through the pages just handed him, "Do you have anything to add?"

"Nothing of note, sir;" he paused. "He kept me at a fair distance most of the day."

Andrew looked up from the third page, looking at Fatik over its upheld edge. "I see he met with Ms. Matthias again today. Were you able to overhear the conversation?"

Andrew alone presently knew the full truth of their mission. Cooley and Fatik were under the belief they were indeed there to protect a High Party member from an existential threat, which of course they would do, if any such threat were to present itself; Andrew would ensure that. That Samael remain alive until Andrew received the order from Michael himself was, for some reason slightly beyond Andrew's explicit comprehension, of the utmost importance. Regardless, the indeterminacy introduced by this stricture certainly made his job more difficult than it otherwise would've been.

He knew Cooley and Fatik wouldn't report any such conversation they may have heard unless its content intersected with their known directive. He also knew they'd be alert and listening to anything they could, including Samael's private discussions, especially those he had with Lilith; they were professional intelligence men. Nothing slipped by them.

"I was not, sir." Grinned, "After we had returned to his home I was able to hear... other things."

Andrew knew well what he meant, having stood an evening post or two himself the past couple weeks.

"From now on I'd like you to make every effort to listen in on any conversation he has with her."

Fatik cocked his head slightly, the edge of a thought upon his lips, quickly sewn up. "Yes sir; of course, sir."

"You have a question?"

"Yes, sir. You think she is involved, sir?"

Tapping the ashes from his cigarette into the tray on the desk's rightmost extremity, Andrew sat back in his chair. "I think she's an important piece of the puzzle now before us, that our charge trusts her perhaps too much, that in their conversations there may be found the information we need to successfully conclude our task."

Apparently he'd learned more from Michael than he'd acknowledged, so easily did the half truths form on his tongue, spill therefrom.

Sometimes the truth and what we want to hear coincide.

Andrew shivered imperceptibly, nodded for Fatik to leave.

He shifted his chair to gaze out the window, cigarette held in his left hand, took a drag.

The snow that had begun to fall nearly two weeks ago had returned, its second appearance since, now collecting enough that plows moved the streets, lone behemoths with flashing yellow lights.

CHAPTER 8
MACCABEUS

JUST REGULAR PEOPLE

The mobilization was proceeding with remarkable speed.

It had been a scant five months since Jonathan had approached him at the market, since he and Amin had begun preparations for what was shaping up to be a rather large popular uprising, and already Peter felt vanishing the incredulity and cynicism with which he'd initially reacted to his proposed role.

They'd visited nearly every major city in the US within the first month alone, establishing contacts, sowing the seeds for further organization, setting the general tone of the movement, the entire tour paid for by Amin, who Peter assumed was funded directly by the IDSC.

That he found himself embroiled in an unfathomable conflict, between powers far greater than he, was undeniable. However, that this conflict placed him in a position of power, with a real opportunity to effect actual change in the nation, was also undeniable. And so Peter, knowing full well the precariousness of his position, had embraced his role, determining to see just how far the avenue before him stretched.

He'd not since found an end. He'd also not found any branchings, nor even side streets onto which he could turn. The path before him stretched on, set. At this point he really had no options, certainly no recourse. He had to continue.

The reception he'd received had be rather surprising; the traction of his message was at times overwhelming.

Growing up he'd lived in a world of set political structures. The unequivocal fact that peaceful protest and nonviolent political action were the only acceptable means of effecting change had been accepted, understood, with such heroes as Martin Luther King and Gandhi shining as beacons of hope in a world full of turmoil, a history rife with the misguided actions of those who'd foolishly turned to violence. He knew he'd not been alone in having had these assumptions.

The world, however, bent on dispelling the naïveté of the latter twentieth century, had changed.

Peter now acknowledged, as one born of earlier times never fully could have, that the success of King, the triumph of Gandhi, had only been realized due to the brute realities of their day.

Gandhi hadn't defeated the British through the sheer formidability of his fasting alone; he'd been aided by the Germans, by a world war.

That the civil rights movement in the US had achieved its ends wasn't the result of King's oratory alone or the thousands who'd stood with him in the face of repression and hate; it had done so simply because the Cold War had necessitated the US become united in at least a semblance of democratic spirit, that it reassert itself as a place of freedom so the war machine could proceed as planned, with the full support of a nation completely confident in its righteousness and commitment to liberty.

That the Vietnam protests had been completely superfluous while protests against segregation had been completely successful, or rather the reasons this was the case, had been overlooked. Neither party had during its tenure done anything at all to end hostilities, until, that is, the demands of the protesters happened to coincide with the plans of those in power.

He could not help but recall Heinlein. "Violence, naked force, has settled more issues in history than has any other factor. Breeds that forget this basic truth have always paid for it with their lives and their freedoms."

The gains of the labor movement, which had brought the nation from the pit of capitalist exploitation to the pinnacle of middle-class prosperity, had only been possible due to the willingness of workers to fight, literally, for their rights, And they'd been empowered by the nature of the market at the time, before mechanization had made the industrial laborer veritably extraneous, before globalization had allowed the alienation of labor markets from consumer markets, the outsourcing of labor to corrupt and impoverished states.

His entire life had been witness to the emerging truth that the people of the United States no longer mattered, yet only now could he see the natural end to which these considerations led.

Having never truly recovered from the depression that had marked the beginning of the twenty-first century, the nation had limped along, carrying a constant structural unemployment rate of over ten percent, now creeping upwards, slowly but surely.

Far from addressing the issue, the government had simply withdrawn from the public sphere, its patrons moving to capitalize on the desperation of the people, stripping the nation not just of stable economy but of dignity. That after nearly two decades of such treatment people were ready to do something beyond mere crying, to move beyond asking politely for help that was not and never had been forthcoming, was understandable.

The majority of Americans hadn't actually made such a movement—Andrew had been correct in his summation of their complacency—yet nonetheless in his recent travels Peter had encountered a not insignificant number of people who'd lost their faith in democracy, people with little care for the sanctity of private property or the wisdom of those who'd done well for themselves in the manipulation of capital.

People ready to act.

Not Marxists radicals bent on the realization of a fantastical workers utopia, not mere disgruntled workers and citizens who'd had a bad year and felt the need to lash out, these were regular people, of all ages and socioeconomic backgrounds, who'd simply seen through the façade of their society and government. For if democracy was the rule of the people, the United States had long ago left democracy behind, settling instead for the base act of voting, devoid of real political force or the possibility of actualizing popular will.

This was nothing new to Peter. However, there was a large distance, a chasm of ideology and will, between simply acknowledging the political machine of the country had oligarchic tendencies and actually accepting one lived in an oligarchy. To move from sentiments of injustice and the despair of economic impotence to a will that fully admitted that neither ideal nor morality had any true bearing on reality was itself a significant progression; to move from this admission to the determination one would actually do something about it was... something else altogether.

The people he'd enlisted in his purpose weren't immoral; they were perhaps the most moral, tempered by the cold forge of reality, no longer hiding from the fact that moral action had no place in the politics of reality. They didn't set themselves against the insidious tyranny of placation and economy because it was the right thing to do, but because it was the only thing they *could* do. Moved not by anger, not by envy or self-righteousness, nor even by the desire to realize a better world for themselves and their children, the companions of the Maccabean Revolution instead set themselves on the path to war because it was the only way in which they could actually be free.

For the few, the many, who'd joined him, given choices—well defined by those in a position to benefit from any taken—were unacceptable. That they could buy a new car or 3-D television, that they could wear the clothes from a certain designer while disdaining those from another, no longer served. That they were periodically given the choice of candidate A or candidate B wasn't enough.

And ahead the avenue stretched.

The revolution Peter fomented wasn't that of class warfare, for he'd found adherents from all walks of life. It didn't spring from religion or ideology; these served not to expand freedom but to limit it. Peter's revolution grew from the need of every man, every woman, to be free in truth, not the freedom of anarchy nor the freedom to do any particular thing, but instead the actual freedom to write their own stories, to be able to determine options themselves and not merely be satisfied and grateful they had choices at all.

The evolution of man had led to this spirit, just as the evolution of economy had established the frame within which the tensions necessary for its expression were able to be realized.

As one man he'd met in Chicago had put it: "I don't care about the future, what this future will be. I don't care if our actions bring about the death of us all, or if in the course of our actions we are lost. Life itself is meaningless without freedom. To live a life determined by others, no matter how comfortable or odious, is to live no life at all."

Peter had pressed him, "Yet certainly being alive is more of a life than being dead."

To which the man had responded, "There's more life in a death chosen freely than there is in simply walking a given path."

Peter had seen to it that the man, Charlie by name, Mr. Charlie by popular opinion, was given broad discretionary powers.

At Amin's urging Peter had also taken a pseudonym for himself, one that invoked the spirit of the rebellion and would serve as a rallying cry throughout the nation.

The name he'd chosen, with due respect to Jonathan, his enigmatic benefactor, was John Maccabeus, after the great general of ancient Israel. Already people had taken to referring to their emerging organization as the Maccabeans, to the coming action as the Maccabean Revolution.

He could only hope the name would remain, for only successful revolutions were deemed such.

ON DIVISION AVENUE

Thorin moved himself far from the edge of the road as the plow passed, having learned the hard way that not doing so entailed wet shoes and slush-covered pants, an uncomfortable mix in the middle of February, one of the coldest and snowiest anyone in D.C. could remember.

He didn't like leaving Aleta alone at the apartment; the baby was due any day now. Yet on this night he was compelled to venture the icy sidewalks and snow-covered streets, on his way to a meeting called by several former members of The Movement who since Mark's betrayal had come to be associated with a new group known as the Maccabeans.

The Maccabeans were a group unlike any with which he'd ever been associated. In the time since they'd first appeared in D.C., some two months ago, there'd been no call to rally, no protests executed or even scheduled. They hadn't, as far as he knew, proposed any actions at all, making this meeting, to which he'd been invited earlier that very day, unannounced and set to occur much later than the usual political forum, all the more intriguing. What could possibly require such an impromptu gathering was beyond him, yet there had been something in Benjamin's voice when he'd called that afternoon, a certain nervous excitement, that Thorin had been unable to deny.

And so he found himself in the not-so-upscale neighborhood of Lincoln Heights sometime approaching 10:30, having taken a bus from Georgetown across the river, searching for an address on Division Avenue that thus far had eluded him.

He shrugged his coat up on his shoulders, ducking within the upturned collar.

Fucking Benjamin.

It was then he saw Marquetta, a sexy Latina and former leading vixen of The Movement, whom he'd recognize anywhere. Even in the dead of winter, bundled in a down parka and scarf, she was unable to conceal her unadulterated sexiness, the fine curve of her ass visible still below its enveloping quilts. She stood before a medium-sized concrete building, the edifice of some sort of warehouse, smoking a cigarette in the yellowed light of a sodium streetlamp.

As he neared, she turned, peering out at him from the updrawn hood of her coat. "Thorin," she smiled, a thing that always had the curious effect of making his heart beat just a little bit faster, "I'm glad you were able to come." She pursed her lips around her smoke, pulling a hit; "Most of the others are already here."

He smiled as well; "Do you know what this is about?" paused, quickly looking away, toward the door of the building, slight stains of red growing on his cheeks.

"I'm not entirely sure," she too glanced toward the building; "The Maccabeans asked us to come here, to invite 'only those we could absolutely trust.'" She pulled one last time on her smoke before letting it fall to the sidewalk, there to be quickly smothered by the heel of her boot. "It's the first we've heard from them in more than a month."

"And what was the word then?"

"That we should determine whom we could trust and wait for them to contact us."

Thorin chuckled, returned his gaze to the woman before him, focusing safely on a point somewhere to the right of, a little down from, her rather enchanting eyes.

"I know, right?" She laughed as well, pulling his eyes involuntarily to the gentle flex of her neck, upward to where her lips, red even in the sickly light of the streetlamp, curved slightly at the corners.

Thorin laughed again, this time at himself.

I fucking need to get out more.

"Shall we?" She nodded toward the door.

Grinned wickedly, "Ladies first."

THE BEST KIND OF FANTASY

Amin directed the car north on the Anacostia Freeway, traveling slightly faster than the general flow of traffic, now in the passing lane, circumventing a rather large tour bus, the kind for tourists not for rock-stars. Peter assumed it must be headed for its home port, as late in the evening as it was, too late to actually be in service.

This is neither the time nor the place for tourists.

He was a little nervous, perhaps more so than he'd been since the first meeting so many months ago in The Bay, when he'd been unsure of his position, incredulous of his purpose.

Those days now seemed distant, those before vague and ill-defined. Sure, he recalled with clarity many moments of the summer, many before, yet his experiences of the intervening Autumn and Winter overshadowed the movements of his earlier life, which now seemed amateur, without object or order.

Amin, his bodyguard and advisor, sponsor, was the closest thing he now had to a friend, which was to say he didn't really have friends any longer, not really. He'd not seen or spoken to either Andrew or Thorin since they'd parted ways. Aside from Amin, those with whom he did speak didn't even know his proper name.

He was Maccabeus, a man with no history and thus nothing to interfere with his purpose.

Amin caught him in the rearview mirror; "You are ready?"

Peter laughed, ashed his cigarette out the window. "Sure," took a hit, "It's not like I've never done this before."

But the truth was this meeting was different. This night found him in Washington D.C., the heart of the beast, where thus far he'd not travelled. The movement, however, had reached the point at which a visit to D.C. was called for, and against Amin's warnings of the treacherous nature of The Capital, he'd decided to make a personal appearance.

When things do begin, the front here will be perhaps the most important of all, where action will be covert, hidden until the last minute.

That he had a plan for the Maccabean Revolution, a fairly detailed blueprint outlining the path he wished to follow, complete with defaults and contingencies, was itself a thing of wonder. That he actually believed the plan would work was a thing of faith, for which another name was delusion.

Self delusion is the best kind of fantasy.

But what of the intrusion of reality?

Irrelevant.

Self delusion, after all, is itself just another word for will. An encompassing delusion, the belief one's vision is true, that it can be actual, makes freedom possible.

The power of realization was his, made potent by a stubborn refusal to admit the impossibility of his end.

A thing is only impossible until it is not.

"How much longer until we arrive?"

"Not long. Perhaps five or ten minutes."

"When we do, I'd like you to stay in the car."

As expected, he didn't like the idea at all, his expression of disapproval clear even in the narrow scope of the reflection. "I'm not sure that is a wise decision."

"The decision is not yours to make. It is mine."

"Need I remind you of the delicate nature of this particular situation? I..."

"The decision is mine, Amin. I *have* to go; you do not. And I'd prefer that this group, any eyes that may be among them, be unaware of your existence." He finished his cigarette, flicked it out the window; "You know as well as I D.C. will be a crucial front in what is to come. I'd like to reserve the possibility of your returning as an anonymous citizen, not as the personal confidant of John Maccabeus."

Amin knew he had no ground to stand on. The IDSC had, for whatever reason, chosen to charge Peter with this task. For now, Peter was in charge, Maccabeus, the unwitting father of the revolution.

He kept his silence, exiting the freeway onto East Capitol Street.

Peter turned from the mirror, closed his eyes, mind encompassing the coming meeting and what would there be said.

I will be honest with them.

REUNION

The building was indeed a warehouse, small as far as those sorts of things went, but still a large space, devoid of internal structure, without even seats to provide direction or focus.

Thorin could recognize a number of those who milled about within, fellow former members of The Movement, yet to his surprise most of the thirty-some people were unknown to him.

Doing his best to mingle, feeling awkward and more than a little apprehensive, he waited for whatever was going to happen. Having no wish to rehash the disappointments of the past Fall, he stood apart, away from the greater mass of people, toward the south side of the space, biding his time and watching the others as they too waited.

People continued to trickle in as the minutes passed, yet he found himself more interested in observing Marquetta, who stood with her back to him, speaking with a group of men he didn't recognize, than he was in cataloging the number of people present he didn't know. The air inside the warehouse, although significantly warmer than the winter chill that ruled the streets outside, was nonetheless fairly cold; she, along with most of the others, himself included, still wore her coat. Regardless, he enjoyed the view.

"What would Aleta say if she could see you now?" A familiar voice shook him from his observation.

He turned toward its source.

"I mean, you're practically fucking her with your eyes." A large smile greeted him, embraced him with a great bear of a hug; "It's been too long."

Lacking words to express his surprise and strong upwelling of emotion, Thorin simply maintained the hug, just a little longer than was perhaps usual for such a reunion.

Releasing his friend, he stepped back, attempting to regain his bearings, blurted, "What the fuck are _you_ doing _here?_"

Peter grinned, taking in the gathering of people. "I'd ask the same of you, Thor." He sparked a cigarette. "I mean, what are _you_ doing associating with this riffraff?"

Thorin laughed, for once glad to hear his not-so-flattering nickname, so long had it been since he'd been with anyone who knew him well enough to use it. "Holy shit, man; it's good to see you," paused, "I... um, well, I don't really know what I'm doing here." He grinned in spite of himself; "I was invited by some old friends."

"So I take it you know the girl with the incredible ass?" He nodded toward Marquetta, still engaged in conversation.

Thorin had no response.

"I see;" he hit his smoke, turning back to face Thorin directly. "Aleta would be quite pissed indeed."

His grin could have devoured Thorin whole.

Just then Benjamin, apparently the organizer of the gathering, slid the deadbolt of the door, the noise echoing loudly enough for everyone to hear.

"I think we're ready to begin," he said with an air of finality, began to walk toward the mass of people.

"To be honest," Peter said quietly in the new still of the place, still soft enough that only Thorin could hear, "I didn't expect you to be here."

He moved away then, butting his smoke on the floor, on a path that would intercept Benjamin, toward the west end of the building, across from the entrance.

Thorin, as yet unmoved by Benjamin's theatrics, remained at the margin.

The waiting people turned as Benjamin passed, followed him with their eyes until all were set in the same direction, to the west, where he met with Peter, shook his hand.

What the hell? Peter doesn't know Ben. He's never even been to...

Turning toward the assembly, "Thank you all for coming here; I know this isn't the most welcoming venue for a gathering such as this." He smiled at Benjamin, back to the gathered people; "It was the best we could do on such short notice, the spontaneity of which was needed to avoid unnecessary entanglements." He turned, arms held behind his back, took a few steps away from both Benjamin and the crowd, rounded on them all. "My name is John Maccabeus."

THE CELL IN D.C.

Thorin watched with dumb attention, listening yet not really hearing what his friend said.

That Peter was Maccabeus, the enigmatic leader of the Maccabean group, was simply too absurd. He didn't believe it for an instant.

What kind of game is Peter playing at here?

Why would he pose to be Maccabeus? Why does Benjamin think he is?

Derision filled him.

Does he not even know who Maccabeus actually is?

That Ben and the others would enlist in an organization about which they knew so little was simply unacceptable. That they'd bring him here to be a part of... whatever this was... knowing they knew nothing, Thorin found insulting, angering.

I should be home with Aleta, not here in this den of fools.

Yet even then he knew he was glad he'd come, so welcome had been his reunion with Peter, long overdue.

Thorin looked at his friend, actually observing him.

Peter was different. He looked stronger, more self-assured; his face bore new lines. He didn't speak in the manner of a stoned philosophy major from Berkeley, more full of ideas than convictions. Standing before more than thirty people, most older than he, with more experience in life and the politics of protest, Peter was confident, assertive. He had the unswerving attention of everyone in the room besides Thorin.

"...in D.C will be at the forefront of the movement, silent, underground, yet all the more so important. It will be here the final battle is waged. I cannot tell you more than this now. But if you trust me, we will have a chance to change this country forever." He paused for a moment, gathering his thoughts. "I've been to every corner of this nation, and I tell you We are strong, ready. There are now more Maccabeans in most cities than there are police; together we form a body greater than the national guard itself. This cell here in D.C. is the smallest, and I ask that you don't involve anyone who's not now present. The nature of your function demands delicacy, tact."

What in God's name is he talking about.

He paused to take a breath. "We are aware many of our cells have been discovered, infiltrated, by the enemy, that..."

A man near the front of the crowd interrupted, "You mean the government."

"...that therefore these groups are more useful for misdirection, misinformation, than for direct action. Yet this is precisely as we have planned." He turned to the man who'd spoken; "And our enemy is *not* the government. The government is a fiction, an abstraction. Our enemy is The Party that pulls the strings of our government. This Party, though clandestine and obscure, is real. Government is *not* inherently an instrument of oppression. Government as it should be is nothing more than the expression of the people's will, bound by rules to ensure equity and liberty; it is nothing more than that. To defeat the government itself is to defeat the people of this nation, and they are not our enemies. The end of The Maccabean revolution is not the dissolution of the government, but a return of the government into the hands of the people."

Then, in an aberration of public oration, Peter, Maccabeus that is, sparked a cigarette.

Thorin grinned.

"The means of achieving this end are not simple, for The Party is entrenched in not just our government but also our society and economy; it is powerful, ubiquitous. In our endeavor we will strive to extricate it from this nation, in all its forms and guises."

He seemed to be approaching a conclusion, hit his cigarette.

"To this end we will spare no measure, however dangerous. We will stop at nothing, and nothing will stop us. You here today will have to watch as our revolution unfolds, silent and waiting, a difficult thing for those with conviction and conscience. This is why I've come here today in person, so you'll know we are not a myth, that Maccabeus is flesh and blood, a regular person as yourselves." Paused. "Look around yourselves. Those gathered here are your brothers and sisters, bound not by authority but by faith. Trust each other. Involve no others in what is to come, and know we are all equal before the eyes of God."

"I trust those of you who do not wish to join us will do us the favor of keeping quiet; I know all here were invited because people in whom I have faith have placed their trust in you. Do not betray that trust now. All I ask is that you allow us the chance to change this nation for the better. Though I cannot ask that you betray yourself, I would ask that you take a hard look within to determine whether the truth of your heart and will is aligned with the path on which we, the Maccabeans, are set."

Thorin began to move closer, momentarily met eyes with Peter as he moved his gaze from one face in the crowd to another.

How my friend has changed in just a few short months.

He looked then to himself, saw the same man he'd been when last he'd seen Peter, unchanged, one among a crowd.

Maccabeus stood alone.

"Those who feel this is not for them, who do not wish to proceed with us, I kindly ask to leave now."

Some of those gathered shifted uneasily; others looked around to see just exactly what everyone else was doing.

A moment passed.

Then, three from the crowd, two men and one woman, whom Thorin didn't know, slowly disentangled themselves, moving toward the door. Benjamin followed close behind, meeting them, shaking their hands, before sliding open the bolt and seeing them outside. He returned to where Maccabeus waited, resuming his place at the front of the group, slightly to the right.

Peter continued; "For the rest of you, I'd like to now drop all manner of pretense and affect." He took a final pull, dropping the cigarette to the floor, smothered it with the sole of his shoe. "This group, of which we are all a part, this cell in D.C., is the only one in the nation I know can be trusted completely."

Here Thorin felt compelled to speak, not as a friend of Peter but as a member of the newly christened group of Maccabeans. "Why is that?"

Many turned toward him momentarily, surprised to hear such a question called from the rear, returned their gaze to Maccabeus, awaiting his response.

"That is a good question, my friend;" the term was clearly used in a general sense. "Because I've personally seen to it that this group will remain off the radar of any and all people and organizations who would or could possibly oppose us."

Thorin nodded, unseen by the others except for Peter, who responded with a slight smile, for Thorin alone.

"Now, gather around. This is not the time for a speech but a discussion in truth. Let us get down to the matter at hand."

PUZZLE RING

Amin sat silently in the black coupe, observing the entrance of the building Peter had entered perhaps half an hour earlier, up a ways, on a side street to the north, Gay Street.

He'd never smoked in his life, yet then, recalling the calm cigarettes seemed to impart people, their ability to keep one occupied when nothing was really happening, he almost wished he did.

For reasons unknown to Amin, Peter had determined this meeting was necessary. That at the last minute he'd decided Amin wouldn't accompany him was disconcerting, unprecedented.

He only half believed the reason Peter had given him earlier.

As he watched, the door to the place opened, with three people emerging, two headed north while the other turned south.

So he has finished his preamble.

Amin knew the following meeting would likely stretch longer than whatever introduction had compelled these three to leave. He hoped, however, that Peter could conclude his business here more quickly than usual. He didn't like being in D.C.. Even in a bad part of town, away from The Capital, the risk of encountering unfriendly elements was high. In D.C. always were the movements of people monitored, mostly by IDSC, but here The Party would have its own eyes and ears. He could only hope those who'd been called to the meeting were of a relatively low profile, that the three who'd just left wouldn't go to the authorities.

He took off his ring, a Turkish puzzle composed of eight interwoven loops of white gold, began to deconstruct its knot. The ring had been with him for many years, and he'd found comfort in its loops and folds, the way they joined perfectly when together, only to fall easily apart once just a few were loosed.

His present assignment, working with the boy Peter to organize a rebellion, had lain on his mind from the start, so different was it from other assignments The Chairman had given him. The involvement of Jonathan, whom he'd only before seen in passing, who always seemed involved in some counterintelligence scheme or another, who like Amin was an operative, marked with a silver seal, quite different from an agent or enforcer, made the matter all the more intriguing. Not that he had doubts; his faith in and devotion to The Council was as strong as ever. He simply knew he wasn't in full possession of the facts.

The Chairman has deemed that I should remain in the dark.

He shuffled the loops of the broken-down ring in the palm of his hand, feeling the coolness that had crept into them.

Regardless, his duty was clear: Keep the boy safe and on the path on which he'd been set. Follow as closely as possible his directions. Avoid contact with both IDSC and Party agents.

This last was nearly impossible, and already Amin had been forced to contact The Tower to resolve more than a few incidents involving inadvertent IDSC exposure, to on one occasion remove the threat of a Party intelligence officer who'd infiltrated a gathering in Chicago. Here in D.C., however, such stopgap measures wouldn't work; requests for help would be denied. IDSC could not be implicated in the Maccabean rebellion. The Chairman had made this explicitly clear.

He began to knot the loops of the ring together, a complex yet soothingly simple operation, one he could do, preferred to do, by feel alone, looked up at the door to the warehouse from which now poured a number of people.

It would appear he had enough presence of self to finish quickly.

Of the people who exited none were Peter.

He'd also, perhaps in a rush to have everyone on their way, allowed them all to leave at once, causing something of a scene so late on a Thursday night. Thankfully, the large mass of people, perhaps thirty in all, did seem to have the good sense to not linger together, quickly finding their ways to vehicles, some hurrying down the snow covered sidewalk, north and south.

Several minutes passed, the street and sidewalk before the building deserted, lightly falling snow marking time, slow and extended,

Still though, Peter himself hadn't exited the building.

Then he saw him walk out with another man, looking to be older by at least ten years, who paused for a moment to lock the door of the warehouse. Amin recognized him as Benjamin Hale, a lesser-known activist in the area and former member of The People's Movement for Democratic Change.

Amin smiled as formerly disparate parts of a large and encompassing puzzle settled into a sort of rectitude, continuities made clear… at least more so than they'd previously been.

From a distance he saw Peter move to stand on the sidewalk beneath the light of a streetlamp, large flakes of snow finding illumination as they settled around him, sparking a cigarette, apparently waiting for the man to join him.

He placed the ring, now fully reassembled, back on his left middle finger, moved to start the car.

Before he could do so two large white SUV's, fully tinted, pulled up before the building, directly in front of the lamp beneath which Peter stood. From their confines burst five large men wearing dark suits, who quickly and rather easily surrounded both Peter and Benjamin, forcing them into the vehicles, one to each.

As Amin watched, unable to act yet knowing full well what was happening, they sped away, south, making a hard right onto the first crossing, fishtailing slightly in the inch or two of snow blanketing the street.

CHAPTER 9
PRELUDE

AN UNEXPECTED VISITOR

A leta looked up from her computer at a knock on the door, grateful for a break from the all-encompassing task of ordering crucial supplies and toys for her expected daughter.

Thorin must have finished early.

He'd left the house perhaps an hour before, on his way to some gathering or another, the likes of which Aleta, in delicate state and somewhat cranky... her back was *killing* her... had long since forgone the pleasure.

The knock came again.

"Just a fucking second!" she barked, finalizing her order of assorted sun dresses and multi-textured, variously-colored rattles, a few cute onesies.

Stupid, stoned motherfucker probably forgot his keys again.

She set the notebook on the coffee table, strode to the door, flicking the deadbolt open, set herself back on the couch, picked back up the notebook.

Again, a knock at the door.

"It's unlocked!"

The door swung slowly open.

Aleta, patience worn thin by a long evening of internet shopping, didn't look up. "Did you get the strawberries?"

Out of season as they were, slightly weird and crunchy, she nonetheless could have devoured an entire flat, two flats.

"Aleta?"

The voice was clearly feminine.

She looked up, craning her neck to peer around the corner of the living room, to where Edith stood awkwardly at the threshold, looking rather pregnant as well in a dark wool coat, jeans and a t-shirt stretched tight by the round protrusion of her belly. She wore a backpack upon her shoulders.

Jumping from the couch with enough speed to bring a sharp pain to her abdomen, "Edith!" She hurried over to where the other woman stood; "I haven't seen you in forever!"

For her part, Edith smiled; "Hello, Aleta."

Backing slightly away from the door, Aleta motioned for Edith to enter. "Come in! Come in!" Noticing the overexcitement in her voice yet too excited to moderate it, "What are you doing here?!" She led Edith into the apartment. "Take off your bag," motioning to the couch, "Have a seat!" She sat down in the loveseat set perpendicular to the couch, on the far side of the coffee table from the door, quickly got back up; "Can I get you something? Are you thirsty?" moving toward the kitchen, a kitchenette really, sharing the same space as the room in which they now stood.

"I'm OK, Aleta;" she lowered herself onto the couch. "Some water would be nice," smiled.

"How have you been?!"

"I've been good; traveling a lot. And you and Thorin?"

Aleta returned, handing Edith a tall glass of water, accepted demurely. "We're well," sat down in the loveseat; "He's out right now at some kind of meeting."

Grinned, "Are you disappointed I don't have any strawberries?"

Aleta laughed. "Maybe a little."

Having regained some of her composure, she reevaluated her guest. Edith looked good, healthy. Her skin, instead of the pale, winter fish-belly of Aleta's, was tanned, and not the reddish-orange of a booth but a deep golden glow, sun-kissed.

She felt a slight tinge of jealousy.

"What have you been up to?" Paused, "What brings you here?" Reevaluated, "How did you know where we live?"

Edith laughed again, a light thing set in marked contrast to Aleta's still slightly excited barrage of questions. "Through the Georgetown website."

Aleta motioned for her to continue.

"I was driving through the area, on my way to New York," took a sip of water, "I'm sorry I didn't call first, but for some reason the site only has your address."

Aleta chuckled, settling herself back into the seat a little. "Yeah... We decided to take the number down after the third call we got offering us *amazingly* low rates on student loans," grinned.

Edith also smiled; "I see," set her glass on the table.

"And where have you been? You look incredible." Looking down at her pallid, sickly-seeming arm, back to Edith, "I take it somewhere far from here?"

"I've been around, down south mostly, New Orleans, Texas; I was in Mexico for a while, visited the Mayan ruins."

"And I've been here, studying and generally having a miserable time at school." She couldn't help the large grin that graced her face; "I'm sooo jealous."

Edith turned from her to gaze out the window, to the right, opposite the kitchen, to the bright, halide-lit space there pictured, where snow had again begun to fall, "I've also been alone." Turned to face Aleta once more, "Don't be so quick to disparage what you have. Be grateful."

Abashed, Aleta sewed up her mouth, stifling the comment about to spring therefrom. "You've changed." Seeing the startled look on Edith's face, "Not in a bad way," smiled, "But you're definitely different, more confident. Stronger."

Edith retrieved her glass from the table; taking a sip she again gazed out the window. "Maybe a little. It's been an enlightening year."

"And your baby, is… it well?" paused awkwardly; "Do you know if it's a boy or a girl?"

"No, I don't, but I've taken to referring to him as a boy. Seems weird to call him 'it,' and I as far as I know he's quite well." She laughed, "I haven't heard any complaints yet, at least."

"We're having a daughter;" excitement, of a different kind, tinged her voice.

"That's wonderful, Aleta." She sounded genuinely happy. "Thorin will make a wonderful father for her," laughed again, "I can totally see him with a little girl."

Aleta grinned, blushed.

"You know he's gonna be the biggest softy ever."

"Have you told Andrew yet?" she asked, immediately wishing she'd not.

"No," a touch of melancholy, "I haven't spoken with him since I left New York." She sat forward on the couch; "Have you guys seen him?"

"…No. I know Thorin hasn't spoken with him at all, with Peter either." She glanced away from the other woman's face. "Those two have dropped off the map completely. Both of their numbers have been deactivated."

"I see." She seemed contemplative; "So you don't know if he's still in New York."

A hint of resignation, "No."

The conversation had, through Aleta's unwitting question, moved to matters just a little too somber.

"Don't feel bad. You're gonna make *me* feel bad." Edith smiled. "Let's pretend it never came up."

Meeting her smile with one of her own, "So what would you then have us do?"

"Do you have any ice-cream?"

Aleta let out a giggle. "Tons."

WTF

What the FUCK.

Thorin was partially dumbfounded, partially full of thundering adrenaline, mostly just fucking scared for his friend, two of his friends, moments ago abducted from before the building they'd only minutes before together occupied.

He stepped out of the shadow of the building beside which he'd been standing, across the street from the warehouse. He'd intended to catch Peter after the meeting, once everyone else was gone..

One of those three who left must have informed the authorities.

The thought touched his mind only briefly; no sooner had it formed than he found himself racing across the street to where Peter had stood, smoking a cigarette.

Looking down now in the bright of the streetlamp, he could see a Camel, maybe half consumed, burning fitfully amid a soft blanket of flakes.

He cast about himself, trying to think, to figure out what he should do, despair beginning to well from within him.

I can't do anything.

The sound of footfalls approaching, soft yet distinct in the snow, met his right ear as he looked from his contemplation of the cigarette to see from whom they came. A man, older than he, with dark skin, was approaching at a run from the north. He wore a dark suit, no jacket or hat.

He reached the province of the lamp, slowed; "What are you doing here?"

Thorin paused a moment, taking in the man, the strangeness of his sudden appearance. He hadn't been at the meeting; Thorin had never seen him before.

"I could ask the same of you." He took a step toward the man; "Better yet, *who* are you, and what do you have to do with my friend's abduction?"

The man stopped where he was, yet a meter or two from the sidewalk, "You're his friend?"

"I am," prepared for whatever horrible fate would surely befall one who made such a claim, not a minute since Peter had been literally gaffled from the very spot he himself now stood.

"If you're his friend, what is his name?"

Thorin quirked an involuntary eyebrow.

He squared his jaw; "I'm not telling you anything."

"I know you were in the meeting with Maccabeus; I saw you leave several minutes ago when it broke," took a step toward him, "so I know you know who he is," another. "Yet I also don't know if you can be trusted, and I'm certain none of *Maccabeus's* new friends can be trusted," stopped, perhaps a meter from where Thorin stood. "So I will ask you again if you know his name."

The man was lithe, poised, certainly alert yet disconcertingly calm, merely an arms length away. Thorin, knowing it could be folly but also knowing that alone he had no way to help his friend, simply responded. "His name is Peter."

"And who are you?"

"Thorin."

The man eased up slightly, a grin cracking slightly upon his face. "Thor... He has spoken of you frequently." He moved beside Thorin, sparing a glance at the cigarette, now wet through, no longer smoldering. "I'm Amin, and I'm Peter's friend as well."

"You were waiting for him?"

"I was."

"Do you know who took him?"

Amin glanced down the road to where the SUVs had disappeared. "Those weren't the police, certainly not the FBI or any official government agency, not the way they simply tossed them in the vehicles like that. The government is... usually more polite." Turned back to Thorin; "But I have a pretty good idea.."

"Do you know where they've taken him?" Thorin sounded on the verge of panic, knew it, purposefully slowed his cognitions, "or rather where they'd be likely to take him?"

"Perhaps... I will have to check a few things." Paused, "I'm sure I can figure it out."

"Let's not waste any time. Do you have a vehicle? Perhaps if we leave now we ca..."

They both looked up as a woman, Marquetta, approached from the south. She smiled, giving Thorin a slight wave.

"She's with you?" Amin looked to Thorin.

Perhaps a little too quickly, "Absolutely not."

Amin flashed a quizzical expression, quickly banished. "She was also at the meeting though."

"Yes."

They both turned to fully address her.

"Where is Benjamin?" She asked, looking to the locked door of the warehouse.

Thorin's countenance bespoke incredulity. "You didn't see?"

She laughed; "See what? I was just down the street there, getting the car. I was supposed to come pick up Ben after he was done closing up." She paused, looking from Amin to Thorin, sharply back to Amin, a question upon her lips, unvoiced. To Thorin, "Seriously, where is he?" Glanced over her shoulder, "Some friggin asshole in a fucking SUV just totally fucked my car, didn't even stop. Just sped off."

"Then you have your answer." Amin studied her, "Maccabeus and Benjamin were taken not two minutes ago, abducted from this very spot."

She looked to Thorin.

Who looked quickly to Amin, back to Marquetta, "We're not sure who. But we think we can find out."

The reality of what they were telling her had apparently begun to sink in, for an edge of worry, a panic akin to that which also beset Thorin, entered her voice; "How the hell do we do that?"

They looked to Amin, who reached inside his suit coat, retrieving what appeared to be a cell phone. "Let me make a call."

FUCK

A hundred times, a thousand, Peter cursed his hubris, wedged in the back of a speeding vehicle with his hands bound behind him by a plastic zip-tie, between two imposing men, there trapped.

I should never have come here.

He'd convinced himself it had to be done, thought he could be in and out of D.C. like the wind. Thus far everything had gone so smoothly, easily. He knew though that this had been in part due to IDSC aid, and now, revisiting Amin's protests that IDSC wouldn't be able to help in D.C., he wondered just how much of his success these past months *had* been engendered by his mysterious sponsor.

Peter had often thought of what he'd do in a situation like this.

He'd tell his captors his real name, that he was part of the Maccabean resistance, secure his release as soon as possible. By his reckoning, anyone who'd kidnap him would be working for The Party; they'd release him after questioning and observe his movements, as they'd done with other Maccabeans who'd been detained. Yet here his abductors likely knew he'd been the one speaking at the meeting, making matters more complicated.

Will they release me if they actually think I'm Maccabeus?

Looking at himself now, he didn't think *he* believed it. He was young, weak, easily manhandled by a couple of thugs in three piece suits, certainly not a revolutionary figure. He looked like a college kid who'd had a rough night on the town.

His captors had taken him across the river, toward downtown, speeding the whole way. They'd seemed to be heading for The Capital, yet instead had come to a large brick building, perhaps six-hundred meters distant therefrom, pulled into an alley that cut along its north side.

He was literally hoisted out of the SUV by his arms, carried to a basement entrance set against the side of the building, double-doors bound with a thick chain and padlock.

The driver exited the vehicle; hurrying around its front to unlock the chain. He pulled it free, swung both doors open to reveal a set of concrete stairs wide enough for Peter's two new friends to toss him down, which they did, slamming the doors closed above him.

He heard the chain being pulled back into place.

Fuck.

The trauma of his fall was momentarily numbed by a dawning awareness of his situation.

Hands still bound, his left shoulder had born the brunt of the force; as he raised himself it gave forth a sharp pain, enough to drop him once again, face first, to the floor.

Not dislocated, but almost.

He regained his feet, slowly, a difficult task without the use of his hands or arms.

Looking around, he could see that the room, although certainly of the basement variety, was more of a stock-room, or rather a receiving room, impeccably clean, capped on the far side by a large, featureless, stainless steel door, without a knob or visible latch.

He was trapped.

Two panels of fluorescent lights cast the room in stark detail, of which there was very little.

He had only a short time to ponder this before the door swung open, revealing a beautiful woman, blond, with eyes like ice and a smirk upon her lips. Who stood holding a pistol, leveled at him.

"Hello... Maccabeus is it?"

"What have you done with Benjamin?"

She laughed, a delicate thing that sprung from her throat, melodious; "He should be here shortly. The drivers were instructed to take different routes." Her laughter resolved into a sadistic smile, "Fortunately, *you* have arrived first."

She motioned with the gun for him to exit the room, trailing him down a long, fairly broad hallway, brightly lit, which reached several meters before coming to an intersection. She flicked the barrel to the right.

"I've wanted to meet you for some time," following him around the turn, "to be honest I'd begun to think you were a fiction." She again laughed. "You're not quite what I'd expected;" derision poured from every word.

He remained silent, set on speaking as little as possible, until he knew exactly where he stood.

Having walked perhaps twenty meters, passed a number of featureless doors, they reached a T. She directed him to the left, where he could see terminate the hallway, less than fifteen meters beyond. The rooms here were fronted by doors of stainless steel, fixed with large deadbolts. One to the right lay open. No handle or knob graced its inner face.

"Into the room, Mr. Maccabeus."

"Who are you?"

She laughed again, poking him in the back with the barrel of the 9mm. "I'm Lilith Matthias, Maccabeus, but I imagine you already know that much."

Peter of course had no idea who Lilith Matthias was or if indeed this woman was she, but it seemed to behoove him then to present an ambiguous front. He entered the room, turned to face her.

She doesn't know if I know who she is; she doesn't know if I actually am who she thinks I am. She's fishing.

"What do you want from me?"

"I'm not sure I want anything from you," smiled.

The door slammed shut in his face, bolt thrown fast.

DON'T WAIT UP

Having exhausted the copious supply of ice cream, as well as nearly all possible topics of conversation, Edith and Aleta had found themselves alone still, nearly two hours into the new day, having heard no word from Thorin, with nothing to eat and even less to do.

Suffice it to say Aleta was none too happy.

Edith suspected that when Thorin did arrive he'd likely wish he hadn't.

After a brief conversation bordering on argument, it had been decided Aleta would take the first shower. She had classes at 10:30 the next morning and thus needed to be in bed as soon as possible, or so Edith's argument had concluded. Aleta had rebutted that Edith had been on the road, that she therefore needed her rest, a point quickly debunked by Edith's claiming to have stayed the previous night, in fact every night of her extended vacation, in a semi-nice to exquisite hotel. "Even in Mexico?" Aleta had asked incredulously, to which Edith had laughed, "Especially in Mexico," told her of the quaint yet superlative hotel in which she'd passed nearly a month in San Miguel De Allende, the lavish resort from which she'd witnessed all of December, in Puerto Vallarta.

At which point Aleta had simply given up, perhaps actually convinced, but regardless without the patience to continue the debate further.

Presently Edith occupied the couch, head leaned to the side upon a large pillow, lazily watching the snow fall.

She didn't plan to stay with Aleta and Thorin too long. What she'd told Aleta was true: She was just stopping through on her way to New York. Yet she'd also been hoping to hear some word of Andrew, possibly get a number. That Thorin had also not spoken with him, didn't have his number or know where he was, had come as a surprise, an initially soft blow Edith now, alone with her thoughts on the couch, felt blossom into fullness.

What the fuck am I doing?

For most of her time abroad, most of her pregnancy, she'd not really thought of him... occasionally, sure, but only in the manner of a vague curiosity. A week or so ago, however, she'd had her first contraction, in the French Quarter, New Orleans, while eating a steaming basket of spiced crawfish, and had simply felt the need to talk to him, *before* she bore their child. Visiting Thorin had seemed the first logical step. It had been the only move available.

For the first time she could clearly remember, Edith felt like crying.

She stood up then, moving to retrieve her jacket from the chair over which it was draped in the kitchen, intent on smoking a cigarette, outside in the calm of the falling snow.

Before she could leave, as she was pulling on her wool hat, Aleta's phone, which rested on the kitchen table, rang. A picture of Thorin, laughing at something out of the frame, graced the screen.

Edith, set on giving him shit for leaving Aleta alone for so long, answered.

"Thorin." She said with an air of grave irritation, likely of the same extent as that which Aleta herself felt.

His voice on the other end sounded unsure, "...Aleta?"

"No, Thorin. This is Edith."

"Edith?... errr... ...um, What are *you* doing there?"

"I stopped by to visit," paused, "nearly four hours ago."

She thought she could hear a slight grimace through the phone.

"Aleta said you were supposed to be home over two hours ago."

Silence on the line, then "It's good to talk to you too, Edith."

"You really shouldn't worry her like this, Thorin. She's fucking thirty-nine weeks pregnant."

A large breath, a sigh, "Look, Edith, something has come up, something serious; I'm sorry I wasn't able to make it home on time."

He actually sounds quite distressed.

Edith's affect vanished, concern for her friend replacing it in nearly an instant. "What's wrong?"

"Nothing. Nothing you can do anything about... I was just calling to make sure Aleta is alright."

"She's in the shower."

"Could you tell her... tell her a friend is in trouble and I need to help, that I may not be home until morning?"

Edith almost laughed; "That's not gonna go over very well."

"It can't be helped," paused, "...what?... Edith, hold on a second."

He was then gone from the line for a duration.

Returned, "How did you get to our apartment?"

"I drove."

Silence for a moment, as if he were conferring with someone, "So you have a car then?"

"Jesus, Thor, how could I have driven here if I didn't have a vehicle?"

"I need to borrow your car."

Sharply, "For what?"

"I'd rather not tell you."

Edith guffawed, quickly silenced herself lest Aleta hear from within the shower. "Thorin, you know I won't lend you my car without knowing what for."

"One second."

Perhaps ten passed.

"Edith?"

"I'm still here, Thorin"

"Well... ...Peter has been abducted."

"Abducted by whom?" Surprise, shot through with shock, colored her voice. "What is he even doing in D.C.?"

"It's too long a story, bu..."

"Why do you need my car?"

Thorin paused then, "We are going to rescue him."

"Who are 'we'?"

"That's also too long a story, but we do need your car."

"Then I'm coming along." Obviously.

"That's out of the question, Edith. It will be far too dangerous."

She smiled, "Do you need a vehicle, Thorin?"

"Yes," sounding quite earnest.

"Can you get one from anyone else?"

More hesitantly, "No... not really."

"Then I suppose I'm coming with you."

Silence on the line.

"Where shall I pick you up?"

Emerging from the shower, Aleta found the apartment empty. She walked to the kitchen table, where lay a note:

> *Aleta,*
>
> *Thorin called while you were in the shower. Bus service where he is has been canceled due to the snow, and he needs me to give him and one of his friends a ride.*
>
> *Don't wait up,*
> *Edith*

She sighed, turned from the kitchen and living room, heading for her bed to find the much needed rest her aching back demanded.

WHAT LAY BELOW

Samael strode through the halls of Party Headquarters, started down the flight of stairs that separated his offices from the rest of the building.

When he'd ascended to his present position more than two decades ago, he'd had a great deal of the internal structure altered, creating three distinct wings.

The first floor was comprised of the great entrance hall and staircase on the south side, with the northern half containing the mail room, offices for low level Party members, accountants, and "lobbyists," public bathrooms, and a large conference room serviced by two offices at either end.

The upper floors were reached by a grand staircase that ascended from the great hall to a landing, there splitting into two branches. Many had thought his decision to not install an elevator odd, given the height of the building, four stories, yet he'd had his own reasons for taking the more traditional, perhaps antiquated, route.

The southern set of stairs, those to the left if one were ascending the main case, led to his wing, comprised of a security and reception area as well as three offices on the second floor, a smaller conference room and three more offices on the third, with his own suite, including an office, a library, a bedroom and full bath, on the fourth. The entirety of the offices therein were dedicated to his personal accounts and interests.

The north stairs led to the greater bulk of the building, which had been systematically separated from his wing. There worked a number of clerks and accountants, lawyers, middling Party members and the more influential lobbyists, and presently the IDSC men, one of whom currently trailed him.

Samael knew he was there, perhaps four meters back, the largest of the three, who looked like he could break a man in two with his bare hands. He took comfort in the man's presence, confident that there was no one, Maccabean Rebellion notwithstanding, with whom he could not satisfactorily deal.

In addition to redefining its internal configuration, he'd also had built a fairly large complex below the building, the western extension of which was greater than the bounds of the structure itself. It was this secret, well, not quite secret but nonetheless restricted, area to which he now traveled.

Lilith, with help from her people, had been able to capture a Maccabean but an hour passed, and not some simple schmuck who'd been caught buying a conspicuous amount of Vaseline or who'd been seen talking with someone who had, but a legitimate Maccabean, one from out of the area who'd just this night had the audacity to hold a meeting right there in D.C..

Samael smiled, satisfied yet disturbed his people had successfully found a D.C. connection when IDSC had been unable to do so. The former feeling was somewhat stronger, given his present reliance on IDSC protection, which irked him terribly even if he did welcome the security provided.

Reaching the landing, he descended the broad steps at its base, crossed the great hall and turned left, into the lower wing.

At the eighth door on the right, four passed the public restrooms, he halted, turning to address his shadow.

"Wait here. I will be below." He moved to the door, found the appropriate key, one among over a dozen on a large chain tucked into his suit coat's front right pocket, inserted its length into the lock, simultaneously placing the thumb of his right hand on the reader to its side.

Waiting momentarily for the door to open, he stepped through to another set of stairs, much more narrow than those he'd just come down, the door closing of its own accord behind him.

He descended the first half-flight, turning at the landing, descended the remaining stairs, at the door there found repeating the procedure that had granted him access above.

His smile blossomed anew on his face.

Of any part of the building, this wing perhaps embodied most fully the various nuances of his personal style. Not only the interrogation rooms but also the cells were completely soundproof, airtight. Stark, sterile, the corridor he walked was dressed in white, trimmed in steel, illuminated brightly by a contiguous alignment of parallel fluorescent tubing, seeming to trace a single blazing road down the center of the ceiling, banishing all shadows.

He didn't come here often, but he did frequently enough to feel a certain comfort, a familiarity with the severity of its ways. Welcoming the diversion, he generally liked to be present at interrogations, if the prisoner were interesting, and this Maccabean, supposed Maccabean, was certainly that.

His destination lay at the far western end of the wing, passed the various interrogation rooms, each of which had a unique and rather ingenious configuration. There were only sixteen holding cells—he hadn't seen the need for more. Fewer than half were currently occupied.

Stays here were often, though certainly not always, short-lived.

Lilith emerged from the southern branch of the cell block, waiting for him at the end of the corridor, a slight smile on her face.

"Are you sure he's one of them?" He asked, yet three meters distant.

She nodded. "Absolutely. We have a concrete match," glanced away from him, down the hall from which she'd just come, "This is the man who called the meeting, from out of town, earlier this afternoon." She turned back, cracked a dry chuckle, "He thought coming with such short notice would keep him off the radar."

"What do we know about him? How did he arrive?"

At this she seemed a little less self-satisfied. "We aren't sure," turned as he reached her, taking him down the hall to stop before one of the steel doors, "It is possible he drove in; however, the call we back-traced from the other's phone originated in Atlanta." She paused; "Although it's possible he had the call made by proxy once he was already en route."

"And what *do* you know about him?"

"He's younger than expected, much younger than our profiles suggest. That he is a lieutenant, or even Maccabeus himself, seems undeniable though. Our operative reports he had a great deal of influence on the other prisoner, and that he spoke as Maccabeus."

"Then again," Samael rejoined softly, "he could just be a proxy himself."

Spoken tightly, "That is a possibility."

"You may leave us." He nodded down the hall; "See to it everything is proceeding as planned."

Acknowledged with a sharp nod, turned to disappear around the corner of the main passageway.

Samael drew open the door, stepped within, leaving it ajar behind him.

CURIOSITIES AND LOGISTICS

Andrew sparked another cigarette, his third in less than an hour, set his right elbow on the desk before him, head thereupon to stare into the finite void of his office, more specifically the space slightly above his desk, focused on an abstract point, eyes crossing.

There was little in the reports he had from Fatik and Cooley, perhaps even less in his own observations, with which to design a way to eliminate Samael without implicating The Council. This, of course, was the main dilemma he had in successfully executing his current objective. Michael had been exceptionally clear, unequivocal and incontrovertible: The Council must not be associated with the man's death.

Andrew's ploy, which had granted him nearly unlimited access to Samael, had at the same time thrown a gigantic monkey wrench into the midst of the greater mission itself—His team was now charged with Samael's security. A convenient breach of this security, with witnesses or without, would invite too many questions, questions he doubted could be simply explained away.

Andrew had trapped himself in a box of his own device.

For weeks now he'd racked his brain for something, a peculiarity in the man's habits and schedule, that could provide an opening without implicating Andrew's team, without his having any idea when exactly the order would be given.

He'd found none.

The situation wasn't helped by Samael's seeming distrust of The Council. Not that he didn't trust their ability to secure his person or even the nation generally, but instead that he seemed to be acutely aware The Council would, if given the chance, collect intelligence on *him*. He'd thus forbidden Andrew's team the use of several standard instruments, foremost of which were the small, in-ear bugs that allowed teams to communicate with complete privacy. Made in sets tailored specifically for a given use, the network they constituted was completely independent, uncrackable; they were a staple of contemporary covert operations. They could also be used to amplify sound and track movement to less than a meter.

Samael knew all of this, and so they'd been the first to go, soon followed by all electronics whatsoever, including phones. The phenomenon wasn't restricted to merely Andrew and his men—At the security office on the second floor of the southern wing, passed which even Andrew could not move without explicit invitation or permission, visitors were required to relinquish all such devices; even Samael's staff had to pass inspection when entering or leaving.

And the man's schedule was routine, cyclical, with no chance of an "accident."

Andrew was beginning to suspect he'd need the help of an outside element, although who or what this could possibly be completely eluded him.

He pulled on his cigarette, which had nearly gone out during the unwinding of his thoughts, tapped the accumulated ashes into the nearly full tray to his right.

Presently the man was downstairs, in the building yet outside of his wing for once, guarded by Cooley, doing God only knew what in the basement, which Andrew had only witnessed him visit once before. He then, apparently Cooley now, hadn't been invited below.

What the Hell is down there?

No one besides Samael and Ms. Matthias, no other, had been seen or reported going below.

That was the truly odd thing, really. No one ever went down there; at least, no one was ever seen doing so. Yet there was below something both Samael and Ms. Matthias, two figures of none too much frivolity, found worthwhile.

Butting his smoke among the other discarded remnants in the tray, he banished curiosities and potential logistics from his mind, retrieved his phone from the far side of the desk, summoning Fatik. It was almost time for Cooley to be relieved, and Andrew had new instructions before Fatik assumed the watch.

One thing he was beginning to learn was that acting was nearly always better than wondering, waiting in the dark. He found himself an intelligence agent, charged with a task both simple and complex, one of counterintelligence and intrigue.

Knowledge is power, and I don't intend to be blind or defenseless as I dare the path set before me.

A MOTLEY CREW

Edith eyed the group assembled before her: a buxom vixen, a rather stylish, seemingly out of place Arab, and Thorin, a fool.

What does that make me?

Of its own accord the wisdom of Kenobi sprang to mind.

Who is more foolish: the fool, or the fool who follows him?

Yet Edith *knew* her involvement here was something from which she could not abstain, not and still be able to live with herself.

Peter was her friend, perhaps more so than any other who could lay claim to the designation. He was kind, innocent in his own way. When they'd first met what seemed so long ago, she'd been instantly attracted to him, not because of what he said but because of what he didn't say, who he was. Later, she'd come to understand he was a friend... and not just a friend who'd failed to become a lover and thus become a friend by default, but a friend who'd never wanted to be anything else. She'd never actually had a male friend who'd simply been just that, and now that she thought about it she'd never really had a female friend like that either. Always with others there'd been some ulterior motive, often on both sides, that having spent itself found them friends. Peter had simply started being her friend from the beginning, with no pretense, no affect.

And so she found herself in the now still air, the dark of early morning, alone with Thorin and these two people she'd never before met, observing them as they observed her and each other, by the shores of the Tidal Basin, at the foot of the Jefferson Monument.

Presently the odd quartet was engaged in conversation, much of which escaped Edith, yet which she was slowly but surely becoming able to follow.

"From what I've been told, other Maccabeans who've been taken for questioning were released;" Marquetta looked to Amin.

Who was unmoved. "Yet how many of those were abducted in the middle of the night, right outside the place of a meeting where it was known, possibly by the abductors, that Maccabeus was in attendance?"

She looked thoughtful for a moment. "So he *is* Maccabeus."

Thorin laughed; interjected, "Yeah, I don't really believe it myself."

Marquetta looked from Thorin to Amin, eyes narrowed.

"*Who* is Maccabeus?" Edith had thus far been unable to determine this on her own.

Thorin turned his head to address her directly; "Peter is Maccabeus."

"Peter?" Marquetta looked intrigued.

"Maccabeus?" Edith was lost anew.

Thorin took a breath, perhaps a mental step back from his two interlocutresses; Amin gave him a subtle yet nonetheless reproachful look, a quizzical eye on Marquetta.

"Let's not worry about that right now;" he met both of the women's eyes. "All we need now discuss is how we are to secure their freedom." He took another, fairly large breath. "Amin is right. They will not be released," turned to Marquetta, "regardless of what has been the case with others." To the group, "This situation is different."

"Then what should we do?" Marquetta seemed a little put-off, not quite pouting.

Edith slanted a look at her..

Not quite used to being corrected, is she.

She grinned inwardly. Beautiful women were amusing, in their own way.

Amin, the tall Arab man wearing a suit when everyone else was dressed casually and for winter, filled the gap in the conversation; "We are going to break into Party Headquarters and free them."

"And how is that?" Marquetta rejoined. "We only have your word to go on that they're being held at this so-called 'Party Headquarters,' and we know nothing of where therein they are being held, what stands between us and them, and how we will deal with whatever does stand in our way."

Edith found the question convincing.

Unfazed, Amin met her gaze for a duration, holding it just long enough to be uncomfortable, for everyone. Addressed the group, "I know where they're being held. I know where *therein* they are being held." Backed off a little, "The place is known as Party Headquarters. They're being held in cells located on the basement level, which has two points of entrance, both of which will be difficult to breach."

"And what would you propose we do?" Thorin was clearly on edge, slightly melancholy, yet seemed legitimately, ardently, curious.

Amin continued. "One entrance is located in an alley; it will be unguarded, yet is impossible to open from the outside. The other entrance is found on the first floor of Party Headquarters, in the building itself; we will find security at the front door and possibly at the stairs to the basement as well. There will be at least one door, possibly two, between us and the detention level; each requires a key and thumbprint identification."

Edith was taken aback. "What the fuck has Peter gotten himself into?" Turned to Thorin, "Who the fuck are these people, Thor?" To Amin, "Seriously, who the fuck are you?"

"I'd like to know that as well," Marquetta interjected, arms folded beneath her breasts.

Edith turned on the woman, eyes steel.

Interestingly, Amin addressed himself to Marquetta. "I'm sure you would."

"Look," Thorin stepped more to the middle of their impromptu circle, "Amin is a friend of Peter; I have no doubt," nodded to Edith.

"And how do you know that?"

He sighed, an edge of frustration, "Because I do." Paused with a glance toward Amin, "He knows my real name," smiled.

Amin, apparently finding great humor in something, burst out in laughter, contained quickly.

The conviction in Thorin's voice was enough to satisfy Edith, who knew that, a stoner as he may have been, Thorin wasn't one to give his loyalty or trust easily or frivolously.

She glanced to Marquetta, who still stood studying Amin, who silently studied her in return.

Thorin turned to Amin, "Continue, please."

"I suggest we attempt to access the internal entrance first; perhaps we will find a means of opening the doors. If not, we can break into the basement from the alley," he paused, "but we will have to use explosives."

Edith couldn't believe what she was hearing.

Marquetta, said flatly, "And you have access to explosives."

All eyes turned to Amin.

"I have a limited amount of RDX plastique."

All eyes remained on Amin.

Who was yet unfazed by the attention. "This is why I'd prefer to enter the other way. Detonating a shaped charge in D.C. is likely not the most prudent thing to do."

Edith rejoined immediately, "I agree."

Seconded by Thorin.

Marquetta stood silent, contemplating Amin, who again contemplated her back. She quickly looked away, over Amin to Jefferson's monument, which rose sharply to his rear.

"And how would you propose to deal with security in the building?" Thorin wasn't dissuaded by the gravity of Amin's suggestions.

He grinned; "*I* will deal with security. You and the woman will go below; you shouldn't encounter much resistance there." He turned to Edith; "You will remain in the vehicle." His tone left no room for argument.

Thorin nodded thoughtfully, gaze set on the ground before him.

Marquetta brought a hand to her chin, partially covering her face, absently stroked the deep brown layers that there fell as a delicate frame.

Edith, alone in her vantage, facing just about north, studied the Washington Monument, tall and bright against a dark sky, white enough to match the snow covering the land below.

CHAPTER 10
ACTION

MACHINATIONS

It had been nearly an hour since Lilith had left Samael alone in the cell with the Maccabean, an hour of waiting, of mostly suppressed curiosity and impatience.

Even with the door open, as she was sure it still was—Samael wouldn't want to become a prisoner himself—not a sound carried from the cell to where she waited, in the main corridor near the passage to the receiving room.

Samael must have been going easy on him, a point reinforced by the fact that he'd not transferred the prisoner to one of the several rooms before which she waited, and although it was a matter of indifference to the plan whether the Maccabean were brutalized or not, she would've preferred the former, just because.

She sighed, turning to pace once more the brightly lit eastern extension of the corridor.

Any time now...

Thoughts interrupted by a soft buzz in the right breast pocket of her jacket.

Smiled.

She pivoted toward the far end of the hall, toward the portal there that led to the stairs to the first floor, drew her phone from her pocket, briefly scanning the message before slipping it back within.

Opening the door, less of a hassle when leaving, she climbed the stairs, emerging through the door at their top to where the IDSC man stood, ever awake and alert.

Fucking grunt.

Lilith didn't care for the three IDSC men, mainly because she felt slighted their presence had been deemed necessary to begin with, but also to a great extent because they'd been witness to her personal shame, her bondage to Samael, body and mind.

That one or all of them could very well be injured or even killed in the coming incident pleased her greatly.

Closing the door behind herself, she approached him. "What is your name, agent?"

She'd never had need to speak with this one before.

He straightened slightly, a semblance of attention, covering a wary, calculated posture. "Cooley, ma'am"

She didn't smile. "Cooley, go and get the others. Tell them we will have company very soon."

He seemed unsure; "Company, ma'am?"

Coldly, "Hostile company." She looked beyond him, toward the great entrance hall, purposefully. "We expect dissidents may attempt to assassinate Samael this very morning, in a few minutes."

"We have received no such intelligence, ma'am."

She then smiled, ice. "*I* have received such intelligence, agent, not two minutes ago. Now you *will* call the other agents down here, and you *will* perform the task with which you've been charged."

He hesitated but one moment longer; "I'd have to go all the way to the upper north wing; I don't have any means of communication."

"I know you don't; depriving you of those contraptions was my idea."

"But I can't leave my post, ma'am. My first duty is t…"

Cutting him off, "Your first duty is to the protection of Party Leader Samael's person," pinned him with her eyes, "and I'm telling you that you'll need the other two men."

"What of The Party's security forces?"

"There are none presently close enough, Cooley." She added a touch of desperation to her voice, "I'm telling you, directly, to go get help now, *before* it's too late."

At this he turned sharply, not quite running but nonetheless moving quite quickly down the hallway, disappearing into the grand hall in the direction of the main stairs.

Fucking grunt.

BREACH OF SECURITY

Thorin had to admit that so far the plan had proceeded without a hitch. Of course, they had yet to breach the building itself, but they *had* been able to find their way to its brick edifice on North Capitol from the far side of the tidal basin without incident or accident over the snow-covered, icy roads between.

Presently they were approaching the front entrance, behind whose doors lay waiting a number of unknowns, obscure and sinister.

Amin had assured them the guard found at the building's front desk would be unarmed, more a formality than an actual measure of security, a clerk really. It was the possibility of other forces, perhaps at the stairs that were their current aim, perhaps in other parts of the building, with which they had to concern themselves.

He didn't know how Amin knew what he did; he simply knew the man had made a single, if extended, phone call, far enough from him and Marquetta that neither of them had been able to eavesdrop, that when he'd returned he'd seemed more confident, informing them that "the next step is to secure a vehicle." When Thorin had asked why they couldn't simply use Amin's car, he'd been told the car was "traceable" and couldn't in any circumstance be used.

He glanced over his shoulder at Edith, just before he, Amin, and Marquetta reached the building's threshold, gave her what he hoped was a reassuring smile, most likely a nervous, worried scowl.

Amin, reaching the doors first, opened the right of the two, holding it for Marquetta and then Thorin and himself to pass through.

It closed gently behind them.

They found themselves in a great, vaulted chamber with two rows of columns running its length to either side, at the end of which lay a single grand staircase.

Amin nodded to Thorin, promptly setting himself toward the north side of the chamber, to a corridor there found, the entrance of which from Thorin's perspective was partially obscured by one of the towering columns.

Thorin walked to the desk, addressed the clerk, who'd risen from his seat to watch Amin disappear down the corridor. "He really has to piss," grinned.

The clerk also grinned; "Happens to the best of us," paused, "Can I help you?"

Remembering the lines Amin had told him, Thorin moved to the desk, set an arm out thereupon. "We're here to speak with Mr. Talencaster."

He had no idea who the man was.

The guard, however, simply grinned again, "His office is down the hall there," pointing to where Amin had moments ago vanished. Laughed, "He's always here at odd hours..." glanced at Marquetta, who'd removed her bulky jacket before disembarking Edith's car "...Never before had visitors this late though."

Thorin laughed as well, a semblance of good natured humor; "Yeah, well, he's reviewing a land-use dispute for us, and the hearing is tomorrow morning." Grinned, "Just stopping through to make sure everything is in order."

Seeming satisfied, the clerk resumed his seat. "It's down the corridor there, second hall to the left, passed the bathrooms, third door on the right."

Thorin raised his hand in a soft salute, nodding thanks, turned and began to cross the chamber, not too fast yet not too slowly.

He felt a stop at the bathroom might be in order after all, knowing there wasn't time. Still...

His thoughts broke off as he cleared the row of columns, coming square with the line of the corridor. Down the hall, perhaps ten meters from its mouth, stood Amin and a thin, blond woman.

Amin held a gun, barrel extended by a slick looking silencer, trained on her.

As Thorin drew closer he could see the woman didn't look scared; rather, she seemed a touch annoyed, turning to amusement as she caught sight of Thorin and Marquetta. Amin was speaking to her, quietly.

"... will escort my two friends downstairs."

"And if I don't?"

"Then you will die right here, right now."

The woman smiled, a slightly disturbing thing that seemed more to slither than spring onto her lips, pure affect. "So I have no choice in the matter." At which point she actually giggled slightly, quickly stifled. "Very well," composure fully restored, "But I must warn you that you may not like what you find down there."

She turned, inserting a key into the lock, pressed her thumb on the plate set to its side. The door unlocked with an audible click, swinging open into the corridor.

First Thorin, then Marquetta and finally Amin followed her through the portal, Amin pausing to gum the lock with a small portion of plastique. Descending the stairs, the woman opened the door at their base, the others following her through into a remarkably well lit corridor, its floor, walls, and ceiling a blazing, nearly blinding, white.

Amin, gumming the lock on the lower door as well, gave Thorin a reassuring touch on his shoulder, quickly disappearing back up the stairs.

With Amin, and his weapon, gone, the woman regained a touch of what Thorin assumed was her usual air of cold disdain and authority, so easily did it reassert itself, banishing the mask of passivity that moments before had graced her rather striking features. She passed an eye over Marquetta, rounding on Thorin, "Do you feel as confident without your keeper, Maccabean?"

"Take us to him." Thorin had no time to bandy words with the woman.

She laughed, turned to begin a slow stroll down the corridor. "Are you sure you want to see?"

He could hear the smile on her lips.

"Perhaps you and your whore haven't the stomach for such things."

Thorin, at once offended by the woman's referring to Marquetta as a whore and disturbed by the vaguely macabre undertones of her taunts, brought himself before her. "What the fuck is that supposed to mean?"

She smiled; "That the woman with whom you keep company is a whore, through and through," she turned slightly, bringing Marquetta into the compass of her vision, "Tell him I speak the truth," nodded toward Thorin.

Marquetta's face flushed a deep red, stain visible still beneath the naturally dark tone of her visage.

She continued, "And that your friend, *Maccabeus*, may not be able to leave this place with you…" smile deepening "…at least not in one piece."

And then, before Marquetta could respond, before the woman could utter a single further odious word about his friend, Thorin, with all his strength, hooked her directly in the temple with his left fist.

She dropped in a heap, head impacting the hard tile of the floor with a dull thud.

Tremens of adrenaline heaving through his body, bringing a slight distortion to his vision, he turned from the woman's crumpled form, literally shaking, suddenly sweaty, in the sterile coolness of the basement corridor.

"Fucking bitch."

Marquetta, taking a step back and giving him a quizzical, possibly concerned look, "I completely agree," broke into a kind of grin.

AMBUSHED

Andrew hurried through the halls of Party Headquarters, hot on the heels of Fatik, who was similarly situated to Cooley.

Both of the other men had unbuttoned their jackets for easy access to their sidearms, Beretta Px6 .45 semi automatics with rounds already in their chambers, holstered in shoulder harnesses, Fatik's on his right and Cooley's on his left. Andrew, also similarly armed, hadn't yet been able to convince himself his following suit was necessary.

He'd fired his gun in training, and was actually a fairly good shot, but he'd never really considered he'd one day actually have to *use* the thing. That entire aspect of his training had been abstract, a formality. He silently prayed it would remain so.

The gravity with which he and his men—he had to pause mentally at that. *He* had "men," with guns no less, who knew how to use them, who *had* used them, successfully… nearly overcome with a sudden wave of nausea—descended from their offices in the north wing, with which they trod its hallways, however, was quite real, and completely unable to be dismissed.

Andrew was possibly heading into a fucking battle zone. Then again, he could possibly just be heading to the first floor and a false alarm, hopefully

They reached the end of the hallway, turning right, toward the north branch of the stairs that would take them to the ground floor and Ms. Matthias, the vaulted ceiling of the great hall coming partially into view.

Upon reaching the stairs, Cooley, ever a wary hound, slowed; descending the first half flight, ducked down in a sort of crouch, he peeked around the corner of the low wall fronting the landing.

Apparently having seen nothing of concern, he rose, beginning a brisk descent of the main case, Fatik and Andrew following in staggered form behind.

As Andrew cleared the wall, took the beginning of his first step down the broad stairs, a shot, muffled by a silencer but still distinctive, echoed softly through the great chamber.

Cooley, who'd nearly reached the bottom, dove to his left, off the stairs to land in a roll, finding himself set low behind one of the hall's broad marble columns.

Andrew threw himself behind the diminutive wall of the landing, struggling to remove his own weapon from its holster.

Fatik, caught unawares not halfway down the case, had nowhere to hide. Blood stained the left sleeve of his jacket, above the elbow.

Andrew waited for the inevitable shot that would, in short order, put an end to Fatik's witty banter for good. A few seconds passed, seeing Fatik turn and begin a lopsided sprint for the top of the stairs. The second shot never came, and the next moment found Fatik slouched behind the low rise of the wall, on the other side of the landing from Andrew.

From what he could see Fatik's left arm was completely useless; agony stained the man's face as he tried futilely to manipulate his fingers.

Was it by sheer luck our assailant maimed Fatik's strong arm, his shooting arm, or had he done so on purpose?"

The precision with which the shot had struck Fatik argued against the former, so neatly had it shattered his humerus. The possibility of the latter opened up a number of questions about the shooter.

Does he know who we are, have intelligence on *us* specifically? Or was he simply able to see on which side Fatik's sidearm was holstered? Can anyone shoot with that kind of accuracy?

He made a mental note to ask Fatik that very question at the earliest convenience, provided they both survived the night.

For now, Fatik, a cold-blooded, former IB agent, was out of the action, able to sit, likely to stand and possibly to run, but certainly not to fight.

Andrew considered his options, the situation he found himself in.

Cooley was somewhere below, and this was their greatest advantage. However, with Andrew pinned-down on the landing, unable to help, it was unlikely Cooley alone would be able to gain an advantage on the hidden shooter... As far as Andrew knew there were multiple enemies below; the great hall was anything but lacking in places for men to conceal themselves, the set of broad columns lining the center of the chamber providing potential cover for quite a few hostiles.

He'd not had the chance to inspect the front desk, where there should have been a guard, albeit unarmed, yet he could only assume the man had been either incapacitated or killed, that possibly he'd fled.

Andrew and Cooley were in this alone against an unknown number of enemies.

He thought back, attempting to place the trajectory of the bullet that had caught Fatik.

The way Fatik was walking, down and across the steps, the shooter must be somewhere on the north side of the hall, possibly near the main corridor.

This made sense with what he knew of Samael's location and Ms. Matthias's warning.

The shooter is guarding the way to the basement.

Shit.

I've failed. This morning will find Samael dead, killed by political dissidents on my watch.

Fuck.

I've no recourse, no way to circumnavigate our hidden assailant quickly enough.

Fucking shit.

That is assuming they've been able to penetrate the lower level, a thing possible only if Ms. Matthias has cooperated.

A moment of hope, that somehow he could turn this situation away from disaster, flickered through Andrew.

Then again, if they'd been wholly unsuccessful this man wouldn't now be here shooting at us.

Motherfucker.

Andrew's thoughts raced, covering much ground but offering very little.

Across the landing, Fatik, no longer struggling to move his arm, looked to have passed out, from shock or blood loss Andrew could not tell.

Is he dead?

If they've gained access to the lower level, they must have in mind a path of escape.

They won't attempt to leave through the main hall; they were waiting for us. They knew we'd be here.

No one ever goes down there, yet there is below something both Samael and Ms. Matthias find worthwhile.

There's another entrance to the basement, a secret entrance.

Now with an object upon which to focus, Andrew's mind worked, potentialities and permutations, a racing calculus of impossible scenarios and undesirable outcomes, searching for a course of action that wouldn't end in debacle.

SHOOTER

Amin had been ready for the men's appearance. He'd been ready to slaughter them where they stood, frozen in time, open and without cover on the great staircase.

And he could've done so. The sloppy, imprudent manner of their descent, unfitting for a trio of IDSC agents, had left all of them vulnerable.

And he would've done so, without hesitation, had he not spotted the young captain with whom he'd worked the past fall, bringing up the rear.

The realization that the men descending the stairs were IDSC agents, that one of them was the enigmatic prodigy, The Chairman's protégé, had given him pause, and so he'd done the only thing he could: He'd halted their progress, separated them and pinned them down in the west end of the chamber.

He could only assume the large one, who'd taken refuge behind a column at the far end of the hall, was now intent on somehow flanking his position. As unlikely as it was he'd succeed, Amin had no desire to have to kill the man, and so he'd retreated to the mouth of the northern corridor, from where he could observe both the landing of the great stairs, on which the young captain had taken refuge, and most of the north end of the hall, in whose blind spots lurked the other agent.

He didn't have to keep them at bay indefinitely, only long enough for Thorin and the woman to secure the boy and the other prisoner.

Perhaps five minutes should do it.

That when he'd called no one at The Tower had informed him of the presence of IDSC forces in Party Headquarters Amin found not quite troubling, more interesting. In all likelihood the intelligence officer with whom he'd spoken, a functionary who likely never left The Tower's confines, except perhaps to sleep, eat, and fuck, had had no idea about whatever operation in which the three men now confronting Amin were involved, which of course meant theirs, like his own, was a secret even within the IDSC itself. That the young captain was in charge, which surely he was—the other two were clearly veteran agents, enforcers and solders—indicated The Chairman himself had an interest.

Amin had no desire to disrupt plans about which he'd not been briefed, although he *would* do whatever was necessary to secure the boy's release. His safety was Amin's primary objective. Nothing would prevent him from fulfilling his duty.

Hopefully this situation will not have to progress any further.

He slid his fingers around the ring on his right hand, feeling the tightness of its woven loops, still knotted as one.

Together the form was strong. So long as they remained as such the ring was whole, a single piece. Only when the weave was broken did the individual loops fall into disarray, a sort of entropy of form and function, in the wrong circumstances, disaster.

He knew this, accepted its truth. Amin had faith that what was unfolding was according to plan, feeling an odd sort of rectitude in the queer realities of the situation.

So long as everyone does what he feels right, in whatever position he finds himself in, the highest end is served.

Just then he saw the captain peek his head around the corner of the short wall behind which he'd taken refuge. Amin, determining he could best deal with the two agents if they actually knew where he was, in which case *he* would know where *they* were—there were but a finite number of viable approaches to the mouth of the corridor, all of which Amin could cover from his present vantage—fired a warning shot just above the captain's head, impacting the wall, causing painted plaster to crumble and fall, likely onto the young captain himself.

That should keep him there for a while, and get the other's attention.

He grinned, patience and irony.

Just four more minutes.

WHO ARE YOU?

They left the woman lying on the floor of the corridor, of no danger to anyone, raced down the brightly lit length.

All these fucking doors look the fucking same.

The thrill of adrenaline had crystallized inside Thorin, effecting a deep energy, anger and vengeance, which filled him completely. He felt deadly, unstoppable.

He paused momentarily, opened one of the doors.

What he found there turned his self righteousness to ashes, wilted and frail.

The room he entered was also brightly lit, also a brilliant white, immaculate. At its center was set a table, below which was found a drain. Above, a large mirror, as long as the table itself, peered down. On the table were straps, white, which looked to be fashioned for the immobilization of a human being. To the side of the table was a mobile cart, like one you would find at a nice hotel. This cart, however, didn't hold anything room service would provide, champagne and strawberries, perhaps a spread of pancakes and waffles, sausages... Upon its surface lay instruments of torture, a scalpel, some sort of drill, what appeared to be a small torch, like what one would use to caramelize a crème brûlée, several other hooked and edged implements, actual hooks.

Thorin, absorbed in the scene, flinched for a moment as Marquetta moved beside him, ducking her head into the room to see what exactly he was so interested in.

She gasped.

Tearing his eyes from the suggestive, if presently empty and sterile, room, Thorin pushed her passed its threshold, exited as well, pulling the door closed behind himself.

If Peter has ended up in one of these...

Thorin shuddered. A vague yet visceral image of his friend on a table like that which he's just seen, strapped down, staring into a mirror as his flesh was peeled and mutilated, burned, passed before his mind. He shook it off, set himself once more on his purpose.

I need to get him the fuck out of here.

From the uniformity of the doors in the main corridor, Thorin surmised they all fronted similar chambers. He moved passed them, refusing to admit even the possibility Peter might be found in one, hopping dearly he would not.

Marquetta followed closely behind.

They reached the end of the corridor, which there branched to the right and left.

A door to the left lay open; Thorin could hear a voice speaking within.

"...know you know more than you're telling me, and I know you did not come to D.C. alone."

Thorin approached the portal with dread, within seeing Peter, thank God in one piece, seated on a steel chair that appeared to be bolted to the floor, facing the doorway. His hands were pinned behind him. A man, older by his voice, wearing a suit, stood with his back to the aperture.

He began once again to speak. "Shortly I will have no choice but to remove you to one of the interrogation rooms, the prospect of which I can't say I find displeasing, but for both our sakes, for the sake of your body and mind and for the sake of my time and patience, neither of which is infinite, tell me now for whom you work."

Peter sat still, silent.

"Whether you are this Maccabeus or not, whether you simply work for him, I know without question there is another who pulls your strings." Thorin could hear the sneer in his voice; "You are a pawn, a puppet. A child. I..."

Thorin, having heard enough, rushed with all of his might into the room, catching the man completely by surprise, slammed his shoulder into his back, sending him literally flying into the left wall of the room, passed a startled looking Peter whose momentary surprise turned to visible relief as he saw who'd come to his rescue.

The man, dazed, his head having hit the wall fairly hard, struggled to raise himself from the floor. Thorin slowly approached, kicked him with the laces of his boot, with all his strength, directly in, under, the side of the head. The man's head snapped back, his body rising slightly from the ground before collapsing, boneless, to lay discarded in the far left corner.

Thorin returned to his friend, helped him raise himself from the chair.

"Are you OK?" he asked, searching Peter's face and body with his eyes and hands, looking for injury or wound.

Peter simply nodded, slowly.

There was a hollowness in his eyes that belied the seemingly innocuous nature of his confinement.

Thorin consciously refrained from questioning his friend about what had transpired, instead drew his Swiss Army Knife, which he'd carried for most of his life, from his pocket, cut the plastic binding Peter's hands.

Peter, arms free, flung them around his shoulders in a great hug, speechless.

Thorin gently disengaged himself from Peter's embrace; "Let's get the fuck out of here." Paused, looked to the man on the floor, "What should we do with this douche?"

Marquetta, who'd until then held back at the steel-framed doorway, took a step inside, turned to look at the crumpled form on the floor. "Is he alive?"

Thorin nodded, "Just knocked out," paused, "I think." To Peter, "Should... ...should we kill him?" The words formed clumsily in his mouth.

Before Peter could respond, Marquetta interjected, "No." Taking a step back as they both turned toward her, "We are not killers," she clarified. "We should simply lock him in here. He's no threat to us now."

Peter nodded, still silent, urging Thorin toward the exit.

Without a backward glance he herded them out of the room, drawing the door closed behind himself.

"If ever I cross paths with that man again, one of us will die."

Marquetta, filling the extended and strange silence that dominated the void left by Peter's pronouncement, "Where is Benjamin?"

Peter stared vacantly for a moment longer, quickly snapping
back to the present. "I think he's in one of the other cells here, from
what that... ...man told me. In one of the cells down there," he nodded toward the northern extension of the corridor.

Together, they walked quickly to the other wing of cells, opening
in order the doors they found there.

The first, breached by Thorin, was empty, the second as well,
opened by Peter. As the two men closed their respective doors, Marquetta screamed, softly, as if the air that had moved to form its burst
had itself become frightened, retreating back into her breast. Thorin
moved quickly, pushing her aside.

It was a man... he thought so at least... long of hair and thin of
muscle, a waif in the purest sense.

His skeletal form made the pictures Thorin had seen of Holo-
caust survivors from the last World War seem amateur attempts at
parody, black and white captures of actors who'd not quite studied
the actualities of extended and inhumane confinement to the fullest
extent. He lay on his side on the floor of the cell, unable to raise himself, smelling of feces and the funky cheese of infection.

Thorin was taken aback.

Peter, coming around behind him, gazed silently into the cell.

"Should we take him with us?" Thorin nearly stuttered the words.

Peter took a step closer, beside Thorin, studying the wretched
figure on the ground. "I don't think he's able to move," glanced at his
friend, "and if *we* move him, carry him running through this place, we
are more likely to endanger our own lives than save his," back toward
the man.

"Well we can't just leave him here;" Thorin shivered, "We just
can't."

"From what I gathered from... ...the man who was speaking to
me, I'd tend to agree."

Thorin was confused, "Then what the hell do y..."

Pushing passed his friend, Peter grasped the man's head gently
between his hands, said something inaudible, barely audible. He quietly and calmly jerked his arms, twisting the man's head nearly 270°,
lowered the now limp form to the floor.

Thorin staggered back in shock, gaping at Peter, his friend with
whom he'd smoked many a bowl, now one to coldly kill, without
comment, without question.

It was then the path of the past several hours came to fully settle
in Thorin's mind.

He looked around himself, verging on panic.

What the fuck what the fuck.

How the fuck did I end up here?

Who is this person before me? Peter? Maccabeus? A killer?

Who are *you*?

Peter's eyes met Thorin's.

What the fuck?

Peter exited the cell, gently drawing it closed behind himself; he set his hands on Thorin's shoulders.

Thorin flinched.

"That was all I could do for him, Thor."

Thorin turned his head away from his friend's gaze, feeling a tear form in the corner of his left eye, tumble down his cheek and along his jaw.

Peter released him, guiding him softly to the side, moved toward the cell opposite the one from which he'd just come. He opened the door.

Marquetta gasped in relief, rushing in to where Benjamin sat as had Peter, arms bound behind his back. She helped him to his feet.

"Thank God it's you and not that horrible woman," he turned toward his savior, kissed her on the neck, unable as yet to embrace.

"Give me your knife." Peter took a step into the room, reaching back toward Thorin.

Who was unmoved, impassive.

"Thor!" Peter snapped at him, "Give me you fucking knife. We don't have time to bullshit."

Dumb, Thorin handed Peter his knife, who proceeded to enter the cell fully, cutting Benjamin free of his bonds.

"Let's get the fuck out of here."

They exited the cell, first Marquetta and Benjamin, followed by Peter, who, with a fleeting look back to where four more cells lay unbreached, tugged Thorin into motion.

Thorin snapped into the present, nodding to Peter before turning to follow him back toward the main corridor.

Benjamin and Marquetta were nearly to the intersection, Peter and Thorin close behind, when the woman materialized from around the corner, a trickle of blood running from her right temple and a gun held in her hand.

Upon seeing her, Benjamin rushed forward, forcing her down the opposing wing, toward the room in which Peter had recently been imprisoned, yelled over his shoulder, "Get Maccabeus out!"

The corridor here was narrow enough that Benjamin completely obscured the woman; the space between its walls not admitting two to engage her.

Having no better alternative, Peter dragged Thorin into the main corridor by the upper sleeve of his shirt.

Marquetta took a step to follow, hesitated, instead turning back toward the intersection, disappearing to the left, toward were Thorin could here sounds of struggle, thankfully no gunshots.

He jerked out of Peter's grasp, "Fuck you, man." Turned back toward the cell block, "We have to help him."

"We can't. Not in this confined space."

Thorin dismissed his words, "You're prepared to simply write off his life as well, *Maccabeus*?"

Peter hesitated, unsure, then turned as well toward the cell block.

A moment later both of them were deafened by the crack of a gun, amplified a hundredfold in the close of the corridor.

They sprinted around the corner.

They found Marquetta, on her knees with her arms around Benjamin, who sagged forward in her embrace, the back of his head missing.

The blond woman lay on the ground in a pool of Benjamin's blood, seeming to again be unconscious.

Marquetta sobbed.

Thorin rushed to her side, without thinking placed his hand in the gooey mess of Benjamin's exploded skull, reeled back against the wall, aghast.

Mother of fucking God.

Peter then gruffly gripped him, impelling him down the main corridor, drew Marquetta upward, his right arm around her back.

Together they broke into a run.

HE'S GONE

For minutes Andrew had been pinned on the landing, unable to advance. He looked across to Fatik, still unconscious, possibly dead, still bleeding.

His concern for his man lay evenly weighted against his determination to execute his orders. Andrew didn't think the bullet had opened Fatik's brachial artery, there simply wasn't enough blood... At least he hoped not. Regardless, his duty to The Council, to which Fatik also owed loyalty, was paramount.

Some things are bigger than a single life.

We have each chosen our paths.

He'd earlier attempted a survey of the hall, finding their assailant alert and ready, the bullet that had impacted the wall just above his position proof enough. Since then he'd remained hidden, hoping Cooley would be able to either provide distraction or rout the enemy himself.

Now, more than three minutes, a lifetime, later, Andrew grew impatient, frustrated. No longer frightened, he was simply tired of crouching behind a wall, watching Fatik slowly bleed to death, out of reach, knowing that somewhere below the man he'd been ordered to protect and kill was likely being murdered by another.

"I think he's gone, sir;" Cooley spoke quite quietly, a lone voice in the cavernous hall, carried still to where Andrew waited, the simple words, simply spoken, breaking the deathly quiet that had moments before dominated the space.

Andrew ventured a peek around the wall, flinching despite himself, however, finding no bullet waiting to fly in his direction.

He paused a moment, scouring the chamber before him.

He stood then, quickly descending the steps, ready at a moment's notice to dive therefrom, take refuge as had Cooley. Yet still nothing of danger presented itself, and he reached the marble floor of the hall without incident, quickly dodging to the right, sidearm trained before him, to the far side of the southern row of columns, across the hall from where he'd determined the shooter to last have been.

Sprinting from column to column, he rounded the reception desk, finding the guard on the ground behind, tied up and apparently unconscious. He ducked behind its mass, moving toward the east end of the building, near the main entrance, crept around its side to peer at the mouth of the western corridor, which lay empty.

He then saw Cooley cautiously approaching the corridor from the left, in a line nearly perpendicular to that of Andrew's sight.

Andrew stood up, bringing a sharp turn from the other man, who quickly lowered his weapon once he saw it was Andrew who'd drawn his attention. He signaled for Cooley to remain where he was, moved to the entrance. Opening the left door, he ducked his head through, scanning the street for potential threats, other dissidents who'd perhaps remained outside, finding nothing but the empty, snow covered expanse of North Capitol. He let the door close, walking to where Cooley waited.

"I think he's retreated down the stairs."

Andrew nodded his agreement.

Cooley smiled; "Then we have them; there's no way out of there."

Andrew remained impassive; "Yet our charge is down there with them."

The other man shrugged. "If their objective was to kill him they've by now surely succeeded."

Andrew could not argue with this, close as it was to his own summation.

"The best we can do is hope to capture them."

Andrew shook his head. "There's another entrance, Cooley; there has to be." Gazed down the corridor, "It's the only way any of this makes sense."

Cooley looked skeptical, yet unwilling to directly question his superior.

"Why else would he simply leave his position here? To find himself trapped below-ground?" He knew he shouldn't, didn't need to, explain his orders. Yet he had to talk this out, if only to himself. "He had us immobilized, would've for as long as he wanted. I know that, you know that, and you can bet *he* knew that, when he set the ambush *and* when he retreated."

Cooley remained silent.

Fuck it.

"We have to go down there, Cooley, first to determine if Samael is dead or in danger, then to attempt capture of these dissidents. His safety is our first priority."

Cooley nodded.

Andrew motioned for him to enter the corridor first, waiting until the man had attained the door to the basement stairs before following, weapon drawn.

A FAMILIAR FACE

Edith lit another cigarette, her second since the others had disappeared within the brick building, using the cherry from the first to induce the noxious leaves into a steady burn.

Fuck it.

She hadn't smoked when they'd been around, hadn't wanted to deal with the questions or eyebrows that would've been raised. Now, with more nicotine in her system than had there been for longer than she could remember, she still felt on edge, apprehensive, as if at any moment something terrible were going to happen.

What she'd been able to pick up from their conversation was nearly impossible to comprehend.

Peter was called Maccabeus; he'd been abducted. Thorin and his two strange companions, the enigmatic yet strangely likeable Amin and the beautiful yet incredibly irritating Marquetta, had entered the building before which she waited, intent on freeing him, carrying with themselves explosives, at least one weapon, and a will to do whatever it would take to realize their end.

The whole thing was surreal in the extreme.

And so she smoked, not with disregard for her unborn child, for she felt the betrayal acutely, but with an understanding, clear, that if she didn't she'd be unable to simply wait in the car, at least not without freaking the fuck out.

She wished she hadn't insisted on coming along, that she'd left the apartment before Thorin had called, perhaps never come to D.C. at all.

Sitting in a cold, running car with the window slightly cracked in the earliest of morning hours, inhaling poisonous smoke just to maintain a grip, gazing across the street at the sheer face of a building that refused to share with her the secrets it held within, she found the prospect of finding Andrew, wherever he was, whatever he was doing, immaterial, sublime, evanescent.

Her cigarette, poised between her lips, slipped slightly as she saw, there across from her, the front door of the building open, a man pop his head out to glance quickly up and down the street. She ducked down, hastily closed her window, just before his gaze passed her position, peering from the shadows at the first face to breach the door since her friends had gone inside.

Her smoke fell completely from her lips, dropping into her lap.

She didn't care, for the face she'd seen, now gone, vanished back into the building, was Andrew's, unmistakable, even in the brief instant it had shone from the opened door.

A moment passed, two, until the sharp sting of the cigarette on her leg brought her back to the present.

She jumped out of the car, brushing the burning brand from her jeans.

She hesitated; time stretched, ill-defined. Large flakes once again began to softly fall, filling the space between her and the building.

Andrew.

She knew it was ludicrous. He couldn't be in the building.

Yet she knew what she'd seen.

Never would she forget his face. That she'd mistaken another for him was impossible.

He must have come to help.

Somehow.

A large flake, crystalline, cold, alighted on her nose, melted, found itself intermixed with the saline of tears, flowing down around her lips, her neck, to rest between her swollen breasts.

She began to run, awkwardly in the way of a very pregnant woman hurrying across a snowy street, a slow, running waddle, toward the door that had moments ago, perhaps minutes, she didn't know, framed the face of the man she loved.

ESCAPE

At the far end of the hallway from the gruesome flesh that remained of Benjamin, Thorin's old friend and Peter's compatriot, Marquetta's apparent lover, they nearly ran into Amin, who, bursting through the door at its furthest extension, set on the direction from which they'd just come, jumped easily to the left, allowing Thorin to pass by, coming back to the center of the passage to confront Peter, still with Marquetta by his side.

"I told you coming here was dangerous."

Peter, seeming untouchable, was not fazed.

"Dangerous perhaps, tragic, imprudent," he paused, moving passed Amin toward the corridor that led to the receiving room, turned to address his three companions, "yet still I do not regret having come."

Thorin stood speechless, eyes darting down the corridor. He brought them to Peter, tried to look quickly away—yet Peter held them. For a moment but nonetheless an eternity.

Amin studied Peter, weirdly enough seeming satisfied by what he found. "We should be going," with a nod toward the door he'd just come through, "Soon we will have company, I'd imagine."

Fuck this shit.

Thorin spoke, eyes still set on his friend, "You don't regret coming? Benjamin is dead. We could have all been killed; we still might be. What the fuck is wrong with you?"

"Ben's death is tragic, but he chose that fate, freely." He broke contact, focusing on the near distance of the hall; "This night has held many truths for me. I hadn't previously appreciated the realities of what I'm doing. I didn't know the face of my enemy, and I didn't know who I was. I didn't know..." turning to look down the far end of the corridor, "I didn't know the truth of this path. Yet now that it's present I find not hesitation but determination, not doubt but certainty: These people *need* to be completely extirpated, and I'd be one to see such an end through, now knowing full well the actuality of what we're about, the reality, unequivocal and deadly, of the choices we make."

Thorin began to respond, cut of by Amin.

"We need to go *now,*" shot a glance at the door.

Thorin began to object, to perhaps shout at Peter, shake some sense into him, yet then recalled where they were, what had happened and what could happen next, kept his mouth shut.

Together, Amin bringing up the rear, they moved down the corridor toward what Thorin could only assume was the exit of which Amin had spoken.

Passing through the door at its end, a thick piece of work, perhaps four inches of solid steel, Peter hanging back to keep it open, they found themselves in a relatively small basement-like room. The stairs at the far side ended at a pair of nearly horizontal double-doors, the kind you would find in the basement of any building in the city.

Thorin rushed up the stairs, attempted to push the doors open, finding the way chained shut from the outside, quarter-inch links slightly visible as he exerted force.

"What the fuck do we do now?" He could hear a building panic in his voice, louder than it should have been in the close confines of the room.

"Hold it open," Amin dug within his jacket pocket, retrieving a small portion of the plastique. Reaching through, he smooshed it into the links of the chain, a moment later sticking a small device into the putty. "Everyone, back through the door." He withdrew his phone, obviously more than just a phone, took a moment to fiddle with it, fingers sliding along the face of its screen. To Peter, "Close the door."

No sooner had Peter done so than Amin inputted a command, the dull reverberation of a small explosion passing through the steel.

Without a word Peter opened it once more. Taking the lead he made haste across the room, up the stairs, throwing the doors wide.

The others followed, emerging into a fairly wide alley, from what Thorin could figure on the north side of the building.

It had again begun to snow, softly, quietly yet heavily, large flakes floating down, between the building and its neighbor, surreal.

They broke into a run, emerging from the mouth of the alley onto Capitol Street, veering right, across the front of Party Headquarters, toward where Edith waited in her Subaru, hopefully with the engine running and ready to go.

However, as they neared the car Thorin could see quite clearly Edith was not waiting within.

Fuck.

He cast his gaze about the street, finding her nowhere, caught up with the others as they reached the car.

"She's not here," spoken desperately to no one in particular.

Amin, nearly throwing Peter into the back seat, slammed the door shut. "This is clear."

Marquetta also entered the rear of the car, from the opposite side of that through which Peter had been hauled, stepping from the snow of the road and into the warmth of the running vehicle.

"We are not leaving without her."

Amin didn't smile. "I'd never suggest we do so."

Again Thorin searched the road, looking for some sign of what could have happened to her.

He was about to succumb to desperation, simply call out her name for the world to hear, when he noticed leading away from the vehicle footprints in the fresh snow covering the road, headed toward the front entrance of Party Headquarters.

Fucking Christ on a fucking crutch.

"If I'm not back in five minutes, or at the first sign of trouble, leave without us."

Amin nodded, moving around the front of the Subaru, opened the driver side door; "I'd greatly prefer we all leave together."

Thorin caught his eyes, cracked a dry grin. "I'd like that as well," sprinted off across the street, toward the building he'd just left and never thought he'd enter again.

TRAGEDY

Of all the idiotic, fucking retarded… Fuck…

He raced across the street.

Motherfucking women.

He reached the doors, started to open them quickly, then, realizing what he was doing and to where the doors led, hesitated. He cracked slightly the right of the two, peering within, half expecting to see armed men in the chamber beyond, perhaps rushing toward him. What he saw was an empty room, cavernous, distinct in its lack of occupancy.

He stepped within, drawing the door closed behind himself.

The still of the place denied the possibility of simply calling out to her. He made his way cautiously across the marble floor, hugging the inside of the southern row of columns. Finding the hall completely deserted, he began to cross toward the main corridor, to where the stairs that descended to the basement were found.

Paused midway.

There was a sound coming from up the stairs, a sort of belabored breath, the sound of someone in trouble, injured.

Without really thinking, he sprinted up the great stair, reaching the landing to discover not Edith but a tall Indian man, mostly unconscious, laid-out to the left behind the low rise of the wall that fronted the landing.

Did Amin do this?

He didn't have time to wonder, needed to find Edith and be gone from this place, yet also he couldn't leave the man where he was, not the way he was. Blood soaked the cloth of his suit on his right arm, also his jacket, the carpet upon which he lay, spreading in a stain nearly a meter in diameter.

Thorin kneeled down, reaching inside his pocket for his knife, found it missing.

Fuck.

He'd given it to Peter below.

Not really knowing what else to do, yet knowing he had to do something, Thorin began to ease the injured man out of his jacket, meeting with struggle, weak yet still enough to complicate his task.

This is taking too long.

He succeeded in removing the jacket, cast its bloody bulk to the side, rolled up the wet, crimson sleeve, a thick reek of iron reaching his nose, bringing bile to the base of his throat.

He found no exit hole.

The bullet must be lodged in his arm, in a bone, most likely.

He'll live.

Thorin removed the man's tie, pressing the wide end onto the ragged hole, wrapped the rest of its length firmly but not too tightly around his upper arm, tied it off with the knot upon the wound.

"That's all I can do for you, man." He spoke more to himself than to his unconscious companion. He stood up.

"Thorin!" Edith's voice rang out, too-loud in the quiet vastness of the chamber.

He turned to where Edith stood, at the mouth of the northern corridor, instantly and without thought barreled down the stairs, reaching her in mere moments.

"What the fuck are you doing in here," his voice carried an edge of anger, not loud but cutting.

"I came in to..."

"Didn't you fucking listen to Amin: You were supposed to wait in the car, safe."

"But, I..."

He cut her off, grabbing her by the arm, began to drag her toward the door. He expected her to be abashed, perhaps to apologize; however, she was not, did not. Instead she tore herself out of his grip, took a step back, toward the corridor.

"Andrew is still in here, Thorin." She not only sounded serious but seemed anxious as well. "I looked for him down there," she looked toward the north wing. "But I couldn't find him."

Thorin had no time for whatever lunacy in which she was attempting to entice him to join her, again grabbed her by the arm. "We have to leave here, *now*."

"But he's still in here." She looked panicked. "We cant leave him behind."

Realizing there was no way he could physically force her to come with him, not without literally dragging her the whole way, he took a breath. "Whom can't we leave behind?"

"Andrew!"

For some reason she seemed to think *he* was being unreasonable.

He released her sleeve; "Andrew?" Thinking for a moment, "Andrew isn't here."

"But I saw him, not two minutes ago, at the door." She nearly sobbed; "He's in here somewhere."

He began to again tell her Andrew was *not* there, that she was mistaken, stopped himself.

As usual, there's no arguing with women.   .

"You and I are in no position to help him, and staying only puts us in danger as well."

"Bu…"

"He came here on his own; he can find his way out on his own." Forestalling another of her objections, "The others are waiting in the car. Tarrying here also puts them in danger. We need to leave. We need to get Peter away from this place."

She seemed to focus then on his words, "Peter is in the car?"

"Yes, and we need to be as well."

"You're sure Andrew will be OK?"

What the fuck is this woman talking about? Jesus Christ…

"He'll be fine;" he smiled. "Trust me."

Which apparently she did, allowing him to guide her toward the doors. He pushed both open, drawing her out into the frigid chill of early morning.

Snow continued to fall softly through the air.

They descended the short rise of steps fronting the building, reached the sidewalk from where he could see Edith's Subaru to the right, Amin in the driver's seat. He led the way across the street.

I'll have to toss her in the front, sit in the back with Peter and Marquetta, I…

Suddenly a shot rang out behind them, from the direction of the alley. Before he could react, before he'd even really heard the percussion of its discharge, Edith roughly pushed him away, sending him flying face down to the street, his footing unsure in the slippery expanse of the snow-packed road.

Amin, quicker than Thorin had thought anyone could be, leaped out of the car, stood behind its open door, firing a number of shots in quick succession, forcing their assailant back into the alley.

"Get her to the car!" Amin met Thorin's eyes as the latter attempted to raise himself from the street. He fired another shot into the mouth of the alley.

Finding his feet, Thorin turned, intent on literally dragging Edith with him, to his horror finding her fallen on the street where a moment before he'd stood.

He reached down, lifting her body from the snow. A dark red stain marred the white expanse. He couldn't tell from where she bled.

Oh no.

She wasn't heavy, not really, even thirty-five weeks pregnant perhaps only 75 kilograms.

She felt weak, too limp in his arms.

Amin remained where he was, gun trained on the mouth of the alley. Peter sprang out of the back seat just as Thorin rounded the front of the car, opened the front passenger door, helped him settle Edith, whose breath was slow, shallow, on the seat. He looked to be completely aghast, horrified.

The two friends crowded into the back.

Amin fired one last round into the alley—Thorin wasn't sure whether he did so at someone in particular or simply as a warning— He then quickly resumed the driver's seat, throwing the stick into first, bringing the Outback into swift motion, speeding north at a decidedly unsafe speed.

Thorin wanted to scream, to shake the man beside him, demand to know if he still didn't regret having come to D.C.. Instead he sat back in his seat, leaned his head back to gaze out the rear windshield, to where in the retreating distance he could see two figures emerge from the alley, come to stand in the middle of the street, watching as they sped off, away from Party Headquarters.

Amin raced onward, slowing infinitesimally to make a hard right onto New York Avenue, the solid grip of the Subaru bringing them around the turn without incident.

"What are we going to do about her?" Thorin sounded much calmer than he felt.

Amin, not slowing but speeding even faster down the deserted street, "My first priority is bringing *him* to safety." He didn't exactly sound pleased.

"Fuck my safety;" Peter retorted, anger in his voice. "We need to get her to a hospital *now*."

Unfazed, Amin continued down New York, slowing a little now that they'd put a fair amount of distance between themselves and Party Headquarters. "And we will do so, as soon as we're out of The Capital."

Peter started to argue, cut off sharply by the older man.

"If we go to a hospital here, they will find us. If we go to a hospital anywhere near here, they will find us." He softened, "There's a place we can go outside of Baltimore, perhaps thirty minutes from here."

Thorin, unsure what to say, looked to Peter.

Whose eyes were set on Edith, lying silently in the front seat. "In thirty minutes she could be dead, her child as well."

Amin responded without turning from the road; "In that case there will be two more lives at your feet. Perhaps in the future you'll think twice before flouting the dictates of good sense and the advice of your friends." He backed off a little, in tone only. "Regardless, even if she and the child perish, they'll not be the last to fall." He turned momentarily from the road, set a hand upon Edith's stomach.

"We travel a dangerous path, Maccabeus, for ourselves and any foolish enough to follow. Never forget that."

Peter sat back, into the middle seat between Thorin and Marquetta, silent.

For his part Thorin unrolled his window slightly, letting the cold air slide across his face.

We're going to Baltimore.

Aleta's gonna fucking kill me.

He laughed then, a dead, mirthless thing, drawing a sharp look from both his friend and the woman beside him.

He took a breath. Another.

Her being here in the first place is my fault. She was shot because she saved me.

Her life or death, her unborn child's, are my responsibility.

He could only hope he was adequate to the burden, whichever end was realized.

CHAPTER 11
THE CENTRE

COMMONS

Daniel cast a slate-blue gaze upon the crowd assembled in the Ithaca Commons. Young and old, male and female, there all were represented, a small sea of shining faces, unmarked by toil or oppression, imagined or physical. The queerly removed, acutely abstracted psychological pressure he'd known his entire life was here absent, those before him looking to have never known its dry, stale presence.

If there was one thing he'd come to know in the months he'd passed in Ithaca, it was that these people were unlike any with whom he'd before ever interacted.

I wonder where Thorin is.

He cast about the crowd, not finding the older man, in fact not seeing anyone he could reasonably say he knew well. Not to say he knew Thorin well; even after six months in Ithaca, talking and working with him nearly every day and most nights, he could not lay claim to that, but at the very least Thorin was *known* to him, mysterious perhaps but nonetheless a bastion of center and stability, a man whose simple presence made most everything a little more real, interactions with others a little less awkward. Daniel had ventured with him from his old life; Daniel's new life, however one would characterize it, now was somehow found premised on the older man's company.

There was one among the crowd he called friend, Charlie, an old man, older than Thorin by at least a few years, likely a decade, who walked with a limp and carried a cane, although as far as Daniel had seen he rarely actually used the thing.

Presently Charlie sat upon a concrete wall at the far side of the commons from where Daniel too waited, dangling his legs idly over its worn, rounded edge.

I wonder when they will begin.

It was Saturday, the day of rest, when in Ithaca was found merriment and diversion, in The Commons a veritable festival, complete with music and refreshment, the heady scent of ganja filling the air.

For Daniel, Saturday had become something to which he looked forward, emblematic of a world far removed from that which he knew, had known, whose peculiarities and microcosms, eddies and springs, offered him a welcome escape, more a redefinition really, from himself, of himself.

So too did the people of Ithaca provide him the context to be himself in a way he'd never before known.

They were just so different from the strangers he'd known in The City, not just in their movements, the way they related to each other, but also in the content of their beliefs, the ordination of their minds.

So strange.

The people of Ithaca seemed to function as a single extended family. Perhaps ten-thousand strong, the community was tightly knit in a way no social structure in The City ever could be. There, surrounded by millions and millions of people, it would be a thing of curiosity for one to know a hundred by name, to interact freely with those one didn't know as easily as with one's friends and family a thing of wonder, suspect. Here, people were familial with all, and here all was provided.

No one ever went hungry in Ithaca; no one was without a home or a friendly ear, welcome arms. It was a utopia, fully functioning, thriving, content in its finitude.

The farmland in this part of New York was expansive, providing plenty for all, as indeed the inhabitants of Ithaca were a small bunch when held against the multitudes the fields there around used to sustain. Unlike Bethel, Ithaca didn't export its produce, for no trucks were granted access to its compass.

And there was wine aplenty, ganja grown under an open sky amidst the endless rows of vine, beside the deep waters of Cayuga.

Those who didn't tend the fields, who didn't care for the animals, large herds of cattle, flocks of sheep, clutches of chickens, some swine, were occupied with matters of their own, from maintaining the city itself to a great many other things, some with which Daniel was familiar, others that he couldn't fathom at all.

The university up the hill, Cornell, lay abandoned. As far as Daniel knew, no one aside from Jonathan, no one with whom he'd spoken, ever really went there. Daniel, from what he could tell Thorin as well, had never been invited to come along, and he'd had need to ascend the hill but a few times during his stay, first to walk the arboretum in the fall, discovering varieties of trees of which he'd never before even heard, later to sled the great slope that lay near its western limit, close to town and away from the larger edifices of the formerly great institution.

Ithaca Commons was itself an intriguing place, where people congregated for functions such as that to which he was now present, where on afternoons a thriving market sprang up and in the evening young lovers and hooligans, old couples and families, came for a bite to eat, coffee and tea, perhaps to pass ganja among themselves, or not. It was a place for meeting and for being met, and it was as alien to Daniel as were those who animated its ways.

The City, for all its immensity, was in essence nothing more than an extremely elaborate, overly complicated, crossroads. Surely, people lived there, or rather had homes located therein, and assuredly people worked there, yet The City in its truest form was a thing defined as extension alone, a distance one must cross to get to where one was actually going.

The City has no Commons.

In Ithaca The Commons marked the center of the universe, anthropocentric in the extreme, where at its origin was found the Sun, ringed round by the other near heavenly bodies, found in relative order and distance, the furthest extension of which lay nearly a kilometer there from.

He again surveyed the crowd.

Where the hell is Thorin?

Not that he *needed* Thorin to be there, but they *had* made plans to meet...

Distracted by a beautiful woman with long, flowing hair, making her way passed him, east and deeper into The Commons. She moved lightly, floating through the crowd; a spring dress, white linen embroidered with roses, graced her shoulders, falling just below the gentle curve of her calves.

Surprised to find himself following behind, a cigarette between his lips and a smile upon his face.

THE WOMAN IN THE LINEN DRESS

Daniel kept his eyes low, navigating the crowd without acknowledging those he passed, set on the flowing garment ahead, beneath which thin ankles met light, leather sandals.

It had been over half a year since he'd left New York, since he'd last seen Alena, and although he could still recall with precision every line of her face, sharp and soft, the way her hair hung gently down, the lightness of her laugh as he became the object of yet another silent, or not so silent, joke, the memory of her had grown ever-so-faint in the dimly lit chambers of his mind, its ways and darkened pathways, potentialities and could-have-beens, receding, no longer felt acutely.

There'd been a time when he'd loved her. He knew this, couldn't deny the feelings he'd had, their reality, visceral and cerebral. He also knew time was reality, that a lifetime had passed since his love for her had had the opportunity to express itself, that expression was fact, actuality.

Then, walking The Commons, pulled along by a nymph, mysterious and beautiful, he didn't love Alena. A cherished memory wasn't love, for his time with her had taught him what love was, and one cannot love a memory.

Love, a reality of a higher order, is predicated on a great many things, essential and incidental, the foremost of which is its object must be present, given, accepted. That love is reciprocated, this is surely necessary, lest love die, yet that the one you love be present is even more so requisite, the love of a memory, a lack, being simple love of oneself, paradoxically, as love found in that which one is not.

Crossing The Commons, trailing an unknown woman set on an unknown destination, he wasn't looking for love; even less was he in search of an Other with whom he could by recourse find himself. Daniel, for once without over thinking things, simply wanted...

He grinned.

He simply wanted to fuck the woman in the linen dress.

Having followed her through The Commons, now finding himself nearing its eastern limit, bordered there by Cayuga Street, away from the greater mass of people and the stage set just west of Commons Center, Daniel slowed, seated himself on a bench, sparked a cigarette as the woman entered a café to the left, a small place that among other things served the best gelato he'd ever tasted.

He took a pull from his cigarette, considered his present situation.

He'd never before seen the woman, odd considering the relatively small population of the city, or at least he couldn't remember having seen her. And he knew he would if he had. She was more gorgeous than any other he'd encountered in the past months, his presence here, now waiting for her to emerge from the café, testament enough.

Sat, puffed. Lost in thoughts, mainly shallow but occasionally of not insubstantial depth.

After a short while she exited the café, holding a small, white, ceramic cup, steaming. She lowered herself into a seat set there to the left of the entrance, perhaps six meters distant from the bench upon which Daniel sat smoking his cigarette, not hiding that he was staring at her intently.

Her hair fell deep, rich, over her shoulders, the darkest of browns yet certainly not black, reached to the base of her spine, itself lain lightly against the woven metal of the seatback, straight and poised, without slouch or arch. Beneath the light material of her dress could be seen a vague silhouette, contours of body suggestively shaping the rose-embroidered shroud, beautiful curves hugging a somewhat, although not quite, petite frame.

For his part Daniel sat silently, puffing the final drags of his smoke, appreciating the presence of a woman in truth. Not a girl, certainly not.

She turned toward him then, jerking his eyes from the curve of her hips, passed the swell of her breasts, to her visage proper, deep almond eyes peering at him from under dark lashes.

Sipped her tea, a smile creeping into the corners of her mouth.

He smiled back.

The woman arched an eyebrow, smile leaping from the periphery to form a soft purse, slightly open, what he could only assume were warm lips curved around the space of a question.

Set down her cup, bringing her right leg over her left, leaned lazily on her right elbow, forward, against the table before her. "Is there something I can do for you?"

The soft melody struck his ears, words as supple and warm as were the lips, the tongue, that formed them.

And with that, thoughts of fucking her fled Daniel, the finitude of his self reasserting itself, awkwardness banishing virility to settle in a familiar form of insecure impotence.

He turned away, moved to quickly exit the scene, hesitated and remained where he was, seated. "I was just wondering who you were;" he attempted a smile, badly executed. "I haven't seen you before."

"Nor I you," she smiled, "not really... though I do know who *you* are." Her eyes sparkled, veritably.

Daniel sighed, inwardly.

What the fuck.

"I seem to get that a lot;" he stood, smoothing his shirt.

"With the company you keep, how could it be otherwise?" She turned back to her tea, retrieving it from the table, motioned for him to join her; "You're the closest thing to a celebrity we have here." Paused at the incredulity that sprung onto his face, "Perhaps *curiosity* would be more apt," laughed.

"What about the company I keep?" He refrained from moving toward the seat opposite her, unwilling to allow the woman, however striking she may have been, to have such power over him.

"Jonathan? Mr. Charlie?" She laughed again, "*Thorin?*" Placed her tea on the table, unsipped, "If you don't see how your coming here with them, Thorin especially, who hasn't been back for more than two decades, makes you a person of interest, you must be blind as well as stupid."

Daniel, silently admitting he indeed was both, walked toward the woman, sat down opposite her. "I have eyes enough to see you're the most beautiful woman in this city."

Not that I've ever seen, certainly not, but... exquisite.

She blushed then, hiding her face behind the cup, setting it down empty. "I'd never have thought you to be such a..." she paused, searching for words, "...such a smooth talker," broke out laughing.

He sat silent, unsure how to respond, unable to move as he'd just then seated himself, stuck, left to squirm.

The feeling was unpleasantly familiar.

Obviously not that which she labeled him, Daniel fidgeted uneasily in his seat, feeling not quite rough, more awkward, certainly not smooth.

Mumbled, "Just being honest," glanced away, toward the bench upon which he'd recently rested, wishing somehow he were still there, better yet still back with the crowd at the other end of the commons. He turned toward her, fighting to maintain contact with the dark orbs, deep wells, she somehow passed off as mere eyes.

Now that he'd made direct contact with them, he could see they were completely black, save but a thin crest of brown, almost indistinguishable at their borders.

He set back slightly, taken off guard.

"How do you know Thorin?"

The sun slid from her lashes, dripped onto her lips, sprang forth as a light laugh, not quite a giggle; "Jonathan introduced us a long time ago." She reached a hand behind her head, seemingly extended in a stretch, in fact retrieving a short, fat length of white from the layered depths of her hair, from behind her ear, from what Daniel could tell.

Sewn round with incredulity, "Decades ago?"

He couldn't believe the woman before him was more than ten years his senior, so soft did her skin look, so youthful was the life she exuded.

She lit the joint with the flame of a candle, oil, set into a small, frosted glass lamp, which he'd not noticed until just then, set it back on the table between them. "Indeed," puffed, "when I first arrived here," again, "back when They made us leave our homes."

This was a topic in which he was much interested, revived after long months.

He sat back in his chair more fully. "Back when the IDSC reformed The Cities."

She nodded, pulling one more hit from the joint, proffered it to him.

He smiled, accepted the smoldering length without hitting it.

"Where did you live before?"

"Here and there," she spared a glance at the spliff, still held between the fingers of his right hand, unhit, "I used to move around a lot, you understand." She motioned for him to return the joint, retrieving it quickly, gently, before pulling a thick hit, exhaled into the light breeze flowing passed, carrying the smoke away readily yet not touching a hair on her head.

He shivered in the full light of the afternoon sun. "What was it like?"

"What was what like?"

He hesitated, also not sure exactly to what he referred. "Being..." paused, reconsidered, "Living back then, before the IDSC."

"If I said it was at once more and less free than my life now, would you want to know why, in what ways?"

He grinned, "Of course."

"Then it was not at once more and less free than my life now."

His brow furrowed, drawing close, a semblance of concentration, or perhaps irritation. "Lemmy have that joint back."

Pulled a few hits, sitting into his chair, head leaned back to puff weary rings through pursed lips.

Then decided to take control of the conversation; "And what do you do here, in Ithaca?"

She looked out, into the empty extension of the commons there, not quite passed him, more to the side, but certainly into a space other than that which he occupied. "This and that;" she accepted the joint, now half consumed, from his outstretched hand. "You could say I'm a spiritual aide," took a hit, "or more accurately a simple helper," laughed; "Mostly I watch Jonathan as he works." She glanced over her shoulder, "Up there, at the old university."

Curiosity now truly piqued, "What does he do up there?"

"He Creates."

"Is that supposed to mean something to me?"

"Does it?"

Thought for but a moment, "No."

Laughter in her eyes, "Then I suppose not."

Memory tugged at Daniel, a half remembered conversation from what seemed a long time ago. He thought, no, he *knew* he'd had this conversation before, or at least one so much like it the difference was moot.

"Does it have something to do with Judging?"

She looked momentarily startled, quickly covered. "Perhaps it does." Passed the joint back to him, "But judging from your question, you have no idea what that means."

He blushed, involuntarily, embarrassed that he was blushing, suddenly just a little too warm, too close to the goddess before him. "Should I?"

Her laughter fled her eyes, burst fully formed from her lips, not quite quickly contained.

He met her eyes again.

Do you?

He knew the answer, the response *to* the answer, left the thread behind.

They sat silently for a duration, the joint passing between them.

She broke the still, gathering herself as if to leave. "I'm Mary, in answer to you earlier curiosity."

Mary. He formed the name in the quiet of his mind.

Then, before he could respond, before he'd finished savoring the unspoken tones, she rose from her seat. "I'll see you soon, Daniel the Dreamer."

Speechless as she began to walk away, an uncomfortable number of questions lodged in his throat.

What the fuck?

Watched as the woman, linen dress and all, disappeared around the corner, north on Cayuga Street.

TO WHICH HE WAS PRESENT

Daniel sat, momentarily stupefied by the woman's sudden departure.

After but a moment he rose from his seat, set himself on her trail, stopped, retrieving a cigarette from his pack and leaning against the east face of the café, around the corner from the table he'd just abandoned. He sparked it, observing as the woman, now crossing State Street, which marked the Commons' northern limit, made her way... wherever it was she was going.

That he'd jumped from his seat to follow her was as much of a surprise to Daniel as had been his interaction with her itself. Both had simply happened, yet still certainly sprung from some hidden volition to which he wasn't privy. He was no puppet; of this he was sure. That he'd followed her then, moved to follow her now, must be a product of his choosing, regardless of his awareness or lack thereof of its realization or intricacies.

The mystery now was why he'd set himself on the path before him.

Leaned against the wall, some thirty meters from her departing figure, he had the opportunity, the objectivity, to examine his course, limited as his perspective was by the shadow of self and the cloudy veil of all, and there was very much, that was unknown, to which he wasn't entirely present yet which nonetheless lay across his mind and spirit, heavy and confining.

Fuck the hidden desires and vague wishes of my sublime self. I will not be so driven.

He turned away without giving the woman a second glance.

The festivities at the other end of The Commons still hadn't properly begun—as yet no music was being made on the stage, which sat silent still amid the crowd, empty.

Peter was at once relieved and incensed to see there Thorin standing before Charlie, who occupied the same seat he'd had when Daniel had left nearly a half hour earlier.

He approached the older men, setting himself perpendicular to their faced meeting.

Thorin turned slightly, sparing him a quick nod, "Daniel," turned back to Charlie and whatever it was he'd been saying to him.

In no mood for pleasantries or the hobbled conversation of old men, Daniel interrupted before Thorin could resume, turning toward him, "What the fuck am I doing here, Thorin?"

Thorin let linger a look with Charlie, slid his gaze back toward Daniel. "Why would *I* know what *you* are doing here," glanced momentarily to Charlie, grinned, back to Daniel, "Perhaps it is time for you to be on your way. Canada, was it?"

At a loss for words, and truly having basically forgotten himself he'd ever been set there on, Daniel felt fade his anger, took in the scene around himself, thought on all Ithaca had been to him since he'd arrived.

His life in The City seemed vague, even more so than it had during his brief trek with Thorin through the lower reaches of New York, poorly defined, a mass of frustrated movements and uncomfortable not-so-silences. Looking back, he could identify no moment to which he could point and say "That was me. That was my life." He could assuredly recall moments he'd experienced, places through which and to which and from which he'd moved, but not a single moment of himself nor any place he could call his own.

Furthermore, he could not recall clearly one conversation or interaction he'd had, save those at the end he'd shared with Thorin and Alena, not one. It was all a mess, half-movements and ill-born instances of truncated being. Mostly he recalled long and pointless internal monologues, dialogues and trialogues, sardony, painful observation and dissection, minutia.

In the dark one tends to speak with oneselves.

The thoughts came to him unbidden.

The compass always points…

He stopped, jerking himself back to the present, to *the* present in which both Thorin and Charlie were present, watching him thoughtfully.

Let slip, "I don't even know what Canada is," sounding more forlorn than he'd intended, drawing clear sympathy from Charlie and a cocked head from Thorin, eyebrows raised in unspoken question.

Quizzicality banished after but a moment, "Then you no longer wish to go there?" No hint of smile touched his face.

Daniel sighed, turned quickly into abashed irritation, "I don't suppose I ever *wished* to go there," to a gruff laugh, "Back then it was simply the only place I could think of," drew a cigarette.

Until this point a silent observer, Charlie interposed, "And this means you now can think of more?"

Drawing another laugh from Daniel, who'd in the past months come to appreciate the man's soft spoken nature and cutting directness, "I'm not even sure what it means," sparked the length held between the first two fingers of his right hand. "I think it means *I* am more than I was."

Unwilling to let Daniel have his moment of simply defined reflection, Thorin pushed him; "So what the fuck are you doing here?"

Daniel, thankfully in the middle of a drag, had a brief duration in which to consider his response.

Exactly zero thoughts entered his mind.

In fact, nothing entered his mind.

Well, not nothing, but *nothingness*. Perhaps that was the correct term to denote the nothing with which Daniel then was occupied.

Then, a beginning.

I'm speaking to Thorin and Charlie.

The present rushed in, a cascade of open space and potential, fresh in a way neither his thoughts nor the mind that housed them could... could have ever been. For Daniel knew then the present was an alien thing to him. Having lived his life in the mere futures of others' pasts, reflected upon the ephemeral plane of their passing, he'd had no way to know what the present was, opened into the now of his self.

It was life, love, freedom and awareness, clear vision and subjectivity, for objectivity, as he now knew, was just a term for living others' stories, abstract and always incomplete, not enough.

It is not enough to simply be a character in a story, a phantom whose existence lies only in the passing tide of enveloping context, set and stage.

I'm more than a sign, to myself and others. I *am* more than the passing play of things, dead and fixed in their relations, mere history playing at actuality.

Dead, eh?

Again the thoughts came to him unbidden.

Yes.

Then why is it dark?

It is light; I see the sun now overhead.

It is dark... It is dark...

The thought sounded mad, in of course the way thoughts *could* sound, which was not at all.

Still...

It is cold.

I stand in the sun.

He could feel the warm tendrils now, touching his face and brow with golden extensions.

They will come for me soon, they...

Daniel paused in the infinitude of his mind, considering that which crossed its space.

Paused.

Who is coming?

Thought.

They always come.

Who?

Why do you torment me?

I don't know you.

I don't know myself?

Absurd.

I...

They...

Silence and still; quiet.

The void of his mind was consuming, inescapable.

"I do not know him!" Daniel screamed, a harsh, cutting thing that crashed through the crowd of people, over and through Charlie and Thorin, who were as though mere filaments, moved by, yet nothing to, the force of his voice.

Opened into the now of his self.

He was in the Commons. Present were a number of people, all contemplating him. Thorin and Charlie, obviously a little taken aback by his outburst, stood, sat, faces inscrutable.

"Whom don't you know, Daniel?" A familiar voice came from behind him.

Thorin and Charlie jerked their eyes over Daniel's shoulder, passed him to the source of the question.

They looked surprised.

He turned, meeting Jonathan's gaze. "I don't know." Took a breath, "I don't know him." Another.

The older man smiled, bringing an uneasiness to Daniel's viscera. "I think you do."

He nodded to Thorin.

"It is time."

TRUTH

The truth of this world is aesthetic.

In the end, in the beginning and middle even, all is simple reflection of personal taste.

How would you like to see the world? Is it hostile, frightening? Is it exciting and new, full of experiences and potentialities? Dead ends and frustration? Is it dead? Is it alive? Does the world speak to you, you to it? Are you in the world or of the world or in spite of the world? Because of it?

The will to truth is enshrined in the mind. It is undeniable, inescapable, mutable only if one's humanity itself is rejected, itself muted. Yet the form of this truth, whether it be elaborate, simple, exclusive and regulatory or comprehensive and positive... this is a matter of aesthetics, taste.

What is it you see?

Nothing save what you want to see.

Somewhere out there, betwingst the flow and ebb of reality, is the final piece, or just a regular piece, of the puzzle that will finally bring sense to this Confusion.

What is the nature of the fit though? Colors, shapes? Concept and continuity? Spirit? Material?

It is all inherently meaningless, the puzzle just as much as the pieces themselves, ephemeral. Yet more than this it is concrete, eternal, heavy and inescapable, a preponderous amalgam of things small and large, the actuality of which is imminent, the meaning of which is too great to acknowledge, let alone comprehend.

So we tell stories. We read stories, write them, consider them and like them, or not. Simply ways, simple ways, to limit the All to that which can be understood.

Still though the truth of any of it is aesthetic only; anyone who tells you different is selling something. If anything, honesty, scientific honesty, presupposes this, even if the manner of presentation attempts with all its formal will to obfuscate the fact.

He trailed his hand along the wall to his right, feeling the repetitive friction of passing brick, now and again tile, a doorway traced in wood trim, sometimes painted sometimes not. No windows though. This deep into The Structure was found no such plane of illumination, simply wall, door, portal and frame.

Not an hour past he'd been outdoors, in the Commons, waiting for the coming evening, the plaintive calm of a spring evening in Upstate New York, music. Before that with Mary, a beautiful woman, smoking a joint in the enveloping atmosphere of her presence, a little awkward yet weirdly comfortable, black orbs, deep wells, drawing him, cut short, left to squirm.

The passages he traveled, walking silently behind Jonathan, Thorin to his rear, were anything but like the Commons, far removed from the freedom and ease he'd come to know. Even less were they akin to the ways he'd walked in The City, where silent eyes observed, recorded, where a million steps marked every street, every corner, unseen, forgotten in the rush of the place.

These halls had no eyes, blank, featureless. They presented no potentials, seeming confining, antithetical to his rightful movement as a free man.

No one, very few at least, had walked these extensions for a long time. Here there were no footprints or scuffs, for here there wasn't even dust. This, more than anything, attested to the utter abandonment of the place.

Yet, the length before him also marked a path, uninterrupted in its finitude, unambiguous, clear.

Had he chosen this path? Had it been forced upon him? Was it given or created?

The point was immaterial.

He walked a line, thin in its own way as it was fairly broad in truth, traced in marble tile and bordered with brick and frame. Any and all sign of what lay beyond its twisting ways was absent, and Daniel, not simply out of his element, as was the case generally these days, but also strangely out of himself, found himself wishing for, needing, though they were presently several meters underground, more, just a moment of vision, a crack of light to lend him a modicum of orientation. Even here that should be possible.

Inspiration.

The word then had no meaning. It was a fraud, a sham, a sick effigy of a mere process, alien and devoid of soul.

What is a soul? Is it a thing, immutable and everlasting? Transient and corrupted, finite? The expression of self? The truth of self? Perhaps a simple reification of compounded relations, itself hollow, void, a lie that allows other lies to gain the appearance of truth? For if truth is anything like what it portends to be, it must be at heart structured about a kernel of imagination, a hard ether itself not about anything and thus a lie.

We lie to ourselves every day. Every moment of life is an elaborate frame for a surfeit of well hidden dishonesty, a great pile of excuses, the only truth of which is that they're being made, apologies all pointed away from the great lie that is the world.

My world.

I'm tired of living a lie.

When one is surrounded, enmeshed, in the never-ending tide of falsity, by the denial of those who live in and take such falsity as absolute, who define themselves with and by the small aspects of their delusions they're willing to acknowledge at all, the lie is real, inasmuch as it is actual.

Yet he knew Thorin was real in truth, a center of truth, secrets hidden so well they must be so. Only lies go out of their way to be seen. Thorin, an enigma of the highest order, must therefore contain much that was real.

Jonathan... Jonathan. Of all those presented in his story, Jonathan was the least defined, a Cheshire cat, disembodied smile and wit, left drifting in the vaporous quiet of all that was not, by extension all that was in truth. Never before had Daniel been in a position to observe the man, always distracted by incidental happenings, occurrence and event. Now though he felt close to him, and not just because he trod behind him, obsequious and subservient, matching his steps in the sterility of the underground compound. They were approaching something, some place to which Jonathan alone knew the way; he could almost hear the great currents, somewhere below, around.

Jonathan was taking him to The River.

Daniel halted then, not his steps but the flow of his mind, startled by his instinctive articulation, unspoken but for this all the more potent.

The River.

What river? Was it so special, this hidden sanctum to which Jonathan led him, that it demanded propriety even in its evocation within Daniel's troubled mind?

Then known, understood, the queer intonations of others that before had been simple anomalies of vocalization, now revealed to be more, greater, measures of respect and acknowledgments of uniqueness.

Realized, he too had done the same. The City was from where he came, given the respect of an individual despite being a mere shadowy form of people's passing. These people he now knew, whom he'd known now for some time, had other respects, Friend, Judge, Creator, Centre, Kind, things that to Daniel were undefined entire, let alone formed in such a way as to demand proper address.

Now, walking an unknown path in an unknown place, itself surrounded by the ludicrous actuality that was Ithaca, an anomaly of space and time as Daniel knew them, set apart from the world by the IDSC, and more than this by a distinction of spirit so real that those not admitted to its compass hadn't even an inkling such a place, such a thing, could exist, Daniel had come forth with a new Thing, itself undefined yet undeniably Real, The River.

It was to here Jonathan led him, Thorin as well, though Daniel knew, felt at least, that the other man's presence was predicated upon his own.

He could hear the heart of some great beast, organism or entity, thundering, pounding, himself caught in the torrent yet untouched by its flow. It pounded in his ears, was felt in his pulse, new excitement and old, ancient, life.

He was alive, the pulse of The River proof, moving through him, carrying him onward.

He was alive.

THROUGH THE DOOR

Jonathan halted before a door set to the right at the end of a long corridor, one of innumerable such ways they'd trod since entering the building what felt like an hour earlier, likely no more than several minutes. The door, no different from the others gracing the corridor's long extension, was affixed with neither lock nor bolt; it opened inward easily under the confident manipulations of the man who, now in the close of his private underground domain, seemed taller, greater, a bear of a man who could certainly rend one such as Daniel easily, without effort and without a second thought.

Daniel approached the portal warily, uncertain what he'd find beyond, vision blocked by the broad sweep of Jonathan's shoulders as he stepped through.

Jonathan glanced back. "Don't be afraid, Daniel. There's nothing *in here* that can harm you," smiled. "Nothing you do not bring yourself."

What the fuck is that supposed to mean?

Again, Daniel felt trapped, inexorably approaching a precipice or perhaps a termination, a constriction beyond which he could not pass yet from which he could not turn, the entirety of personal history and force impelling him toward certain demise. Already he could feel himself shying away from… himself, as odd as this seemed when actually considered. Yet the sheer was palpable, reified layers of self, karma, peeling away.

What the hell is happening.

His episode in the commons, so publicly displayed, would have, should have, been embarrassing, such an accidental outburst of inner reality simply unacceptable, inappropriate. He too it seemed naturally hid his truth, whatever truth this was, desiring with all his being to remain unknown, to himself and others. That Jonathan had then arrived, whisking him away to this place, into Its bowels, had seemed a blessing, alleviating the need to explain his outburst, to himself or others.

Now, however, Daniel was possessed with the building awareness that his present course was somehow related to the strange intrusion he'd experienced, somehow connected to the mysterious voice with which he'd spoken, to the dark side of himself that was utterly afraid, in pain and alone. The dissonance within him stood in stark significance, inarguable fact.

Daniel was on the verge.

But of what?

He did this to me; I know it.

What are you?

I am nothing, the voice of between.

Silence.

Be silent.

Silence consumes me!

Go away.

There is nowhere to go. I am trapped.

Captured.

They will come for me soon.

Who will come?

No one ever comes.

They always come. Always...

We are here.

He stepped through the doorway, finding himself in a fairly large chamber.

The thunder, flow, of The River felt now quite close, among the capillary of self, the artery of truth flooding him, rich and viscous.

He bled away, back in the manner of a receding dawn, banished from himself as surely as the bolder shades of grey dissipate in the growing dawn.

"I know this place." He spoke before he could consider his words, unaware of not only their meaning but also he who spoke them.

The truth, hidden always, must not remain so.

Thorin entered behind him, brought himself to Daniel's side, a hand on his shoulder.

Daniel then didn't know whether the hand was in comfort or restraint, whether it supported him or pushed him forward. Then all blended together, seeming indistinct, sharp and defined, vague.

"I'm sure you do, Daniel;" his friend spoke, far away, directly beside him. "You've been here before, long ago."

He turned then to Thorin, forgetting Jonathan as he receded into the room, moved toward a table, no, a bed, flat and white, set around with leather restraints, metal fasteners, found there at its center. "When have I been here?"

Looking around, he didn't recognize a single aspect of the place, felt still its familiarity.

This is fucking confusing.

Jonathan returned, a soft smile on his face. "I'm sure it is, my young friend."

Fuck. Again.

"What is the meaning of this?" He turned to Thorin, his one ally in this madness, a man whom he knew he could trust... wait... he could not trust him. Thorin had betrayed him; he'd...

What had he done?

The old grievance seemed small, barely remembered yet sorely felt.

Turning to slight panic, "What is happening, Thorin?"

Thorin smiled, itself, himself, receding into the distance of the near present.

A rustle, a slight breeze. Another entered the room.

Light linen, soft roses brushed passed him.

Mary.

What is she doing here?

"Hello, Daniel;" the dark of her eyes consumed him.

"I'm sure you remember Mary," Jonathan welcomed the room's new occupant, turning her with a sweep of his hand to face Daniel, the two of them set directly to his fore, Thorin to the right. "It was she who brought you here."

"I came here with you." Certainty, clarity, recollection and path.

I came here with you.

Jonathan then laughed, a great thing that filled the room, Daniel's ears, not menacing, even less joyous. It was the laughter of complete and total understanding, encompassing Daniel, filling the cracks of his being in ways he could not comprehend, in places he didn't know existed, yet somehow knew, felt. "Certainly I led you here; your friend," a nod to Thorin, "did so as well, yet it was Mary who opened the door."

"You opened the door. I saw it with my own eyes."

Again The Laughter owned the chamber.

"With whose eyes did you see this?" He brought himself close, so very close to Daniel's petrified form. "Yours?"

Dismissed with a thought.

"Through whose eyes do you see?"

Then, standing stock still, presented with people, Kind people whom he both did and didn't know, Daniel was unsure.

A Break.

"I do not know him," whispered into the growing void of himself, now extending beyond, into and around those before him, about the room, the fixture that graced its center.

Jonathan smiled, brought forth a cup, simple, plain, hewn of a single piece of maple, grain dark, vivid, brimming with clear liquid.

Daniel could feel the transcendence of the liquid, a twinge at the base of his throat, his spine, moving through him, around him, bringing gooseflesh to every inch of his body.

"Now," the word carried the significance of singular truth, singularity and synchronicity, comprehending the whole of this life, this single life, known then as merely one of many, of few in the grand scheme, revealing him as a babe, pure, "you do."

Daniel watched, reached for the cup, draining it to the dregs.

Opened into The Real of himself.

THE CENTRE

He awakes early, shades of dew clouding his vision, rolls over onto his side, finding there a flower, red. Blood red, dotted with droplets of moisture, perfectly round, tiny, refracting the rays of the fully risen sun, spectrum encapsulated in the whole of their minuscule volumes, deep, drawing him in.

He draws back, away from the universes of color, diamonds left to evaporate in the manner of all dew, slowly and unseen.

I must have been sleeping for a long time.

His back hurts, and raising himself he can feel still the stiffness of the ground along its length, a subtle restraint on his limbs that prevents him from realizing complete movement.

Overhead the sun shines, bright and full, speaking to a fully risen day that belies the moisture set around him, on his face and clothes, the flower beside.

Before him spreads a field of green, extending to the east as far as he can see, beyond even, although he does not know how he knows that it does, but indeed it does. Endless. Nearly so.

Then again, in infinity anything short thereof is in effect a vanishing dimension, lost in the limitless abyss.

Mountains to the southeast stand, monolithic, polylithic, great and tall, their rocky heights lost in the azure dome above, not so much hidden as simply sublime, meeting the earth in broad and sweeping forests of dark green, distant, ill-defined, expansive, lending perspective and scale, silently testifying to the sheer immensity of the scene.

North... He does not look north. Nor does he know where indeed north lies, yet still, north he does not look.

Yawns.

The dream from which he's awoken had been dark, a vague, now dimming, nightmare. From the little he can recall he's glad to be back home.

Shivers involuntarily.

He turns from the escaping green, west toward the sea there, a crystalline blue expanse, pale aquamarine, disappearing over the far horizon, pristine, cold in the manner of a beautiful woman—untouchable, unreachable, impassive. Inescapable.

Walking toward its shores, a bright expanse, not sand but instead small quartz pebbles whose lack of translucence is more than made up for by the light they throw back toward his eyes, pure white, a softness born of chaos, potential, he notices a diminutive, leafless bush before him, at the edge of the crystalline lining, moves to walk around.

Skirting its tough, weathered form, he sees the bush is actually a tiny tree, intricate in its miniature twists and gnarls. On closer inspection it does have leafs, new buds, minute protrusions of light green, the green of new growth, not tempered yet by the sun's radiation, not yet productive.

Then known, I am as these buds.

From what tree do I spring?

He reaches out, touching the light ruffles, brings his hand down to the trunk, feeling its sturdiness. Its bark, tiny as it is, feels of wrinkled parchment; the delicate, dry ridges of its surface convey a sense of age, the ancient skin of life, of many seasons, the elements having lent it a character that surpasses the supple newness of the field around.

He tugs gently on the trunk, whose roots put forth a brief resistance before pulling free, the tree now found in his hand, estranged from the bank that had for so long nourished it.

He is taken aback, aghast at what he has done.

The tree, before his very eyes, withers; the new buds lose their vibrancy, turning to ash, a fine dust that disintegrates between his fingers.

He casts the dead thing into the pure waters of the sea, unable to look upon what he has wrought.

He follows, wading out into the shallow waters, feels the lap of gentle waves upon his shins, his thighs, reaching to his breast.

Turns then, onto his back, stroking away from the scene of his crime yet carrying still its mark, his body, with him, out into the deeper water, coolness born of the depths sliding passed below.

After a time, or perhaps a duration, for time here is moot, immaterial, he finds himself a lone figure, set upon the placid surface of an endless blue expanse, horizon indistinguishable from sea, air still as is water, each an aspect of himself, soft.

He sinks below, into the growing dark of the deep, not knowing or caring what lies below or if he has breath enough to sustain him.

Drifts into the ether of his soul.

He walks the loop of the garden, drawing himself about the courtyard. A beautiful woman, Alena, stands on the far side; he can see her through the blooded branches of the maple.

He increases his speed, toward her, only to find she too has moved, still on the far side of the tree, obscured.

He hears a soft laugh, her laugh, drift through the boughs.

Looking down then, he sees he is before the bench upon which together they'd so long ago sat, close with unspoken thoughts, a lifetime ago if it were a day. Inscribed there are the mysterious characters, alien still, yet, he can see them for what they are, now.

The words ring out, crystalline, clear.

ONLY BY LETTING GO OF YOURSELF WILL YOU BECOME WHO YOU ARE

Alena is there, beside him, gazing at him as he stands transfixed.

He breaks away, looks up, mouth dry with too many words, tangled in silence. The weary grief of a lost sailor, far from home and alone, stranded on some desolate island or another, creeps through the cracks of his being.

She looks more amused than anything. Her pony tail hangs to the side as she stands with head cocked, waiting for him to do something besides gawk at her and mutter excuses.

Silence.

"Now you know;" soft words drop into the still of the place, hovering in the twilight.

He cannot respond nor articulate even a sputter, tongue cast in iron, heavy and too slow to move.

Pauses.

The scene is familiar, two dreams, two realities meeting as one, presented here, one in three, again in one.

She smiles, laughs, filling the courtyard, the spaces of the garden therein. Turns; "Do you know what this is?"

He knows the answer, knows still he doesn't know.

"I do not know him," reflex, an articulation of its own, inured, instinctive. He has been here before.

She lets slip her hand from the statue's forearm, closes the space between them.

His arms find themselves around her, she herself into his. Looking down he sees his angel, cradled there, so very close, looking up at him with eyes, warm, brown, deep yet not dark, holding love for him.

Spoken softly, ever softly, "You do."

They kiss then, stretched into the thin mesh of the moment, the greatest depths of eternity, one in the same.

Time is an affect.

It only exists as a function of movement, distance. It is not real on any fundamental level, a mere form of intuition, limited by reference, forms of denotation, *necessities* of experience.

Laughs.

Its ties bind our minds, yet in this vice our spirit, which is another name for the truth to which we testify, is free.

Can you tell me the you seven months ago is different from the you present now? Would you do so based on distance? Can not one thing exist in two places? More?

Time is but a relative distance.

That I see you here now, in The Cell, just as I saw you then, silent, scared in your mother's womb... This is what Is. You were there, then, and you are here, now. You were here, then, and you are there, now. All is *then*, ill-defined and poorly distinguished.

A thing is what it is.

He moves toward him, across the small space between.

Are you more than a thing?

I am a man.

What is a man?

Laughter forms in the recesses of his eyes.

A man is free.

Free to be more than what he is.

Really.

A break.

Do you know me?

I don...

Pauses

You are me

I am mad.

The two both break off then, back away from one another, each unsure who has spoken, both knowing quite thoroughly neither has.

He feels the rough of the cell wall behind him, pressing against his back, sees across the other, himself, his wretched self, doing the same.

Fills with the horror of inescapable darkness, without even room to stretch out, not even alone but kept company, always, by others, countless others.

Peter screams, turns, dashing his open palm upon the wall, sobs.

Daniel stands, silent, observing.

We are not the same.

Peter.

The man turns, eyes atwitch. You speak my name?

Daniel nods. I do.

You are Daniel.

I am.

A pause.

I do not know you.

A pause.

I know you completely.

Time stretches.

The man, wretched man, turns away, head upon stone.

Why do you torment me?

I...

Brings his face toward him.
It is my fault.
Tears in his eyes.
Silence.
What is your fault?
He moans then.
She was so young. So innocent.
Rises, moves toward him, grasps him by the lining of his jacket.
You must forgive me.
The depths of his soul open through his eyes, the void of perdition there stretching beyond comprehension, framed purely, repentance.
Whisper, forgive me.
The Other dissolves.

Below passes a taxi, quaint in the way of all taxis here, slightly dingy and obviously not originally intended to be a taxi at all, turns right at the next crossing, heading down the hill.
The street is lively for this part of the city, at least it is for this time of night, now approaching 11:00.
Glancing to the left, away from the disappeared vehicle, she cannot help the small smile that springs onto her face. Nearly two weeks now has she stayed at the hotel, nearly every night retiring to the calm vantage of her balcony to enjoy some wine, observe the city around, yet still the scene brings her joy.
It is the feel of the place, more than anything.
Simple, unconcerned. Forthright.
And still, when she rises, taking in the gentle warmth of morning, she sees Gabriel walking the street below, on his way to the bakery, to the square that lies at the top of the hill, inevitably, perpetually, climbing toward his Dasta, though yet he knows this not.
It is funny how different a place is when known oneself, not merely in another's story. Not once did he speak of the taxis here.
She knows that her story, if ever it were told, would certainly make mention thereof.
A story, you see, tells more about the teller than it does about its subject.
It is not that his story had been incomplete or lacking; I still feel its fullness acutely.
I know the reason for this is that he'd been in the story, had *been* the story itself, himself.
The stories you tell do not mention me.
Startled.
She is talking to me.
I do not know who you are.

I know who you are.
Do you not know me, even now, with me as you are, always?
Silence.
My story... You are in it. We are there now, inside, and thus I am inside you, as your are inside me, as together we *are* the story.
You know me.
He breaks down, falling toward her swollen womb, sorrow so great it encompasses him, strangles him.
He is suffocating.
The walls of his sanctum, formerly soft and supple with the vigor of life, full of love, the strong pulse of The River all around, tighten.
The world becomes pain; the sound of The River slows, quiets.
Ripped into the eternal damnation of life everlasting.

A leaf turns, one of many, a page of life lies open.
Of a sudden a girl is standing there.
My story...
The story.
The world quiets.

I send you into the world.
Into a den of lions I cast you.

What story would you have?
I would have my own.

We have lain in shadow long enough.
Into the Valley of the Shadow I send you.
For My Name's sake.

Tear at him.

Alone in a cell.
Tear at Him.
I will not forgive you.

Is this the end or beginning?
Tear at him.
Screaming.

All the print is blood.

I do not know Him.

Tear at Him.

He rends himself, open.
Is made anew.

He raises himself, struggles to find footing.

The beautiful quiet of impending dawn has captured the scene, all the stars of early morning banished save one. Over the water, to the northwest, a small point of light remains, the morning star, Venus, shining bright, clear.

He wades toward the shore, cognizant of exactly where he is, where he has been, has been all along.

He knows this place.

Before him burns a fire, there at the edge of the crystalline lining. Gazing at the fire, gazing....

Into its forking form he plunges, delving into the flames.

Only to be rebuked, cast out. Unwelcomed.

The fire burns, bright and pure, awesome.

Radians of dawn begin to break the horizon beyond, a golden crown, trimmed in magenta, meeting cool blue, grey and indigo, spreading over the field, framing the mountain heights.

He turns from them.

Toward the expanse beyond.

Below the dark dome of The West, before the pure light of the morning star, rises a sword, known then as the small tree he'd destroyed so long ago, just then.

Its branches spread above a proud trunk, gnarling ways made straight although not cast aside; still can be seen its age, the forms of its growth, there, below the spreading boughs.

He makes his way toward it, extends a hand to feel the green of new growth that graces its branches, the cold of hard steel that forms its cross.

Opening his mind, his hands slide down, find themselves grasped around.

He thrusts the sword through his forehead, blood running down its cool length, a spidery messianic script, black, lit yet in the fading twilight of dusky dawn.

He falls to his knees, forward, driving its length deeper, into the firmament of his mind, feels it there take root.

The risen sun finds him beside the water, death and new life met as one.

FAITH

Thorin sat back against the low wall, tracing the flight of a hawk, high in the sky, headed northwest toward the lake, even as its form became indistinct, obscured by distance, vapor, the ineptitude of his vision.

He'd come outside for a moment to regain his bearings on the world, having spent the better part of three days below, in the room there found, tending Daniel, although he knew his ministrations in this capacity were sorely ineffectual.

It was Spring, fully realized; crocuses poked their way from beneath debris, the untended recesses of a flower bed running the length of the building behind him. In Ithaca, Spring meant rain, which had for most of the past three days thoroughly inundated the place, now gone, a respite that found the sun high in the sky, clouds barely visible on the eastern horizon.

The sun was so bright, its glare intensified by ocular weakness born of Thorin's long duration below, that he had to shade his eyes, unable to face the light.

Even then he still found himself squinting, passed the rising smoke of the joint held in his right hand, crossed before him over the left, a semblance of humility.

What have we done to him?

Truth be told, he had no idea. Only his trust in Jonathan, in his knowledge and intent, kept him from breaking down entirely.

If anything happens to him...

But something will happen to him, something has been happening for some time, days, still now.

Daniel lay as he had since moments after drinking from The Cup, strapped to a table, lost in the infinite Being of the Centre.

Looking at the boy one could almost think he were sleeping, peacefully. Most of the time. No mar touched his brow; no sound escaped his lips. Yet being in the room one knew, viscerally, acutely, that Daniel didn't sleep.

In the room, beside Daniel's supine form, the terrible immensity of all that was there *not* seen was enough to steal one's breath, time frozen, marked by the slow and steady rise and fall of the boy's breath, then allowed to follow suit.

He knew Jonathan was there now.

They'd at first tried to give him fluid, nutrition, orally, yet his teeth were set, clenched, immovable, at times giving forth a dull grind, never parted. Jonathan had then come forth with an IV, complete with a hanging rack and an inexhaustible supply of fortified saline, apparently having anticipated, planned well.

Thorin felt like a fool.

He'd known this had been coming for some time, months, since he'd decided to bring Daniel here. He'd known what it would entail, the risks involved. He'd also known, understood, the necessity, having finally been reacquainted with the boy after so many years, as he'd always known he would be.

When he'd first lain eyes on him again, that night at the bar, having previously heard from Alena of their earlier encounter, he'd been unsure, untrusting of the hand of fate even as he knew all moved according to a Will, a singular, inescapable Will that moved men such as he like so much flotsam. Speaking with him then, Thorin had known what must happen, and he'd tried his best to prepare him.

Now, having seen, felt, with his own eyes, his own heart and spirit, just exactly what Daniel underwent…

There'd been no way to prepare him.

In Daniel alone lies the answer, the inner strength and coherency of spirit that will allow him to come through a whole person and not a blithering madman, forever tormented by the fury of inner hell.

Faith. Thorin had faith Daniel would emerge whole, new, reborn in spirit and mind, awoken after a lifetime of indistinct daydreams and all too acute nightmares.

It was a faith born of necessity, as any belief, rooted in the grim uncertainty of spirit's progression, the twinkling fragments of all that was ill-aligned, as well the deep wells of parallax that riddled his representation, brought incoherence to his mind.

Thorin laughed, the peculiar turn of his thoughts lightening but a little the burden that rested thereupon.

He too had been altered in the days past. Not only because he too had touched The Source, although to a far lesser extent than Daniel, but because in the spaces left thereby he'd found time to grow, become more, himself as well.

He pulled on the joint one last time, flicking its short, brown-stained length to lay among the sprouting flowers, turned to reenter the building and face his own personal purgatory below.

AWAKENING

His head felt heavy.

Not the heaviness of fatigue or confusion, nothing like that, instead simply a tightness at its base, muscles stiff, tender to move.

He opened his eyes, attempting to rise, a feat accomplished easily, although for some reason he felt the bed upon which he lay itself should have put forth some sort of protest.

Looking down he saw the restraints, knew that not too long ago he'd been in them confined.

Given the... Given from where he just come, where he'd been, the things he'd there experienced, the...

Thoughts came too quickly, faster than could be acknowledged, the thin film of his awareness unable to capture the entirety of the torrent.

...He well understood such measures had likely been necessary.

He felt a lifetime had passed, knew it had *in fact* been only a short while, knew nonetheless the spaces of his being then expressed measured vast distances, infinities, deeps between brief moments of clarity, moments in which there'd existed in him enough reference, allusion, to bring coherence to what must have been but tiny portions of The Reality passing through him, there being changed, bent and reformed, emerging unique, an aspect of him even as they were aspects of The Source from which they sprung, met together in the mutual expression of life, a story told as one.

Thorin was there, to the left, between the bed upon which he sat and the door he'd entered so long ago.

He cast his gaze about the room, searching for Mary, whom he didn't know yet for some reason felt the need to lay eyes on.

She was absent.

Instead he found Jonathan, to the right, met his eyes, his smile encompassing him in welcome. Daniel thought he could see relief, contact broken as the man turned to Thorin, gave a slight nod.

No one said anything. The quiet of absolute silence filled the place, a thing that usually would've set him ill at ease, now accepted, embraced, known as peace.

He moved to the side of the bed, sliding his legs over the edge, stood up.

His feet found the floor, confident, set slightly wide, Jonathan before him.

Silence maintained itself.

He walked away from the bed, turned, bringing himself around to face the two men, Jonathan to his left and Thorin to his right.

For his part Thorin looked as though he'd had a tough time. Weariness creased his face; his shoulders looked drawn down, burdened, tired. Yet still his countenance spoke a different story, one of knowing wisdom, satisfaction, perhaps a touch of relief, tinged with apprehension, there at the edges of his being.

Jonathan was impassive, signature smile absent, a touch of mist apparent in the corners of his eyes.

Daniel stretched his back.

Silence.

The three of them stood, observing each other, themselves, three points of awareness, estranged in body yet one in spirit.

Fully realized, the moment stretched, set in the evanescence of actuality, adrift in the concreteness of the sublime, passed on, an eternity thrown aloft in the building progression, brought low by the tide of occurrence.

Daniel could hear the steady pulse of The River, life flowing through his body, met there by...

Paused.

He was there, beside the flowing waters, now with perspective enough to see that the shores beside which he'd lain, from which he came and to which he went, were not those of a sea, instead known as the banks of a mighty river, The River from which all came, was found, and into which all went, was lost.

The immensity of Reality surrounded him, resided within him.

His mind remained placid, even presented as it was with the implacable swell of Spirit within, around, running through him, sprung from him, from which he sprung.

The moment passed, replaced with another, another, the cascade of infinity then acknowledged as real, known to be omnipresent, each a duration of limitless Being.

There's so much time. So much space.

He focused, limiting his attention to the bare reality of the small room in which he stood, to the men before him who seemed all but unaware of the immensity of the place they occupied.

He smiled, a small thing, carrying the power of The Centre that then was with him, which always would be, always had been, bringing an audible sigh from Thorin, a wide grin from Jonathan.

And then, the silence was broken.

"We have lain in shadow long enough."

THE END

AWAKENING

IF YOU ENJOYED EPOCH AWAKENING,

Leave a review at **amazon.com/dp/061592462X**

Like us at **FACEBOOK.COM/EPOCHTRILOGY**